JEFFERSON PARKER

Jefferson Parker is an award-winning journalist and the author of nine previous novels, including *The Blue Hour* and *Red Light*, both featuring Merci Rayborn, and *Silent Joe*, winner of the Edgar Award and the *Los Angeles Times* Best Mystery/Thriller Award.

He lives in Laguna Beach, California. When not working on his books, Parker spends his time with his family, hiking, hunting and fishing, and haunting the public tennis courts.

Visit Jefferson Parker at his website:
www.TJeffersonParker.com

BLACK
WATER

JEFFERSON PARKER

HarperCollins*Publishers*

HarperCollins*Publishers*
77–85 Fulham Palace Road, London W6 8JB

www.**fire**and**water**.com

First published in Great Britain by
HarperCollins*Publishers* 2003

1 3 5 7 9 10 8 6 4 2

First published in the USA by
Hyperion 2002

Copyright © T. Jefferson Parker 2002

T. Jefferson Parker asserts the moral right to
be identified as the author of this work

A catalogue record for this book
is available from the British Library

ISBN 0 00 712217 9

Set in Times

Printed in Great Britain by
Clays Limited, St Ives plc

For Rita

ACKNOWLEDGMENTS

I'd like to thank Larry Ragle, retired head of the Orange County Sheriff-Coroner Department crime lab, for pointing me in the right directions, again. Getting tired of this, Larry?

Thanks to Cro-Magnon Music for permission to put the prescient lyrics of Tom Bagley and Cat Parker into the voice of Gwen on pages 192 and 268.

Also, I'm grateful to Dee Harvey of the Brain Imaging Center of the University of California, Irvine, for inviting me to the Robert and Margaret Sprague Symposium. This was a heady conference for a mere storyteller, but filled with interesting people. Thanks in particular to Dr. Sam Gambhir for his fascinating lecture on molecular imaging as well as his casual observations on the dangers of using MRI on gunshot victims. And special thanks to Dr. Larry Cahill for his riveting presentation on the emotional components of human memory. Long live the amygdala.

BLACK WATER

ONE

Archie pushed the gearshift into third and set his hand on her knee. Coast Highway, southbound. Man in the moon big and close, like he was tilting his head for a peek down into the convertible. Archie glanced up, couldn't tell if the guy was smiling or frowning. Didn't care because Gwen's skin was warm through the dress, a few degrees warmer than the breeze gusting through the car.

He looked at the speedometer then at her. Saw her hair moving, her face sketched in the orange glow of the dashboard lights. A silver champagne flute in one hand, a smile.

Archie pretended he'd never seen her before. Pretended he was trying to look at something else—the squid boat off of Crystal Cove in a pool of white light, say—only to have this Gwen creature drop into his world like some special effect. There she was. What luck.

He lifted the hem of her dress up over her knees and slipped his hand under. She eased back in the seat a little and he heard the breath catch in her throat. He caught the faint smell of her, windblown but unmistakable. Archie had a sharp nose and loved what it brought him. Like right now, the milk-and-orange-blossoms smell of Gwen, bass scent of his life. All the other notes that came to him—coastal sage and the ocean, the new car leather—were just the riffs and fills.

She smiled and tossed the plastic champagne flute in the air, the darkness stealing it without a sound. Then she slid her hand under there with his, popping up the cotton dress and letting it settle like a bedspread while she trailed a finger down his forearm and over his wrist.

"Long way home, Arch."

"Five whole miles."

"What a night. It's cool when we mix our friends and they get along."

"They're all great. Priscilla drank a lot."

"The cops put it away, too. Thanks, Arch. You spent a fortune for all that."

"Worth it. You only turn twenty-six once."

Gwen's curls lifted in a random swirl and she pulled his hand in a little closer. She didn't speak for a long moment. "Twenty-six. I'm lucky. Will you love me when I'm thirty-six? Eighty-six?"

"Done deal."

"I'm really sorry about earlier."

"Forget it. I have. Damned temper."

A serene moment then, as the roar of the engine mixed with the comfort of forgiveness.

"I can't wait to get home, Arch. I'll be outrageously demanding, since it's my birthday. It *is* still my birthday, isn't it?"

"For about three minutes."

"Hmmm. Maybe you ought to pull over."

Archie downshifted and looked for a turn off the highway. There was one at the state beach, one for the trailer park, another one back by the juice stand. They'd used all of them, just one of those things they loved to do. She'd sit on his lap with her back to him. Up that high she looked like a tourist craning for a view of something, one hand on the armrest and the other on the dash. The great thing about the new convertible was he could look up past the back of Gwen's head at the stars, then at her again, put his nose in her hair or against her neck and wonder what he'd done to deserve her. For a young man, Archie Wildcraft was not a complete fool, because he understood, at thirty, that he'd done nothing at all to deserve her. Dumb luck, pure and simple.

"There's the turn," she said, pointing.

"I love you," he said.

"I love you, Arch. You're always going to be my man, aren't you."

It wasn't really a question so he didn't answer. He braked and steered off the highway and into the darkness.

Four hours later, Deputy Wildcraft jerked awake when he heard something loud in the living room.

Gwen slept right through it, so Archie cupped one hand firmly over her mouth as he raised her from sleep. Her eyes grew large as he whispered what he'd heard. He prodded her out of the bed and toward the bathroom, which was where Archie had told her to go if something like this ever happened. All the time Archie was trying to listen but he heard nothing from the living room, the house, the whole world.

He watched as she pulled her new purple robe off the floor and moved through the room shadows toward the bath. Archie got a nine-millimeter autoloader from under the bed. He set it on his pillow while he pulled on his underwear—comic, "Happy Birthday, I'm Yours" boxers with a big red ribbon printed around the opening. They'd made her laugh. Him too, and they'd made love again and fallen asleep damp and tangled in the sheets.

He put on his robe and picked up the gun. Then he got the phone and carried it toward the bathroom, where a thin horizon of light shone under the door. He opened it and gave her the phone and whispered *don't worry this guy picked the wrong house to burgle maybe just a bird flew into a window if something goes wrong call 911 but let me check it out first.*

I'll call it now, Archie.

Don't call it until I tell you to call it. Turn out the light the twenty-two's under the sink with a full clip and one in the chamber. The safety's down by the trigger guard push it 'til the red shows.

Be careful.

I'll be careful.

Archie got his flashlight and walked out of the room and into the familiar hallway. Carpet, bare feet hardly making a sound. There was a light switch at the end of the hall, where it opened to the living room. He flipped it on but didn't step in, just stood there scanning right to left then back again over the sights of the automatic: wall, sofa, window blinds with a big hole in them, chair, wall with a painting, Gwen's birthday presents on the floor. Then the same things again, but in reverse.

He looked down at the big rock in the middle of the living room carpet. Size of a grapefruit. Saw the shards of glass twinkling near the sliding glass door. Saw where the wooden blinds had been splintered when the rock came through. Offed the light and listened. The refrigerator hummed and car tires hissed in the distance.

Archie moved quietly into the kitchen and hit another light. Empty and undisturbed. Breakfast nook the same. Little family room with the TV and fireplace looked fine, too, just the VCR clock glowing a steady 4:28 A.M.

He checked the bath and the laundry room. Went back to the living room and shined his flashlight down on the rock. Kind of a rounded square, red and smooth with clear skinny marbles running through it like fat. Gneiss, thought Archie, veined with quartz. Common.

He wondered who'd do something infantile and destructive like this. Kids, probably—don't know who lives here, just want to bust something up, video it, have a story to tell. Maybe some forgotten creep he'd shoved around in Orange County jail when he started work eight years ago. Cops make enemies every day and Archie had made his. They all came to his mind, though none more than any other. The crime lab could get latents off that gneiss.

All of this sped through Archie's brain as he unlocked the front door, slipped outside and quietly pulled the door shut behind him.

The moon was gone so he turned on the flashlight, scanned the porch and the bushes around it. A rabbit crashed through the leaves and Archie's heart jumped. He stepped down to the walkway. It was lined with Chinese flame trees and yellow hibiscus and bird-of-paradise. The drooping branches of the flame trees made a tunnel. Archie followed the walk around to the back, moving his light beam with his left hand, dangling the nine millimeter in his right.

He stayed on the walk and it led him around the swimming pool. The water was flat and polished and Archie remarked for maybe the millionth time what a beautiful home they lived in now, big but plenty of charm, on a double lot in the hills with this pool and a three-car garage and palm trees fifty feet high leading up the driveway. An extra room for his viewing stones. An extra room for Gwen's music. An extra room for the baby someday.

He continued along the curving walkway then stopped in front of the slider where the rock had come through. The beam of his flashlight picked up the big ragged hole and the gleam of fissures spreading in all directions. He saw no footprints, no disturbance of the grass.

Archie stood still and listened, clicked off his flashlight. Never did hear a getaway car. Kids, he thought again: they would throw the rock, haul ass giggling along the west fence, jump it at the corner and be down the hill before he'd gotten Gwen into the bathroom. He thought of her just then, standing in the hard light with her robe on, hair all messed up, scared as a bird and listening to every little sound, the twenty-two probably still in the cabinet under the sink because she didn't like guns. And he thought what a jealous little jerk he'd been for a few minutes at the party. Married to her for eight years and he'd still feel his anger rise when his own friends hugged and kissed her.

He missed her. Wondered what in hell he was doing out here with his happy birthday boxers and a gun and his wife afraid in a locked bathroom a hundred feet away.

He turned back up the walk. Past the pool. Into the tunnel of trees. Then a beam of sharp light in his eyes and by the time he found the flashlight button it was too late.

Up close, an orange explosion.

Bright white light and Archie watching himself fly into it, a bug in the universe, a man going home.

TWO

Sergeant Merci Rayborn nodded at the two deputies standing at the front door of the Wildcraft house. One of them handed her an Order-of-Entry log, which she signed after checking her watch. She was a tall woman with a dark ponytail that rode up the orange letters on the back of her windbreaker as she wrote, then down again as she handed back the clipboard.

"Who got here first and where are they?"

"Crowder and Dobbs, Sergeant. In the kitchen area, I believe."

The other uniform looked past her head and said nothing.

In the entryway Merci Rayborn stood still and received. Smell of furniture wax and wood. Smell of flowers. Murmur of voices. She looked at the entryway mirror, the living room furniture, the carpet. She looked at the hole in the blinds, which suggested a hole in the glass behind. She looked at a rock the size of a newborn's head lying near the middle of the floor. At the little pile of gift boxes. No alarm system—kitchen, maybe.

"Merci."

Paul Zamorra came softly down the hallway, light on his feet. And dark in his heart, Merci thought. He had the gentle deliberateness of an undertaker. And the black suit, too.

She turned to her partner. "Paul. Do you know this guy?"

"Not well. You know, just a friendly face. We'd talked."

"Wildcraft. I'm sure we talked, too."

Though she wasn't sure of that at all. The department was sharply divided into people who approved of what Merci Rayborn had done and people who didn't. Everyone had an opinion. Some of the deputies wouldn't talk to her, nor she to them unless she had to. This hurt Merci deeply, as if the two halves of her heart detested each other. She had come to distrust all opinions, even her own.

But Deputy 2 Archie Wildcraft? She remembered nothing about him but his unusual name. Now he was in the hospital with at least one gunshot to his head and little chance of living.

"His wife is the other, Merci. Gwen Wildcraft. She's in the bathroom."

Merci led down the hallway, noting the textured plaster, the black-and-white Yosemite photographs in brushed stainless-steel frames, the way the track lights were aimed to display them. She stopped at the thermostat and saw that it had been set at seventy. She walked past another deputy then down into a large bedroom with French doors and gauzy curtains. Big sleigh bed with the covers messed up. Smell of perfume and human beings.

The bathroom door was open. The door frame was splintered and the lock plate dangled by two screws. Merci leaned over the crime scene tape and looked in.

Here, very different smells—the sharp afterburned scent of nitrocellulose and something faintly metallic and sweet. Gwen Wildcraft lay beside the toilet, back to the floor but her head against the wall at a hard angle, facing down and to her right. Eyes closed, mouth open, arms and legs spread, purple robe almost matching the blood on the wall, the floor, the shower door, the counter and mirror. More from her nose and mouth. Merci noted the cell phone lying faceup in the right-hand sink.

This was Rayborn's sixty-seventh homicide scene as an investigator for the Orange County Sheriff's Department. For the sixty-seventh time she told herself to see, not feel. Think, not feel. Work, not feel. But, not for the first time in her life, Rayborn told herself she couldn't keep on looking.

"Let's get Crowder and Dobbs."

"All right," said Zamorra.

———

The four of them stood in the breakfast nook. Looking into the kitchen, Merci noted the fresh pot of coffee on the maker, unpoured, the machine still wheezing. A timer, she thought, confidently programmed to make coffee that Archie and Gwen Wildcraft would never touch. A red colander filled with oranges sat on the counter and a curved wooden stand dangled a bunch of pale bananas. The word *waste* came to her mind, as it often did.

Crowder was a big man with short gray hair brushed into a severe 1950s flattop. He reminded her of a man she'd been in love with many years ago—three to be exact. Crowder watched as Merci brought out a new blue notebook and her good pen, and she wondered if he hated her.

"We were down on Moulton, stopped for coffee. Dispatch said possible gunshot reported in Hunter Ranch. Wasn't a nine-one-one but we rolled right then. It was five-ten. We came in quiet because it's a good neighborhood, wasn't a hot call. Got here at five-fourteen. The house looked okay from the outside. Nobody around, no neighbors, nothing. Houselights showing from a couple of places inside."

"What about outside?"

"No."

"The driveway?"

"No."

She asked twice because two floodlights had been on when she first walked up the Wildcraft driveway. That was just after six, on the cusp of sunrise.

Merci made notes in a loop-crazy shorthand, her subjects separated by slashes like lyrics quoted in a review. <u>CK</u> meant check, always capitals and underlined, sometimes circled if the question seemed extra important. She wrote, *drive lights mo-det? <u>CK</u>/*, then looked up at Zamorra.

"Paul, how many cars in the driveway when you got here?"

"Four."

"Let's have a look where they're *not* before we leave tonight. The concrete's new and it could hold a track. Make sure the CSIs examine it before the battalion moves out."

"Yes."

Crowder looked out one of the mullioned breakfast nook windows. Merci followed his gaze to a large fenced yard, patio and orange trees, all sharp with color in the August morning.

Dobbs let out a short sigh. He was young and hard-jawed, with arm muscles that almost filled out his green uniform shirt. Smooth, ruddy face. "Look. We called for backup and paramedics when we found Archie on the other side of the house. We searched the house and found his wife in the bathroom. We taped it off. And by that time the driveway was full of vehicles, new concrete or not."

Merci looked at him. "Next time think before you open a parking lot."

Dobbs looked away.

"Anyway," said Crowder. "We rang the bell but didn't get an answer. Porch lights off, but lights on inside. Decided to walk around the house, see what we could see. Wildcraft was on his back on the walkway, about halfway around. Bleeding from the head but still breathing. Wearing a robe. Handgun beside him. Then, like Dobbs said, we called in, went inside and found the wife. I left two footprints and a kneeprint in that bathroom somewhere. You know, checked her artery, but there was nothing."

"Was there a bathroom light on when you went in?"

"Yeah," said Crowder. "I could still smell the gunsmoke."

Merci smelled nothing of guncotton out here, just the faint sweet smell of wood polish and coffee.

"What did you see driving up?" Zamorra asked.

Dobbs crossed his big arms. "Yes, sir. A black, late-model Cadillac made the north turn at Jacaranda when we were turning up. That would be an expected car in this neighborhood, but it was still just a little past five in the morning. Two white males—early-to-mid-thirties, plus or minus five. There's a streetlight at the intersection, but it's weak."

"See faces?"

"Very briefly, sir. Passenger was dark-haired, bearded, big face, thick black glasses—you know, I mean the frame part was black and thick. What I thought was, *heavy*. The driver was blond, and I thought *businessman*. I mean, these were instant impressions, sir, just . . . flashes. But they both looked unusual."

"How?" Merci asked.

Dobbs ignored her and spoke only to Zamorra.

"Unusual facial structures."

"What do you mean?" Zamorra asked.

"You know, like when you're down in Laguna on the boardwalk and you can spot the tourists from other countries? Just the faces, you know, the way they formulate. I read in a magazine it's from the facial muscles used to pronounce different languages. You know, like a French face looks different from an American one because their face muscles help make different sounds."

"So, they were French?" asked Zamorra, with a small smile.

Dobbs chuckled. "I couldn't say, sir."

"Take a guess," said Merci.

"I wouldn't guess with so little information," Dobbs said, finally looking at her. "That would be pointless."

Merci felt the blast of anger go through her. After thirty-seven years of trying to stop it she still couldn't, but she'd learned to put her anger into thoughts that could contain it. And sometimes amuse her. What she thought about Dobbs and his condescending arrogance was *give him the guillotine*.

"Since you're big on points, Dobbs, what was the point of parking your car in the driveway of a homicide scene and letting everybody else do the same?"

Merci felt ashamed at harping on this but she had to say something and that was what came out. It was her nature to grab and not let go. If Dobbs disliked her for what she'd done, that was even more reason for him to suck it up, get along, do the job. In her opinion, anyway.

"Look, Sergeant Rayborn," said Crowder. "I'll take the blame for that. I thought about the concrete and figured this was another report that would come down to firecrackers or an engine backfire. I should have said something. I just let him park where he wanted. By the time we found what we found, the backup and medics were here. We were in the bathroom."

"I understand that," she said.

She walked around the quaint little breakfast table and stood in front of Dobbs, got up close and looked straight into his eyes. She saw the uncertainty there and enjoyed it.

"I might have parked there, too," she said. "I don't care about the driveway. The driveway is history. What I care about is you treating your fellow cops with respect, instead of something stuck to the bottom of your boot. It's still *us* and *them*, Deputy. If you don't like me, fine. If you don't like what I did, fine. But keep it to yourself and we'll all be able to do our jobs better. You saw Gwen and Archie. I think we've got bigger things to worry about than our own opinions of each other. What do you think, Deputy?"

"Right, Sergeant," said Dobbs.

Merci heard a somewhat reduced hostility in the man. It was the best she could expect. In the year since her actions had publicly torn apart the department she loved, Merci had basically shut up. She'd taken the oath and told the truth. After that she had little left to say, and no one in particular to say it to. And she'd found that silence confuses the enemy.

But when it came to this, a subordinate officer trying to belittle her in front of fellow professionals, well, this was stomping time. It had happened before. In the last year she'd learned that confrontations were like haircuts—there were good ones and bad ones but none of them changed the essential truth. And the essential truth was that there were many people on the force who would never approve of what she'd done, never forget and never forgive.

So if the man piped down even just a little, it was good enough.

"Thank you," she said.

"I'm pissed off about this, Sergeant. Archie wasn't a close friend of mine but I liked him. He was a good guy."

"Then let's work together and get the creep who did this a nice stiff death sentence."

"Yes."

"Okay. Now—French, German, Latvian, Croat, Russian, Finn or Dane? I'm confident that any Orange County sheriff deputy could tell the difference in two seconds at five in the morning under a weak streetlamp."

Dobbs smiled but still colored. Merci stepped away with a very minor grin.

"Deputies," she said. "Call Dispatch and get us an all-county stop-and-question on that car. Sheriff's Department only. Tell them to use the computers and not the radios, because Sergeant Rayborn doesn't want any gawkers involved. We're one hour cold but it's worth a try. If they're tourists, maybe they got stuck in our famous traffic."

"Yes," said Dobbs.

"Then, go round up the caller. If he won't come over, tell him I'll be knocking on his door real soon and real loud. On the way back, one of you should count your steps between his place and this one."

In her small blue notebook—blue because the man who had taught her to be a homicide detective used blue, and because she had loved him—she scribbled the name and address of the caller who'd reported hearing gunshots, tore off the small sheet and gave it to Dobbs.

"Go ahead, and hear him out on your way back here."

She saw that Dobbs understood her vote of confidence, her encouraging him to informally question the witness. She winced inwardly at what the muscular but not stupendously bright Dobbs might come up with on his informal interview. But in her experience two versions from the same witness were always better than one because contradictions stood out like billboards.

Dobbs nodded and they walked away. At the front door they parted and stood back for District Attorney Clay Brenkus and one of his prosecutors, Ryan Dawes.

Merci swallowed hard, tried to keep her blood pressure from going berserk. Dawes was the DA's most aggressive and best homicide prosecutor and he had a conviction rate of ninety-six percent. He was mid-thirties and looked good in what Merci considered a men's magazine kind of way. An "extreme" athlete, whatever that was, rock surfing or sky skiing or some such thing. His nickname was Jaws and he liked it. He was the only person in the district attorney's office who'd spoken out when Merci was going through her own public and private hell less than a year ago. Jaws had told the Orange County *Journal* that what Merci was doing was "a self-serving disgrace."

Rayborn and Zamorra watched the crime scene investigators shoot video and stills of Gwen Wildcraft and everything around her. The coroner's team removed the thermometer and fastened clear plastic bags around her hands, feet and head. Then the CSI's turn again, to measure the distances between body and wall, body and door, body and tub, etc. Then, grunting and slipping in blood, four of them pushed and pulled her into a plastic bag. Rayborn saw two small, round wounds—one at the hairline, just above the left temple; one under, and toward the inside of, her left breast.

Rayborn felt great disgust and pity for the human race. She imagined a pink *casita* on a white beach in Mexico. She had never been to such a place but liked to picture it sometimes. She could see it now. She pictured her son, whom she had seen less than one hour ago, splashing happily in the ocean by the pink house. She watched the engagement ring on Gwen's finger, a small diamond caked in dark red, disappear as a tech worked her arm inside the bag ahead of the advancing zipper.

"Rectal temp ninety-seven degrees, Sergeant Rayborn," said the deputy coroner.

"Then she's been dead for less than an hour."

"Maybe longer, if her BT ran high."

A CSI Merci had never worked with handed her two small clear evidence bags. Each contained an empty cartridge case—a nine millimeter by the look of them. One was labeled "1" and the other "2." The CSI stared at the bags as he gave them over. The writing on the cartridge bottoms confirmed her guess: S&W 9mm.

"I marked the floor tile with circled black numbers, and arrows to show the direction of the openings. Had to get them out of there before they got kicked around and lost. Both were to her right. One in the corner and one next to her knee. I've got a sketch with the relative positions and time. I made sure the video guys got close-ups."

Rayborn glanced at the glass shower door to see if the casings,
ejected by an automatic pistol, could have bounced off and left a pit
or nick. But the lights glared off the glass and she could see no marks
at all. Just the faint outline of herself: square shoulders, strong body,
an almost pretty face.

The CSI had placed a small wad of toilet paper in the mouth of
each bag to keep it open, keep the moisture from building up and
maybe wrecking a print.

"What's your name?"

"Don Leitzel."

"I'm Merci Rayborn. Thank you and good work."

She looked at the dresser in the Wildcraft bedroom, noting the
sapphire earrings in a still-open box.

They stood in the rock room. Scores of stones, most of them dark in
color, all of them elegant in some way that Merci Rayborn couldn't
describe. Some small as golf balls, others a couple of feet long. Many
of them rested in form-fitting stands. Some of the stands were wood.
Others were plaster or clay, some even brushed steel.

"What are these things for?" she asked.

"I don't know," said Zamorra.

"They look Japanese," said Merci. "Maybe Bob would know."

"I'll get him."

She waited in the quiet room. Her gaze went from a rock that
looked like a mountain with rivers running down it, to a rock that
looked like an island with coves, to a rock that looked like nothing at
all. Collections bothered Rayborn because she'd once interviewed a
man who kept a collection of hollow, decorated birds' eggs. In a
nearby apartment, he kept a collection of hollow, decorated human
beings. But as she considered the rock that looked like nothing she
thought it was the most graceful nothing she'd ever seen.

Bob Fukiyama and Zamorra stood on either side of her.

"Suiseki," said the assistant pathologist. "Viewing stones."

"What do you do with them?" asked Merci.

"You view them. Appreciate. Meditate."

"Then what?"

"Sergeant?"

"*Then* what do you do?"

"I think that's all."

Rayborn looked incredulously at the assistant pathologist. She had never meditated. Thought about things, sure, like a tough case she was working, but everyone did that. Appreciated, yes, occasionally. She appreciated her son and looked at him a lot, but Tim Jr. wasn't a rock.

"Collecting and displaying *suiseki* is an ancient Japanese pastime," Fukiyama said. "My grandfather collected stones. There are societies, shows and displays. Some *suiseki* can be very valuable. Some look like islands. Some look like mountains with snow and streams. Some are more abstract. People in crowded cities keep the stones in their homes, ponder the shapes and what they suggest. The stones take them away from the city and into nature."

"Do they have any left?" she asked absently. She was staring at one that looked like a water buffalo, curled up with its head on its flank, resting.

"Left, Sergeant?" asked Fukiyama.

"In Japan, Bob. If it's an ancient hobby and a small island, have they found all the good ones?"

"I don't think so, Sergeant. And they're collected all over the world."

"I like the buffalo."

Fukiyama stepped forward and looked at it. "You know, that's a really good stone," he said. "If I remember right, water buffaloes are an entire category in themselves. Hard to find. Grandfather's was a good one, but not as good or as big as that. Or as jadelike."

"See?" Zamorra asked her. "You understand *suiseki*, you just don't know you do."

"I know a good rock when I see one," she said, still looking at the buffalo stone.

The men laughed quietly but Rayborn didn't. She could still smell Gwen Wildcraft's blood every time she took a breath.

———

Across the hall was a music room. Merci looked at the keyboards and speakers and mixing board, then at the twisting river of cables, jacks, plugs and cords running beneath them.

There were two CD towers full of discs. Merci looked to see who the artists were, but didn't recognize them.

"How old was she?"

"Twenty-six," said Zamorra. "Yesterday was her birthday."

Merci figured that a musically inclined person ten years her junior would listen to an entirely different kind of music than she did.

"What about Archie?"

"Thirty."

On the walls were bright oil paintings of beaches and hills. They looked like the work of one artist and Merci checked the bottom right corners on three of them: GK. She made a note to confirm Gwen's maiden name.

There were several photographs of Archie and Gwen. Archie had a strong neck, a broad, genial face and big dimples. Straight short hair. Good teeth. Gwen's face was compact and beautifully proportioned beneath a high forehead. Strong eyes. Intelligent and sexual. Eight of the photographs were professional portraits with brass date plates at the bottoms of the frames, going back to 1994. The '94 portrait was from their wedding.

Merci looked at the dates and the photographs and watched the Wildcrafts age over eight years. First they looked like a couple on the high school homecoming court. Last they looked like a couple you'd see in a celebrity magazine. In between, six years of gradually evolving handsomeness and beauty.

Dead in her bathroom on the night of her birthday. Shot in the head in his own backyard.

One of us.

Merci stood behind the synthesizer looking down at the keys and controls, then over at the knobs and slide controls of the mixer. She noted the microphone, which was on a stand beside the keyboard. The black paint on the mesh had been worn away by Gwen Wildcraft's lips, and the metal was touched by a red substance that Merci realized was lipstick.

"I'm firing up this tape deck," said Zamorra.

The speakers crackled and Merci watched him turn down the volume. A tentative four-chord intro, then another one, tighter, like the player was figuring it out as she played. The woman's voice was high-pitched and clear. Not strong, but breathy and light:

> *We went out and got it all*
> *Gold and diamonds wall to wall*
> *And I got you and you got me*
> *We're who everybody wants to be*
> *Turn it up loud turn it up high*
> *Do what you have to*
> *But don't say good-bye*
> *Don't even joke about saying good-bye*

Rayborn pulled out her blue notebook and wrote, *Dep. 2 30 at $40K base/Wife 26 paints and plays/house a mil plus/pool, furns pricey/CK$.*

Zamorra clicked off the music mid-chord.

Merci stood in the terrible silence for a moment, then turned as a green uniform full of muscles came into the room. "The wit's waiting outside," it said. "One hundred and fifty-five steps from where he heard the shots to the front door of this house."

"Good work, Dobbs."

THREE

It was a large-caliber handgun," said the witness.

His name was William Jones and he was sixty-eight years old, a retired schoolteacher. Merci thought he looked like Dean Martin, and acted like him too, but the drunk part wasn't an act. She could smell it on his breath. He was wearing brown plaid shorts, a blue plaid shirt and a pair of Ugg boots. His legs were luminescent white and skinny. It was now 7:34 A.M. and they were standing on the street opposite the Wildcraft driveway. Some neighbors had congregated outside the tape.

"How do you know?" she asked.

"I shot a million rounds when I was young. Twenty-two. Thirty-eight. Forty-five. I was in the service, nineteen fifty-one to fifty-three. I know my firearms. And the sound carries up here in the hills."

Jones said he lived in the garage of his son's house here in Hunter Ranch. He said he was welcome in the house, but preferred the garage because a man needs his own place to call home. Actually, he didn't get along with his daughter-in-law, but that was another story, wasn't it? He had been awake at five o'clock because he was a light sleeper and his stomach was bothering him.

When he heard the shot it was exactly 5:06 and he knew exactly what it was.

He went into his son's house, found the Sheriff's Department number in the front of the phone book and called.

Merci remembered that Crowder had marked the Dispatch call at five-ten. Good enough, she thought.

William Jones went on: "After I called I went to the bathroom, relieved myself, washed my hands. Then I went back into the kitchen—that's where I'd made the call from—and watched out the window for the cops to come."

Merci noted all this then looked up at Jones. He was lighting a cigarette, peering cagily through the smoke at her.

"Everybody okay?" he asked.

"Archie was shot but he's alive. His wife died."

"Gwen? Oh, damnit all, you couldn't have found a nicer couple of kids. Oh, *damn*it."

Jones froze a beat, then kicked the air and nearly fell over, his cigarette trailing sparks. The boot almost came off and Jones balanced on one thin leg while he worked his foot back in. He steadied himself, sighed and looked up toward the Wildcraft house, then back to his garage, then at Merci.

"Shit," he said. "You don't mind, I hope."

He pulled a flat dark bottle from the rear pocket of his shorts, took a drink and put it back. Canadian Mist, Merci noted.

"What did you see?" she asked.

"Nothing at first. Then, after I went to the bathroom and came back, I saw a black Cadillac STS heading away from Archie and Gwen's place. I know my cars, too. It was five-eleven."

Merci looked hard at Jones because she wanted him to be as good a witness as she thought he was. So he's drinking whiskey at seven in the morning, she thought: that doesn't mean he can't see straight.

"California plates, and I got the first two letters," said Jones, peering at her again. "They were OM."

"Did you see the driver?" asked Zamorra.

"No. Couldn't see anyone at all. Much too dark."

"How fast was it moving?" he asked.

"Twenty, maybe. But accelerating."

"Like it was just pulling away from the house?" Zamorra asked, looking at Merci.

"Precisely. And no, it didn't come from the driveway—I'd have noticed it. It could have been parked on the street across from Archie's, but the magnolia tree right there blocks that angle. It was heading down the hill, right in front of Archie's place, when I first saw it. I looked out the window and there it was."

Merci looked out at the expensive neighborhood: big lots, big trees, horse corrals and stalls, houses set back and hardly visible. One property even had a pond. The morning sun tinted everything gold. She could see the Jones garage across the street, at the end of a long drive lined with Italian cypress that looked eighty feet tall.

A hundred and fifty-five yards from Wildcraft's house to Jones's ear, she thought, more or less. And farther from the Wildcraft bathroom to Jones's ear, plus the walls and ceiling, which was probably why Jones hadn't heard the shots that killed Gwen.

"What about Wildcraft's driveway light?" she asked.

Jones said it was on. He squinted his eyes at Rayborn again, and at first she thought it was the sun. But the sun was behind the magnolia tree and the tree was behind Jones.

"No," he said.

"No what?"

"No. In my opinion it was not a murder-suicide," he said.

Suicide had come to her mind as soon as she learned that they were dealing with two gunshot victims. And come to her mind again when she learned they were a deputy and probably his wife. Rayborn was acutely aware that far more cops die of suicide than are killed in the line of duty. It had once been her opinion that the law enforcement suicide problem was due to low hiring standards. Then, one year ago, Paul Zamorra came very close to killing himself and Rayborn had seen beyond this narrow conviction.

"Why not?"

"Archie's a good man, Sergeant Rayborn. Sharp. Looks like a young Gary Cooper. And his wife wasn't just beautiful, she was sweet as a girl can be. You hear about perfect couples, well, that was one. They had everything."

"We don't know what happened," she said.

"You can rule that out," said Jones.

"You ever hear them fighting?"

"Once in a while."

"How many times is once in a while?"

Jones considered. "Twice in six months."

"When was the last time?"

"Yesterday afternoon, around three. I was pulling weeds. It was coming from their yard."

"What was?"

"Yelling. Mostly her. Gwen yelling but Archie quieter. He wasn't saying much."

"Who said what?"

"I couldn't make out a single word. Just two people arguing. I went back in and got another beer. I can't stand couples fighting. Worst sound in the world. Reminds me of my ex."

They thanked him but Jones just stood there and stared at the Wildcraft home.

Merci looked at the little crowd forming outside the yellow ribbon that sealed off the driveway. She and Zamorra took a few minutes to walk over and find out what they had seen and heard: nothing. She got names and addresses and phone numbers for later, just in case.

They started back toward the house. One of the CSIs slowly walked the side of the driveway—long strides, head steady, cap down low—staring hard at the concrete. To Merci he looked like her father used to, working the East Walker for trout.

She stopped and watched him. She liked his focus and intensity. "Paul, I think we should get that black Caddy to all Southern Cal enforcement—first two letters OM. I know it's late. I know it might be nothing. I know Jones drinks his breakfast. But it's worth the try."

"I'll make the call, Merci." Zamorra hesitated. "You think Archie might be our guy here?"

"I hope not."

In the last year Zamorra had become a department suicide counselor. Merci had heard good things about some of Paul's work, though he'd hardly said two sentences about it.

"What do you think, Paul?"

"I want to talk to his friends. Family, if he's got any. First I'll have Gilliam send a tech to the hospital. We should do a GSR collection on Wildcraft before they clean him up. And get his robe for blood samples."

Gunshot residue, thought Merci. They'd do an adhesive lift, then swab and dissolution. If they came up with barium, lead or antimony, that was a strong indicator that Wildcraft had fired a gun. If they found residue *and* Gwen's flesh and blood on Archie's robe or hands, look out.

Though Wildcraft could have been at the range that day, she thought, practicing with his service weapon. He could have been close to her when she was shot by someone else, taken off running and made it outside.

Or he might have gotten off a round at the guy who shot him.

"Good."

Merci stood in the tunnel of trees and looked down at the bloodstains left by Wildcraft. She had expected more volume from a head-shot adult who was still alive. Still, the amount was substantial. Most of it had pooled, indicating that he wasn't moving much. Zamorra stood slightly behind her because the walkway was too narrow for both to stand shoulder-to-shoulder. Behind Zamorra were Crowder and Dobbs.

"Archie was on his back," said Crowder. "Arms more to his sides than out. Like he never had time to even get them up, just fell right where he was. Wasn't moving at all that I could see. His head was away from us, his feet toward us."

Rayborn squatted in front of the pistol lying not far from the blood. An S&W automatic, she saw—a nine millimeter. Four feet from the gun lay a long black flashlight, the head of it on the walk and the body in the dirt. The light was off.

"Where on his head was he shot?" she asked.

"I'm not positive he *was* shot. I couldn't tell with all the blood and hair. I wanted to slow it down so I wrapped his head in my windbreaker. I didn't see any wound. I thought maybe through the eye. But at one point he opened them both and they looked okay that way."

"Did he say anything?"

"No. Pupils huge, way down in shock."

She looked at the slope of the narrow walk and figured that Wild-craft was facing toward the front door of the house when he was shot. The slope would have been uphill for him, sending his weight back-ward, which would land him as they'd found him. But for all she knew he could have been walking away from the house, fallen forward and facedown and rolled over. Or spun with the shot. Or staggered a one-eighty. Or went spastic and done something unexpected, as many gun-shot victims do.

Maybe Archie will wake up in a few hours and tell us what hap-pened, she thought. Scalps bleed a lot. Maybe the bullet took out a little meat and knocked him cold but left his brain in one piece. Maybe it bounced off.

She thought of a case she'd worked her first year on patrol, where a creep took a hit in the head with a nine millimeter and they found the slug in his thigh. It had bullied its way down there, bouncing off skull and bone, burning through muscles and cartilage, careening through solid matter like a monster out of control. Which, Rayborn thought, is basically what a bullet is once it gets inside you. The guy ended up fine as he ever was: they got him on a narco charge and he did time. Cortera, thought Rayborn—Reuben Cortera. That was ten years ago but Rayborn never forgot a creep's name. Never.

She stood and looked at the trees. Their trunks were a few yards back from the walk and the morning sun was still low enough to sneak in under the foliage. Still standing on the walk, she moved aside a branch and stared down at dark soil and the few violets and sparse alyssum that were scratching out a living in almost constant shade. Someone had worked the area recently. There were rake marks, and a shiny new brass emitter on one of the risers.

Then she saw the two shoe prints less than a yard away. They startled her. They were side by side, facing her. Close. Clear. Big. Like someone had rested or waited there, or an invisible man was there right now, offering his hand to shake. Or pointing a gun at her head. To Archie's left, if Archie was coming up the walk the way she thought. Ten feet away she saw more prints. Many partial indentations and apparent overlaps—signs of movement. But they were in harder soil and not as clear.

She nodded Zamorra over and he took the branch and looked in.

"Has anyone been in here?" he asked.

"No, sir," said Dobbs. "Can I see?"

Merci stood aside and let the young deputy look.

"So excellent," he said.

Crowder looked next and let out a low *hmmm*.

"Ike's going to love this," she said. Ike was one of the good CSIs, someone who took her side in what had happened. He was terrific with imprint casts. "Please tell him I need him here, Deputy Dobbs."

"Yes, Sergeant," he said, and walked briskly back toward the house. She couldn't tell if he was mocking her or trying to be efficient, and she didn't really care. Her heart had sped up a notch when she saw the foot imprints and it was still thumping good and hard and she thought *I'll use this cast to put your ass on the row, you big ugly bastard.*

Rayborn and Crowder spent the next ten minutes looking for brass on the big footprint side of the walkway. They worked mostly from the cement—squatting and reaching out with ballpoint pens to lift the leaves of the violets and to part the downy blossoms of the alyssum. Occasionally they took a step into the foliage, keeping well away from the footprints. They looked like naturalists. Merci didn't care what they looked like as long as they got the job done. The bullet scar on her side hurt. It was eight months old now, flat and hard, like a thin piece of aluminum grown into her skin.

She glanced back once at Zamorra. He hadn't left his place on the sidewalk. He slouched, loose and still as a cat, with his back to the sun and his hands in the pockets of his black suit pants.

It was Zamorra who spotted the nine-millimeter cartridge case glinting next to a violet bloom. He pointed to it with a straight steady finger. It stood upright and poised, like a gymnast who has just finished her routine. It was ten feet from the sidewalk, opposite the footprints. Not where the big man had waited under the tree.

Rayborn looked at the blood on the cement, the casing ten feet away. Right where you'd expect to find it if Wildcraft had shot himself.

Merci and Zamorra watched Ike photograph, then make casts of the good shoe imprints. He fixed the soil with hairspray to hold the looser particles, poured the plaster of paris mix over a putty knife to break its fall into the precious hollows. Then he shored them up with broken tongue depressors before filling the shallow indents to the top. When he was done, Ike sat back, lit a cigarette and waited for the casts to set up.

They watched the CSIs video, photograph and sketch the place where Archie Wildcraft had been found, treating it like the homicide— or suicide—scene it was almost certain to become.

While they photographed and collected the brass casing, Merci called her watch captain for a condition on their wounded deputy: minute-to-minute, nonresponsive.

And nothing yet on a black Cadillac STS with plates that started with the letters OM.

They watched the fingerprinters working the bath and bedroom. Both rooms were loaded with latents, as she expected. The print techs had found a small twenty-two automatic under the sink, placed it in a paper bag and set the bag on the counter for Merci. She held the bag and looked down at the shiny, heavy little weapon. Stainless finish, white-checked grips. A chick pistol. She wondered why Gwen hadn't used it. Rayborn figured the chances of Gwen Wildcraft knowing how to use it were fifty-fifty.

She took the tiny autoloader over to the evidence log and thought about the gun they'd found outside, just inches from Archie Wildcraft's hand. Murder-suicide weapon, or the deputy's home-protection gun? Both? Again, her stomach sank at the thought of Archie Wildcraft shooting his wife and then himself. The idea bumped the edge of her soul, like a shark nudging a swimmer.

You could put this together a few different ways, she thought: Wildcraft heard the rock come through his window. He got his flash-light and his sidearm, went to check it out. And when he came down the walkway the big bastard standing under the tree put a bullet in his brain, took the deputy's nine, went inside and got Gwen. Then put Archie's gun back in his hand. It sounded like a tall tale.

Or this: the rock was already there, heaved in a rage earlier by either husband or wife—the fight that William Jones had heard that afternoon, the incident that finally let out the demons. Police science writers would call it the precipitating stressor. Something to do with her birthday maybe. Archie boiled until his wife was getting ready for bed. She took the phone into the bath and locked the door. Felt safe. But he crashed the door and shot her so fast the cell phone flew from her hand before she could push 911. Then he went outside, staggered around, and finally took care of himself.

She went back out to the driveway. The cars were gone. She noted the news vans parked on the street—two networks and two locals. The number of curious neighbors had doubled, mostly due to kids on scooters. The moist, late-August heat sent waves up from the roof of William Jones's garage.

She paced the big rectangle of new concrete, knelt to examine a rough spot in the finish, thought of the woman in the bathroom with the bullet holes in her.

The driveway floodlights were tucked up under the eave of the garage. Rayborn stood under them and looked up at the sunlight/motion detector module. She got out her blue notebook and wrote *CK mot det after dark.*

What set off the motion detector? Jones had seen the lights on at five-eleven but Crowder had seen them off three minutes later. Neither had seen a car in the drive.

She walked back around the house to the glass door where the rock had gone through. She didn't see any rocks like it, no rocks at all, in fact, except for very large round gray stones that were set in concrete around a whirlpool. Besides that, there was a small covered patio with a cafe table and two chairs, some potted plants, a lap pool, a little section of bright green lawn, then a slope of late-season wildflowers leading down to a white post-and-rail fence.

A path made of railway ties led through the flowers and Merci followed it. There was gravel between the ties, and the flowers grew right up to the edges of the wood and the stones. Bees hummed from bloom to bloom and for two seconds Merci felt like she'd entered a scene from one of Tim Jr.'s Winnie-the-Pooh stories. She thought of her boy and wished she could walk with him into one of those scenes and stay there for a year or two.

She went all the way down to the fence, then back to the patio without finding a rock you could throw through a window. She wondered if it had come from Wildcraft's collection of viewing stones. What a view that one had, she thought.

Zamorra was sitting at the cafe table, legs crossed, staring at the hole in the glass.

"Let's walk it tomorrow," he said.

"All right."

"We'll know by then if Archie fired the gun or not."

"Yeah."

He studied her with his unsettling calm. "Stay open, Merci. He might have done it."

"I know. I will. I'm trying."

Merci thought how easy it was to be wrong. She knew how wrong she'd been about a deputy named Mike McNally, and the terrible price they had both paid. Mike was part of what had happened a year ago, the heart of it. So she said nothing more. Because even if she was wrong now—even if she was being fooled by her heart, as she'd been so spectacularly fooled before—at least it was speaking to her again.

Plus, and more to the point, she thought, Wildcraft was one of us. *Us*. We protect and serve. We do what's required. We kick ass and take names.

We don't kill our mates, then ourselves.

"I know you are, Merci. I know."

At nine that night, Merci returned to the Wildcraft home. She had had dinner with her son and her father, played with Tim Jr., read him three of his favorite books, then tucked him in.

She was tired by then but she had to find out one thing. She wouldn't be able to sleep until she knew.

She parked shy of the driveway and walked in, flashlight in hand just in case. When she got up near the garage the lights went on, big floods—one angled right and one left. It was nine-twelve and eight seconds, by her watch. She turned toward the house, following the walkway that would lead to the front porch and door, then around to the back, where Archie's blood marked the concrete.

But she stopped about halfway to the door, turned around to see if the driveway lights were still on. They were. So she backed off into the bushes and stood in the darkness under a big sycamore.

She listened to the crickets, and a far-off barking dog. From here, she couldn't see any other houses. Out in front of her, over the roof of the garage, there was a section of darkness and a few stars. It had irked Merci for almost ten years that she could only identify one star: the north. She'd promised herself to take a junior college class in basic astronomy someday, one of many such promises not yet kept. Rayborn put herself far down on the list of people for whom she'd do something pleasing.

At exactly nine-seventeen the lights went off. She stepped from the darkness and walked back to the driveway, forcing them on again. The motion zone was wide—from the middle of the drive all the way to the start of the walkway.

She tried the garage door, got resistance, didn't want to force it. Around the side was a convenience door but it was locked. She shined her light through the small window. Hard to see with the light bouncing off the glass, but there were two cars. One was an SUV of some kind, the other was small and low and hidden beneath a fabric cover.

She went back to her car, ran the beam of her flashlight along the back seats before getting in. Just a habit by now. She listened to the police radio turned down low, thought about Tim Hess and Tim Jr., dangled her arm into the darkness behind her seat.

The lights stayed on for exactly five minutes again.

The timer was perfect. And the motion detector was good enough to sense human movement twenty feet away.

FOUR

Just after six the next morning Archie woke up. He'd felt himself swimming upward for a long time, but he had no way of telling hours from years. All he knew was he was rising through water and stars, earth and fire, toward something necessary and far away. A woman's voice told him: *Swim. Breathe. Rest. Swim. Breathe. Rest.*

And that was what he did.

He broke the surface and looked up to an intensely red ceiling with bright blue lights. Quivering air, shadows forming and vanishing. Space collapsing. Space expanding. Sounds, too, punishingly loud: mechanical, electronic, pneumatic, ethereal.

"Unbelievable," said a voice.

"Hello, Archie," said another.

"I'll get Dr. Stebbins."

The conversation was much too fast and complex for Archie to follow. He understood two things. One was that he was terrified. The other was that he had lost something huge and it would never come back.

He looked and saw monsters over him: eyes, nostrils, teeth. He tried to open his mouth but his will gave way before it could happen. His lips burned and his throat burned and the ferocious colors made him close his eyes and settle back down into where he'd been for so long, hovering just below the surface, protected, safe in his river.

Swim. Breathe. Rest.

FIVE

Wildcraft's fingerprints are on the Smith nine. His right index finger, thumb and web were marked with barium, antimony, copper and lead. With corroborating evidence you can make a very strong case for him having fired the weapon. We do it all the time in court, as you know."

James Gilliam, director of the Sheriff-Coroner Forensic Services Department, looked at Merci over his glasses, then at Zamorra leaning against the back wall of Gilliam's office. He was a quiet, scholarly man until you got to know him.

It was eight the next morning. Merci had already talked to Sheriff Vince Abelera, who had talked to a neurologist at UCI Med Center. Archie Wildcraft had made it through the night. He had opened his eyes for approximately fifteen seconds. X rays had shown a small object lodged deep in his brain, smaller fragments throughout. The doctors would not let anyone interview the patient at this time. The man's life was in the balance. Merci had begged Sheriff Abelera to make the doctors tell them what caliber bullet was inside Archie's brain. But the x ray wasn't clear enough to measure fractions of millimeters, and the object, apparently, had fragmented.

"I can't tell you what he shot with that gun," Gilliam continued. "Until we finish with the bullets from his wife. And unless they retrieve the bullet from his head."

Rayborn felt her stomach sink: Gilliam was already believing that Wildcraft had done it. Plus she'd had her usual big-eaters' breakfast, which her father cooked every morning for her, Tim Jr. and himself. She ate a lot, burned it off in the gym. But now it felt like she'd eaten nails and washed them down with battery acid.

She tried to fight her dread with details. "How many micrograms of lead in the residue, James?"

"Point six five. After two hours, that's the persistence level you'd expect to find from a discharged nine-millimeter autoloader. Like the one they found next to him. Good thing they hadn't washed him up at the medical center yet."

"Good thing," she said. "What about the blood on his robe?"

"We're still cooking it to check against his wife's DNA. Give me a day or two."

"Okay, I'm ready for Mrs. Wildcraft now."

"I figured you would want to see her."

"Absolutely."

"Because it will make you angry and make you work harder."

"Make me angri*er*."

Gilliam smiled, then colored slightly and stood. A year ago he would not have smiled. That was back when he had a schoolboy's crush on her and didn't know what to do with it. At first, Merci had been too obtuse and inexperienced to know what it was. Then, one day, right out of the blue, he just told her. It seemed noble but comic. Gilliam confessed that even his wife was teasing him about her. Things got better. It was further proof that she understood men poorly.

"Ready, Paul?" she asked.

Zamorra nodded and eased himself away from the wall with a little shrug of his back.

Merci hated the autopsy room. Its stink of formaldehyde, bleach and blood. The hard edges of drains and blades, saws and suctions, scalpels and scales. The stainless steel and chrome and plastic. And those bright overhead lights that presented this torture chamber as just science. But most of all she hated it for the lightness it always brought to her head, for the cold sweat it brought to her temples, for the way it made her want to throw up, then sleep.

Gwen Wildcraft was still tabled, but there was a sheet over her. All Merci could see were her feet—small and stiff and white as fence pickets.

Gilliam lifted the sheet from Mrs. Wildcraft's face and pulled it down to just below her chin. Her skin was gray white and her eyes were closed. From the left side of her head they'd shaved a large patch of wavy dark hair. The shorn skin surrounded a small hole with ridges swollen around it. Above the hole was a brief vertical dash, like the top of an exclamation mark.

"Don't be fooled by the skin blowback," said Gilliam. "That's the entry point."

As always, Merci found it hard to fathom that a body without life had once been so full of it. Such an immensity of difference. It was like standing in a desert while the sun beat down on you—how could you believe it was once underwater? She noted with rising anger that even dead and mutilated, Gwen Wildcraft was almost beautiful.

"Now, two gunshots," said Gilliam. "One to the heart and one to the head. Both *apparently* nine millimeter, fired from up close. We recovered both bullets, and Buckley's working them up with the crime scene gun. The one here in the brain was a real mess, I can tell you. Mushrooming, fragmentation. Heads are hard, thank God."

Not hard enough, thought Rayborn.

Late yesterday afternoon she had run the serial number of the weapon found beside Wildcraft, confirming its registered owner as Archibald Franklin Wildcraft.

"Excuse me," muttered Gilliam, pulling the sheet down to the waist. Merci swallowed hard when she looked at the inverted Y incision, obscenely large, loosely stitched back together. The final insult, she thought.

"The other shot," Gilliam continued, "bounced off a rib and stopped inside her heart—back in the right atrium. It cut the pulmonary artery on its way by. Cause of death was coronary failure. Hard to tell whether it stopped because a bullet tore through, or because her brain was ruined. Either shot would have been fatal—the heart certainly, and the brain almost certainly. The shots came very close together in time. She died quickly, that from the histamine level and the blood loss. She still had almost four liters of blood."

"How close was the shooter?" asked Zamorra.

"Very. The heart was a Zone Four—the barrel was somewhere from six inches to two feet away. From the powder particles on her robe I'd put it at the closer end, but there still isn't any sooting. I think the heart shot occurred first—farther out, bigger target, gave the shooter a chance to get even closer for the next. The head shot was a Zone One, direct contact, significant blast destruction. There's even a front sight impression above the flesh tear, caused by the flesh ballooning back against the barrel. The gun you got at the scene did have a very small particle of bloody flesh stuck to the top of the front sight. And the barrel is heavy with blood and flesh particles. DNA to come. She might have been supine by then, and he just pushed the barrel right down against her head. There was some powder driven into the wound. We're running the same DNA comparison for Mr. Wildcraft, also."

Merci stared and let the ugliness fuel her. The waste. The arrogance. The sickness of spirit that it takes to regard another life as cheap and disposable. The fact that he would do *this* to another body, while his was still out there, alive and eating and smiling and sleeping and shitting like the rest of us.

She nodded almost imperceptibly, eyes steady and unblinking, lips pressed in tight between her teeth.

"You personally removed both the bullets, right, James?"

"Yes."

"Then are they nines or not?—God knows you've seen enough of them."

"I'm almost sure they are, but Buckley's the man for that."

"Okay, James—you figure Wildcraft is good for her, then himself. His gun, his prints. Is that what you're seeing?"

"It fits, so far. But I wouldn't presume to do your job, Merci. Mine is enough for me."

"Paul?"

Zamorra hesitated. Merci saw that he was looking at Gwen Wildcraft's face too, with an expression that looked like hers felt.

"I talked to a couple of Wildcraft's friends last night on the phone."

He held her gaze and she knew this meant more bad news, news
that Zamorra didn't want to give her in front of Gilliam.

Fucking great.

She felt her anger coming but couldn't stop it. Didn't want to. It
wasn't sharp and clean like they tried to say in the books, wasn't
purifying. It was heavy and cumbersome as a wagon full of rocks.
Like once you pointed it in one direction and let go, you'd never get
it back, never change its course. She wanted to point it at Wildcraft,
for making her suspect him. She wanted to point it at Gilliam and
Zamorra, for smugly assuming the worst about a fellow deputy. She
wanted to point it at Mike McNally, for helping her make the worst
judgment of her life, a judgment that kept on judging.

Most of all she wanted to point it at the killer of Gwen Wildcraft,
but she didn't know who that was.

Yet.

"Give the woman some privacy," she said. "We'll finish in your
office."

"Whatever you want," said Gilliam.

"Whatever I want is not a guilty deputy."

"I understand."

"Since the last one I arrested for murder was totally goddamned
innocent."

"I do understand," said Gilliam.

"I know you do."

With two hands he replaced the sheet over Gwen Wildcraft, looking
at Merci, the gleam in his eyes lost in the glare of the lights overhead.

Back in Gilliam's office Merci stood against one wall and Zamorra
another. She felt anxious and nervy and physical, like she wanted to
kick somebody.

"Was she raped?"

Gilliam flipped back through his notebook, then stopped and
smoothed a page.

Merci wondered why you'd have to look up the answer to a ques-

tion like that, but she knew Gilliam was only finding his facts. Still
it irritated her that he couldn't just get to the bottom of things sometimes.

"She'd had vaginal intercourse within the last three hours of her
life. There was no genital bleeding, bruising, tearing or abrasions. No
sign of a struggle. No semen in the mouth, throat or anus. Mrs. Wildcraft did have some light scrapes, perhaps bite marks, on the back of
her neck. I can't explain them. They may be sexual in nature, or they
may not be. This doesn't appear to have been a sexual attack. It's
possible that she was coerced into intercourse some other way than by
force. Or maybe the killer was interrupted. Maybe it was never his
intention. That's just speculation."

"I guess that means she wasn't raped."

"That's my opinion."

The anger fanned by seeing Gwen Wildcraft's tortured body
wouldn't leave her, it just sped her up, made her want to fight. "Well,
is it Deputy Wildcraft's semen or isn't it?"

"I'm cooking the DNA gels right now, Merci."

"What did the tech see on the driveway—any good tire tracks?"

"Nothing he could use."

"What about the footprints under the trees?"

"The imprint casts came out beautifully," he said. "Size-sixteen
casual shoes made by Foot Rite. They're not widely available—not
like the same shoe in a size ten, say. You're looking at specialty stores
and catalogues. Ike might be able to get some useful manufacturer's
information for you."

"Fingerprints from the bathroom?"

"Lots of them, as you'd guess. We're running them all against his
and hers, but nothing's popped out at us. That's eyeball work, so it's
taking time. Vince told me last night he wants all this fast-tracked.
Buckley did the test shooting last night, so he might have some findings by now."

When they walked into the firearms examination room, Buckley was
sitting at a table next to one of the comparison microscopes. He'd been

looking across the room, his chin up on one fist, and seemed slightly apologetic for it.

On the table beside him was a two-foot square of plastic bubble wrap upon which sat Deputy Wildcraft's gun, the brass casing found by Zamorra and the two casings from the Wildcraft bathroom. A clear plastic box held what looked to Merci like a small-caliber bullet sheared into two fragments. The box beside it was empty. A larger one held perhaps fifty empty nine-millimeter casings: Buckley's comparison brass, Merci thought, fired through various guns.

Buckley was a wiry Georgian who had what Merci thought were impeccable manners, and a skeet shooting medal from the '72 Olympics. As usual, his shirt was plaid and his tie was a solid knit and his hair was sprayed into a perfect brown helmet.

"All three nine-millimeter casings from the scene were fired through the automatic registered to Deputy Wildcraft," he said quietly. "The breech face left two easily distinguishable marks. I haven't photographed any of this yet, so you'll have to take my word on it until I do."

"Your word's good, Buck, even if it isn't what I wanted to hear."

He sighed and shook his head. "It wasn't what I wanted, either. Makes me wonder if I could have done something. Should have seen something. But I didn't. Locked in my own little world, I guess."

Buckley's shoulders slumped. Merci saw him draw a deep breath and straighten his back.

"The slugs from inside Mrs. Wildcraft came from cartridges fired through that gun, too. The land and groove marks are good because the original cutting blade had a big anomaly that shows through on every bullet the gun projects. I say big—you need a microscope to see it. To a good examiner it looks like a street sign."

Tracking the freefall of her hope, Rayborn said nothing.

And looking for refuge in details again, she thought to point out that the cutting tool used to create the rifling in the gun barrel would have been used to create the rifling in the *next* barrel on the S&W production line. And the previous one. But she knew the chances of any two of those barrels showing up in the same state at the same time in the same murder investigation were smaller than the breech face marks. By quite a bit.

It felt dismal to find herself thinking like a defense lawyer.

"I guess there's some flesh and blood that Jimmy took off the barrel end of the automatic, which he's going to try to put with the cut in her forehead," said Buckley.

Neither Rayborn nor Zamorra spoke until they were outside the Coroner's Facility. It was almost noon and the late-August morning was humid and hot.

Merci looked up at the pale blue sky and wondered what Tim Jr. was doing exactly now. Watching TV. Helping Grandpa do something around the house. Driving his favorite birthday present from three months ago: a stationary carlike contraption with a mock video obstacle course he could "steer" through. It had sound effects: start, idle, and an engine shriek that rose in pitch and volume according to what gear you shifted into.

She loved the way that Tim Jr. carefully locked the seat belt around his waist before he turned on the ignition, took the wheel then floored the accelerator and threw the shifter down into third. She interpreted this as a mixture of intelligence and courage. But then, she'd come to see that he was marked for greatness. All her acquaintances who had children thought the same of theirs, but in Rayborn's opinion Tim was superior in obvious ways.

"I'm ready to hear what you got on Wildcraft from his friends. I don't suppose it's terrific news, if you didn't want James in on it."

Zamorra shrugged. "He was high-strung, happy and worried."

It was like a window had been opened in a sweltering room and a puff of cold clean air had blown through.

Happy?

"Worried about what, Paul?"

"They were spending a lot of money. He liked nice things and so did she. He worked all the overtime he could get. Did some bodyguarding and security work once in a while. I'd expect to find some nice credit card bills when we check their finances."

She waited while a faint smile crossed Zamorra's face. "And he was in love. Still is, technically."

She braced herself even as the words came out. "With whom?"

"Gwen. All three of the guys I talked to told me they'd never seen a guy that much in love with his wife. Two of them actually used the word 'insanely.' She was just out of high school when they got married. He had just graduated from state college with a degree in geology. Baseball scholarship. Gwen helped put him through the Sheriff's Academy singing in a rock band. Archie was proud of all that."

Zamorra laughed quietly. It wasn't something that he did very often and it made him look different. The darkness fled and he looked like a guy you wanted to know, maybe even touch.

"Okay, Paul, cough it."

"Archie has strong opinions and he stands up for them. A temper, too. There's a group of young deputies he hangs out with, some cops he met in the academy. Archie and one of them got pissed off at each other, had a fistfight in a bar and Archie knocked him out with one punch."

"What was the fight about?"

"You. The guy said you were wrong and Archie said you were right and it just got out of hand. They made up later but, according to the friends, neither one of them changed his mind."

For just a moment, her dread wavered and Rayborn enjoyed the warming breeze of approval. From a guy she didn't know. A guy very possibly guilty of murder, a guy with a bullet in his brain and not likely to live out the day.

"That's funny," she said, hearing the lameness but not caring. "Well, was Wildcraft a good candidate for a murder-suicide or wasn't he?"

Zamorra looked at her and shook his head. They had a running dispute about the way they looked at things. Merci tried for black or white, and absolutes. Zamorra was prone to colors and gradients. Merci judged quickly; Zamorra sometimes didn't judge at all.

"Was he or wasn't he, Paul?"

She looked at Zamorra with a small smile because she knew how long an answer might take. Hess had been like her and Zamorra put together: he'd bury himself in details and facts, gathering instead of judging, then his gut would kick in and guide him through. She wished she could be more like Hess, less opinionated and huffy, but decisive and effective when she needed to be. He had told her to be kind to herself because that's who she was stuck with for the next fifty years.

"I need to keep looking," he said finally. "Some people have other levels, whole lives that take place in secret. Those are the tough ones. No one sees it coming. Rare, but it happens. They don't ask for help. They don't announce it. They usually leave a note."

Merci tried to imagine a life that secret, an intention so perfectly disguised.

"I don't see that he could kill a woman like that. His wife. What a beauty. What a voice, and she wrote songs. Look at those rocks he collected, the *suiseki*. He had, what do you call it . . . *appreciation*."

"You can have all that, Merci, and still be desperate. That's what they all have in common—they don't see a choice. It's the last thing they can think of to do that's positive."

"Blowing your brains out is negative."

"I don't mean morally. It's positive in the sense that you do it. You act. You take back control of your life by ending it."

She thought this over, trying to split atoms like Zamorra. "Ass backwards," she said.

"Don't judge what you don't understand." Zamorra glanced at her and she saw the quick flash of anger in his eyes.

SIX

Merci stood in the Wildcraft bathroom for the first time. She held the crime scene photographs, looking down, then up. It no longer smelled of blood and guncotton, but, faintly, of soap and potpourri. The room was smaller than she'd thought, but plenty big for two. White walls, a shiny tile floor, a high ceiling with a skylight. Thick white towels, lavender accents. And now, without the glare of light off the shower door, one nick in the glass that might have been made by an ejected casing.

She'd gotten there an hour early because she liked some time alone. Hess had told her how he saw his way into some tough cases by imagining a picture relating to what had happened. He'd let the picture grow and change, even if it wasn't making sense. He'd led them to a killer called the Purse Snatcher that way—the first thing he'd pictured was a woman in a cocoon. In the end, there were no cocoons involved in the case at all, but that picture kept growing and changing until Hess understood what the Purse Snatcher was doing and how he was doing it. She'd been in awe of him for that. So she'd practiced until she was tired, then practiced more. It was alien to her way of thinking because she'd never—even as a child—had any interest in make-believe. At first she couldn't do it, then she could. She realized that to understand some things you have to let them come alive in your mind first. This idea was the second most important thing he'd left her.

Merci needed to be alone for it, with only the ghosts for company.

Now, alone in the house, it was easy for Rayborn to see Gwen in her purple robe. Alive. Vibrant. Frightened. Small face, smart eyes, but eyes that are afraid.

What is she doing?

Does she come in here to take her face off, use the pot? Or does she immediately back to the far wall?

She has the phone with her because she's afraid, but how afraid? She locks the door because she's afraid, but how afraid?

Fear of the next moment? Or cautious, just-in-case fear? Did she have the phone in her hand when he came through the door, or did she reach for it?

Either way, it ends up in the sink, which is the "his" sink because the cabinet beside it houses shave gel, an athletic-themed antiperspirant, aftershave and a box of condoms. They're all economy sized, generic brands, except for the prophylactics, which are ribbed for her pleasure.

And either way, Merci thinks, Gwen is not afraid enough to get the little white-handled twenty-two from Archie's sink cabinet. Maybe she's afraid of it. Maybe she doesn't know how to use it. Maybe she doesn't know it's there.

Or maybe *she just wasn't fast enough.*

It all could have happened in seconds: Gwen runs in and locks the door, looks down to dial the phone, the door splinters off its hinges, something clubs her chest then a pistol is jammed against her high, intelligent forehead so hard the front sight takes a divot from her ballooning skin, one-two, bang-bang, you're dead.

Shot by her husband—a dimpled hunk she had had consensual sex with a few hours earlier, the man she'd fallen in love with in high school, helped through the Sheriff's Academy, posed with for portraits every year, with whom she shared a bed and a home in the hills?

She couldn't see it. Couldn't see Archie in this room with Gwen. He wasn't a player, not at this point.

But why not? She thought she knew why not, but that would wait for later.

Right now, this first time through, she was going to try to see it like Gilliam and Buckley and probably everybody assumed it happened.

So she stepped back into the bedroom. August sunlight flew through the blinds, landing on the carpet in widening bevels. Smell of sheets, raised by the afternoon warmth. Bed unmade, blanket thrown back, pillows close enough together to make her wonder if Gwen had been sleeping on her side, face up against her husband. Or maybe the other way around.

> *Do what you have to*
> *But don't say good-bye*
> *Don't even joke about saying good-bye.*

Okay, she thought. Archie did her and Archie's going on his death march now, out to the walkway. She tried to picture him but she still couldn't. It would have helped to have seen him in the flesh at some point, but Merci couldn't remember ever seeing the man. Which was hard to believe, with a face like his. Just the dimples were enough to make you remember.

She checked her notes to get the lights correct: one bathroom light on; one kitchen light on; one TV room light on; all other houselights off. The driveway light was on when Bill Jones made his call at five-o-eight in the morning but off when Crowder and Dobbs arrived at five-fourteen.

She walked down the hall, feeling the deep padding and springy carpet under her duty boots, nothing like the creaking hardwood floors of her rented house in the orange grove. She could hear the *cats* walking down the hall at home. So quiet here, she thought.

But Archie, she tells herself, has just murdered his wife and he comes down the hallway, leaving the lights off.

She sees no reason for Archie to stop in the living room. His ears would be ringing and his nostrils would be sharp with burned powder and his eyes could see nothing but the red life of his bride spraying into the bathroom air. He would have some of her on his right hand, probably, maybe some on his face and robe. Archie doesn't

see the stack of presents. Archie doesn't see the rock in the middle of
the living room, thrown earlier that day in the terrible argument. Archie, she thinks, doesn't see anything but the black vastness that waits
for him outside.

Why outside? He's already made a bit of a mess in the bathroom.
Why not kill himself in the rock room, with his mute, graceful *suiseki*
around him? Why not do it in the immaculately polished silver Porsche
Boxster convertible that sat *covered* in his garage? Why not sit on one
of the living room couches, get comfortable?

But no, Archie walks outside.

Merci opened the front door, stepped onto the porch and closed the
door behind her. There is no sun at five in the morning, she thinks.
She tries to picture the world dark, with the help of just a flashlight
beam, just like Archie saw it. But this is difficult. In fact, she's thankful
for the summer light because the walkway is steeper and narrower and
more sharply curved than she remembers. If you weren't familiar with
it, you could walk right off.

But Archie, she thinks, fresh from slaughtering his wife, and pass-
ing up a half dozen sensible and meaningful places to slaughter himself, takes a flashlight outside with him so he won't veer off the
walkway and . . . what? Stub his toe? Get his bare feet dirty? Bang his
head on the branch of a Chinese flame tree?

Apparently so. Because, as Gilliam demonstrated with the GSR and
Buckley with his tool marks, Archie stops on the walk, understands
that this is the place of places, turns around to face the direction he's
come and fires, hitting himself in the head.

Sure. Maybe.

Merci stood over the spot where Wildcraft had been found, the
bloodstains darkened almost to rust on the concrete. Ants swarmed
over it, thick in the cracks.

Sure. Maybe.

Bullshit.

She walked briskly back to the front door, swung it open and continued on to the master bath. She stood there again where Archie would
have stood. Looked at the lavender hand towels, the blood on the tile
floor, the fingerprint dust everywhere in sight.

Take it fast, now, Merci thought. Take it like a man who's just killed his wife and now plans to kill himself.

Down the hallway then, not turning on the lights because he's walked this hallway thousands of times. He's got the gun and the flashlight. Gun in the right hand, light in the left. At the door he slides the flashlight under his right arm to free a hand. Steps outside, closes the door behind him.

No lights on still, and he doesn't bother with the flashlight because he knows where he's going.

But where *is* he going?

Merci stopped just short of the place where Archie bled. She looked at the walkway behind her and at the walkway ahead of her. She looked at the near wall of the house, saw the big bulge of the chimney and the windows on either side. Saw the wall of trees to her right. She looked down at one of the photographs.

A possibility: this was as far away from her as Gwen would allow him. Any farther down the walk, he'd be circling back in her direction. *Pulled* back in her direction. Even dead, she's more powerful than he is, that's part of why he had to do this. But here, right here, Archie is at the apex of his orbit. The end of his leash. And he can't be seen from inside. Gwen, the insufferable witch, the monster who finally got what she asked for so many years, won't be able to see him right here because he's behind the chimney. She has no idea what he's up to. He's free now.

Merci sees that, having come down the walkway this far, Archie's back is to his wife. This seems natural, that he would turn his back on her one final time.

He's shivering by now, she thinks, his fury and resolve and mad logic are delaminating and he's beginning to feel true horror at what he's done. And what he still has to do.

He turns around, facing the way he came. Why? As if he could go back, undo things? Make a fresh beginning? Go confess to Gwen that he really doesn't hate her? Say a simple hello? Or good-bye?

He takes a deep breath. He swings quickly and confidently, and fires.

Never hears it. Sees nothing. Feels nothing. Maybe an owl watches the brass flicker into the violets, the brief puff of smoke as the gun clatters on the walk at the same time the heavy human bulk of Archie Wildcraft slumps like a fountain turned off for the night.

Thus, just what we found, Merci thinks: one brass nine-millimeter casing to the right side of the walkway, where the ejector on the Smith would logically throw it.

Okay. I can believe this. I can believe this. But I still can't see it.

What about Size Sixteen, waiting under the Chinese flame tree? What about all the footprints on the other side of the walk? Who made them and what were they looking for?

She felt her heart beating fast and the sweat cooling on her scalp. Her fingers were slick on the photographs so she wiped them on her chinos. She smelled herself and her perfume and the sweet stink of some flower or vine and the rich damp smell of earth with things growing in it.

She continued down the walkway, trying to clear her thoughts. She stopped by the swimming pool for a moment and watched the clear blue water. She looked at the two chaise longues, touching lengthwise, and the little round tables on either side. So they can touch, she thought. Drowsy in the sun. Sweet smell of flowers. Reach. Touch. Quiet words. Eyes still shut, sun orange and warm on the lids. Let's go inside. Oh, *yes*.

Near the far end of the pool were two eucalyptus trees. Stretched between them was a hammock big enough for two. Merci looked across to the patio, where Zamorra had sat at the end of that long first day here. There was the little cafe table and, of course, two long-legged cafe chairs.

It's everywhere I look, she thought: two young people in love. That must be what it's like, you arrange the world around yourselves. Us. Us. Us and them.

She started out in the bedroom again. But this time, Archie wasn't going to be the shooter.

And the first thing she thought was: Gwen wasn't shot first. The rock hadn't been lying on the carpet since afternoon. It had come through the window just after five in the morning, and Archie got out of bed when he heard it. He made sure his wife was in the bathroom with the cell phone. He wouldn't let her call 911 yet because he's a cop, a young cop with a handgun and a flashlight ready for something like this. If there's a dragon in his castle, Archie's going to slay it himself. Chop off its head and parade around the grounds with it.

Merci rechecked her lights list, imagining Archie as a home defender instead of a murderer. But the lights wouldn't tell her much about what Wildcraft had done because, if she was right, someone had been in the house after him.

Down the hallway again, flashlight in his left hand and gun in his right. He's alert, heart beating hard. Quiet on the carpet in his bare feet.

She could picture Archie now, even though she could not remember ever seeing him. The portraits, she thought. The big boyish face and the dimples and the strong neck. But more than that, too. He was easy to picture because he'd done this. He had been here. He was true.

Or so her imagination said. Which won't cut ice in court, she thought.

In the living room she stared again at the carpet where the rock had been. Archie would have stared too, would have seen the rock and the shattered wooden blind.

Outside now, Merci walks along behind him. She remembers the moon phase map from today's paper and knows it was gone by two that morning. So it's easy to picture the flashlight and its beam moving from the crooked little walkway to the bushes to the trees, then back again.

She heads down the walkway to the place where Archie has fallen. She wonders if Wildcraft heard something here, something that made him turn around. Or if he just kept walking out and around to where the rock had come through the window. He'd want to see the point of entry. Human curiosity. A cop's training. Absolutely, that would have been his destination.

She tries to picture him but can't get details now. Can't tell how far he would have walked. Can't tell if he'd stopped and turned just before he was given the surprise of his life, or if he was walking back from the broken window. Might never know, she thinks, unless Archie wakes up and has enough of a brain left to remember.

But this was where he bought it. Almost bought it. Facing up the walk, in the direction of the front porch, the front door, the entrance to his home. In the direction of his wife, who has just turned twenty-six, whom he has recently made love with and left alone and frightened in the bathroom at five in the morning with a cell phone that probably doesn't work well in these hills, and a gun that she's not likely to use.

All this is charging through Rayborn's mind as she looks down again at the ant-covered blood, then to where the size-sixteen shoe prints lie, still visible, back under the down-hanging branches of the flame tree.

I will identify you, she thinks.

I will know who you are and will deliver you to experience the full course of criminal justice: special circumstances, lying in wait, capital crime, guilty as charged, your honor, a lethal hot shot and you're *gone*.

You got one of us, but the Orange County Sheriff's Department isn't done with you, you bucket of piss.

She stands under the tree where Size Sixteen has stood. Places her feet where his have been.

What a view. Not just hidden behind branches heavy with leaves, but hidden *between* them. Easy to slide through, when you were ready. Archie came past here, she thinks. Size Sixteen would have trouble seeing him on his way by. But coming back Archie was an easy mark. Maybe Archie was less alert by then. Maybe his eyes were used to the dark and he'd turned off his flashlight. Maybe he was shining it somewhere else. All it took from Size Sixteen was, what, two long strides?

Quickly, she slid from the green to the edge of the walkway. Easier and faster than she thought it would be. Little resistance, little noise.

Yes, two giant-sized strides brought her to the edge of the cement walk. For what—a three-foot shot at a human head? Give him another year and Tim Jr. would be able to do that. He could probably do it now. God, I love him.

She took the two steps again with her nine millimeter out in front of her, just one hand to aim it because the other held the photographs.

And because Size Sixteen had probably done it that way. Leave one hand free to part foliage, she thought. Did he have a flashlight too? In the dark, on another man's property, on another *armed* man's property? Oh, yes. He did.

But the trouble with all of this was the casing. If it had gone down this way, and if the shooter had used an automatic of some kind, his ejected shell wouldn't have landed where Zamorra found it.

No. It would have landed where all the overlapped, partial footprints were.

And the bullet that was still inside Archie Wildcraft's head—was it from his nine or something else? That was the key. Still no word from Sheriff Abelera. Still no word from the hospital.

She heard a car pull up and park on the street. Zamorra, she thought. She walked toward the driveway and saw Ryan Dawes slamming the door of his convertible.

Merci watched him come down the sidewalk toward the drive: gray suit, black shirt open at the collar, sunglasses and a black briefcase. Tall, lean, strong in the leg and butt. He ran a hand back through his honey-colored hair.

She backed into the foliage again. Found the size-sixteen prints, placed one duty boot in each and stood still as Dawes walked past her. On his return trip, Merci stepped out and aimed her finger at his head.

"Gotcha, Jaws!"

Dawes jumped backward and dropped his briefcase to the walk.

"Shit! You scared me, Ray . . . scared the shit out of me."

"What are you doing here?"

"My *job*."

"You're just a lawyer."

He said nothing but he was breathing quickly and there was sweat on his forehead.

"You'll be fine, Mr. Dawes. Look—when you get the pee scared out of you, breathe deep. Deep."

"Yeah, yeah."

"Got it?"

"I get it."

"What are you looking for?"

He said nothing while she tried to look past his glasses and take a read on him. But the silver-blue lenses threw her own face back at her.

"This is a crime scene and we're still processing it. So stay on the beaten path and don't touch anything. Not one thing."

He smiled and let out a quick little snort. "Cut the crap, Rayborn. I know what to do with a crime scene. We don't like each other. Fine. I can play this your way if I have to."

"My way is not to whine to the papers."

"I should have kept my mouth shut."

It didn't sound like an apology, or even the preamble to one.

"You kicked my ass when it was down, Jaws."

"I should have stayed quiet."

"Don't mess up my crime scene."

"I won't. I need to get the evidence right this time."

She could have killed him. Thought she might. But she held her tongue and imagined Jaws slipping from a toe-hold and pinwheeling down the face of Half Dome toward his death.

Then she heard footsteps on the walk. It took her a moment to recognize Al with no sport coat on, and a pair of aviator shades hiding his eyes.

Al Madden was former head of the Sheriff's Department Homicide Detail, and now the district attorney's top investigator. He was big, smart and tireless. Hess had spoken highly of him.

The DA prosecutors used Al when they needed more than what the case detectives got. Or to tie things up, nail things down. Clear up the details, connect the last few dots.

Or when the DA thought the detectives just might have gotten something wrong. Al was there to help them win cases. And to keep the People from getting humiliated in court because of bad police work. Or sued into oblivion by the ACLU.

She nodded and shook Al's hand but said nothing. Like greeting your executioner, she thought. She wasn't going to make polite chatter. In the uncomfortable silence Al pulled off the sunglasses to reveal gray eyes rimmed in red.

"Look, Merci, everything looks tight on the reports. I'm just here to take some measurements, confirm a couple of small things. Clay knows this is a delicate one, with Wildcraft being one of ours."

"I understand. Small things like what? Measure what?"

"Nothing in particular."

Then everything in general, she thought: a wholesale dismissal of my casework.

"Let's do it, Al," said Dawes.

"Do you mind, Sergeant?" Madden asked, a hint of apology in his voice.

She shook her head and walked past them toward the driveway.

She walked through it again with Zamorra, once with Archie as the shooter and once with him not. Then again as burglars, noting all the things they could have taken but didn't. When they were finished they stood for a moment near the swimming pool and watched Al Madden and Ryan Dawes.

The two DA men were kneeling, Al on the walkway and Dawes over where Zamorra had found the casing. Dawes checked one of the crime scene drawings on the clipboard beside him, dropped his end of the tape and spread both arms to point out where the brass had been found. Madden nodded. Then Dawes hooked his right hand toward his head, pointed a finger and jerked his head.

"Did Wildcraft shoot himself, Paul?"

"I still don't know."

"Well, does he fit the damned profile, or whatever you call it?"

"Not so far. But the evidence fits *him*. You know that. Merci, if we have to take down a guilty deputy, nobody's going to crucify you for that."

"And what if he isn't? Then that's two in a row. I hurt a good man and lost half my department on the first."

"Talk to the sheriff."

"About what?"

"Giving it to Wheeler and Teague. Let somebody else take it."

Merci understood that she wanted Wildcraft's innocence for herself

as much as anything else. As a way to show the people who hated her
that she was a good cop, one of them. One of us. If she was proved
wrong about him as she'd been wrong with Mike, she'd resign. Probably wouldn't have to, she thought: reassignment to traffic would be
swift.

"No," she said.

"I knew you wouldn't."

"What would you do?"

"Find out more about Wildcraft. Nobody does this without a reason. Usually, more than one."

She said nothing as she watched Jaws run his hand through his
hair, then absently scratch his head. Cute little puke, she thought.

"Merci, I got some of their banking records, canceled checks and
credit card statements. The last two months of last year, and the first
two months of this year, the Wildcrafts spent about a hundred and
twenty thousand dollars on fun stuff—the new Porsche in the garage,
new furniture and carpet, a remodel on two of the bathrooms. Trips to
Grand Cayman, Tahiti, Costa Rica. That's beside the fact that they live
in a million-plus house in a million-plus neighborhood. Wildcraft was
making fifty grand a year and his wife made eight."

Hard to get more obvious than that. She shook her head and said
nothing.

Zamorra shrugged and glanced outside. "I've got us lined up with
her parents for five o'clock."

"What about his?"

"They came in last night from Northern California. The father said
they'd be at the hospital all day tomorrow. He said they'd be here until
we put the guy who did this in a coffin."

"That will be a wonderful day."

Rayborn had no guilt over her beliefs on crime and punishment.
You do the crime, you do the time. So far as murderers lying in wait,
well, off with their heads.

She once had the idea that there should be a countywide tax fund
for victims of the worst crimes. Their survivors would get lots of
money. Even at only five dollars per capita, you'd come up with fifteen
million a year for the fund. She would implement it when she was

elected sheriff, sometime around the age of fifty-eight. But she'd thought of all the people who'd kill each other just for *that* money and shook her head. Human nature, she thought. Don't get it.

And she'd never be sheriff of Orange County anyway. That had been a dream. Before Mike McNally and a man she'd killed, before the grand jury testimony she gave.

Now she was awake.

SEVEN

That afternoon Archie woke again for a few seconds, heard the sounds, saw the faces. So bright here, so loud.

He understood that he was Archie Wildcraft, Deputy 2, Orange County Sheriff's Department. That he was married to Gwen. That they lived in a nice home in the hills. These facts struck him as weightless and breakable.

Then dark water.

An hour later he woke again, to see his father and mother looking down at him. He felt tears burning down his face. His father held his hand and told him that Gwen had been shot that night, too, didn't make it. Archie knew this was what he had lost that would never come back. This was the huge thing that he was missing. Gwen. His wife. He couldn't picture her face, exactly. And her absence left in him something very large and very black.

So he swam down, deeper than he'd ever been. Trying to get to the bottom and stay there, to just join the darkness forever. Struggling to get to the depths. Down in the murk, burrowing through the silt and mud and rock, Archie heard the woman's voice again.

Swim. Breathe. Rest. Swim. Breathe. Rest.

The voice had the ring of authority so Archie, a young man used to taking orders, obeyed it. He trusted. He believed. He turned around, pushed off the black hard bottom and swam back up.

53

EIGHT

Rayborn drove her Impala down the on ramp to the Riverside Freeway, looking ahead at four lanes of crawling, belching cars. Like the border at TJ, she thought, everything but the kids selling piggy banks and *churros*. What a mess. She barged her way in and finally got over to the car-pool lane, which was doing thirty.

Zamorra sat neatly beside her, suit coat still on, looking out the side window. She'd never seen him with his tie so much as loosened, even when he'd come back from seeing his dying wife in the hospital and his face looked like he was dying too.

In the eight months since then Merci had come to love and respect him. For the first two months after Zamorra's wife had died, Merci had watched him thicken with booze and lassitude. He never complained about what he was going through. He seemed hungover every day, though she didn't think he always was. She suspected he had a string of temporary girlfriends, and some evidence to support this suspicion, but she never asked and he never told.

Everything else, they talked about. Tentatively at first, like panelists. But as the early months dragged on, Merci was able to talk to him about the death of Hess, and Zamorra about the death of Janine. It was easy, talking with someone who'd lived through something similar. Like exchanging terrible, valuable gifts. And though Merci blamed herself for what had happened to Hess and Zamorra blamed God for Janine, there was enough loss, rage, sadness and guilt between them to begin a friendship. It never felt to her like the losers' club, though. The Loss Club, maybe. She thought there was something noble in their sufferings, hard as it sometimes was to locate.

After a couple of months Zamorra must have quit the heavy booze. She knew he'd gotten himself back to his beloved boxing gym in Westminster. He started to look like himself again, even if he often seemed to be a thousand miles away in his mind. She admired the toughness that allowed him to climb out of the hole that he'd fallen into. And she admired the depth of feeling that had allowed him to fall into that hole to begin with.

A secret love began to grow. Secret because she still loved Hess and because Paul still loved Janine. Secret because only a few short months earlier she had been fooled into betraying Mike McNally, whom she knew—even while she was betraying him—loved her. How do you offer an unfaithful, mistaken heart to someone who'd remained so true? And secret because they were partners. Their arrest record was eighty-four percent, highest in the detail. Why risk screwing up a good team and complicating the life of yet another man? Were her uncertain emotions worth that?

But Rayborn couldn't reason away her feelings. As the weeks went by she was struck by all of Zamorra's good qualities—his good manners and good looks, his skill as an investigator, his personal neatness. He was gentle, unselfish, considerate. He was sensitive to other people's feelings. He was slow to answer but concise when he did. He was observant, often gathering more than her in shared encounters. He understood subtleties that, in her opinion, would have to be explained to most other men. She was also drawn to the darkness in him—not the grief, but the violence he concealed. The anger. More than once she saw it flare up in him at suspects and informants and convicts and belligerent citizens. He always controlled it, but it was there. She believed it to be considerable. And she respected him for keeping it safe but ready, like a gun.

She liked the way he smelled. She liked the little curves that made double parentheses around his occasional smiles. Even the nasty lumps he got in the gym. And how in profile his eyelashes looked sad.

She imagined touching him and being touched. Wondered how his cleanly shaven cheek would feel against her neck. Wondered how his wiry arms would feel around her, what his flat boxer's chest would feel like against hers. Sometimes she'd picture him and herself together and she'd smile inwardly because he was two inches shorter than she was. This amused her and made her think of the famous actors she'd heard about who were shot from heightening angles. In particular Yul Brynner standing on a box in *The King and I*, according to her mother, who saw the movie something like twenty times.

Merci couldn't help imagining what their children might look like. And how terrific it would be for Tim Jr. to have a brother or sister. She liked to picture that pink house on the beach in Mexico, but instead of just her and Hess and Tim Jr. staying in it, now there were also Paul and *their* child, a girl she'd named Ann, in fact. Ann and Tim Jr. got along beautifully. As did Hess and Zamorra. Merci loved them all equally but in different ways and they were always exceptionally happy.

So she waited to see if Paul was feeling the same way. She doubted it. She pictured him with someone petite, blonde and not associated with law enforcement. She would be elegant and feminine, but not showy about it. She would be devoted to him instead of her career. She would have that little bit of class that Paul had—a genuine appreciation for fine things. She would be eager to please him and would instinctively understand how, or find out. Merci tried not to be prejudiced toward the moronic slut. If she was good for Paul she would support them in every way she could.

But Zamorra showed no signs of interest in Merci. At least any that she could find. She toyed with the idea of telling him, or showing him what she was feeling. But it seemed wrong. Zamorra would love her when he was ready, or he would not. She believed there was nothing she could do about scheduling a man's heart, nothing she had a right to do. Love was an act of nature. Nature would take care of itself, as it had been doing for quite some time.

Then, in June, just a couple of months ago, Zamorra had shocked her.

After lunch they were walking around the old courthouse and

Paul had told her that he'd found someone. Her name was Kirsten.

Merci was thankful she'd had her aviators on because she was certain her eyes would betray her disappointment. But she kept everything else under beautiful control—her voice and choice of words, her mild exclamation of joy for him, her gently protective questioning about this, this . . . *person*.

She'd never known what a good actor she was. And the longer she walked along on that warm spring morning and played the part of happy friend, the better she got. By the time the walk was over, Merci had arranged a three-way lunch when it was convenient for Paul and *Kirsten*. She also revealed to Paul that she was seeing someone, too. He was in real estate, she said, mentioning his name only once: Frank.

Zamorra looked at her oddly, then. The only thing she could read for certain in his eyes was relief.

Zamorra had known.

By the time she got to one of the ladies' rooms back at headquarters her heart was pounding and she was sweating but cold and she had only just lifted the toilet seat when she vomited. After wiping up she'd sat on the seat and wept into a huge wad of toilet paper that shredded and broke away and stuck to her face. She hadn't vomited since the night she'd seduced Mike McNally in order to gather evidence to charge him for murder. This felt worse but she didn't know why. Maybe because back with Mike she'd been disgusted by what she was doing but she had believed it was the right thing to do. Now she was just crying for her own wretched, pathetic little heartbreak.

Before leaving the ladies' room she'd looked at the mirror and seen what she always saw: a tall, big-boned woman with unruly dark hair and a face that was not quite pretty. She had nice skin, correct? Looking back into her own dark eyes she saw anger and disappointment and humiliation. Zamorra had *known*. She took a deep breath and thought, screw it: I've got Tim Jr. to think about anyway, and the last thing my sorry ass needs is a romance with another cop whose wife has just died of cancer.

And that was that.

———

"What did you get on her family, Paul?"

"I got their names and address off one of the Wildcraft loan forms. Earla is the mother, Lee's the dad. Last name is Kuerner. Earla said they'd be there at five. They had funeral arrangements to make."

Merci remembered the GK in the bottom right corner of some of the paintings in Gwen Wildcraft's music room.

"How did she sound?"

"Numb."

The Kuerners lived in Norco, a small city not far from the county line. Zamorra used a map to navigate. Merci got off on Lincoln in Corona, picked up River Road, made a right on Second Street.

"I've never been out here," she said, looking out at a dairy farm, rows and rows of black cows lined up at the feed bars.

"It's interesting."

The houses along Second were mostly beat-up, the grass mostly dead. Chain-link fences, cars on blocks, corrugated metal tool sheds with brown rain stains on their flanks. One place still had the Christmas lights sagging from the roofline and faded, once-red bows sagging from the stucco. A spray-painted sheet of plywood advertised pygmy goats for sale. Merci looked at the stubby, big-bellied little goats, wondering what they were good for and what they cost. One yard was nothing but junk—automobile doors stacked like pancakes, dozens of rusted-out lawnmowers, piles of old steel fence posts, a collection of decrepit cement mixers. An ostrich stood in a child's wading pool and looked at Merci like a cop. The smell of the dairy farm came through the air-conditioned car, dark and mammalian and foul.

"Scenic," she said.

"Norco's a contraction for North Corona," said Zamorra.

"It looks like a contraction."

"They're poor on this end of town."

"Lazy, too, by the looks of it."

"There you go again, Merci."

He had a point. She'd enlisted Zamorra to help purge herself of glib opinion and rapid judgment. She'd gotten so exhausted with the endless opinions of others about herself—*she busted Sheriff Brighton for her career, she did it because she hated him and he didn't promote her, she busted her father because she hated him, too, no, it was because she loved him, she got suckered about McNally and had to blame it on somebody else, she did it because she's amoral, because she's too moral, blah fucking blah, blah, blah*—that Merci had even grown exhausted by her own.

It was just so hard sometimes, to keep from making up her mind before she had all the facts. You saw what you saw, thought what you thought, smelled what you smelled. She thought of Archie Wildcraft, and what he had either done or not done to his wife and himself. There she was again, making up her mind before all the facts were in.

"Yeah," she said. "Yeah. I'm sure a lot of them work hard for what they have."

"I wore the same shirt for my second- and third-grade school pictures. My big brother had worn it for his second-grade shot."

"How many wrecked cars in your front yard?"

She smiled slightly and Zamorra did, too.

"I know," she said. "I just have to remind myself to, when in doubt, shut my trap."

The Kuerner house off of Cherokee was a pale blue bungalow with white porch columns. There was a white picket fence around the small front yard, stepping stones leading to the porch. Two big pine trees stood on either side of the stones and held the house in shadow. The place was neat and clean.

The driveway gate was open so she pulled in and parked in front of the garage. When she got out the smell of cattle hit her hard and so did the heat. Ninety-five at least, she thought.

Earla Kuerner answered the knock and let them in. A little bell jingled when she shut the door behind them. She looked to be in her early fifties, average height and weight. Wavy gray-black hair and a good face.

The living room was cool and the windows were draped to keep out the afternoon heat. An air conditioner hummed. There was a small

TV with the sound turned down and two recliners set up in front of it, with a round occasional table between them. Green carpet. A brown plaid print sofa with heavy oak arms, a bookcase neatly stocked with paperbacks, family pictures on one wall, a china cabinet against another. Two framed paintings by Gwen hung beside the cabinet. One was of the front of the house and the two big pine trees, the other a kitten sitting in front of a barn. Merci noted that the stereo system still had a turntable.

Lee Kuerner rose from the left chair, offered his hand to each detective and introduced himself.

"Have a seat," he said.

"I've got lemonade," said Earla.

"I'd like some of that," said Paul.

"Yes, that would be great."

"I'll get it, honey," said Lee. Merci watched him walk toward the kitchen, a tall, slender man with a slowness about him that she instantly liked. Glasses, plaid shirt, jeans. Reminded her of her father, though Lee Kuerner was probably almost ten years younger. His hair was graying brown and full, long enough to touch his shirt collar.

Zamorra carried the burden of small talk while they waited. Merci looked at the pictures on the wall. It looked like the Kuerners had four children, all girls. Gwen was either the youngest or second youngest, Merci saw, but she couldn't say for sure. The girls were all bony and toothy, pretty faces.

Lee Kuerner came back with two glasses of lemonade balanced in one hand, and a TV tray under the same arm, which he snapped open with the other. To Merci it looked like the tray practically opened itself and locked its own legs into place. Well used. Lee set the tray between them, put the glasses on the tray, went back and got two more.

"We got a tree in the back," he said. "Earla makes good lemonade off it."

Merci sipped hers and agreed. Then, after a long pause: "I'm sorry."

Lee looked away and nodded. Earla looked down into her lemonade glass. A tear ran off her cheek. A tissue appeared in her hand and she dabbed her face.

Merci led, as usual. "Mrs. Kuerner, tell us about Gwen. Tell us who would want to kill her."

"Oh, oh my. I'm just hoping and praying it wasn't Archie. Was it?"

"We don't think so, but we don't know," said Paul. "There is some evidence pointing to him, and some evidence pointing away."

"No," said Lee. "It wasn't Archie. The papers made it sound like he was a suspect."

"The papers don't make that judgment," said Merci. "We do, and as of right now, he isn't."

"But a neighbor said he'd heard them fighting earlier that day. Her birthday, the twentieth," said Zamorra.

"People do fight sometimes, don't they?" asked Earla.

"Gwen hadn't made any domestic violence complaints," said Zamorra. "Did they fight a lot?"

"We don't know of anything like that," said Earla.

Neither Zamorra nor Merci spoke for a long moment. Merci picked it up again, which was how they usually worked—Rayborn leading and exploring, Zamorra clarifying, following up, shaping.

"Tell us about your girl, Mr. and Mrs. Kuerner," she said. "And tell us about Archie." She slipped her blue notebook from the pocket of her sport coat, got a good pen ready.

Gwen was easy. Gwen was happy. She was beautiful from the hour she was born. She was a good student, a good girl. Beautiful voice and liked to sing. Good at drawing. When early adolescence came she was still a good girl. Had a lot of friends and earned them. Still had friends from back then when she . . . Never any drinking or drug problems, though she probably tried things. Worked Pizza Hut, Sirloin Stockade, then a music store. Liked horses, clothes and music. Especially the music. Bought a guitar with her own money and taught herself to play it. Had the knack, and nobody knew where she got it from. Didn't have steady guys, seemed to use good judgment that way. Fell in love with Archie Wildcraft when she was sixteen, a sophomore in high school. Archie was playing scholarship college ball for UC Riverside, a sophomore also. Met him at a theater in the mall, Gwen was there with two of her girlfriends. Archie with two buddies. They went out for ice cream after the show, traded phone numbers. Lee and Earla weren't happy at all about this older guy. Name like Wildcraft spelled trouble, said Lee. Archie was twenty. They allowed him to come over and meet them and had a "pointed" discussion that night about whether to let him in the house again. Agreed that he was clean-cut, well mannered, handsome and head-over-cleats for Gwen.

Lee voted no; Earla voted yes.

So Archie started coming over for an hour, sometimes two, every evening he wasn't traveling for ball. He lived on campus, maybe half an hour away. Earla and Lee never let them be really alone, which wasn't hard with two of their other girls still in the house. Though after a while they gave the young people the privacy of the living room to watch TV, or the family room to study together. Archie never brought her home late from a date, and the curfew was always early. He brought Earla flowers and Lee some choice bass plugs Archie's father had carved, helped him overhaul the outboard on his little fishing boat. Helped them paint the house three weekends running. They never smelled alcohol on either of them, never saw any affection between them except for hugs and reasonable kisses hello and good-bye. All the Kuerner girls liked him, thought Gwen had a catch. Gwen actually colored when he was there or when his name was spoken around the house. Named a kitten Archie so she could say it a lot. She was seventeen when she said she wanted to marry Archie after she graduated.

Lee voted no; Earla voted yes.

Two months after her graduation Lee walked her down the aisle of a little Methodist church in Riverside. One of the happiest and saddest times of his life. Down to his last two girls. But he liked Archie and thought he'd be good to his daughter. Trusted him. Liked him. Archie's ERA was 2.18 and the bass plugs worked.

Earla got up and gave him a tissue and Lee turned his head away and pulled off his glasses in one motion.

Merci quietly cleared her throat. Zamorra looked at Earla, then away.

"How'd the marriage go?" asked Merci.

"It went fine," said Earla. "Gwen called every day, then every week, right up until . . . Archie missed baseball at first, but he got on quick as a deputy and really took to it."

"Why did he quit ball?" Zamorra asked.

"He thought he'd get drafted but he didn't. Never had good control of the fastball and the forkie wasn't working his senior year. Tendinitis, too. Tried out as a walk-on but knew it wasn't for him. No offers."

"That's too bad," said Paul.

"He took it good, though. He was ready to try something else."

"Was Gwen working then?" Merci asked.

"Gwen had a band and made a little money, too," said Earla. "She wrote a beautiful song that got accepted for a TV movie. They paid her good money for it, but got somebody else to sing it."

"Then they were doing okay, financially?"

"Gwen didn't grow up with a lot," Earla said carefully. "And neither did Archie. So, compared to what they came from they were doing fine. They had enough. She was happy and Archie was too, unless he was fooling us. All of a sudden, then, middle of last year, they hit it big with this stock and made a lot of profit. Bought a nice house in the hills, new cars. Took trips. Heck, they offered us a hundred thousand to remodel this place, or just sell it and find a better neighborhood. We didn't feel right about it. They weren't greedy people. Not in the least. But both of them liked nice things. And they worked hard to get them. And when they got them they enjoyed them."

"Stock in what?" asked Merci.

"OrganiVen," said Earla. "Then it got bought up by B. B. Sistel and everybody made a lot of money. You probably read about it."

Merci hadn't, though of course she knew B. B. Sistel Laboratories. They made everything from the stuff she took for headaches to the birth control pills she'd taken during her months with Mike McNally.

"Some doctors started it, down in La Jolla. They made this tumor treatment using rattlesnake venom. The idea was old but they found a way to make it work. Gwen and Archie told us that they'd seen slides and videos, and this stuff made from poison could kill those tumors in just minutes. Said it was like watching a miracle. The company called it MiraVen. Anyway, Gwen and Archie invested twenty thousand dollars early last year. Really scraped to come up with it. Then the company went public. Then Sistel bought it. There were splits and options and dividends and all sorts of stuff. And they made two million dollars, practically overnight."

Merci made a note of that. "Invested twenty thousand, got back two million in less than a year?"

"Half a year. All these young geniuses put the OrganiVen company together, based on the cancer treatment. Doctors, business geniuses, marketing geniuses—they were all friends from college."

She exchanged glances with Zamorra. Slowly, almost absently, she wrote CK *OrganiVen.* Somebody turned twenty grand and snake poison into two million in less than one year, she figured fraud. But something like that could happen legally on Wall Street, or the Nikkei, or the Pacific Stock Exchange right here in Southern California.

Merci wasn't sure what to ask next, so she went with the obvious. "Did the big money make them happy?"

"Very."

"Because sometimes, people are fine until they hit it rich. Then problems start."

Lee nodded quickly, as if he'd thought of that a long time ago.

"I saw no signs of that," he said. "They both seemed kind of . . . relieved. That twenty thousand was hard to get. They used their retirement money, borrowed eight hundred from us. Borrowed from friends. Got a second on their little house in Santa Ana. So when it all happened just like they wanted it to, they seemed almost to not believe it. It was like they'd hit a slot in Vegas, rather than making a sound financial investment."

Merci wrote *couldn't believe it.*

The Kuerners looked at each other. Lee broke the gaze and turned to Merci. "Do you think it was something to do with all that?"

"Do you?"

"It worried me that they made so much," he said. "It was all legal, I know that. But it worried me."

"We're modest people," said Earla.

"Were Archie and Gwen keeping different company last year, when the money started coming in?"

"Not that we know," said Lee.

"Did they ever mention taxes, or getting out of taxes, or hiding the money from the government—even just joke about it?"

Lee frowned and looked at Merci. "No. Once Archie told me that if they made the two million, he'd still have to figure on the government taking almost half. But he didn't say it like he had to hide the money. Or bitterly. Just matter-of-factly."

"So far as you know, did they declare all that income to the IRS?"

"Yes, so far as I know."

Merci let a silence punctuate her change of thought. "Mr. and Mrs. Kuerner, did Gwen ever talk to you about having affairs with other men?"

"No," said Earla.

Lee was looking at the dead TV, his hands folded on his lap. "No," he said quietly.

"What was the maddest she ever got at Archie?"

Earla sighed and looked up at the ceiling. "Once, she told me he was awfully darned nice to some of the women he worked around. Said he always had a smile and a nice word for the pretty ones. Said half the women Archie ran across wanted to take him away from her. She was feeling insecure right then, I think. I don't think she was talking about any girl in particular. And she wasn't accusing Archie of being unfaithful. She was just down at the time."

"Do you know why?"

"After that one song she sold to TV, she didn't sell any more. Her band was getting fewer bookings. This popular nightclub down by the beach—the Nut House—they wouldn't book Gwen's band anymore. After three years, they just stopped booking them. She felt like she wasn't any good at writing and singing. Those things were important to her."

Merci looked to Zamorra again. "When was the last time you saw Gwen alive?" he asked.

"Her birthday," said Earla. "She drove all the way out here to take us out to lunch. It was a tradition."

"How was she?"

"Oh, she was in good spirits. A little thoughtful maybe, like you can get on a birthday, looking back at the years. But Archie had gotten a reservation for dinner that night at a nice restaurant in Newport Beach. She was looking forward to that. It was actually a party but she didn't know it. Our youngest, Priscilla, was at the party, if you want to talk to her about it."

Rayborn made a note. "What time did Gwen get here?"

"Noon, almost exactly."

"And what time did she leave?"

"A few minutes after three."

Merci looked at Zamorra. He held her eye and she knew he was wondering the same thing she was: if Gwen was here at three on that day, how could she be at home, arguing with Archie in the back-yard?

"We came back here after the restaurant and talked," said Lee. "She wanted to see some old family pictures. Like Earla said, Gwen was thoughtful that day. Had something on her mind. I don't know what. I didn't ask. I wish I had."

There was a moment of silence. Zamorra gave Merci his all-finished nod.

She rose and went to the wall of family pictures. "Tell me about your family. Four girls. And Gwen was what . . . second youngest?"

Earla nodded, rose and walked over to the picture wall. "Next to youngest, that's right. Priscilla is our youngest, then Diana and Lizzy. More lemonade?"

"Sure."

Half an hour later Earla was finished with her quickie family history. Merci followed along via the wall pictures, then looked at the photographs that Earla Kuerner had shown Gwen on her birthday, less than eighteen hours before she was murdered in her own bathroom.

Zamorra and Lee stayed in the living room and Merci caught stray snippets of their conversation: the aggressiveness of large-mouth bass versus smallies; Martinez's phenomenal August so far; speculation on Archie Wildcraft's capacity for spousal violence. *No, I don't think so, Detective. Good man.*

Merci had just handed Earla her empty lemonade glass when the little bell jingled and a young woman in a business suit came through the front door. She looked so much like Gwen that Merci blinked: same smart eyes, same wavy dark hair, same good figure. She looked quickly at Merci, then Zamorra.

"These are the police," said Earla.

"How do you do," said the woman. "I'm Priscilla Brock. Soon to be Kuerner again."

She looked at her mother. "Did you tell them I was at the party?"

"They know."

Priscilla nodded. "I was one of the last people to see them before it happened. Arch threw a nice party at the Rex. There were twenty of us."

Arch. Merci made a note of that, too.

Priscilla seemed to evaluate her, then Zamorra. Her chin quivered, then set hard. "Now there are what, eighteen and a half of us?"

"Can you take a few minutes and tell us about the party?"

"Give me five."

She walked over to her father and hugged him, then disappeared down the hall.

Priscilla came out a few minutes later in the same clothes, but no nylons or shoes. She'd pinned up her hair and taken off her makeup. They sat with her in the little dining room while Lee and Earla watched the news. Priscilla got more lemonade for them and tap water over ice for herself.

She told them about the party at the Rex, how Archie told Gwen it was a birthday dinner date for the two of them, but when she walked into the private room they were all there and she just about fainted. Everybody toasted her and brought presents, some really nice ones, then ate a lot and drank some. It was ten couples—everybody from musician friends of Gwen's to cop friends of Archie's. Priscilla was the only sister to make it—one was out of state, the other was working nights and couldn't switch shifts.

"How did they seem that night?" asked Zamorra.

Priscilla took a moment. "Archie was a little worried, a little controlling, as he tends to be. I think he got a little upset at some of his friends, for hugging and kissing Gwen. Nothing big—it passed. Gwen was happy. A little embarrassed at the expense of it all, but happy. Her friends were important to her. She looked exceptionally beautiful."

Priscilla looked down at the table. She took a deep breath and let it out slowly.

Zamorra again: "Do you know what Archie was worried about?"

"That's his personality. I don't think he was worrying about anything big. You know, if the prime rib was right or the drinks were coming fast enough. If Gwen was really having a good time."

Merci mostly listened and made notes. She saw quickly that Priscilla responded better to Paul, so it was best for him to lead. Priscilla twice mentioned the decorations in the private room. Beautiful, lots of work, a couple of the women had helped her and Archie set them up that afternoon while Gwen was here with her folks.

Norco to Newport Beach, she thought. Idea.

"Did you pick up Archie at home, on your way to set up the room?" Merci asked.

"Yes."

"A lot of work getting all those decorations out there and put up. So what time did you get to Archie and Gwen's place?"

"Two, two-thirty."

Merci waited and let the silence work on Priscilla. Zamorra did the same.

"So what did you and Archie argue about in the backyard?"

Merci saw the anger flash into Priscilla's eyes, but not back out.

"We didn't argue about anything."

"Oh," said Merci. "One of the neighbors said he heard loud voices—a man and a woman—about three that afternoon."

"Well, those would have been Archie's and mine. But it sure wasn't an argument. What it was, was me going off on my stupid sonofabitch soon-to-be-ex-husband. And Archie trying to calm me down. I've got a temper. I lost it then."

"Why?"

"What do you mean, why?"

"Why then, with your sister's husband?"

Priscilla colored and Merci made a quick scribble then looked up, hoping to aggravate the woman.

"Because we're *friends*?" she asked with a quiet acidity. "Because I trust him and respect him? Because he's been like an older brother to me since I was fourteen?"

"Those are good reasons, Priscilla. I was just asking, trying to get the feel of the conversation."

"I apologize. I feel like I could bite somebody's head off. May as well be yours."

"Accepted," said Merci. "And I apologize for being blatantly suspicious about everything and everybody. It's my job, and I'm good at it."

"Yes," said Priscilla. "You are."

"Who threw the rock?"

"Again?"

"Who threw the rock through the living room window?"

Priscilla eyed Merci with fresh suspicion and held the look for a long beat. Merci expected her to color if she knew about the rock. If she didn't, Merci wasn't sure: maybe a big surrendering sigh.

With no change in color, Priscilla smiled a thrifty little smile. "What rock?"

"The rock on the living room floor. It was thrown through the window and the blinds."

"No. There was no rock. I think I'd have noticed. I will say, however, that I'm capable of missing things. But no rock, Detective, that I saw."

An uncomfortable moment then, while the two of them cooled down and Zamorra said nothing.

"Tell me about the future ex," said Merci.

"Charles Brock of the Riverside office of Ritter-Dunne-Davis Financial. That's all you need to know. That's all I wish *I* knew. Believe me."

Merci waited. Then, "Sure. Thanks for everything. Really."

Priscilla walked them to the door. Lee and Earla rose and came forward and shook their hands and thanked them.

Merci had a parting idea. "You know, Priscilla, just a long shot, but did Charles Brock sell Archie and Gwen the OrganiVen stock?"

Priscilla sighed. "Yeah. Charlie can sell anything to anybody. In fact, he sold some of it to himself."

They stopped at UCI Medical Center and found the neuro ward. They waited for almost twenty minutes to speak with Dr. John Stebbins. Stebbins was short, young and tight-mouthed, looking at the detectives as if they were surgical complications.

"We can't do it," he said. "We can't determine the *caliber* of bullet in Mr. Wildcraft's head."

"We can, Doctor," said Merci. "If you just show us the pictures."

"You don't understand. The spiral CT will give us a very close measurement of the object, down to one millimeter. But the bullet has fragmented. And if you figure in the one millimeter margin times four fragments, a caliber measurement becomes meaningless. See?"

"When are you going to take it out?"

He laughed curtly and sighed. He looked up and over her head as he spoke, as if it was easier for him to believe she didn't really exist. "The edema has been reduced somewhat. There is no infection at this time. Surgery now would be inadvisable. It's possible that we'll never remove the bullet from Mr. Wildcraft's brain."

"And it's possible he'll die tomorrow," said Merci.

"His condition is extremely critical."

"I want to see him."

"Absolutely not."

"I'll push you aside and go in anyway."

He still wasn't looking at her. "I will allow you exactly thirty sec-onds. Only one of you. Just one."

"How about both of us, for fifteen?"

"This way."

"You just did the right thing, Stebbins."

NINE

A woman with dark eyes and hair looked down at him. Archie sensed that this must be Gwen, that she was in fact not lost and this was all just a very long bad dream.

He looked up at her. Her expression was pitying but the pity looked like something she had to work at. More than anything else, she looked angry.

"I'm Sergeant Merci Rayborn, Homicide," she said. "I'm investigating the murder of your wife. This is my partner, Paul Zamorra."

When he realized it wasn't Gwen his heart wilted and he thought about going under again. Then Archie recognized them—minor players in ancient history. He wanted to say something but words exhausted him.

So he closed his eyes and ducked under, hovering in the cool, pellucid river.

We just wanted to introduce ourselves, Archie. That's all. You're going to get better. I promise.

How do you know that? he wondered.

He thought of Gwen and vaguely remembered a birthday party and a drive up Coast Highway and a rock through the window and a bright light in his eyes. Where had he last seen her? Was it in the bed? Wasn't she sleeping? Hadn't they made love? Or . . . the bathroom? Didn't they go into the bathroom for something?

Gwen is dead, he remembered. My huge thing, gone. Why can't I see your face? Please let me see her face.

And again he tried to picture Gwen but he could see nothing but the black immensity that had swallowed her.

I got shot in the head, didn't I?

No one answered, so he asked again.

No one answered this time either, and he realized he was thinking, not talking. He realized he was far away from everyone. But he also realized they were right there, just a few feet away from him. It was like existing in a world that was taking place in the same time and place as theirs, but not connected to it.

He tried to swim back up so he could talk, find out what had happened, maybe help Detective Rayborn.

Up. *Up.*

But there was still water over him and he couldn't go the last few feet.

Then the voice that had gotten him through all this:

Breathe. Rest. Breathe, Archie. Rest.

TEN

"Awchie is okay?"

"Archie is in the hospital."

"He's not in the hospital?"

"He *is* in the hospital."

"He's not in the hospital?"

"I just told you, Tim, he's *in* the hospital."

Tim Jr. looked away with false disinterest. "Oh."

Merci squeezed the washcloth over his head and Tim smiled up at her.

"Awchie is not in the hospital?"

At twenty-seven months of age, Tim's new favorite thing was to be negative and contrary. He loved to defy Merci, even when it was counter to his self-interest. He loved to say he didn't like things that he clearly did. Loved to ask questions that contradicted information he was just given. Over and over and over. Merci enjoyed it: Tim's first taste of the power of no.

His other new thing—this had started a few months ago—was that he was developing sudden deep interest in people who seemed far from his daily experience. For instance, the ranch manager who occasionally worked in the Valencia grove that surrounded Merci's house. His name was Rodas, and Tim, after meeting him once, still asked about him constantly. Or Tad, who ran the breakfast house Merci occasionally took them to on Sunday mornings. Or Paul Zamorra, who had come over to the house a few times—though never with Kirsten.

Tim's new passion was Archie Wildcraft. Just the night before, she had told Tim a little about what had happened. She always tried to talk to him as a young person rather than as a toddler, for reasons she wasn't completely certain were good. Something to do with giving him a realistic sense of the world and what happens in it. Mainly, she just figured that if he asked how her day was, he deserved a halfway accurate answer. Not that she got graphic about things, and there was plenty she just left out. She always tried to explain things in gentle ways, ways that wouldn't harden or frighten him. *Archie got hurt in the head and went to the hospital. And his wife is now all gone.*

"All gone" being the term she applied to Tim's father, Hess. A bit more of her heart crumbled away every time she had to use it.

Last night, after Merci's first long day on the Wildcraft property, Tim had asked many questions about Archie. This morning he'd asked more. After lunch, when Merci had called Tim, as she did almost every day, he'd asked immediately if Awchie was in the hospital. For reasons that Merci clearly understood, her son had fastened his interest to a man he knew almost nothing about and had never met.

Which is exactly what his father was.

Whatever, thought Merci: better than asking about the moronic toys and junk food he saw on kids' TV.

"Awchie is all gone?"

"No, Archie is okay."

"Is all gone?"

"Is okay."

"Awchie is . . . a car?"

"He's a policeman."

"Is not a policeman?"

"Time to get out of the tub now, Tim. Let's get out."

Clark, her father, heated up the night's dinner while Merci sat at the table with Tim. It was an old farmhouse with a big kitchen and this time of year they left all the windows open in the evenings to take in the cooling air. A black cat jumped onto Merci's lap and she petted it once, then set it down on the squeaky old floor. They had six or eight cats but Merci could never remember their names. She liked them in a general rather than an individual way, as she did most human beings. And likewise found them annoying more often than not.

She had the newspaper open in front of her but no interesting crimes had made the pages this day. Out of curiosity she checked the business section for the B. B. Sistel activity. The ticker symbol was BBS and it was even at fifty-three and three-quarters dollars a share on the NYSE.

"What chances are the doctors giving him?" asked Clark.

"Apparently he's stabilized. So that makes him extremely critical rather than hour-to-hour."

"Where did it lodge, exactly?"

"I don't know. It's all just yellow goo to me."

"Goo?" asked Tim.

"Goo," said Merci. "Your brain."

"Oh."

Clark pulled a baking dish from the oven, his ropey arm lost in a huge mitt. Merci thought of Lee Kuerner and his bass fishing. She wished her father had some hobby he loved, some passion, even for something as silly as fishing. The only thing that seemed to matter to him anymore was being useful.

"If it damaged the left side of his brain," he said, "the right side of his body might be impaired. You know, one side of the brain controls its opposite side of the body."

Merci thought about this. She could see the B volume of the encyclopedia open in the cookbook holder. Clark liked to think of himself as helpful in her work.

"That bullet could take away his memory," he said. "Or his math skills, or his ability to see colors or to reason deductively. Anything."

"I wonder if it can lodge in there and not really do any damage."

"A lot of brain matter goes unused."

"The doctor said that they might not even try to remove it. That would be riskier than leaving it where it is. I thought the lead would dissolve and kill you, but that's not a big problem. The leads in paints can kill you but not the lead in bullets. That's a surprise."

"It has no feeling, the brain. They can operate on it with the patient sedated but awake, carrying on a conversation. They'll do that if they're near the speech area. If the guy starts talking funny, they back off."

"Big of them. What's for dinner?"

"Chicken."

"That moron Dawes brought in Al Madden to check my work. Says he wants the evidence properly handled this time."

He looked at her steadily. "Dawes took advantage of you to make a splash for himself. What he said about you was really about him."

It never failed to astound her that her father defended her side in an action that brought shame upon himself and disgrace to two of his friends. And it wasn't as if the whole miserable thing had come as a surprise: both Merci and Clark had known that if she testified to the grand jury, Clark's head would roll. Over something that had gone down thirty-three years ago, she thought. Thirty-three *years* ago: a prostitute with secrets, powerful men frightened for their careers and their families, a deputy forced into doing the unspeakable. And a soft-spoken gentle man who closed his eyes to what he knew was going on. Clark. What was it he had said? *I knew there was blood on my hands, but I didn't know how much.*

"Moron?" asked Tim.

"It's a person who is not very smart," said Merci.

"A person who *is* very smart?"

"Never mind," she said. The idea of Tim obsessing about Ryan Dawes curdled her nerves.

"I'm not going to put my soup on my head," her son said thoughtfully.

"Very good, Tim. That's excellent."

Clark checked something steaming in a pot, stirred it with a big wooden spoon, then set it back on the stove. The kitchen smelled of roasting sage and chicken. It was warm so Merci held up her hair. Tim took one look at her and slid off his booster seat, claiming that he'd be back. Tim loved missions.

"Did you get any fingerprints off the gun?"

"Wildcraft's. He came back with GSR, too."

"Could the lab match the gun to the bullets in his wife?"

"They could and they did."

"And you said the gun was registered to the deputy?"

"Dad, you know exactly what I said."

"Her blood on his clothes?"

"Gel cooking, jury out."

Tim sprinted back into the room with a small elastic hairband in his hand. Merci took it with a smile and got her heavy dark hair up off her neck. He climbed into her lap.

"Looks bad for him, doesn't it?"

She sighed and looked at Clark. "I don't think he did it. I don't think he put that bullet in his own head. Someone shot him, then took his weapon and shot his wife. Then came back and put the gun in his hand."

"Fired it once, to get the metals on his skin?"

"Yeah."

"Why?"

"I don't know. But Archie had no motive for any of this. He was happy, in love with his wife. Or so his friends say. Pretty house they lived in—you could tell they took pride in it. Someone threw a rock through the slider in the living room, and I think that's what got Archie out of bed that morning. I think that's why it was thrown. Neighbor saw a black Caddy driving away, just after he called in the shot. Patrol saw a black Caddy with two guys in it, leaving the vicinity at the same time. Cal plates, first two letters OM. We put out a countywide all-enforcement but nothing popped."

Clark stopped whatever he was doing and stared at her. "That's a heck of a frame job."

She looked down at the paper. "Yeah. We're smelling for enemies, but nothing hot yet. They had some big stock winnings last year— they ponied up twenty grand and made two million."

"That kind of money creates its own problems."

"The parents say it was all legal, all aboveboard."

"But still—you turn a little money into a fortune in a few months, and all sorts of reactions take place. It's almost chemical."

She nodded and noted that the stock market arrows were all pointing down on the business page. "The sister's kind of interesting," she said.

"Oh?"

"Younger than Gwen. Just as pretty. Was over at Archie's the day of the murder when Gwen was with her parents in Norco. The neighbor heard them arguing. Loud. What do you argue with your brother-in-law about, on your sister's birthday, while she's not there? The sister says they weren't arguing, it was just her going off about her future ex. Feels . . . not right. These two beautiful major babe sisters, this young hunk who's just raked in two million. I don't know. Just one of those feelings you get. But Archie doing that to Gwen and himself? That feels flat-out wrong. I hope to God he wakes up with a clear head and can tell us what really happened."

Clark said nothing for a moment. His expression said *don't count on that*, but he had the good sense not to say it out loud. "Your instincts are good, Merci."

"When they're not bad."

"Come on."

"Well, yeah, they're getting better, I hope."

"Daughter, do something nice for yourself—be a friend to you."

"Yeah yeah yeah."

Tim followed this conversation but said nothing. He stared into the space midway between his mother and grandfather with a dazed expression, which meant he was concentrating. She used to think he was drifting or working on a bowel movement until he started repeating things or asking about things she never even knew he'd heard. She loved the way his eyes looked when he was drinking in the world.

"I had one of the records deputies burn me copies of Wildcraft's felony court transcripts in the last two years," she said. "I brought them home for some light reading tonight. Besides the huge income, one thing you make being a deputy is an enemy or two."

"One of those fringe benefits."

"I wonder why nobody calls them fringe anymore."

"I call 'em fringe," said Tim, snapping out of it.

"Prove it."

"Fringe."

"You do. Very good."

"Very not good?"

She smiled and leaned forward, right in his face. "Okay, Mr. Negative."

Tim laughed and pinched her nose and Merci asked him for a kiss. When he said no, she faked a pout and he gave in. His hands were soft and warm on her cheeks. It seemed like he got heavier every day, but still, she loved him on her lap, right up there close where she could smell his breath and his hair and touch the small parts of his perfect body. When she looked at Tim, then thought about her job, she wondered what happened to people. To start out so sweet and end up so dismal. She'd seen a lot of what the world does to people, and what they do to the world, but it had never engaged her sympathy until Tim Jr.

Precious little man, she thought: what will it do to you?

"First week I worked the jail an inmate promised to kill me when he got out," said Clark.

"You never told me that."

Which was typical of her father: he'd rarely spoken about his work when she was a girl, and he rarely spoke of it after he retired. Merci wondered at how different they were with regard to their work. For Clark, being a deputy was just a job. For Merci it was a passion. Clark left the job at headquarters. Merci dreamed it. Clark hardly talked about his work at all. But work was just about all Merci talked about. She understood that she'd gotten her drive and enthusiasm from her mother. Her stubbornness and general misanthropy, too. And she understood how difficult it must have been for them, such opposites in so many ways.

"It was strange," he said. "This guy was in on an assault charge. He was a biker, one of the Hessians, a skinny guy with red hair and freckles and a straggly little beard. Smitty. Smitty Cole. Cole took one look at me and started working me. Dissing me, you'd call it now. And he did a good job of it—he saw right through me. He called himself the Prophet, claimed that God told him what other people were thinking. He was maybe twenty-six or -seven, I was twenty-one or -two.

Talking trash about me, talking trash about the job, talking trash about your mother. It got directly under my skin and one day I lost my temper and hit him in the stomach. Then across the chin. Hard. Knocked him clean out."

Merci's father suddenly took on a new respect in her eyes. "You punched him out?"

"Well, yes."

"That's great, Dad."

He looked at her with mild disbelief, an expression that she'd known as far back as she could remember.

"Back then, things were a little looser in the jail. We didn't pit gladiators like the guards up at Corcoran, but you know, it was tit for tat."

"And you'd been tatted."

"That was the only time I ever struck an inmate."

"Well, I'm glad you clocked the creep. When he woke up, he said he'd kill you?"

Clark glanced at Tim on her lap. "A few days later. Looked at me in the mess hall, pretty much rabid, and told me he'd, ah . . . deal with me when he got out. I believed him. Maybe because I was young. But it registered in a way I didn't like. Maybe because he'd said other things that were true."

Merci waited for the punch line, which was fairly obvious, but she wanted to hear details, if there were any.

"Died in a drug deal gone bad," said Clark, forking the chicken onto plates. He glanced at Tim again, then at Merci. "Someone . . . removed his head area with a ten-gauge item made for waterfowling."

"Bummer. Hungry, Tim?"

"Not hungry."

"Too bad, little man. Let's eat!"

After dinner she poured a substantial scotch and water and turned on the living room TV for Tim. He liked *Teletubbies*—a PBS children's program that Merci considered hallucinogenic but harmless. It was about cuddly creatures with televisions implanted in their stomachs living in tunnels under a phony golf course that grew big plastic flowers and had radio broadcasts coming out of evil-looking speakers. The Teletubbies themselves scurried around like potbellied oldsters, squeaking to one another. Cottontail rabbits loitered on the greens. The accompanying music was repetitious and infantile in a bizarre way and Merci figured the creators were '60s acid casualties with fat grants from the Corporation. Then she tried to remove this idea from her head, just another useless and probably inaccurate opinion. So many of them. She watched the Teletubbies go to bed in their underground sleeping pods and saw how this absolutely fascinated her son.

What could it hurt? You've got tubbies and I've got scotch.

She sat on the floor beside him and stroked his back while he watched. She wouldn't let him see the next show, which sent him into a tantrum—Tim's new reaction to being denied even the smallest desire. Merci figured it was a phase.

Tim bawled it out and she let him, then took him into his room and read him three of his favorite stories. He fell asleep on her lap in the rocking chair and she carried him to his bed.

She showered and put on a light robe, then came back to Tim's room and sat in the corner in the dark. The remnants of the ice cubes clinked rhythmically in the glass as she rocked. The sweet aroma of the orange blossoms wavered in on the warm breeze. She closed her eyes and said the same prayer she said every night, to a God she believed in but wasn't sure she trusted.

Watch over him. Watch over him. Watch over him.

In the living room she turned down the volume on the police band radio, already set to the Sheriff's frequency, down low. Listening to it was a holdover from her old days on patrol, the days when every crime seemed to require her attention, on duty or off.

She sat forward on the living room sofa, some of Archie Wildcraft's court testimony spread across the coffee table, the lampshade tilted out to throw light over her shoulder. The windows were still open and the white tip of a cat tail twitched from a shadow on the seat of Clark's old recliner.

Then she started with the criminal felony cases, going back a year.

The People versus Vomastic Washington, multiple homicide, responding deputies Archibald Wildcraft and Damon Reese. Archie testified that he'd found the defendant hiding in a bathroom cabinet at the crime scene. Conviction to Ryan Dawes, two life sentences to be served consecutively, appeal filed and pending.

The People versus Stephanie Mai, attempted murder of Marilyn Mai, her identical twin sister, wiretap testimony from Deputy 2 Archibald Wildcraft. Apparently, Archie had been assigned to an undercover sting at the sisters' favorite Garden Grove disco. He'd gotten some incriminating statements from her. Conviction to Lisa Musick, twelve years, appeal filed and pending.

The People versus Felix Mendez, possession of illegal narcotics, conspiracy to distribute narcotics, possession of illegal automatic weapons, attempted murder of a police officer. All of this grew from a domestic disturbance call, responding officers Archibald Wildcraft and Damon Reese again. Reese was about to take a bullet from Mendez's hidden derringer when Archie shot him through the hand, kicked away the gun and cuffed the defendant. When the prosecutor asked if Archie considered himself a hero for saving his partner's life, Archie said he was just a deputy doing his job. Conviction to Ryan Dawes, life in prison without parole for Mendez: strike three.

Merci scanned back through the Mendez transcript and saw what she thought she'd see: Mendez was heavily implicated in *La Eme*— the Mexican Mafia—though he steadfastly denied knowing anything about the organization. Dawes presented testimony that Mendez was a ranking member of *La Eme*, having earned his way up by dealing narcotics and handling enforcement, intimidation and murder contracts. Mendez's attorney aired a symphony of objections, the judge sustained half and overruled the others, allowing Mendez to deny it all.

Merci knew that *La Eme* had climbed into power in just the last two decades, as the Hispanic prison population had grown. In the California prisons, they ruled. They were exceptionally violent, well organized and thorough. They were loyal to each other, and all but silent to the law. And although their power base lay hidden in the cells of the huge penal system, their reach went far beyond the walls and razor wire.

Sure, thought Merci, *La Eme* could hit Archie Wildcraft if they wanted him hit. And sure, Felix Mendez would not have been too happy about having his left hand blown apart in his own home while his wife watched, by a handsome young deputy with dimples. But why Gwen?

Merci flipped back through to read about the disturbance call. An anonymous neighbor had phoned it in, and the deputies had walked into the middle of a cocaine-addled dispute between the couple. Sure enough, when Michelle Mendez had spit in his face and bitten him, Archie Wildcraft had shoved her into a wall and cuffed her. Made her nose bleed. And that was when Mendez produced the pistol from under his bathrobe.

Merci flagged the transcript with a red paper clip.

She leafed through *The People versus Goudee*, a rape case, but rapists were cowards. And *The People versus Viznaska*, a car thief, but Viznaska was twenty years old, apparently not mobbed up, had no violent priors. And *Rhonert*, a burglar; *Nelson*, a boiler-room phone fraud scammer; *Vasquez*, a fugitive female shot-caller whom Archie and Reese had easily matched to a briefing mug while she walked three pitbulls down Fourth Street, about five blocks from headquarters, in broad daylight.

Another hour and she'd finished off the felony criminal cases in which Wildcraft had testified in the last two years. She fingered through the arrest forms—mostly drunk-in-publics, drunken drivers, disturbing the peace, fights. The same shit that's coming over the radio right now, she thought. Meat and potatoes, everyday stuff.

One drunken driving stop almost two years ago was of a man named Trent Gentry, who happened to work for the Newport Beach office of Ritter-Dunne-Davis Financial. She pulled and flagged this with a red paper clip too, strictly on the coincidence of Priscilla Brock's beloved Charles working for the same global company. Small world, she thought. *Small World, Big Opportunity*—wasn't that the

RDD slogan you got sick of on TV? At any rate, Archie had done the right thing and busted the drunk.

She sighed and sat back and looked out at a bright moon checkered by the window screen. So many creeps, she thought. But how many of these are capable of this? One? Maybe two?

She clicked off the radio, checked Tim, made another drink, sat outside on the back patio. She looked out at the dark groves and marveled at how they just ended a hundred yards in three of four directions, at the ten-foot salmon-colored wall of a housing development. Merci loved the wall for all the people it kept *in*. She had not chosen the farmhouse for aesthetics, and in fact she didn't care for orange juice, but she'd grown to like the still sweetness of the trees and semiferal cats that moved silently through the grove, like thoughts. Her father had been offered the place by an acquaintance who owned it, and the rent was cheap. That was long before Clark had entertained any notions of moving in. The old farmhouse came with the warning that it could and would be sold to the first bidder with the right price, but that had yet to happen. Merci wondered how many millions her five acres were worth. What, six or eight grand for every orange?

Zamorra called at eleven-fourteen.

"You weren't listening to the police band."

"What."

"Irvine cops found a black STS, license QM742JN abandoned at the end of Sand Canyon. You know, out there by the strawberry fields—past the new hospital."

"Jones said OM."

"*O*s and *Q*s—not the first time."

"I want to see that car."

"Gilliam and Ike Sumich are on their way."

"I'm on mine. Thanks, Paul."

She poked a cat out of the way, tossed the drink and nuked a cup of instant coffee, dressed quickly, told Clark the score. She kissed Tim. She remembered the CSI who was doing such good, thorough work at the Wildcraft scene, Don Leitzel. So she called him and told him to get on it double time. He said, "I'm there," and hung up.

Twenty minutes later Merci came to the end of Sand Canyon Road, braking her Impala well outside the ring of white light cast by three big tripod floods. The floods were being run by a big generator that half deafened her as she got out of her car. It was so loud she could barely hear herself think, but the light was bright and true, and Zamorra came from light to darkness to greet her.

ELEVEN

The STS was parked off the road, on a wide beach of dirt and loose gravel that separated the asphalt from the strawberry field. When Merci stepped out of her car she could smell the fruit. The roaring generator had been set up maybe twenty yards from the front end of the Caddy. One light tripod was positioned a solid ten yards away from each end of the car, Merci noted: good.

She also saw the crime scene tape, a big rectangle of it with the car in the middle.

"You'll like this," said Zamorra.

"A confession letter and video evidence?"

"Not quite. Your pal Dobbs was first one here again."

"My luck."

"Look at the crime scene he marked off, it's the size of Yankee Stadium."

The floodlights made her think of a baseball stadium, too—the bright, clean white light. She followed him to the tape, then under it, but Zamorra took her by the arm and stopped her.

Then Merci saw the flashlight in the gravel, pointing toward the road. Less than a yard away lay a citation book. Then a sunglass case. Then, closer to the STS, a bundle of road flares, unlit.

Her heart sped up and she thought of young Dobbs and wondered what all this debris was.

"What's this stuff doing everywhere?"

"He'll want to tell you."

Dobbs was already trotting toward her—head steady, up on his toes—but staying way out by the perimeter of the tape. She saw the triangle of his torso, the big chest and arms.

"Sergeant Rayborn," he said crisply.

"Deputy."

He knelt and picked up the flashlight and aimed its beam down into the dirt and gravel. It barely showed up against the fierce light of the floodlamps. She knelt, too.

Dobbs traced a small circle on the dirt with his light. In the middle of the small circle was a large footprint.

"I found a total of ten indentations, leading from the car toward the road. I marked the best ones with whatever I had handy. None of them are very good, but the first four, up by the car, are better. Two people. One set starts from the passenger side of the Caddy. The other from the driver's side. I took the liberty of holding my duty boot over the ones from the passenger side—don't worry, I didn't even come close to touching one."

Dobbs stared intently down the beam of his light.

"I wear a twelve," he said. "And these are bigger than mine. A lot. Big dude."

"Very."

"I approached on the passenger side, from the rear, checked for anything suspicious, then taped the whole scene off before I called in. Got into kind of an argument with one of the CSIs over how close the generator should go. After that driveway thing, *nobody's* getting too close to my crime scenes. Including me."

"You with Crowder tonight?"

"He called in sick so I'm solo. Sergeant, guess what's laying on the front seat of the Cadillac?"

"That could take a while."

"Today's *Journal*, folded into quarters, with the article about Archie facing up. About Archie and Gwen, I mean."

"Nice work."

"Thank you. I'll be over there with the order log, if you need me."

Merci picked her way over to the rear end of the car, following

Zamorra, avoiding Dobbs's markers and the footprints. She glanced out at the strawberry field, saw the furrows converging back toward a hill with the moon above it. The furrows were lined in plastic to protect the berries and the plastic shined like water in the moonlight. The fruit smelled sweet on the air, not heavy like the Valencias, she thought, but higher in pitch and less determined. She could see the Irvine Medical Center from here, which was where Tim Jr. was born. She thought of how small and red and afraid he'd been, of the plastic ID bracelet that dwarfed his wrist, of the little blue-and-white-checked cap they gave him to keep his head warm in the New World. And she remembered the great fear and anger she felt when she was being wheel-chaired to the pickup area to take Tim home.

She shined her light on the STS plates and the registration sticker.

"It's not on the hot list," said Zamorra. "Registered owner is George Massati of Lake Forest. His CDL says forty-four years old, five-ten, one-ninety. No criminal record. I sent two uniforms to his place. There are twelve models like this on the state hot list—three of them here in this county. If somebody got fancy and swapped out plates and tags, this still might be a stolen vehicle."

"You seen the trunk yet?"

"Not much to see, but here."

Zamorra popped the trunk from inside the cab and Merci ran her light across the recess in a slow back-and-forth motion. Not much was right: a bungee cord, an old red shop rag, three paper funnels with the Union 76 logo on them. The trunk liner was clean.

"George runs a tight ship," she said.

"Even adds his own oil."

"Then drives his clean Caddy out here and ditches it? I wonder."

"I do, too," said Zamorra. "If he ditched it, he probably got picked up. Maybe the getaway car left us some tracks."

"The crime scene guys probably set up the generator on them."

"You can't blame Dobbs for that," said Zamorra.

"He's a good kid," said Rayborn.

The front passenger door was open and Ike Sumich was bent into the opening, hands on his knees, not touching the car. He turned when he sensed her and she saw the tight anger on his face. "They were either wearing gloves, or they wiped the interior. All the slam dunks—steering wheel, shifter, door handle, headlight switch, turn signal—clean."

"Too hot for gloves," said Merci. "They probably wiped. They used one of the red shop rags from the trunk, then threw it over in the culvert there. I know just where to find it."

He backed out, shaking his head. "I already looked."

Ike had blond hair that fell over his forehead and he was as thin as a wire hanger. He was a terrific CSI, the best sketcher she'd ever worked with. She'd decided years ago that he was to be one of *her* people, one of the then-under-thirties who—along with her—would be running the department someday. That particular plan had gone bust with the Mike McNally arrest, but that had nothing to do with Ike. She remembered Hess telling her once that he wished he was Ike's age again. She wished he had been Ike's age then, too. And about her age now. And hadn't gotten cancer. And hadn't taken from a scumbucket punk the bullet that ended his life.

Dadda is all gone?

Dadda is all gone.

Dadda is here?

Dadda is not here.

Is in the picture?

Is in the picture but is all gone.

Is not all gone?

Dadda is all gone. Good night, Tim. I love you. Good night. Good night, little man.

"Sergeant, I might be able to dust up something from the door handles or body, but it's getting damper and damper out here. I suggest towing this thing into impound as fast as we can, put it in the covered part. I can try tomorrow, when it's dry and clear and warm out. If the print dust won't raise anything, I can try alternative light source on the big parts, maybe superglue some of the controls."

"You've got it."

Then Sumich changed subjects without missing a beat, something that often caught Merci off guard. "Al Madden has been hanging around my crime lab. In conference with the Big Man. Doors closed."

This was news, not good. "And you heard the name Wildcraft."

"I did. Gilliam has to give him what we find. I mean, that's our job. To *not* give him the findings would be awfully damned strange."

"I understand."

"Dawes, too."

"Shit."

"I dislike telling you this kind of thing."

"If you didn't it could hurt me."

"I see what I see. I think I detect unhappiness in Gilliam, for what it's worth. He . . . well, you know how he likes you."

"The proud, the few."

He smiled again, shook his head to get his hair back. "You say what you think and you're the best detective in Homicide Detail."

"Thanks."

"I see what I see."

"You'll be making more footprint casts tonight."

"I'll be up a while. Gravel and sand are tough. I hope the breeze stays down."

"What are your chances of matching them to the Wildcraft ones, if they came from the same shoes?"

He thought about that a moment. "I'd need luck—some visible anomaly that would make that pair of shoes unique. Or almost unique."

"You're lucky, Ike."

"I try to be."

Merci looked into the car. She noted that the front passenger seat was adjusted far back. *Very* far back, she thought.

"Did you move the seat to get at the floor mats?"

"Not yet."

Right where Size Sixteen left it.

Don Leitzel was doing the photography. He'd opened the driver's door for the interior shots, which he took with the limitless patience of a professional cameraman.

"Be sure to shoot the front passenger's seat," she said.

"Already done, Sergeant."

"And make a written note of the height adjustment before you change it, okay?"

"I've got all the light, window, door and seat positions written down. Lights to lighter."

"Where was it?"

"Height-wise? All the way down. And the back was reclined to about forty degrees. If you need the seat all the way back and forty degrees of recline in a car this big, you're a very large person."

About what you'd figure for Size Sixteen, she thought. "Did you guys find anything good in here?"

"You mean like a driver's license or a checkbook? No."

Merci ran her light over the dashboard and the puffy-looking leather seats. Pale gray interior. Some shiny wood. It looked almost familiar, though, and she realized it was like a fancy version of her Impala. The keys hung in the ignition.

Her light beam caught the LCD face of an onboard navigation unit. That was one thing the Impala sure didn't have.

"Can you program that navigator thing to bring up the last map it was asked for?"

"Sure. And I definitely will."

"How about right now?"

"Might have to get in for that."

"No. Get Ike to hold you."

Ike held Leitzel and Merci braced Ike and Leitzel leaned in, switched on the key and had the navigator showing the last requested map in about thirty seconds. He never touched a thing but the buttons. Merci loved guys who could figure out basic stuff like this: gadgetry usually threw her, though she could fieldstrip and reassemble her nine—blindfolded—as fast as anyone she knew.

"Some place down in La Jolla," said Leitzel. "It looks residential."

"Go back one more."

He leaned in again, did his thing, looked back over his shoulder at her. "Newport Beach," he said. "Up on the bluff there, above the bay."

"Go back another," she said.

A moment later she saw the Newport map vanish, replaced by a new one.

"University of California, San Diego," he called back. "The School of Medicine."

Merci thought about those three specific geographical points, and came up with nothing whatsoever. "That gadget will give you an address, won't it?"

"Yeah, sure," said Leitzel. "That's how you cue up the map in the first place."

Leitzel gave Ike his hand and Ike gave Merci his other and Leitzel leaned in again. She heard the click of the controls, could see the changing lights on the LCD screen.

"Here's the UCSD address."

He started to read it to her, but she stopped him and called Zamorra over. He looked at them with some amusement as Merci told him to get the blue notebook and pen from her windbreaker pocket, take down some addresses and wipe the smirk off his face.

Merci could find no useful tracks left by a pickup vehicle. Tracks, yes, but too many of them. And too faint, also, with the gravel content high and the summer too dry to let the shoulder pack down hard enough to hold a pattern. Dust to dust. She had to figure that Ike's foot casts would also be too vague to help.

Still, she had Leitzel photograph what looked like two distinct sets of tire tracks.

Then, with her flashlight quartering the darkness in front of her, she walked to the culvert that ran along the road between the dirt and the strawberry fields. The ditch was wide and steep and she could see a trickle of liquid down at the bottom. The moon was behind the hill now. The smell of the fruit hit her again. Funny how it comes and goes, she thought—not like the oranges.

She took two long steps down the bank and stopped again, surrounded by the dank rounded smell of old water. Quiet here. Brush and weeds to her left and right, cattails down near the stream. She could hear the frogs and crickets now, with the noise of the blasted generator trapped above her. Something rustled in the grass, then splashed.

She took four more long sideways strides, which brought her to the bed. The scar on her side felt tight and irritating. She thought of being surprised from behind, remembered the awful realization that she was about to get shot and how long it took to go down.

The culvert was lined with concrete. Her light picked up the dark shimmer of water and the black shine of mud. She slowly turned a circle with the flashlight beam leading the way. A soft drink can, smashed. A foam fast-food container, partial. One tire, automobile. One refrigerator, doorless. One garden hose, cracked and faded.

On her way back up the side, Merci kept moving her flashlight beam left to right, then back again, hoping to find a little swatch of red in the darkness and the brush.

Near the top of the embankment, she did. She climbed her way through the brush, then settled on her knees for a better look. It was a red shop rag. Half wadded, half loose. When she lifted it with a stick the wadded part stayed together, like it was held with glue. Or God knew what, thought Merci.

She slipped a new paper lunch bag from one of her hip pockets— always carried three on a crime scene investigation—and popped it open with one hand. It took five tries. Then she teased the shop rag inside with the stick. Dropped in the stick for good measure.

Too bad you can't get fingerprints off a rag used to *wipe* finger-prints, she thought. But there was plenty else Size Sixteen might not have thought of when he tossed the rag: skin particles, hair, fiber from clothing or furniture or carpet or cars, dandruff, sweat. And what's holding the wadded-up cloth together, Size Sixteen? Did you blow your fat murderous nose before you chucked the rag into the bushes? Maybe I can send you to death row on snot evidence.

She stood on top of the embankment, a few yards back from the edge, looking again for footprints. None. Too much brush, too many weeds. And the generator noise again, rattling her nerves.

Suddenly a shadow rose behind her, clear in the floodlights.

Her heart jumped and she wheeled. Her hand found the nine but she caught herself.

"Oh, *Paul!*"

He stopped dead, hands up. "You okay?"

"Perfect."

He looked at her but she saw he understood. Understood that a memory can be heavy as an engine block and sharp as a razor. Through the thumping in her chest and the ringing in her ears she could see again what she'd loved first and best about Zamorra: all the things he didn't need to be told, all the things he just *got*.

"The deputies interviewed George Massati," he said. "George was angry because he'd been sleeping. George claimed his car wasn't stolen, that it was in the garage. Guess what? It was. But the plates were different. So our friends were thorough enough to steal one car, then slap on plates stolen from another one, figuring it might take the owner a while to notice his plates had changed."

"Cute," she said. Her heart was still racing and part of her felt like a hysterical dope. The other part of her felt like a ghost had just run his fingers up her thigh. She took a good deep breath of air into her lungs.

"What's in the bag?" Zamorra asked.

"A red shop rag. I think it was thrown into the culvert so we wouldn't find it."

He nodded, smiled slightly. "You're better than perfect. You're good."

TWELVE

Early the next morning Archie opened his eyes. In the half-light of the ICU he saw the silhouettes of the monitor and drip trolley, the crimson swoosh of someone leaving the room. He lifted his head, rising just slightly on his elbows, and backed up onto his pillow.

Gwen is dead, he thought. The huge black nothing that was now Gwen opened up to him and he felt his heart falling down into the center of it. It was still beating as it fell, but it felt reluctant. He thought it might stop. He waited for it to stop. He saw that bright flash of light in his eyes, the one that had greeted him on his walkway under the trees.

And he heard the voice again, the one that had been telling him what to do for these last forty-eight hours, now saying: *Your heart is strong. I'm above you in the sky. You will find me if you look.*

Archie realized it was Gwen's voice, even though he still couldn't picture her face.

Another red rush of movement outside the door, then it came straight at him: "Oh, Mr. Wyocraff! Mr. Wyocraff! It's so good! You be careful, you be careful with a IV." Warm hands on his shoulder then and a dull pain that registered as a flash of lime green. "You take it easy, Mr. Wyocraff. You our miracle. You take it easy."

"Sure," he heard himself say. The voice was sandy and tan and seemed to come from far away.

Four more people suddenly crowded into the room. He felt the energy they brought with them, as if their bodies contained fires. Hands on his shoulder again, and another throb of pain.

Another nurse, then: "Archie, we're going to move you back down in the bed, then raise the head, okay? You just relax now. . . ."

They pulled him down by his ankles. A nurse steadied his head and it felt like she wore oven mitts, and he wondered if his head was wrapped. A motor ground and the bed rose slightly, bending him at the waist. His head hurt only a little. But a burning match touched the tip of his penis and he very slowly tilted down his head for a look. *Catheter*, he thought, and tried to say the word but it wasn't worth the syllables.

He strained his neck for a look down at his shoulder. Through the hospital smock he could see the plastic gadget with an intravenous line hooked into it. He ran his right hand across his cheek: hard stubble. He raised the hand slightly and felt the soft turban of gauze that came down to his ears. When he slipped the finger under it he realized they'd shaved his head.

He remembered that Gwen was dead and he waited for his heart to stop.

The four bodies parted. A man in a suit stopped beside the bed, looked at Archie and said, "I'm John Stebbins. How are you feeling?"

Archie managed a nod.

Dr. Stebbins stared into his eyes like he was looking for a treasure. "Vision blurred?"

Archie shook his head very slightly, the turban resisting the pillowcase.

"Color?"

Archie nodded.

"How many fingers am I holding up?"

"Two," he said. It seemed like such a long word, stretching on for miles, like a beach.

"You can obviously hear me. How's your head feel?"

Archie nodded again. He watched the doctor's eyes move to the monitor, then back to him.

"Look at the ceiling, please. I'm going to touch you with a pen. When I do, just raise a finger for me. Okay?"

The nodding was wearing him out. He looked up. He felt something touch his toe. Ankle. Kneecap. Fingertip. Stomach. Thigh. Hip. Chest. Upper arm. Palm.

"Move your right foot. Good. Left. Good. Raise your right knee—that's enough. Now the left. Fine. Raise your right hand. From the shoulder now—excellent. Can you smile?"

Archie tried to smile but his lips were tight and his teeth felt huge and dry.

"Fine," he said. "Welcome back."

Archie just stared at him: a pale blue man with peaceful eyes and a tight mouth.

"How much Decadron is he taking?"

A nurse said something and Stebbins nodded. "And how much Tegretol?"

Archie heard her answer but couldn't calculate what it meant.

"Seizures?"

"A sharp decline, Doctor. None for four hours."

Dr. Stebbins turned to one of the nurses and ordered a spiral CT scan immediately, tell Bixton it was priority and call me as soon as they're ready.

They parted and the doctor left in a comet of trailing red. All four stared at him like he was the most interesting thing they'd ever seen. A fifth person craned her neck from the doorway.

"Soup," said Archie.

He drank three cups of broth and fell deeply asleep. Then they were trying to wake him and he was able to come up through the clear warm water and join them.

One nurse wheeled his bed from the room and the other pushed the drip trolley.

"You be very famous when you get out," said the nurse, the one who had called him her miracle. "Reporter all want talk to you."

Her face was enameled yellow. Orange hair, an indigo uniform that he knew was either white or blue. He saw these colors clearly even though he knew they were wrong.

"Did they bury her?" he heard himself ask.

"I don't know. You think of life, Mr. Wyocraff. You don't think of death."

But that was almost all Archie thought about while they ran the CT on him. Death and Gwen. Gwen and death, now together. He tried to pull them apart but they wouldn't come. And he still couldn't remember the last time he'd seen her face. He knew he loved her. He knew she was gone forever. He knew that she was the largest thing in his heart, his life, his history. Why couldn't he see her?

Would she talk to him again?

The scan was painless. The doctors hovered a few yards away and talked about things inside his brain that he couldn't see. He wondered if they could see what he was thinking. Then the one called Stebbins told him all sorts of information about what might be happening to his brain, about fragmentation and edema and infection and amnesia and pain, about the thalamus and the amygdala and the pyramidal tract, and colors and confusion and the emotional components of memory.

Back in his room in the ICU he closed his eyes hard and tried to burst out of his nightmare. He used to do this when he was a boy and having a bad dream—just scrunch his eyelids down hard and blast out of it and into the comfort of his bed. It was like space travel. But it didn't work because this was not a dream.

So he tried to transport himself back to that night. To get himself onto the walkway under the Chinese flame trees just one second before the bright light hit his eyes. To change what happened.

God, what I could have done, he thought.

But Archie couldn't take himself back. And he wondered what good it would do if he could. He knew he'd come up that walkway again, be caught in the light again, take a bullet in his head again.

And what had happened to Gwen would happen to Gwen again.

He'd have no power to stop it, really. Because he didn't know *why*. He didn't know why any of this had happened. Until you understood why, what was the point of going back?

Archie twisted quickly to the side and vomited the meager content of his stomach. Tears burned from his eyes and the catheter pulled a green arrow of pain through him. He smelled the foul aroma of his body. He heard a buzzer go off, and another.

Then the crimson rush of motion again, and hands upon him, voices bubbling forth. More of this horseshit about being someone's miracle. He lay back and shut his eyes tight and tried to go under to the warm deep water where he was safe and invisible. But he couldn't get there. Just couldn't slip beneath himself.

Then her voice again, ordering him not to descend, not to go down.

Up, Archie . . . that's where I'll be. Free and open in the sky.

So Archie lay on the bed while they handled him and imagined himself in a beautiful blue sky. So hard to go there, though, with the noise and activity all around him. And he realized this was his world now. It was the only place that would have him. Loud and painful and shot with colors that made no sense. Gwenless and loveless and stripped of everything that was valuable. Indifferent, needle-happy and catheter-mad. Urgent but pointless. This is the world he was part of now.

There was nothing he could do about that. It was like being born again.

Then, in his nauseous despair, Archie heard Gwen's voice again.

I love you, Arch. I'm still your girl.

I want to be with you, he thought to her. I want to be with you so badly.

Be with me. I'm up here waiting.

If I can find out why, maybe I can go back and make it all come out right. If I understand it I can make it go our way.

Find out why, Arch. Make it go our way.

I will. I can.

When Archie woke up again it was early afternoon and Sergeant Rayborn was sitting next to his bed. Again—though for only a split second—he thought she was Gwen, that this whole stupid thing was only a nightmare and everything was really very okay.

But it was just the sergeant. She didn't look as angry as before, but she had the kind of face that could get that way fast. Standing back near the wall was her partner, Zamorra, the Golden Gloves guy who dressed like an undertaker. More history, coming back to his mind one image, one memory at a time.

He let his eyes roam to the small framed picture on his bed tray—a dark-haired beauty with smart eyes. That's her, he thought. *Gwen.*

"How are you feeling?" the detective asked.

Archie raised his eyebrows and let them fall. "Good," he whispered. He wasn't trying to whisper, it just came out that way.

"Can we talk for a few minutes?"

Archie nodded. He saw her little notebook and her pen. He remembered wanting to be a homicide investigator someday. She had tough eyes and a pale blue face. Zamorra's was pink.

"May I have your full name?"

"Archibald Franklin Wildcraft."

"Address?"

He gave it. It was strange, bringing up this bit of information. It was inside him and true but not substantial.

"What did you do in college, Archie?"

"Played baseball. All my life." This was a much heavier memory. He looked again at the little picture on his stand.

"What's your rank, Archie?"

"Deputy Two."

"What's your assignment?"

"Patrol. Days."

"Can you tell me the name of your partner?"

"Damon Reese."

"Describe him to me, can you?"

"Six feet, one-ninety. Brown and brown, big nose."

Rayborn waited. Then nodded and wrote.

"Archie, what happened the night that Gwen was killed?"

It took him a moment to think of the words, order them, then gather his strength to form them. His memory of that night was filled with gaps. Chasms. With the same black nothingness that was now Gwen. He thought he could fall right in. The older stuff, like playing baseball, was clear.

"I don't remember everything."

She didn't look up from her notebook for a moment. When she did, her eyes fixed on his and Archie felt like he was being seen without his clothes on.

He watched her make a note, then look at him, waiting. "Tell me what you do remember."

"I remember that Gwen was there. It's hard to picture her that night. I can see her from years ago, but not from that night. She's like a . . . ghost. A good ghost. A party. Friends. A rock in the house. The walkway by the pool. A bright light. Then this."

"Do you know how the rock got into your house?"

"I remember a noise."

"Someone threw it?"

"I didn't see."

"Did you throw it?"

"I don't remember throwing it."

Rayborn looked at her partner. Archie was sure that something was being communicated but didn't know what. It was hard to understand. His mind seemed to follow things, then there was a big soft gap, and the meanings fell into it. And he knew the meanings were there, but he couldn't reach them. Like trying to touch a ball that's just out of reach.

"Did you shoot your wife?"

Archie looked at the picture before he answered.

"I don't think so."

"Did you shoot yourself?"

"I don't think so. No."

Rayborn waited for those last two answers before looking down at her notebook and scribbling something.

"Archie, were you having an affair?"

"I don't remember having one."

"Was Gwen?"

"I have no memory of that. No."

"Would you be willing to take a polygraph test, answer some questions like these?"

"Yes."

She was nodding now, biting her bottom lip, which is what Gwen used to do when she was thinking through a problem. Isn't that strange, he thought, that I can remember her biting her lip but not what her face looked like on her birthday? He took a deep breath and let it out slowly.

"Do you remember having a gun with you that night?"

He thought about this for a long time. "No."

"Did you know she was killed with your gun, a Smith and Wesson nine millimeter registered in your name?"

Archie felt a funny pull in his guts. Then an awful sinking. He thought for a moment he was going to slide back under the warm dark water to hover just below the surface, looking up at these people. But no—Gwen had told him she was up, not down. He tried to elevate above all this, above the room and the cops. Up to where she was. Into the blue. Nothing doing.

"No."

"Your prints were on it. And on the cartridges inside. And on the empty casings found at the scene. Nobody else's prints were on them. Just yours."

He said nothing.

"In fact, we've only identified two sets of prints from your home and your entire property, so far. Yours and hers."

"Someone wearing gloves?" he asked.

"Maybe," said the detective. "But that leaves us with just about zero evidence of a third person ever being at your house. We've got a set of footprints that might belong to the gardener. We've got a black Cadillac that may or may not have anything to do with this case. And that's it. No physical evidence of another person being on your property that night. No witness. Just your gun with your prints on it."

He said nothing. It hadn't occurred to him until just now that he would be a suspect. If it weren't for Gwen, it would be comical. He'd actually laugh. But, ridiculous as this was, it was about Gwen, too, and Gwen was murdered, and nothing about the murder of Gwen would ever, ever be funny.

Archie stared back at Rayborn and felt an almost blinding anger spreading through his body. Like something boiling out from his heart.

He'd felt this before and he'd always believed he was capable of murder on anger like this. He'd learned to hide it. And along with the anger came an overwhelming wave of guilt.

I couldn't protect her.

He blinked. He smelled a draft of his own body odor swelling up around him. "I couldn't have killed her, Detective. I loved her. I don't kill people I love."

She was watching him hard. Archie thought she knew he was furious, thought he saw a look of impressed understanding cross her features. Maybe she's got the temper, too, he thought.

"Answer this," she said.

He waited.

"Our lab pulled enough barium and antimony off your hand to establish that you'd fired a gun very recently. That would be your gun hand. So, when did you shoot and what did you shoot at?"

Archie had to think. First, to let that anger settle down a little. When the temper hit, it was like something heavy and smooth starting downhill. It just pulled you along.

But even with his fury tamped down, it took him a while to turn around and wade backward into time, past what had happened that night. It was extremely hard for him to get beyond that point. It lay back there behind him like a dam on a river. It was huge and black and heavy and absolutely immovable. On the far side of it lay memory, Gwen and strong feelings. On the near side there were just spotty images with no emotion attached to them at all.

"I went to the Sheriff's range recently. If I had my calendar I could tell you when."

"That day?"

"No."

"The day before?"

"No. Two weeks before. Maybe three or four. I'm not clear on some things."

She looked straight at him again and those eyes rooted around inside him like they were hungry. "I guess you wouldn't be, Deputy."

"No. I'm not."

"Barium and antimony usually wash off in a day or two. Just with regular showers."

"I can't explain it."

"Maybe you fired the gun and don't remember doing it. That happens in brain injuries, Archie. Parts of your memory get taken away."

"That doesn't seem possible."

"What doesn't?"

"That I could remember loving her but not remember shooting her."

He didn't say that he also remembered loving her but could not remember exactly what she looked like the last time he'd seen her. Except that it must be something like Sergeant Rayborn looked, because he'd twice wondered if Rayborn was Gwen. He looked at the picture and saw a slight resemblance.

She looked back at Zamorra, then at Archie again. "That's not hard to understand. One memory is ruined. But another stays."

Archie realized that, based on this theory, he could have done just about anything on Earth in his life but not remember it now. It was like having a cage lowered over you.

"Did you shoot her, Archie?"

Again, that hot rush of fury moving through him. A fury with its roots in the old Archie, the part of his life on the far side of the dam. "No. Am I under arrest?"

"No," she said. Then she exhaled slowly, like she'd been waiting a long time to do it.

Archie watched Zamorra move closer to his bed. Zamorra looked like a man who could hurt you, and people said he could. But right now, this furious, Archie knew he could rise from his bed and yank the man's head off before he could make a sound.

"Do you know what *suiseki* is, Archie?" he asked.

"No."

"Tell me, did Gwen ever write music?"

"Yes." He remembered some words from a song she'd written many years ago, right after they'd met. She'd been sixteen. She'd given him a tape of it, with her playing guitar. He still had that tape in a cigar box in his closet.

Don't speak, don't say a word
We're just dreaming
Words get in the way

He wondered how he could remember those words from ten years ago, but not her face from the last time he'd seen her. It was starting to drive him crazy.

"When was it?" Archie asked.

"When was what, Archie?"

"When did she die?"

"It was early Wednesday. The day before yesterday. Today's Friday."

Archie tried to find somewhere to put this information. But he couldn't remember much of that day. Or the day before. And even less of the two days since, here in this bed—just a seamless stretch of sleep and dreams and voices underscored by raw, physical fear and deep dread. But he clearly remembered shutting out Cal State Fullerton in a pre-league game in April of 1993, scattering three hits in seven innings, and clubbing a home run to left center. Could still see that ball sailing over the 385 mark. He clearly remembered the white hairs that grew between the toes of his boyhood black lab, Clunker, when he got old. Could clearly see the face of his father while he reeled in a smallie on one of his hand-carved plugs: whiskers on his chin, a hard glint of pride in his eyes, mouth in a tight smile with a cigarette in one side and the smoke welling up under the brim of his hat.

And he could clearly, effortlessly see the face of Gwen Kuerner, age sixteen, when he knocked on the door of her house for the first time and she and all three of her sisters answered it.

He closed his eyes. "I'm very tired."

"Thanks for talking with us," said Zamorra. "Is there anything we can get for you?"

"Please bring me another picture of Gwen."

Zamorra paused and looked at the picture on the bed tray before he answered. "Okay. Anything else?"

"I just remembered what *suiseki* means. They are rocks you collect and look at. Viewing stones. I have a room full of them. I always liked rocks as a kid. But the viewing stones, I think I bought those kind of recently."

"You didn't know that three minutes ago."

"I just remembered it now."

"Archie," said Zamorra, "when does your gardener come?"

"Huh?"

"Your gardener, the guy who rakes the leaves and pulls the weeds."

"I don't really know."

"Do you know his name, or how to get in touch with him?"

"I don't remember."

"Can I ask you one more question?"

He nodded but he felt himself gliding upward into a clear blue sky that was Gwen.

"When you think about that night—Gwen and the party, the rock and the light in your eyes—do you remember being sad? Angry? Happy? Afraid? How did you feel, then, that night? What was in your heart?"

"I was happy. We made love by the beach. Stars in her hair. I just remembered that, too."

Merci sat at her desk at headquarters and played her messages. The Homicide pen was empty now, almost seven on a Friday evening. She liked it this way.

George Wildcraft confirmed their Saturday breakfast interview. He had a clear sharp voice and for whatever reasons she pictured him with a suntan and good teeth. Natalie, Archie's mother, would be there also. But Zamorra wouldn't because it was Saturday and he refused to work Saturdays or Sundays. *Kirsten.*

Gilliam had called but not said why. He rarely left information on a tape. She called him at home and apologized but he cut her off.

"You know you can call me anytime, day or night, Merci."

"Thanks, Jim."

"Look, I didn't want to leave it on the machine, but we finished up the DNA on Gwen and Archie today. The semen inside her was his."

"I could have told you that."

A silence. TV news in the background.

"And some of the blood on his robe was hers."

"Shit."

"Yes," he said softly.

"There's an explanation, Jim. He loved her. He had no reason."

"I hate to be the one to point this out, but—"

"But we've convicted lots of creeps with less than half the evidence we've got on Wildcraft."

"Less than a quarter," Gilliam said.

Merci felt a little chill go up her back. She pictured a jury listening as Archie tried to reassemble his blasted memory: *I have no memory of that . . . wait a minute, I just remembered . . . no, I didn't kill her. . . .*

So she wondered if a piece of lead might speak more convincingly on his behalf. "Can you tell me the caliber of the bullet in his head?"

"I can't do it. The scans just aren't precise enough. We're talking fractions of millimeters in bullet size. Plus the fragmentation and distortion. I need the slug."

"Why not use a—you know, Jim, a . . ."

"A what, Merci? God knows I'm open to ideas."

"I don't know, some gadget that measures bullets in brains."

Another silence. "I wish I could."

"It's possible."

"What is?"

"That someone else shot them both."

Gilliam chuckled. "I'm trying to see it your way. In spite of the evidence, I am. But I'm not getting very far."

"Shit was going *down*, Jim. Somebody chucked a rock through his living room window. We've got some monstrous footprints from under that tree. What if Gwen was *alive* when Archie went outside? What if Wildcraft went outside to find the rock thrower and got off a shot at Size Sixteen? That accounts for the residue right there."

"Okay. But your witness heard one shot, not two."

"Simultaneous."

"I'm stretching hard here."

"Okay, then Archie came out with his weapon when he heard the rock through the window, walked into a bullet from the giant under the tree. He's down and bleeding. The shooter takes his gun and uses it on Gwen. He comes back outside and fires a sky round through it, with Archie's hand in a shooting grip. That's what Jones heard."

"Why didn't he hear the shot that put down Archie?"

"A small caliber—twenty-two or thirty-two. A silencer. Maybe Jones sneezed right then, was flushing a toilet. I don't know yet. But it was an autoloader. That accounts for the mess of footprints. Because the shooter had to find the casing."

"It wasn't just the gardener who left those prints, or one of us?"

"Not just the damned gardener, and Crowder told me that nobody'd been in there. It was the shooter, looking for the brass."

"And at some point this guy wipes Gwen Wildcraft's blood on Archie's robe?"

"Exactly."

Gilliam sighed. "Maybe."

"What's wrong with it?"

"Not really wrong, Merci, but we've got a young, financially troubled, very jealous deputy who kills his wife and shoots himself. It happens. We all know it happens. Or, we've got a giant throwing rocks, hiding under trees, switching out weapons, planting evidence and driving away without anyone seeing him. I'd go with Occam and his razor."

"Fuck Occam, and his razor too."

"And this Jones witness? I understand he was drinking hard stuff in the morning."

"So? He heard what he heard. The two shots to Gwen, they happened inside the bathroom. The bathroom was on the far side of the house, away from Jones's garage. And where did you get that Wildcraft was extremely jealous?"

"I was extrapolating."

"Because Gwen was beautiful."

"Correct."

"And what's this *financially troubled* crap?"

"It's a million-dollar home, Merci. Wildcraft was good for about fifty or sixty, and his wife was unemployed."

"They invested in OrganiVen, the cancer-cure guys. Made two million in less than a year. They weren't troubled—they were flush."

"It's easier to spend than to make. They could have been way over their heads."

"Jim, something's wrong. Help me. I'm no damned good, trying to think like a defense attorney. But I can't go after an innocent deputy just because he looks guilty."

Like I went after Mike.

"You know, Merci, that entry wound in Wildcraft's head—right side, behind the temple and above the ear—is where a lot of right-handed suicides place the gun."

She felt her anger leap from her heart to her mouth, like a spark jumping a gap. "Stebbins gave you scan copies already?"

"Slow down—you'll get yours tomorrow. You're free to look at mine if you can't wait that long."

She swallowed down the anger, saying nothing.

"Ryan Dawes isn't seeing it quite your way either," said Gilliam.

"Yeah. And Al Madden's hovering over me like a driving teacher."

"Look, Merci, whether to arrest and charge Wildcraft with this is Vince and Clay Brenkus's call. Let them do their jobs, and we'll do ours."

Again, she pictured Wildcraft in court: *I have no memory of that . . . I don't think so . . . we made love by the beach that night . . . wait, I just remembered.*

Christ, she thought: and his fingerprints all over the gun that killed her, and her blood on his robe? The jury may as well bring an electric chair and an extension cord with them.

She thought for a moment. "Okay, you think he did it. But what would you do if you were me? If you believed in your heart that he didn't?"

Gilliam said nothing for a beat, then he cleared his throat. "I'd just ask him lots of questions and listen hard to his answers. If Wildcraft did it, it's going to come out. He can't talk his way out of it with a bullet in his head. I mean, he'll never be able to keep his story straight. The way I see it, he tried to kill himself. He wasn't planning on being around to help with his defense, so to speak."

She agreed with that, but said nothing.

"And I'd look for a pair of size-sixteen Foot Rites somewhere on his property. The bottom of a trash can would be a likely place to start."

"Do you really think he set it up to look like a third party?"

"No. But it's possible, and if he did, he didn't have to work very hard at it—some footprints and a rock through his own window."

"Then off himself? Why bother with all the extra work if he was going to do that?"

"Because he didn't want to get caught. He's a cop. Even dead, he didn't want to get caught."

"Death before dishonor."

"That's part of it. Vanity, arrogance and pride come to mind, too."

"I thought *I* was cynical."

"Give yourself about twenty years."

She thought about that. Twenty years from now she'd be fifty-seven. Once, she believed she'd be running for sheriff of Orange County about then. Now, after her grand jury appearance, the dream seemed bitter and comic.

"The rumor is, he had a temper," said Gilliam.

"I've heard that, too."

"Used to, anyway. God knows what that bullet left him with."

She thanked Gilliam and punched off, feeling the exit of sweet hope as it pinwheeled down and away.

She got out her blue notebook and dialed William Jones's number. She got a rather ditzy sounding young woman who laughed and said she'd check but usually Bill was, well, not exactly sober this late.

Actually, he sounded pretty good to Merci, and he remembered her immediately. She asked him if he knew what day the Wildcrafts' gardener usually came.

Mondays or Tuesdays, pretty sure, said Bill. Could always tell by the little truck and the loud leaf blower.

"What's he look like?" she asked.

"Like a gardener. Mexican, regular size. He gets here around seven, leaves about three. I'll call you next time he's here. Tell me how Archie's doing. The papers don't tell you very much and the nurses say the same thing every time I call."

"I just saw him. He's awake and lucid, but tired."

"He's going to make it. Archie's strong as a horse. I'd see him washin' his car out here on Sunday mornings and he had muscles on him you wouldn't believe. Not the gym kind, the baseball kind. Long muscles for running and throwing. I know because I played some ball back in high school. That was quite a while ago."

"For me it was, too."

She gave him her office and pager numbers, then thanked him again and hung up.

THIRTEEN

George Wildcraft was a tall, wiry man with an outdoorsman's face and patient green eyes. Merci was right about the teeth and tan. She'd made him for a salesman by his phone attitude, but now saw that she had been wrong. Weathered hands with dark creases, scarred fingers. She put him at sixty and in one of the building trades—carpentry, maybe, or electric or plumbing.

Natalie looked ten years older. She was very petite, leathery, and pretty in a miniaturized kind of way. Her hand seemed no larger than a monkey's when Merci shook it. Her engagement diamond was enormous.

They sat at a round glass table in the atrium coffee shop of a hotel in Newport Beach. The August sunlight filtered down through a frosted skylight and reaching palm trees. Merci knew they were staying at a Best Western in Santa Ana but it didn't matter to her where they talked.

The waiter who took their drink orders looked like a guy from a magazine ad.

"What do you have?" asked Natalie. "What evidence?"

Merci sat back. "We have a lot of evidence, Mrs. Wildcraft."

"Natalie."

"Natalie. Too much to go into specifically. Not all of it seeming to point to the same thing. That's the way it is in lots of cases."

"Who did it?" she asked. For a small woman her voice was rough

113

and low. From that and the lines on her face Merci figured her for a thirty-year smoker. Rayborn herself had smoked a pack a day for ten years but had quit four years back. She missed the cigarettes heartily and still dreamed about smoking. But she wanted to live longer for Tim and had always hated the smell of tobacco smoke on her fingers and clothes. And the wheeze high in her lungs when she lay down at night. She still thought that the smell of a freshly opened pack of cigarettes was one of the three best in the world, right behind a pouch of fresh good coffee and the top of Tim's head.

"We don't know."

"Is Archie a suspect?"

"No."

"That's a common thing for cops to do, though, kill themselves and their wife."

"Not common, Natalie. But law enforcement officers do end their lives more often than others."

"He didn't."

"I don't think he did, either. But there's some hard evidence that points at him."

"What evidence?"

"I can't tell you."

"Can't or won't?"

"Both."

Natalie latched her hard brown eyes onto Merci's. "No one knows him like George and I know him. From when he was young until right now, he's been honest and truthful and good. *Completely* honest. I can read him like a book. He never could fool me, not for a second. He told me he didn't do it, and I guarantee you he didn't."

The waiter brought the coffees but nobody wanted breakfast. He looked disappointed.

"What did you think of Gwen?" Merci asked.

Natalie sat back, looked at her husband, then at Merci again. "We thought she was a wonderful girl. George?"

George Wildcraft nodded. His green eyes were full of expression. "She was a fine girl. We loved her and so did Arch."

With this, George looked down at the glass tabletop, as did Natalie.

Like it had said something. Merci watched them, attuned to their private frequencies of grief. Neither spoke.

"Tell me about Archie," said Merci. "You said he was honest and truthful and good?"

Natalie finally looked up, a tear in the corner of one eye. She smiled. "Well, not *all* the time, Detective Rayborn. He was a handful when he was young. He was all boy. You know what I mean."

They lived in Willits, which was Mendocino County, California. Second generation *Northern* Californians, both of them. Merci noted the pride in the *northern* lineage. Northern meant you didn't waste as much Colorado River water, weren't narcissists, Hollywood weirdos, bodybuilders, faddists, etc. George did framing and drywall and firewood. Natalie worked a drill press at Remco, day shift. Archie was their only child.

He was a big, content baby and a big, content toddler. He was a terrific athlete, even then: George remembered him throwing wiffle golf balls around his room when he was six months old, "could really zing them." Walked at nine months, *ran* at ten.

Went off to kindergarten at five, was "unimpressed" by authority and only played with a few hand-chosen friends. He was a bit of a bully and fairly physical. Had a friend that was a lot like him and they were always cooking up something. Kevin was the other kid. They signed Archie up for T-ball at age four—a year early—but nobody cared or said anything because he was the best player on the team. Orioles, that year. Looked a little like Will Clark, stroking the ball off that tee. They got him into Pinto League early, and he was the best player on that team, too.

Natalie said that for his first four grades of elementary school Archie had some problems. Nothing too serious, but he fought a lot. Didn't participate in anything but sports. Wasn't popular with other students or teachers. He and Kevin were still raising hell together. Always seemed a year or two ahead of the others physically, but academically he "struggled." Around the house he was polite because he knew his mother would "paddle his pointed little fanny" if he showed disrespect. George "took the belt" to Archie when it was necessary, which was not too often, according to Natalie.

"How often was not too often?" Merci wanted to know.

"Maybe once a month back then," George said. "Just a few good swats and Archie would bawl and mind his manners for a while. No welts or bruises or anything like that. I loved my boy. I couldn't hurt him. But I wanted him to get some common sense through his head."

Then, when Archie was halfway through the fifth grade, something in him changed. Natalie and George both saw it. He started dressing sharp, wanting the latest fashions. Took extra time with his hair. Brushed his teeth twice in the morning, wanted underarm deodorant. Had a funny little hop in his step—hard to describe but it was like he was walking more on his toes or something. Even changed his route to school in a way that added a full ten minutes.

"Her name was Julia," said George. "A transfer student from Dayton, Ohio. Little dark-haired girl with a bright smile. Cute as you can get."

George smiled and Merci smiled with him. Natalie looked down and shook her head.

"It changed him," she said. "He wrote letters and poems to her. Called her all the time. He sent her pictures of himself, his dog Clunker. Had a giant fight with Kevin—stitches on both boys—but that was the last fight he ever got in. Archie's report card went from all fairs to all excellents because he wanted to impress Julia. And she'd call him and write him little love notes with red kiss stickers on the back. They held hands on the way to school and back. George and I, we talked to Julia's mom about it—she was a single mom—and we agreed it was okay, so long as Arch and Julia didn't start kissing or hiding together or . . . well, you know. We wanted to encourage a friendship, maybe even an early form of romance, but not physical affection. We kept an eye on them, you can believe that."

"Yes," said Merci. She wondered, very briefly, what she would do when Tim Jr. developed a crush like that. Handcuff him to my wrist, she thought, or maybe in his room. Probably be a Kirsten like Zamorra's, she thought: another qualmless blonde.

"Then," said Natalie, "she disappeared."

"Julia?"

"Yes. Somewhere between her apartment and where Archie would meet her on the way to school. People saw a white pickup truck that wasn't usually around. Some people said Julia got in, some said she didn't. Anyway, she was never found. Neither was the truck. She was ten."

The waiter checked in with more coffee, but still, nobody wanted breakfast. He concentrated as he refilled Merci's cup, then smiled without looking at her and backed away.

Merci made sure she had the girl's last name and the year and city and school right: this would be worth another look.

"Police questioned Archie for quite a while," said George. "We were present, of course. It was nothing accusatory."

All questions are accusatory, thought Rayborn.

"How did her disappearance affect your son?"

George sighed and looked at her. "First he got real quiet. And while he was going through that quiet stage, he brushed his teeth *three* times before school, he asked us for even *more* of the name-brand clothing, he spent even *more* time on his hair. Wrote her more letters. Months later, Julia's mom gave them back to me. He didn't say much of anything to anybody. A whole dinner and he'd only speak if you asked him something direct. That lasted the rest of the school year, through summer and into the next. He'd go to the public library almost every day on the way home from school and read the papers from around the country. Librarian told us that. He told me you never knew where she'd show up. That summer he played baseball harder and better than I'd ever seen him play. Really cracking that ball. Really throwing it hard—clocked at seventy-four miles an hour when he wasn't quite twelve. I could see the . . . what was it? I could see the *passion* in him. The frustration. The anger. By the end of the next school year—sixth grade—he seemed to be pretty much over it. He was talking again, making friends. Even some girlfriends. He was popular. Good grades, still. Nice-looking. A good boy."

"But after that he always had a blank spot inside him," said Natalie. "Like something had gone away and wouldn't come back. Which was exactly what had happened."

Merci knew about blank spots from Hess. She often thought of a person's soul as something lunar—the craters were good things lost, the mounds were good things not lost, and the plains in between were things that didn't matter that much. "How did he react when the police questioned him?"

George chuckled. "He told us that night that if he couldn't be a major-league pitcher when he grew up, he was going to be a missing-persons detective. And he wasn't joking. Archie wasn't a joker that way. Always was real serious about what he was going to do. Well, that's exactly what happened, isn't it? He dropped out of ball and became a deputy."

Merci made a note of this, circled it, watched her pen form the long oval on the paper, once, twice. *Be a missing-persons detective.* Because his first love disappeared off the face of the Earth. Because he loved her enough to change himself for her.

"Tell me about Gwen."

Archie knew immediately, said Natalie. Told them a couple weeks after he met her that he was going to marry her. Was a little embarrassed that she was sixteen and he was twenty, playing college ball for UCR. But that was all. He had the long view. He knew four years wouldn't be anything when they were older.

George and Natalie weren't too happy about the age thing, Natalie said, but when they met her they couldn't help but like her. When two people love each other like that you pretty much have to get out of the way. Gwen looked like Julia.

"We had to trust Archie," she said. "We *did* trust him. It's not much of my business but I'd bet she was still a virgin the day they got married."

"What about Archie?"

Natalie shook her head and looked at her. "Lots of girlfriends in high school and early college."

"Before Gwen," said George.

George looked into near space as if his son's lack of honeymoon virginity was a problem that needed solving. Natalie looked at Merci blankly.

"You going to charge him?"

"Nobody's been charged."

"I said are you *going* to?"

"I don't know."

Natalie's hard eyes locked onto Rayborn's again. "Well, there's one more thing we should talk about. Just so you know. Long time ago Archie took out life insurance policies on Gwen and himself. Seemed smart, with the profession that Archie had chosen. I think her policy was worth about a quarter million. They told us about it, because if something happened to both of them, the money would be split between Gwen's parents and us. George and I don't need the money, so that's not what I'm getting at. It's just something else you should know."

Merci thought about a quarter million dollars, what it would do and wouldn't do. "I wonder if they increased those death benefits when they hit it rich with OrganiVen."

Natalie looked over Merci's face from bottom to top. "Far as I know, they spent their money on nice things. Archie bought us a new car. A Mercedes C430. Red. We'd loaned them two thousand dollars to buy the start-up stock, before the big drug company bought them out."

"Archie and Gwen bought us a computer, too," said George.

It sounded to Merci like they believed the more things their son had bought for them the more innocent he was. And it must have sounded that way to them, too, she thought, because of the awkward silence that followed.

"He wanted to fly," said George. He looked at Merci with a wry smile. "Not professionally, just, well . . ."

"He jumped off the garage roof when he was seven," said Natalie. "Had broomsticks with cloth on them for wings. Broke an ankle, climbed up and jumped again, broke the other. Just hairline fractures, they didn't have to be set."

"Lucky," said George.

"Stubborn," said his wife.

"Loved rocks, too," said George. "Brought them home in his pockets, then later, in backpacks. Read up on them. Bought some fancy Japanese ones when they got rich."

"The *suiseki*."

"Yes."

"Imagine that," said Natalie. "Buying rocks."

Another pause then as the Wildcrafts' memories of their son collided with the reason for them being there.

"Well, thank you," said Rayborn, wondering at the passions of A. F. Wildcraft. "You've both been very helpful."

"Gwen's funeral is Wednesday, Detective," George said. "The Catholic cemetery in Laguna Hills. Two o'clock. On behalf of Archie and Gwen's family, we're inviting you."

"I'll be there. And let me get this, please."

She paid and they stood.

"What are your chances of catching the guy who did this?" George asked.

She thought about that while she put down another dollar on the tip tray. "Better than anyone else's."

"Yeah, he was worried," said Damon Reese, Archie's patrol partner. At thirty-six, he was six years older than Archie. He had a thick, handsome face, a strong nose and the scars of adolescent acne still sharp on his cheeks and neck. When he looked at you, you got all of his attention.

"Archie's a worrier. He worries about his appearance. He worries about gaining weight, losing muscle tone. He worries about the things he owns—his house and cars and all of that. What color paint. What kind of trees to plant. What kind of carpet to get. He worries about his investment in that company that's supposed to cure cancer. He worried about Gwen being happy. About Gwen's music. About Gwen's family. And that's for starters."

"Quite a lineup."

"Merci, Archie's a fix-it guy, an improvement guy. He thinks he can fix anything, and I'll give him credit—he does everything guts-out, does his homework and he never gives up. Me, I'm just the opposite. I know I can't improve hardly anything. I don't care what color my house is painted, and I can't change people. I don't have a wife to worry about anymore. So I take things easier. I'll bet my blood pressure is half of Archie's, and I probably sleep a lot better than he does. I'll never live up there in the hills, but that's fine. I like it where I am. We make a good patrol team because we're different."

Merci listened and watched Reese turn the hose on the hull of his Boston Whaler. The boat was on its trailer in his driveway. Damon had gone fishing out of Dana Point this morning and he was back by ten for their talk, just like he said he'd be.

The water drummed against the aluminum and dripped off in glittering streams. It was too loud to talk over, so Merci just watched Deputy Reese hose the ocean off his boat and the life vests and the bait tank and the tackle. When he was done she watched him back it into the garage and helped him lift the trailer off the ball on his pickup.

Reese carried two big plastic bags of bass fillets into the house, unworried about the pink drips. Merci carried his Lowrance sonar.

"Just set it on the counter there, Merci. Thanks."

"What about Felix Mendez?"

Reese stopped in the middle of the kitchen floor and looked at Merci with his considerable attention. "He would have killed me if it wasn't for Archie. There's one thing I'm glad Archie was able to fix."

He smiled, shook his head at the memory, got a clear baking dish out of a cabinet and set the bagged fish in it.

"Mendez wasn't a punk. He was a made guy, a ranking *Eme* lieutenant. He was loaded to the gills that night, or none of it would have gone down. Fighting with his wife, jacked up on coke, drunk. When his wife tried to go off on Archie and he pushed her against the wall and cuffed her, Mendez went for his iron. He had a one-shot, twenty-five-cal derringer in his bathrobe pocket—so small it didn't even weigh the pocket down. At least not enough for either of us to notice. So Mendez had it out quick, took us totally by surprise. Swung on me because I was closer. But Archie was fast. Blew a hole in Felix's hand about the size of a pea going in and a quarter going out. Bones sticking out all over, what a mess. Made the shot from ten, twelve feet away. Saved my life. Fantastic."

"Did Mendez threaten to kill him?"

"Right there, in all the pain and noise, he probably said something to that effect."

"What about later, in jail or the courtroom?"

Reese shook his head. "No. Mendez wouldn't do that. The *Eme* puts a hit on a guy, they're not going to pound their chests about it. They'll just make sure it gets done."

Merci knew he was right. "Does the *Eme* have a shooter so big he wears size-sixteen shoes and has to recline a Cadillac seat just to get in and out?"

Reese's full attention again. She liked the bright humorlessness of his eyes. She'd always thought a cop's eyes should be like that.

"Not that I know of," he said. "But you could talk to Gang Interdiction about that. If they've set foot in this county, Quevas knows them. The *Eme* would probably do what the other gangs do—use someone up-and-coming to do the hit. So, they could have a bigfoot coming up the ranks, somebody we don't even know about yet."

"A youngster," said Merci.

"Yeah," said Reese, with an echoing sarcasm. "Where did you find shoe prints that big?"

"Under one of Archie's trees. About ten feet from where he fell."

Reese shook his head. "I talked to Ryan Dawes yesterday. He's trying not to let it show, but I think he's gunning for Archie on this one. He spent a lot of time trying to discover that Archie had *lost* considerable money on his stock investments, not *made* considerable money. I told Jaws that the Wildcrafts were not in any kind of unusual debt that I knew about. They made a killing and that was that. Dawes still seemed to want to cast Archie as desperate. It's like he's got this story in his head and he's looking for facts to make it true. I told him considerably less than I told you, without seeming unhelpful."

"I'm glad."

"Why is he thinking Arch? Jaws wouldn't say one thing about the evidence, but he must have something."

He looked at her and they both knew he was asking for information she shouldn't give him. But she trusted Reese and she liked him and he was the kind of guy she'd want in her department if she were in charge. You give to get. But sometimes you give just to give.

"The physical evidence is almost all against him, Damon. Prints on the weapon. His gun hand was loaded when we did the GSR test.

Her blood is on his robe. No solid evidence of anyone else being on their property at the time."

"*Jesus*. Archie's gun kill her?"

Merci nodded.

"And the big footprints, what, something that might or might not be relevant?"

She nodded again. "They could be the gardener's, for all we know."

"His memory's all messed up, isn't it?"

"Well, it's somewhat messed up. Holes. Then, vague in some places but fine in others. It seems like the most recent things are hardest for him to recall. But the older things—things from years ago—they're still in place."

Reese looked away. "So Jaws sees an easy one. Prints on the murder weapon, GSR on the gun hand and a guy too messed up to take the stand in his own defense."

"That's what I think. And high-profile, too. If you prosecute Archie Wildcraft for this, you're guaranteed headlines. I mean, it's been front-page news for three days. Imagine a trial."

She saw the uncluttered conviction on Reese's face. "I don't think he'd kill her," he said. "No way on Earth he'd kill her."

"But if you're the prosecutor and you get the conviction, everybody's going to know your name for fifteen minutes. And that's what it takes to fill Brenkus's empty DA's chair. Brenkus is old. Jaws wants his job, whether he'll admit it or not."

Reese shook his head again. "Yeah. That's the way it goes, isn't it? Something like this happens and people use it to move up. The Wildcrafts—rungs on a ladder."

"Did he ever mention Julia?"

"Never." Reese looked at her with guarded interest but nothing more.

"Tell me about his temper."

Reese nodded, as if he expected this question.

"Yeah, he's got one. I've been his patrol partner for a year and a half and I still don't know exactly what's going to set him off. He's peaceful. He's alert. He's in the moment. Then, wham. You know those carnival games where you take a giant mallet and try to ring the bell with the weight? Well, that's Archie's temper, sometimes. Something just hits him a certain way and off it goes."

"Is he violent with it?"

"Only once, with me around. But you see it. You hear it. You feel it. You also feel him controlling it."

Like Zamorra controlling his, Merci thought.

"So, you don't know exactly what's going to set him off, but how about in general?" she asked. "What gets him?"

Reese nodded again. "Bad treatment of women or girls. That royally pisses Arch off."

Merci thought about that for a moment.

"We roll on a domestic, Archie won't pay much attention to the guy's point of view. He's always pulling for the woman, no matter how drunk or violent or wrong she is. I mean, he took a lot of verbal abuse from Michelle Mendez before he cuffed her. If Archie smells a woman-hater, look out."

"He got in a fight defending me."

Reese nodded. "That was the one time I saw him not control it. One minute, a somewhat rational talk about whether the department is better off under Vince Abelera or Chuck Brighton. Next, some wiseass and not very fair words about you, Detective Rayborn. Next, Deputy Mark Stump coldcocked and lying on the floor. Archie already bending over him, trying to slap him awake."

"Where did that happen?"

"High Rollers, down on Katella. We tried to keep it quiet. That's just a regular bar we were in, not a cop joint."

"Sticking up for me. That's funny."

"Why is it funny?"

"Unexpected, I meant. Surprising."

"A lot of people think Brighton had it coming to him, and God knows McNally's dad did. And your father, well, he was involved and he admitted it. It was one of those rare times when people got what they deserved."

"Some got a little more."

"You got fooled on Mike. You *almost* got fooled."

"That's a generous interpretation of events."

"And Brighton's house needed a little cleaning, Merci. You were the one who did it."

She liked hearing Damon Reese sum things up that way. It put her in a good light and made things seem simple. The truth was a lot more complicated than that, and part of the truth was that she had been fooled into the unfair treatment of a fellow deputy—a man she'd been trying hard to love. She'd believed the worst of him because the evidence had told her to. Some people forgave her and some didn't. Mike had forgiven her as he shut the door of his Modjeska Canyon home on her one very cold night last winter.

Since then she had forgiven herself, but she didn't trust herself. Not all the way. And what good was trust if you couldn't, well, trust it? She second-guessed now, and second-guessed again. It was humiliating. That's what was yanking her chain about this Wildcraft thing: she was trying *not* to believe the worst of him even though the evidence was telling her to. Her self-trust was trying to outmuscle her self-doubt but it didn't have the heft and the whole thing was being pushed by what had happened before. What if she was wrong again? What if Archie's innocence was just another one of her useless opinions?

Shut the fuck *up*, woman, she thought. She sighed, feeling the heat rise into her face. "Thanks for saying that."

"I should have months ago. I figured I was more valuable with my mouth shut."

"Not being a fix-it guy."

"Correct," he said with a smile.

Damon Reese insisted that she take a small cooler filled with ice and a bag of the bass fillets. Then he walked her out. She saw two little boys with scooters standing on the sidewalk not far from her car.

Reese stopped at the planter beside the garage and used his pocketknife to cut a few white daisies. While she held open the lid he set them inside the cooler with the bag and ice.

He shook her hand and looked at her with a calm intensity.

"Call if you think of anything," she said.

"I will. I'd call just to say hello and talk, if I thought you'd pick up."

She'd seen the question coming, but the directness of Reese's phrasing still caught her not quite ready. It wasn't the kind of question you had to think about. You knew the answer, whether you could predict it or not.

"I'd pick up."

He touched her cheek very softly with his fingers and brushed the hair off her forehead. She stood still for this, the sensation of his skin on hers much stronger and more exact than she had expected. She could smell fish and ocean and just a trace of gasoline.

In the rearview mirror of the Impala she watched him wave good-bye, and without thinking she raised her right hand off the wheel and waved good-bye back. She glanced at the two young boys standing on the sidewalk, silver Razors propped against their legs. Both smiled: gaps and gums, teeth too big for their faces. One blew a kiss at her and they both took off, laughing and furiously pumping away down the concrete.

FOURTEEN

Saturdays were usually Merci and Tim time. But with this Saturday cut short by work, all they had time to do was go to a fast-food kids' place for lunch, then down to Laguna Beach to cool off in the brisk ocean. Tim chased seagulls until he was panting. Merci sat in the sand and let the sun tingle her bare shoulders and her back.

I'd pick up. God, now what?

That night was a typical one in the Rayborn household: a big dinner cooked by her father, popcorn, videos, scotch and water on ice, the police band scanner turned low in the background.

Tim, brandishing a now-stringless bow that Merci had bought for him at an amusement park, wanted to watch *Robin Hood* for the some-thing-hundredth time. Merci put it in.

"Robin Hood is real?"

"Robin Hood is not real. He's a character in a movie."

"Prince John is real?"

"Prince John is not real. He's a character in a movie also."

"He's in a movie also?"

"Correct."

"Oh."

Tim bellowed and gushed tears when the endless coming-to-video clips started, so Merci fast-forwarded it to the feature presentation.

"He's got strong opinions," said Clark.

"Wonder where he gets those."

Still blubbering and clutching his bow, Tim climbed into his grand-father's recliner—his new favorite place to sit. Merci stretched out on one of the couches, taking most of it up, nothing but shorts and a tank top in the hot August evening, her hair up in chopsticks. She balanced the cocktail glass on her stomach, which soon made a ring of sweat on the material. *I'd pick up.* She looked down at her legs, and her big feet propped one on top of the other on the arm of the sofa. She wondered if her legs were good ones. She'd been told they were good ones, but that was back in college.

She browsed the newspaper but found no good crime stories. She checked to see how the Angels were doing: fair. She had no interest at all in baseball but felt obligated to follow them because so many of the deputies did. She checked the stock page for B. B. Sistel's Friday performance: up a buck and a half.

She watched Robin Hood and Little John outrunning the sheriff's cartoon arrows. Merci didn't approve of entertainment that glorified lawbreakers, but her father had shown Tim the animated movie one day while she was gone and Tim had glommed onto it like something holy. It was too silly to take seriously, and the actors reading the parts were funny.

But she didn't really watch the movie, and she didn't really listen to the dialogue, or even to the police band scanner on the shelf just behind her. She thought instead about Archie Wildcraft and Gwen Kuerner. And their parents. And Julia and Priscilla and making two million dollars in six months on an investment of twenty grand. And what it must be like to lie in a bed knowing your wife was murdered two days ago, and that you have a bullet in your brain. That you may be a suspect. To ask for another picture of *your own wife*, for Chris-sakes, because one wasn't enough to jog your bullet-riddled memory. She felt her blood pressure rise, cooled it off with a swallow of scotch.

"The Sheriff of Nottaham is bad?"

"Yes, he's bad."

"The Sheriff of Nottaham is good?"

"No, he's bad."

"He's good?"

"You know what he is, Tim."

Dinner was good and it left her feeling heavy and warm and a little restless. She watched Tim watch *Robin Hood again* and sipped her third drink.

Around nine, Gary Brice from the *Journal* called, something he'd been doing on most Saturday nights for the last couple of months. At first she had just let the machine pick up, but then she started answering because Brice amused her. He'd been trying to date her for almost a year now, and she'd always said no. No because he was flip and a womanizer and ten years younger than she was and she didn't find him attractive other than as an intriguing form of male energy. The calls started off as chides about her being home on Saturday nights, then escalated into crazy invites to join him, *right now*, at whatever club or lounge he was drinking in. Or join *us* right now. Gary had "tons" of friends, both female and male, and had guaranteed her she'd like *somebody* in his circle. She wondered why she just hadn't told him to quit calling, but the answer lay at the heart of her Saturday nights and she wasn't sure she wanted it.

"I don't hear drunks and bad music in the background," she said. "Did you take your date to the morgue?"

"I'm at the office. I've got a Sunday 'Lifestyle' piece that needed sudden attention. Our heroine, fighting an inoperable lung tumor but living life to its fullest by counseling psychotic bums—I mean mentally disordered homeless persons—just went into sudden cardiac arrest. Doesn't look good."

"So your article will either get a little longer or a lot shorter."

She wondered at how easily Gary Brice's glib pessimism rubbed off on her. And his curt delivery.

"Yes," said Brice. "These 'Lifestyle' articles are tough sledding. I loathe the upbeat do-goodism of this paper. But I love the police beat. Give me a petty scammer or a psychopath instead of someone trying to make society better. Any day."

"You comfort the afflicted, but finance the articles with ads for liposuction and plastic surgery."

"Precisely. You should have been a cynical reporter instead of a cynical cop."

"I can't write," she said.

"Come have a drink with me. We'll meet somewhere you'll feel safe."

"I always feel safe around you."

"Then it's settled. We'll drink single malts at the speed of light, then, when you can't resist me anymore you can take me into your car and have your way with me. That big Impala would be perfect. Or you can take me to a nice hotel."

"Do you actually have sex as much as you talk about it?"

"Almost. There's no refractory period between sentences."

"You deserve someone racier for your Saturday-night calls."

"This isn't about sex, Merci. It's about degradation and suffering."
She smiled. "Whose?"

"Merci, let's experience those beautiful things *together*."

"You ever try the phone sex numbers?"

"You're cheaper."

She smiled again. "What's new in the news?"

"I can tell you what isn't."

She stiffened a little, felt it coming.

"An arrest in the Wildcraft killing," she said.

"Correct. My editor asked about it. The *publisher* even asked about it. Believe me, by the time my bosses think of something, a lot of other people have too."

"And what are they thinking?"

"They see a guy making fifty grand a year as a deputy, his wife not working at all, and they live in a million-five cottage in Hunter Ranch. He's got a temper and an earnings cap. He's got a new Porsche. She looks like a movie star and wants more pretty things. He can't pay the bills or take the pressure, and he's sure enough not going to let her divorce him. Wham—he ends it for both of them. Or tries to. But he flinches at the last second and wounds himself. Three days later, no word of a suspect. No talk of a motive, not even the afore-mentioned obvious. Awfully damned quiet in the Sheriff's Public Information Office. So people do what people do—they start to wonder, are the cops trying to protect one of their own?"

"I can't talk to you on the record. Not before an arrest, you know that."

"So he *is* a suspect."

"We're questioning everyone who knew her."

Brice was quiet for a moment.

"You really think there's a chance he didn't do it—off the record?"

"At this point, the evidence is pointing away from him," she lied.

"You must have fingerprinted the weapon by now."

"Inconclusive."

"It wouldn't happen to have a registered owner, would it?"

"Stolen from a gun shop in Arizona," she lied again. "And this is all absolutely off the record, Gary."

"Sure. I've never burned you, Merci."

"I understand that."

"So if there's evidence pointing away from him, what evidence is it?"

"I can't tell you that, Gary. You know I can't go into the particulars."

"Even off the record?"

"Even off the record."

"But you've got them?"

"Don't call me a liar, Gary."

"I'm not. But you can make mistakes. You can see things the way you want to see things. I mean, we all—"

She had felt the need for a little levity on this, a hot summer night. She did not feel the need to be reminded of things that she'd been wrong about and had paid for with flesh, blood and spirit. Was still paying for.

She hung up on him and didn't pick up when he called right back. When he called yet again, she picked up on the first ring and Brice started in again.

"Okay, I have a big mouth and a small brain. I'm sorry. You're the best investigator they've got and you know it. I love you and always will."

"Good night, Gary."

"Cuddles."

She clicked off, shaking her head.

Tim jumped up on the seat of Clark's recliner, bow in hand, a defiant gleam in his eyes. "Wicked Prince John is good!"

"He's wicked. And guess what, beautiful little man? It's bedtime."
"Is not bedtime?"

After reading him three stories and carrying on a long conversation about who is real and who is a character, Merci fell asleep on the floor beside her son's bed. At midnight she awakened to find a pillow under her head and a light sheet over her. She gathered them up and took them to her room.

She lay down on her own bed, the door open to the hall and the distant light of the kitchen. She thought about Hess and wondered what they would be doing now if he'd lived. Who knew? She thought of him asleep in his chair in his Thirteenth Street apartment, the moonlight hitting his face and how she'd wanted so badly to touch the little white wave that grew in the thick gray of his hair. She thought of that hair later falling out in big handfuls and how she'd tried to put it back, tried to keep him from knowing. She thought of what she'd done next: made love to him, having convinced herself that it was a way of breathing life back into him but knowing it was mostly for herself, because she wanted every bit of him, from the twinkle in his eye to the cancer in his cells. She thought of him in his box in the ground now, an image she couldn't shake from her mind no matter how many times she banished it. Out. *Out*. She thought too of Paul Zamorra, lost in his Kirsten tonight, no doubt. And of Archie Wildcraft listening to the beeps of the monitors and the thumping of his heart. Of a fisherman's hand on her face. And of Tim, too, as always. Tim, connected to all of them but with little idea how, the youngest player in this minor history, a pure light in a world of shadows.

FIFTEEN

That Sunday afternoon, Archie asked to use a telephone. A nurse was happy to help him out, in fact it looked like Archie could leave the ICU for a regular bed sometime very soon. His vitals were stable, there was no infection, and the edema had come down dramatically. He'd been regularly conscious for a day and a half. Just that morning they'd removed his heparin lock and replaced it with a small neat stitch. He'd been eating like a wild boar since Saturday morning.

When Archie was done with his call, he asked to shower. He didn't seem to need help to and from but they helped him anyway. He smiled and thanked them for the plastic shower cap to keep his dressing dry. None of the staff had realized what a large, strong man he was during the five days he'd spent flat on his back with them. And they were amazed at how he'd come in with seemingly so little chance of living, only to be shuffling around five days later like someone raiding the pantry. Life was a tenacious miracle.

At ten minutes past five, an attractive young woman who had visited several times before brought Archie a small suitcase. She was Gwen Wildcraft's sister, the one who had brought him the small framed painting of his murdered wife. Over the questions of the nurses, Archie took the suitcase into a bathroom and a few minutes later came out dressed and smiling, smelling of aftershave and toothpaste.

He checked himself out of the UCI Medical Center at five-forty.

The nurses and doctors couldn't talk him out of it, the orderlies and security guards were afraid to use force due to the bullet in his head. Not even Archie's doctor, Stebbins, who by phone ordered Archie back to his bed, had any effect at all.

At six, Archie and the young woman were down in the medical center pharmacy getting his prescriptions filled. Four Sheriff's Department deputies clunked into the pharmacy waiting area, but they had no warrant to arrest him, suspected him of no crime and found him to be in decent physical and mental condition. There were smiles, handshakes, pats on the shoulder and a lot of quizzical looks. One talked on the radio for almost five minutes.

At six twenty-five, the woman drove him away in a white four-door Saturn she'd left in the red of the curving main entrance.

Two Sheriff's Department black-and-whites fell in behind them, running without color, giving the Saturn plenty of room.

Archie felt a cool wash of sweat break over his forehead as Priscilla turned onto the street. Up the hill. Past the big Norfolk Island pine tree on the corner, past a blue house with the riding arena and hot-walker, then up to a vaguely familiar stretch of street. The sun was lowering and it shined bright yellow beyond the trunks of the date palms. He looked at Priscilla and her face was neither blue nor red, but a believable shade of violet. Funny how some colors registered as he knew them to be, while others were wild but convincing.

His driveway? Must be. It was distant but familiar. He couldn't remember a lot of particulars from those last few hours, not as many as he should. But he remembered enough of them—and had been told enough of them—to feel a dread of this place and of what had happened here.

Gwen.

"Thank you, Priss."

"I'll come in for a while if you want."

"I'm going to do this alone."

"What exactly are you going to do, Arch?"

"I don't know," he said, not taking his eyes off the closed garage door in front of them. "I'm not sure. But it's important that I be here, isn't it?"

"I think I understand. I'm going to call in one hour. Here, I had this made after you called. It wasn't easy, getting the locksmith out on a Sunday."

He took the shiny new house key and smiled. "I do need this."

With that, Archie got out and retrieved his suitcase. He felt oddly strong as he pulled it from the trunk and set it down, which made him wonder if his pain receptors were damaged, as Stebbins said they might be. Or if it was just the strength that a week of bed rest can give you. He pulled out the long handle and started up the walkway.

He turned to watch Priscilla back out of the drive. When her car disappeared down the street, the two Sheriff's cruisers pulled along the driveway entrance and parked end-to-end so no cars could get into the Wildcraft driveway and none could get out.

Two of the deputies hustled down the drive to him. "Need a hand, Archie?"

"I've got it."

"Rayborn told us it's still a crime scene. She's on her way. She said we can keep you out, legally."

"It's my home, guys."

As at the hospital, they smiled and nodded and looked at each other uncertainly.

"I'll talk to her," said Wildcraft, starting toward the front door. "Don't worry."

They were right. The house was designated a crime scene by a notice in a clear plastic envelope from the Orange County Sheriff-Coroner Department. It was taped to the front door. There was no barrier ribbon or sentry. Archie saw the fingerprint dust heavy on the shiny lock and plate. He felt the roughness of the newly cut key in the lock, saw the little flash of sunlight play off the alloy and onto the varnished oak.

He stood in the living room and looked at the loose pile of gifts. Gwen's birthday, he knew, and remembered that there had been a party. Then his eyes moved to the black electrician's tape marking a rough circle in the middle of the room, where the rock had been. The window was still broken and the wooden blinds still splintered where the rock had come through. It startled him. It all seemed so long ago, another age entirely, but everything looked so fresh, as if it had just happened.

Leaving his luggage upright beside the presents, Archie walked down the hall and into the bedroom. He stepped down into the room and looked at the big sleigh bed. He saw the tangled sheets and blanket and felt a dizzying descent into the blackness where Gwen had gone. He could not picture her here, in this bed. He couldn't clearly picture what she would look like. Or how it would feel to be here with her. He could feel the powerful emotions of being with her at the Kuerners' in Norco, or in their old place in Santa Ana, or on their honeymoon, but not here in this big and new—for them—house. The bullet had blown them away. He wondered if such large and wonderful emotions would ever come to him again, except in the diminishing potencies of memory. His breath went shallow and his heart sped up.

A picture, he thought: *please show me another picture of her. A big one.*

Easy. There she was on the wall of the little sitting room off the bedroom, a photo portrait of Gwen in a low-cut black evening dress, her hair up and earrings dangling and her smart eyes staring back at him with conspiracy and desire. The long and elegant neck, the pearl choker. That was Gwen. He knew it. *Gwen.* The reason. The beginning. The original.

He stared at it for a long time, remembering Gwen at sixteen and eighteen and twenty and even twenty-two, trying to project these hard memories forward to create Gwen at the age of twenty-six, just five days ago, before she died. According to the date at the bottom, the portrait was done just last year. Still, even this wasn't quite enough to bring her most recent face into his mind's eye.

It's to protect you, Archie.

Gwen's voice again. Unmistakable. So actual and alive he felt her breath on the back of his neck. He turned and looked around the room. Then up behind his shoulder.

"But I couldn't protect *you*," he whispered.

But there was no voice then, just the happy chatter of a mocking-bird in the coral tree outside their back patio.

"Gwen?" he whispered again. Then felt a little embarrassed, be-cause he knew she was dead and he knew the dead don't speak except maybe to each other.

The air around him suddenly felt hot and spoiled so he pushed open the French doors to the patio.

He turned to face the bedroom again. When he saw the bathroom he understood that the center of what had happened that night had happened there. From this angle all he could see was the half-open door and part of the big tiled shower. He walked over and looked at the doorjamb ripped loose from the doorway frame. They must have broken this in, he thought. He pushed the door open with the tip of his finger and looked inside.

The smell of spoiled blood tapped him softly at first, then hit him hard. The flies lifted up around his face with brief interest and began to settle back to the hard black pool down by the toilet. Archie looked at the drag marks and shoe prints. Like a battlefield. He saw the blood splatters on the wall and the glass shower door. More on the counter tile. And the little handwritten labels with a strip of adhesive to keep them true: 08/21/02/7:49 a.m./bathroom #3.

He pulled the door closed hard, turned and walked outside, his eyes burning and his heart beating clear up into his throat. The mockingbird in the coral tree bent forward accusingly to face Archie, flipped his tail into the air and shot off a warning.

So Archie walked a wide arc around the tree and then across the backyard to the window where the rock had come through. The break in the glass didn't look like much from here. In the bright light of the lowering sun he could hardly make it out.

He picked up the walkway and followed it past the pool and then around the side of the house toward the front. When he went into the shaded tunnel made by the Chinese flame trees he could feel memories trying to come back to him. It was like facing a closed door and knowing there were people on the other side, waiting for you to let them in. But where was the knob?

He stopped at the big bloodstain on the concrete walk, dried to rust-brown now and just beginning to fade. He thought of the bright light in his eyes and remembered that this was where he had seen that light. Yes, right here, as he walked back toward the front door.

Then he realized this blood was his. He knelt and looked at it, touched it with a finger.

The detectives came briskly down the walkway toward him, like workers late from lunch. For the first time, Archie did not mistake the woman for Gwen, even for a second.

"Deputy Wildcraft," she said. "Exactly what are you doing here?"

He stood and wiped his finger on his pants. The tone of her voice grated on his nerves. It was condescending and bossy. And he didn't trust either of them because they very clearly did not trust him. They had treated him like a suspect.

"Looking at the blood," he said.

"You've got a bullet in your head."

"I can't feel it."

"You can't stay here."

"Why? This is where I saw the bright light."

Rayborn stood there with her mouth half open, her head shaking slowly in disbelief, but said nothing.

Zamorra simply waited with his arms crossed, looking like an undertaker, Archie thought.

"Priscilla brought me some clothes," he said. "I showered and shaved and signed out. I got my prescriptions. I think everything's in order."

"*Damnit*, Archie," said Rayborn. "You can't stay here."

He saw the anger in her eyes and knew she was serious, but immensely flustered. Even Zamorra, who always looked so calm, had a look of mystified doubt.

"Why not?"

Archie watched Merci step up close to him and hook her dark unhappy eyes into his own. Like they had claws in them.

"You need to understand just two things, Deputy Wildcraft. One is that your wife is dead, murdered in this house. Your gun killed her.

Your prints are on that gun. The gunpowder was on your hands. Her blood is on your robe. There are very powerful people who want to see you charged with that murder. This is the first thing. Am I getting through to you with this concept, this concept of you being charged with killing Gwen?"

"You are."

"You're clear on it?"

"I am."

"Good. Because you're about one breath away from being arrested. If you say or do the wrong thing, you're going to end up in Mod J, in the protective custody of your own jail."

Archie's anger jumped. He said the first thing he thought of, as a way of hiding it. "I used to work Mod J."

She shook her head and thinned her lips, like somebody had forced her to taste something bitter. "Number two is *this*, Archie—somebody shot you in the head, right here, five days ago. He left you for dead. He wanted you dead, Archie. Chances are pretty good that he hasn't changed his mind about that. When he hears you're here, it's possible he'll come back and shoot you some more. How's that sound?"

"I'll keep a weapon ready."

"That didn't help you the first time. Are you even close to hearing me, Deputy Wildcraft?"

"Very close."

"Close but not quite hearing me?"

"I hear you very well."

"Are you close to *thinking* straight?"

"I think so, yes. There are the black-and-white cars out front. Nobody would come after me with them around. I'm not under arrest, Detective. I'm a sane adult with no criminal record, occupying my own residence. I'm a man whose wife just died, and I came back here to this house because it was our home. I came here to think about what happened and to remember her."

"Wait until the reporters find out you're here," she said.

Archie had no firm opinion on how he should feel about reporters. "Would you mind leaving me alone now? I want to spend some time here, trying to remember my wife."

She still had a disbelieving look on her face. "Archie, do you even know what day it is?"

"Sunday."

"Do you remember how to tell time?"

"Look at my watch."

"And whether you're hungry or not?"

Archie felt his anger stir. "I'm not hungry."

"Or what to do if that bandage of yours starts to show blood?"

"Call the doctor."

"What's your doctor's name, and where can you get him?"

"Stebbins, at, ah . . . the medical center."

"UC Irvine Medical Center."

"Correct."

"How do you get that number?"

"From the prescription bottles. Or nine-one-one if the blood is gushing out."

She sighed, but her eyes still held his tight. Archie clearly felt her power and the strength of her will. Slowly, her pupils relaxed and he felt her hands on his shoulders.

"You are going to talk to Paul and me, here, at eight tomorrow morning. We'll walk through it, together. Be rested and fresh. You're going to tell us everything you remember about that night. About your life up to that night. About Gwen and the two million and Felix Mendez and a girl named Julia. You're going to tell me everything you know. And you're not going to tell anyone else *squat*. Correct?"

"Yes, okay."

"Call me if you need something. Don't call Priscilla. Don't call your friends. Call me."

"Okay. I will."

"If anyone else calls you, don't talk to them. Not to reporters, salespeople, Jehovah's Witnesses, *anybody*. Understand?"

It rankled him to be talked to like a killer, then a child, so he cracked a joke. "How about Mom and Dad?"

She sighed, blinking slowly. "Yes. Of course."

He watched her take a card from her purse and write something on the back.

"Office and pager on the front, cell on the back. Archie, I want you to call me if you remember something new about what happened to you and Gwen before we meet tomorrow morning. Even if it's small. Even if it doesn't seem important. Call me."

"Okay."

Zamorra had already turned away and was heading back up the walk.

He sat out by the pool and watched the sun go down. He brought the telephone with him and talked to Priscilla when she called. His father and mother called too, frantic with concern, but Archie told them he was fine for now, well protected, please come over for lunch tomorrow.

A few minutes later he got Trent Gentry's number from his personal phone book and punched it in.

"*Shit*, man," said Trent, "I've been thinking about you every second. I'm so goddamned sorry about what happened. I just . . . I just . . . Can I call you back?"

Archie said okay, gave him the number.

A few minutes later Trent was on the line again. Archie heard traffic in the background.

"So, man," said Trent, "what can I do, Archie? I really feel bad about all this."

"Does it have to do with OrganiVen?"

"How could it?"

"I was just wondering. OrganiVen keeps coming into my mind. As something that was good for us, and bad for us at the same time."

"What do you mean?"

"I don't know what I mean. I'm hazy on things."

"Stay hazy, man. Just stay hazy, be careful and take care of yourself."

Archie thought about this. "Okay," he said.

"I'm going to Hawaii tomorrow. Be back in a couple of weeks. I'll call you then."

"What about one of the OrganiVen guys, on the business side? I think I should talk to one of them. It's just a feeling."

"Well, fuck, Arch, they're back in Switzerland by now for all I know. I mean, I don't know those people. Or they're out on some yacht off of Greece. They weren't OrganiVen guys anyway—they were just investors."

"The car."

"What car?"

"The car they came to that meeting in. It looked normal but it wasn't. God, I wish I could remember."

"Man, you're talking nonsense to me now."

"Sorry."

"Aren't you supposed to be in the hospital?"

Archie had vague memories of Gwen meeting two men one night in a bar in Newport Beach. Long ago. A year? Maybe more? She had asked Archie to be there without the men knowing it. Because she was uneasy, uncertain how they would react. React to what? He searched his memory for an answer but it was like trying to get water from an empty bucket. Still, he remembered sitting across the room dressed like a beach bum and looking at the three of them occasionally from behind a pair of sunglasses. One man was blond and clean-shaven. The other was dark-haired, with a beard and mustache, one of the biggest people Archie had ever seen in his life. His head was enormous. Archie could remember being afraid for Gwen, just her being that close to him.

Gentry hung up.

Archie called Merci Rayborn's cell number and told her that he had just remembered Gwen being upset by a man with a monstrous head.

"Explain," she snapped.

He did—maybe something to do with OrganiVen, a meeting in a Newport bar, Gwen asking him to be there without them knowing.

"Monstrous?" she asked.

"Very. Dark hair, and a beard."

"Big enough to recline a Cadillac seat just to get in or out?"

"I don't know. Along those lines, I would say."

"What else?"

"The car they came in. Something about it was different. But I can't remember what."

"Make and model?"

"I can't remember."

"American or foreign?"

"Large, that's all I see."

"The way it looked? Sounded? A custom paint job or body work? A sign, a bumper sticker?"

"I'm sorry. Just that it was different than other cars."

A silence.

"Archie, I'm going to come by and take you back to the hospital. Right now."

"I won't go."

"I'll call paramedics for you, if you'd be more comfortable that way."

"I won't go."

A long silence over a clear connection.

"Archie, are you all right?"

"I'm fine. The deputies are still out front."

"They'll be there all night."

"I'm not afraid."

"I wish you were."

Archie sat and stared at the lights twinkling in the hills before him. He had no appetite. When the night breeze came up it was cool and clean off the desert so he went into the house to put away the phone and get some blankets.

The phone rang just as he was putting it into the charger.

"Hello, Deputy Wildcraft?"

"Yes."

"This is Gary Brice, Orange County *Journal*. How are you feeling?"

"All right."

"How about we do an interview tonight? I can be there in less than half an hour."

"No. I'm tired."

"I can sure see why. How come you checked out of the hospital?"

"I felt better."

"Were the police putting pressure on you?"

"They questioned me about what happened."

"What did you tell them? What *did* happen, Deputy Wildcraft?"

"I won't talk now. I need some privacy and time to think."

Archie punched off. The phone rang again immediately—then off and on until he fell asleep hours later—but he didn't answer it.

From the kitchen window he could see part of his driveway and the two black-and-whites still blocking it. Good, he thought: safe for now. He got a gun, too, a Remington composite-stock twelve-gauge automatic cut down at both ends, with the magazine plug removed to hold all five rounds. He checked to see it was loaded and safed.

He went back out and set the shotgun on the pool deck, then lay down on the chaise longue, pulling the blankets over him. He saw a falling star, then another, then more. He remembered, as a boy, count-ing one hundred and nineteen of them one September night while lying in his backyard on a sleeping bag.

Archie listened to the palm fronds hiss in the breeze.

I'll remember, he thought. And tell Detective Rayborn everything and she'll arrest whoever did this and it will make no difference at all.

I'll remember you, he thought. Someday I will remember every-thing about you and never forget again.

And I'll remember you, Arch.

"Gwen."

A little after six the next morning, just after first light, Archie sat up.

He heard the branch snap, then soft, careful footsteps on the walk-way. They came from down on the property, not from the house but from the direction of the steps and the wildflowers that led down to his fence and the road.

His blankets were damp. The clothes he had slept in were damp. So was the bandage around his head. Archie shivered quickly as he listened to the footsteps getting closer. He lifted the Remington, stood and moved toward the walkway with the stubby barrel held out and his finger on the safety beside the trigger guard.

Archie saw him first. A young blond guy in jeans and sneakers, a light jacket. He held a camcorder up to his face as he picked his way along the walk. He swung the camera to his left, then his right, then aimed straight ahead, at the house.

Then at Archie, who stepped from beside a hibiscus plant and extended his arms and put the barrel of his riot gun under the guy's chin.

The man froze, one foot just coming up to begin a step. "Fuck," he whispered. "Please don't shoot."

The camera lowered very slowly and Archie saw the boyish face— the pale cheeks and young blue eyes, the weak mustache and rosy, astonished mouth.

Archie left the barrel where it was.

"I'm Gary Brice, Deputy. I'm a reporter with the Orange County *Journal*. Please don't shoot me."

"Show me your ID."

"It's in my wallet. My wallet's in my pants pocket. I'll get it."

"Move very slowly."

"Can I put my other foot down?"

"No."

The man calling himself Brice produced ID and Archie glanced at it. It looked good. Brice still stood with one foot lifted almost off the ground, and this made him waver because his balance was bad.

Archie still hadn't moved the gun barrel.

"You're trespassing," he said.

"I wanted you to tell me what happened."

Archie's temper spiked. It was like a rocket being launched. He couldn't account for it, really, other than that he'd been shot and his wife murdered and he'd been poked, prodded, needled, scanned, questioned, doubted, threatened, treated like a child and now trespassed on by a reporter.

Still holding the gun under Brice's chin, Archie ordered him off his property. He could hear the ice-cold anger in his voice and he knew it for what it was.

"I'm absolutely getting off your property, Deputy. I'm going to back up now, and just go away. Okay? So don't shoot, and I'll be gone and I won't come back unless you invite me."

Brice lowered his trembling foot, then backed up one step, then another. Archie kept the gun pointed at his chest.

"Deputy Wildcraft, what happened that night?"

"Get away before I lose my patience."

Brice kept moving back, trying to keep eye contact with Archie and not trip.

"Did you see who killed your wife?"

"Get out."

"What are you going to do?"

"I'll kill them myself."

As Archie spoke, Brice veered off the walkway and backed into an orange tree. He flinched, swung back his hands for balance, almost dropping the camera. He finally steadied himself and re-aimed at Archie.

Archie smiled.

"Did you shoot her and yourself, sir?"

"Go to hell, you little shit."

Brice was halfway through the wildflowers now, backpedaling faster. When he thought he was out of shotgun range he whipped around, tucked the camera under his arm like a football, sprinted down the hill and jumped over the fence in one big leap.

Archie watched him scramble into a little silver four-door and drive away.

SIXTEEN

The walk-through with Wildcraft was a bust. Rayborn took careful notes and Zamorra made sure the tape recorder was always within pick-up distance of their subject, but Archie offered almost no new information. He was vague. He was forgetful. He was emotional, then oddly flat, then emotional again. To Merci, it seemed like the deputy was trying to weigh anchor through molasses.

As they walked the house she noticed that Archie had done some light housework. He had cleaned up the bathroom, taken away the old towels and opened two windows. He had also stacked the birthday presents more neatly in the living room, pushing them up against one wall. He had leaned a twelve-gauge riot gun in the corner of the entryway a few feet from the front door. He had placed his medicine bottles on the kitchen counter by the coffeemaker, spread out in a neat line of four.

The bed was unmade, though, and the bedroom had grown warm and stuffy. Rayborn caught the scent of something musky and sexual and it embarrassed her.

Archie was sweating visibly.

"Who took care of the finances, bills, money stuff?" Merci asked.

"Gwen. Ever since we were married. In the music room, there's a desk and file cabinets. It's all there."

"Tell us about OrganiVen."

Wildcraft sat on the bed. He looked around the room like he was new there. Merci could see it in his posture, in the earnest, uplifted face, the inquisitive eyes. Like he was discovering new things every second. Maybe he is, she thought. Eyes like Tim's.

"It was a company that was new. We invested some money, but I'm not sure how much. It was called that because they made a cancer treatment from snake venom. We got to see slides and pictures of what it did to tumors and it was amazing. So, then the company got bought up by a bigger company and we made a lot of money by selling our shares."

He looked at her, raised his eyebrows unenthusiastically, then looked away.

"How did you find out about it?"

"I'm not sure. I believe we worked with Priscilla's husband, Charlie Brock. He works for a big stockbroker, but I can't think of the name."

"Ritter-Dunne-Davis."

Archie smiled and his eyes sparkled. "Yeah. You should have seen that stuff, eating those tumors. It would kill the cancer, right while you watched. On a camera, I mean, a video."

"You and Gwen put almost everything you had into that company. Didn't you?"

"I think so. I don't remember particulars. Or maybe I never knew them, because Gwen did all the finances."

"I'd like to see those financial things," said Zamorra. "Take some with me to look over closely."

"You're welcome to them. I'm sorry I couldn't help more. I feel sleepy and thick. Kind of dumb. Maybe the swelling started up again."

"Let's get you back to the medical center, then," said Merci.

"I'm thinking about that. But I want some more time here. I look at her pictures and I see her things. And I smell her. And it feels like a light is about to go on. Like I'm about to bring something up out of black water."

"We can't post those deputies outside forever, Archie," said Zamorra.

"I know."

"You'd be helping us if you went back to UCI," he said. "Yourself, too."

"I need to do a few things here. Make a few calls. Look at some pictures. Try to . . . try to just remember."

Zamorra left the room with a hard look at Archie.

Wildcraft was still sitting on the bed. He touched the sheet as if for the first time, rubbing the fabric between his thumb and fingers. When he looked at Merci, his hand stopped moving.

"You going to charge me with it?"

"If you did it, I will."

"Then you don't believe me."

"We're still investigating."

"I can see why you suspect me. With all the evidence you told me about." He smiled. The light caught his eyes and filled them with something innocent and childlike and sad. "I feel guilty."

Rayborn's antenna snapped upright at one of her favorite words. "Why, Archie? Tell me what you did to feel guilty."

At first he looked angry, then offended, then just defeated. "I let it happen. I didn't protect her."

"They call that survivor's guilt."

"Do they?"

She studied his guileless eyes, trying to see behind them, into his mind. Nothing like this had ever happened to Rayborn, and it unnerved her. She'd never chatted with a suspect about whether or not she was going to arrest him, except to disarm. Or talked about the evidence, except either to intimidate or mislead. Or stood in a suspect's bedroom and smelled his tangled sheets and wondered if this was the last place he'd had sex with his wife, or if it was in their car, pulled off of Coast Highway, *stars in her hair*.

All of that was bad enough. But what made it worse was this was the only time she'd ever looked at a suspect and thought he was beautiful. Something to do with those dimples and the nice baseball muscles? Maybe. Something to do with him defending her in a bar fight? Okay. And something to do with the bullet in his head, too, and all of the sad mystery it signified? Yes. But mostly the fact—the apparent fact—that this guy had loved his wife with passion. That was what made Wildcraft seem so genuinely, naturally, uncomplicatedly beautiful.

Christ, she thought: *get a grip*.

"What's wrong?" he asked.

"Nothing. Why?"

"Your expression. I don't know."

"No, you don't." Then, anything to break the hold of this moment. "Why isn't your gardener here today?"

"He must not work here on Mondays."

"Describe him."

"Dark skin and dark hair. I think he's Mexican but I'm not sure."

"How tall?"

"Short and heavy. Maybe five-eight, two hundred. Why?"

"I was wondering who left size-sixteen shoe prints under your tree out there."

"I don't know."

Wildcraft turned to look at the pillows. He leaned over, picked something off one of them, then held it out to her. She could see the hair: four inches, dark, a gentle bend in it.

"That's Gwen's," said Wildcraft.

"Who else's would it be?"

"Well, either hers or mine. But mine was short before they shaved it."

Wildcraft turned to the pillow again and placed the hair back where it had been.

"Were you happy with her, Archie?"

He studied her for just a moment. "Yes, I think so. If she's this large to me being gone, I think she must have been even larger being here."

"How big is she, gone?"

"Huge, Detective. Gigantic."

She believed him. But she still pressed him. Maybe he was just fooling himself.

"But you didn't want more, Archie? Run up some numbers, like some of you guys like to do?"

"I don't remember ever doing that."

"Gwen inclined that way?"

"You mean make it with other guys?"

"That's what I mean."

He shook his head. "Oh, I don't think so. No. Do you want to hear something very weird?"

"Sure."

"She talks to me. I hear her voice in my head, so clear I turn around and look to see where she's standing. Once I felt her breath on my neck."

Rayborn knew other people who heard from their departed. Personally, she'd only heard Hess's voice one time after he was gone, and that was in a dream. He'd said: *It's okay*. At first she'd felt bad about her deafness, attributed it to some failure of emotion or imagination. But as the months passed she learned to forgive herself for what she didn't hear. Why should she be blamed for the silence of the dead? It was one of the things she'd talked about with Zamorra. He had never heard from Janine, either, except once, like her, in a dream.

"You're lucky," she said.

"But it's kind of torture," said Archie. "It . . . gets your hopes up."

"I can see how it would."

"I wonder if there's a way to see her, too. If you can actually hear, why can't you actually see? I don't think it's impossible."

Merci said nothing. What *could* you say to that? But for one extremely brief moment—the time it took to let out one breath and take another one in—Merci pretended that she could see Hess again if she wanted to. She felt spooked and giddy. But would she see him, if she could? Oh, yes. So much to talk about.

"Well, I'll let you know if I find a way to do that," Archie said, reasonably.

"Do that, Archie."

Zamorra came into the room carrying a cardboard box in two hands. "I've got plenty to get us started. I found what looks like videos from OrganiVen. Maybe we'll get to see the rattlesnake cancer cure in action."

Merci heard the sharpness in Zamorra's words. She knew that as

Janine had faded, she and Paul had gone to a clinic in Tijuana. They had come back two days later, Zamorra quietly boiling with contempt for what they'd found down there. He'd made an unfunny joke about demolishing the place and killing the quacks with head-and-kidney punches.

"You'll like that," said Archie, unaware.

"I bet I will." Zamorra headed down the hall with his booty.

"Do you want me to give you a ride to the hospital?" Merci asked.

"No, thank you. I've got a few hours of things to do. I'm feeling better right now. My parents are taking me to lunch."

She looked at him and nodded.

"You're a good detective, Sergeant Rayborn," he said. "I think you're intelligent and thorough. You seem to like your job. You're attractive. You don't smile very often, but you're not in a smiley kind of business. The first couple of times I saw you, I thought you were Gwen. You have very similar eyes. Intelligent eyes. The difference is Gwen's eyes had something generous and inclusive, and yours don't. Yours have something judgmental and private. Something unwelcome to other people, or maybe just to me."

She thought about these statements but it was like being hit by different things in different places.

"I don't really care what you think of me or the way I look, or who I remind you of."

"No, you weren't supposed to. I was trying to be factual."

"See you later, Archie."

"Okay, sure. Something weird just happened, Sergeant."

She waited, feeling her anger rise.

"I just remembered what it was about that car. You know, the car the men drove to the meeting with Gwen?"

Again she said nothing.

Archie was nodding, frowning a little and looking past her. "It was a Lincoln Town Car, black. But it had livery plates. That's what made it different. It was registered as a limousine. When I looked at the plates I saw it."

"So they took a car to the meet," said Merci.

"But one of them drove it. That was another thing that seemed odd. The big guy drove it but he was part of the meeting, so he wasn't a chauffeur, right? And the blond rode up front, not like a customer but like a friend or something."

To Rayborn, it seemed odd, too. And Wildcraft hadn't mentioned the blond before. "Describe the blond man."

"Average build, mid-forties. Hair a little longer than usual. More like a seventies look."

"When you first saw him, did you happen to think, businessman?"

"That's exactly what I thought."

Just like Dobbs, thought Merci. "You wrote down the plate numbers, didn't you?"

"I believe so."

"What did you do with them after you wrote them down, Archie?"

He was already shaking his head.

"You can't remember."

"I can't remember."

"Do you have a regular notebook?"

"Yeah, I *think* it was regular. Here, I'll give it to you. Just a second."

Archie came off the bed and went into his closet. Merci could hear coins hitting coins, the rattle of change in a container, then pages being flipped.

He came out a second later with an inexpensive three-by-five notepad with a spiral binding at the top and a green cover. "Good luck," he said. "I couldn't find anything that looked like plate numbers."

"No. And you can't tell me anything more about that meeting?"

Archie shook his head, frowning, biting his lip. "I wish I could. Just that it had to do with our OrganiVen stock, I mean, I associated the car and the stock but I don't know why. And Gwen wanted me there. I remember that very clearly. I'm really sorry."

"Me, too."

"Oh, wow! I just thought of something else. The light came down at me."

"What do you mean, Archie?"

"The light. That night. I'm six-three. Most people would have to shine it up at me. That guy, he aimed down. I just remembered."

Halfway back to headquarters, her cell phone rang. It was Sheriff Vince Abelera, speaking in his usual soft tones.

"I want to meet with you and Paul at five o'clock."

"Yes, sir. Can you give us a sneak preview?"

"Whether or not to arrest Wildcraft. Brenkus and Dawes will be there. They want to file, they say that it's a good case. Better than good. Everyone's got strong opinions about this crime. For obvious reasons, I need yours."

Her heart sank. "I look forward to it, sir."

"You and Zamorra have my complete trust and confidence on this."

She wondered about that last statement, wondered why Abelera would bother to make it if it was true. She clicked off and sighed, told her partner.

"I was wondering when they'd lower the boom," Zamorra said.

"Me, too."

She looked at him and tried to read the thoughts behind his trim face. "Paul, you've let me lead the charge on this one. Or the *non*-charge. But am I missing something here? Am I blind? Am I the only person not ready to charge that guy with murder?"

Zamorra was quiet for a long moment. Merci watched a man talking on a phone swoosh into the car-pool lane in front of them at about ninety, wished she could pull him over and cuff him.

"I think Wildcraft is running something on us."

"This is news to me, Paul."

"This morning clinched it. He doesn't remember anything more on the walk-through. But he remembers livery plates at a meeting that may or may not have taken place. He suddenly remembers the light came down on him, not up. He gives you that speech about what a good detective you are, and so beautiful too, you remind him of his wife who's been dead six days. I thought you might swat him silly for that one."

"I almost did. Nice eavesdropping, by the way."

"I started down the hall with the box and thought I'd listen in. Just the way he was sitting on that bed. It set off an alarm. Sorry."

"Hey—you're my partner, listen in any time you want."

"I didn't like what I heard. I don't like him and the little sister at Archie's place while Gwen was gone. What was going on then—I don't buy the mad-at-my-soon-to-be-ex outburst. I don't like the little sister showing up with Archie's clothes and helping him check out of the hospital. I'm going to poke around a little, have a closer look at her."

"With an eye for her getting the cute hubby once big sister is out of the way."

"That comes to mind."

"I could see it. All right. Okay. I'm with you."

"I think we should keep looking at him. Hard. And surveil him while we do. Not a twenty-four/seven—but selective—see where he goes and who he talks to. I don't think he's going far with a bullet in his head. But he might go somewhere interesting."

"They're going to want an arrest, Paul."

"Then let's just tell them the truth. We're not ready and we're not moving until we are."

"Good. That's fine. It's clean and decisive and that's what we'll do. Thanks, Paul."

"I don't trust him and I'm beginning to think he did it. He botched the suicide and he's improvising now, trying to keep off of death row."

"I don't think he did it. But I don't necessarily trust him."

She smiled and Zamorra smiled.

"We're a wholesome, humane, optimistic, trusting pair, aren't we?" she asked.

"That's us."

"You really think he did her?"

"He did something."

Back at her desk Rayborn drew up a list of county limousine services, starting with those in Newport Beach. She only had time to make three calls but all three people told her the same thing. There was no very large, bearded driver employed by Executive Plus, Air Glide or Limo-Dream services. Sorry we can't help you, *Sergeant*.

The Limo-Dream guy asked for her badge number and she told him, making a note of his nosiness in her blue notebook.

SEVENTEEN

A minute later Merci sat in one of the headquarters' conference rooms and watched a dazzling blue wave break beyond a pale sand beach. Then another. Zamorra adjusted the volume on the television and sat across the table from her. He pushed aside the box of financial records he'd collected from Wildcraft's house, making room to take notes.

The title of the movie appeared over the breaking waves—*MiraVen and the Treatment of Malignant Blastomas*. Produced by OrganiVen Biomedical Research Partnership and the University of California, San Diego, School of Medicine.

A factual male voice talked over the waves:

"Cancer has been with mankind since the dawn of civilization, if not history herself. It is an organic disorder that afflicts not only human beings, but virtually all of the higher vertebrates and even some plants and trees. A cancerous cell is a cell that has broken free of healthy DNA programming, to metastasize—reproduce—without control within the host body. Such reproduction eventually kills the very host in which the cancerous cell has been thriving."

The screen went from elegant waves to surgically opened bodies showing tumors of various size and location. Merci felt a quiver of nausea go through her, and a little tremor of lightheadedness. Surgical scenes and autopsies bothered her in a way that crime scenes rarely did, something about the slow precision of the former versus the explosiveness of the latter.

"Treatments for cancers have evolved from the primitive to the sophisticated. But until now, no one treatment, or even a combination of treatments, has shown itself to be effective on the deadly blastoma— or budding—forms of the disease. The common problem in all previous treatment modalities has been the concomitant destruction of healthy cells as the tumor is resected by surgery or laser, bombarded with radiation or chemotherapy, even cooled or heated.

"Enter *MiraVen*. Developed by OrganiVen Biomedical Research Partnership, MiraVen treatment modality is so effective that Dr. Stephen Monford of the University of California, San Diego, Medical School has called it a . . ."

The picture cut from a tumor-riddled lung to a white-haired, white-coated man sitting behind a gleaming wooden desk. Merci saw the diplomas on the wall behind him. He was sixty-ish, lean and lightly freckled, with rimless glasses and beautiful blue eyes.

"People in my profession don't use the word *miracle*," said Dr. Monford. His voice was soft and slow. "But I do now. I've seen what MiraVen does and there's no better way to describe it. Two things were necessary to bring about this treatment. The first is nature's simple genius: MiraVen does *exactly* what nature intended it to do—it destroys cells. The second is the work of the OrganiVen biomedical research team, which discovered a way of totally preventing collateral tissue damage. The results are, well . . . miraculous. I could talk for hours on the medical aspects of MiraVen, and what OrganiVen Biomedical means to the future of cancer therapies. But why don't you see for yourself what MiraVen can do?"

On-screen, Dr. Monford gave way to a cobra, head raised and hood spread, casually tracking the sway of a turbaned man who kneeled in front of the snake and played a flute.

The first male voice came back then, stern with factuality.

"The snake. The serpent. Wrapped in mystery, shrouded in fear. Some ancients believed the snake was Satan. Some believed he was a god. But they all knew the dramatic effects of snake envenomation on human beings. However, not until the late nineteenth century did modern science begin to explain what happened when a poisonous snake injected its deadly venom."

The monitor showed a drawing of a human being with only the major components of the nervous system illustrated. A cartoon snake injected a drop of black liquid and the liquid started to constrict the spinal nerves, working its way to the heart and brain.

"Early biomedical researchers determined that snake venom was of two basic types: neurotoxic—which attacked the nervous system, and hemotoxic—which attacked the blood and tissue. It was the fearsome killers—the cobras and mambas and kraits of India—that possessed the neurotoxic poison that could kill a man in less than half an hour after introduction. But a far different venom is possessed by other poisonous snakes of the world: the rattlesnakes, the adders, the vipers. The venom of these snakes *works directly on the blood and tissue of the victim*."

Now the screen showed a simplified illustration of blood: red cells, white cells, platelets. A cartoon snake injected a little pool of black liquid into the blood and the various cells began to wither and vanish.

The Voice of Truth and Reason continued:

"In nature, a bite from one of these serpents can lead to a slow, painful death. But in the OrganiVen research laboratories, under the direction of the University of California, San Diego, School of Medicine, scientists set out to find a way to turn this deadly hemotoxin into a *killer of cancer cells, not healthy cells*. Years later, their dream became a reality, and a potential treatment modality for most forms of mankind's most deadly and feared disease."

Merci watched the picture change to the insides of some kind of animal, but the camera was up so close she couldn't tell if it was a human being or a lab rat.

"I wish that pompous ass would tell us what we're supposedly looking at," said Merci.

"The image modality is yet to be revealed by the OrganiVen bio-technical AV presentation team," droned Zamorra.

Then, Mr. Ass again:

"*The neuroblastoma, or heart tumor—an almost invariably fatal tumor when treated by conventional therapies.* But watch closely as University of California researchers inject this canine neuroblastoma with MiraVen."

Merci watched. The camera moved in close. A rubber-gloved hand, a syringe, a silver needle pushing through the mush of a black tumor on the beating heart of the dog.

"Things like this make me queasy," said Merci.

"Close your eyes and I'll tell you what happens."

"I can cut it."

Merci took a deep breath. The needle slid away from the tumor and the rubber-gloved hand disappeared. The dog's heart throbbed earnestly and the black tumor attached to one side of it jiggled along with each rhythmic beat.

The Voice of Truth was back:

"You may follow the elapsed time on the screen timer while we speed up this videotape in the interests of time. What you will see in the next minute actually elapsed over fifty-seven minutes—*less than one hour.*"

Merci saw a timer blip into action on the right side of the screen, digits counting the sped-up time.

She watched the black tumor bouncing rapidly with each heartbeat.

She watched it turn dark gray.

She watched it turn ash gray.

She watched it lose its firmness and discontinue its rhythm with the heart.

She watched it break up. The parts crumbled into smaller parts, then smaller parts again. And again.

Like a muffin soaked in water, Merci thought.

The rubber-gloved hand came back in preposterous fast motion. With a nozzle of some kind, it sucked the loose, soggy pieces of tumor away from the heart.

The on-screen timer stopped at fifty-seven minutes and four seconds. The Voice again:

"And this is the same dog's heart six months later."

Merci looked at the apparently perfect organ, still thumping away. It wasn't scarred or discolored, or damaged in any way that she could see.

A final clip showed a black cocker spaniel leaping after a red ball on a green lawn.

"I'm supposed to believe that?" Merci asked.

"Sistel Laboratories did," said Zamorra. "They bought OrganiVen for stock and cash that totaled four hundred million dollars. You can bet they had an army of doctors, lawyers and money men who looked at that video pretty hard. And everything else, too."

"Then they've really got a cure for cancer?"

"They've got something. That's why the Wildcrafts made two million on twenty grand. That's why Sistel bought the whole outfit. Happy start-up company. Happy investors, like Archie and Gwen. Happy international pharmaceutical giant."

Merci crossed her arms and sat back, looking at the dead TV screen. It was not in her nature to believe that wildly good news could be true. Wildly good news did not add up in the real world she'd lived in for thirty-seven years.

"There are some interesting things in this box," Zamorra said. "OrganiVen letterhead and OrganiVen envelopes—nice heavy paper, thermal-raised letters. OrganiVen thank-you notes and matching envelopes. A long list of names and addresses that came off a laser printer—some of them with lines penciled through them, some not. Clean copies of newspaper and magazine articles on the venom cure. OrganiVen newsletters. Clean copies of the OrganiVen business plan, bios on the founders and doctors. Four videotapes, like the one we just saw. Same title, anyway."

"What did the Wildcrafts need all that for?"

"Two possibilities come to mind," said Zamorra. "One is they were shilling for the company—raising capital. That's what this tape would have been used for."

Merci nodded. "And the other is that they smelled something wrong—maybe afraid their twenty grand was going to vanish. That stuff could be evidence if OrganiVen wasn't on the up-and-up. Or if Archie and Gwen thought they weren't."

"Exactly," said Zamorra. "Let's talk to that Monford doctor at UCSD. And at least one of the OrganiVen founders. They're listed in the bios here."

Zamorra pulled some papers from the box. "Here," he said. "Wyatt Wright, Cody Carlson, Sean Moss."

Merci thought for a moment. "Wyatt, Cody and Sean. They sound like Tim's friends from the park."

"I'll take Monford and Wright. You get Cody and Sean. I'll call the Securities and Exchange Commission and see what they know."

"Sistel was solid on Friday, Paul—up a buck and a half, I think it was. I looked."

"So did I."

"They got a real treatment for tumors, I might want to buy a few shares myself."

"No, you wanted to buy shares in OrganiVen Biomedical Research Partnership, *before* it got sold to Sistel."

"How much were those?"

"A quarter apiece. It says right here in the business plan. Archie and Gwen bought eighty thousand of them."

Merci did the math on that one, figuring the increase on a per-share basis. Her notepad was too small so she used a piece of OrganiVen stationery. She did her division the old-fashioned way, counting off the zeros with the tip of her pen to keep things straight.

"The stock was worth twenty-five cents a share when they bought it, and twenty-five dollars a share when they sold it."

She looked at the figures and tried to put two million dollars into real-life terms: a fancy home, cool cars, presents for everybody.

"We need to talk to the sister's beloved hubby," said Merci. "Charles Brock. He was the one who brought it to them. Right?"

"Wrong, actually," said Charles Brock of Ritter-Dunne-Davis Financial.

He had insisted on meeting them outside his air-conditioned place of employment. He had told them he was in an incredible hurry today, had about five minutes, at best. So the three now stood in the sweltering shade of a downtown Riverside magnolia tree two blocks away from the RDD building.

"What happened was, they brought it to *me*."

"Explain," said Merci. Charles Brock was stocky, dark-haired and dressed in a navy double-breasted suit. He stubbornly left the coat on.

Merci thought he had too much gel in his hair to be handling large amounts of other people's money. She noticed the little band of white around his finger, where a ring used to be. He was sweating in the heat but Merci guessed that he would be sweating out of the heat, too. His eyes were fast and furtive so he put on a pair of sunglasses.

"Priscilla and I had lunch with Gwen one day early last year," he said. He spoke quietly, sliding his hands into his pockets and pitching his head toward the detectives. "Gwen said she'd heard about this start-up, OrganiVen, a biomedical outfit based down in San Diego. I looked over the business plan and prospectus and the stock proposal and the founders' curriculum vitae, made sure things were right. I mean, any flake can try to issue stock these days. But OrganiVen looked solid enough so I told them if they wanted to take a nice fat risk with their money, go ahead."

"So you weren't in favor of them investing?"

"Not really. I didn't think OrganiVen was for them. I'm in favor of good investments. I'm in favor of blue chips and that's mainly what I sell. I look at people trying to get rich overnight and it makes me nervous. Especially family."

"How did Gwen find out about OrganiVen?"

Brock shrugged. "One of our guys."

"Which of your guys?"

"Trent Gentry, Newport office. He knew one of the OrganiVen founders from school. If I remember right, Trent met Wildcraft in a bar or something. I think that was it."

Brock looked at them from behind his shades. He checked his watch and pursed his lips. "I'm sorry, but I really got to go."

Merci tried to get a look at his eyes behind the dark lenses. "Do what you have to do, Mr. Brock. Thanks for taking five minutes to help solve the murder of your sister-in-law."

"You bet, not a problem."

"Did you know Gwen well, Mr. Brock?"

"Not really. I only knew her for three years. I didn't see that much of her."

"I guess you weren't invited to her birthday party, the night she was killed."

"No. Just Priscilla."

"Mr. Brock," said Merci, "I just thought of something. Did you buy a few shares of OrganiVen for yourself?"

Brock took a deep, honest breath, then exhaled. "Yes, I did. I purchased twenty thousand shares for five thousand dollars."

"So you did okay when Sistel stepped in?"

"I did just fine."

"Mr. Brock, did you ever have any reason to think that OrganiVen, or the people who ran it, were not honest?"

"None at all."

"Did you know any of them?"

"None of them."

"Did Archie and Gwen know you bought in?" asked Zamorra.

"No."

"And Priscilla?"

"Of course she did."

"*Eventually* she did," said Zamorra.

"Exactly."

"Because you and Priscilla weren't getting along," he said.

"Right. That's all I'm going to say about that."

"Thanks again for your help. We're going to have more questions."

"How about by phone? I don't need any office gossip. The other guy from your office doesn't mind just using the phone for this thing."

It took Merci just a second to figure it.

"Al Madden."

"Yeah," said Brock.

"The phone's fine until it isn't," said Zamorra.

"Whatever." Brock nodded but didn't offer his hand, then hustled back toward the RDD building, staying on the shady side of the street.

"Very broken up about his sister-in-law," said Zamorra.

"So broken up he wasn't even curious about who might have killed her. And so broken up about Priscilla that he's sneaking an investment or two he can hide from the divorce lawyer. He's already taken off his wedding ring."

Merci watched Charlie Brock round the corner at Market Street. "He was sweating kind of a lot, Paul."

"Not the heat."

"No, the bank thermometer says it's only a hundred and two."

They walked back to the car, keeping to the shady sides of the streets. Merci could feel the heat from the sidewalk coming through her shoes.

"Ready to go see what Dr. Stebbins has to say about Archie's brain?" she asked.

"Yes. If we're expected to arrest him, we at least should know how his mind works. What's left of it."

Zamorra drove. When they hit the freeway it was backed up to a standstill so he got into the toll lane. Zamorra hit eighty and Merci watched the chrome of the door handles flashing by beside them. She thought Brock was untrustworthy and Wildcraft was trying to tell the truth. She remembered how he'd described the "monstrous" head of one of the men who had met with Gwen.

"Paul, Wildcraft thought his wife's meeting had something to do with OrganiVen. He said there was the blond businessman and the big guy, in a car with livery plates. Archie thought the big guy might have been a chauffeur. But chauffeurs don't sit in on meetings. So, say both of those guys were tied in with OrganiVen. They could have been part of the company, right? And if so, then a lot of other people would know who they are."

"It's worth a try."

She found Wyatt Wright's number in her notebook, dialed, and got a forwarding number from the operator. A receptionist answered "BioLucid, Mr. Wright's office," then put Merci through when Merci said she was law enforcement.

Wright sounded young and unhappy to be talking to a cop. He said his former company, OrganiVen, never used a limousine service. They had to borrow money just to pay the *rent* back in those days, he said. He said this with pride.

"You ever do business with a huge man with a beard?"

"Never."

"What about a blond man, mid-forties, possibly foreign-born, looked like a . . . well, like a businessman."

"No. My business was research, pure and simple. I didn't deal with anybody else but the other scientists. That was among the terms of my employment."

"Were a very large bearded man and a blond man, mid-forties, employed there also? Whether you *dealt* with them or not?"

"Not that I know. I had my head in a test tube the whole time. Really."

"Thanks."

Click.

"Never trust a businessman under thirty," she said.

Next, she tried OrganiVen cofounder Cody Carlson, but his secretary said Dr. Carlson was out of the country and could not be reached.

Cofounder Sean Moss had no office number so she called his home phone and got a machine.

She tried Dr. Stephen Monford—the voice of authority on the MiraVen promotional video—but he was on sabbatical in Norway.

She sat back and thought about the big man and the blond, perhaps tied to OrganiVen but perhaps not, meeting with a nervous Gwen Wildcraft, spied upon by Archie. A new black town car with livery plates. The big guy maybe a chauffeur but maybe not. She couldn't get a baseline, couldn't come up with one fact to build on. The whole thing seemed hazy and dreamlike, which she figured was exactly how it seemed to Wildcraft. But it wasn't in Rayborn's nature to let things go. Zamorra had once compared her to the Gila monster, fabled to hold its prey until the sun goes down.

"If the big guy and the blond were connected to OrganiVen but weren't founders, maybe we could trace them through the incorporation papers filed with the state," she said.

"Well, okay."

"But we've got the limo angle, so I'm going to burn some more department cell minutes."

Merci made eight more calls to limo services that might cover Newport Beach. She asked again about a very, very large chauffeur. And whether the car company had done regular work for a biomed outfit called OrganiVen. The calls were on the department cell phone but Merci didn't think you could catch bad guys on a budget.

None of the companies employed or had ever employed such a huge, bearded, bespectacled chauffeur. None had ever done business with OrganiVen as a regular client, so far as they remembered.

When she was done she wondered what the charges would be for those nine calls, for learning absolutely nothing except that Wyatt Wright was a smartass and Red Carpet Limo had a late-summer special where you got the first hour free, three-hour minimum.

EIGHTEEN

D r. John Stebbins welcomed them into a small office in an old building behind the UCI Medical Center. A floor fan worked diligently from one corner but it couldn't break the heat. The floors were old and wooden and Merci could hear footsteps and voices from the hallway outside.

Stebbins wore a white doctor's coat like the last time Merci had seen him, but a considerably more relaxed expression.

"I apologize for last time," he said. "I . . . when you have a bad day in my profession, it's, ah . . ."

"People die," said Merci.

"Yes. Thank you. Same as yours, in some ways."

"I haven't cured anybody recently," Merci said. "And we're sorry that Deputy Wildcraft decided to check himself out. He didn't consult us and we can't keep him here or anywhere else for more than forty-eight hours unless we arrest him."

"I'm concerned. The edema could easily increase. Infection is possible. If a cranial vein leaks or breaks, the resulting hematoma would be fatal. And besides this organic damage he's sustained, well, I'm not sure if he's capable of taking care of himself. Whether he can remember to take care of himself."

"I'm not either," said Merci.

"Have you seen him?"

"Three hours ago. He seemed a little slower, mentally. Said he was tired, not thinking straight. He said he'd check himself back in this afternoon."

"He hasn't."

"What's going on inside that mind of his, Doctor?"

Stebbins shook his head and sighed. He leaned back from a desk cluttered with papers. The fan oscillated his way and the corners lifted like spectators watching a home run.

"It's easiest to show you."

He rolled back on his chair and stood. Behind his desk was a wall-mounted x-ray screen that he flicked on with a toggle. Archie Wildcraft's x rays were already in. Dr. Stebbins darted a red laser pointer across the image, stopping it suddenly on the outside of the skull.

Merci was startled by the dark chaos that the bullet had brought to Archie's brain. A shadow the shape of a tornado issued from high on the right side, with the narrow funnel touching ground near the bottom of the skull. Around the tornado was a border of pale gray.

"This is Archie's right hemisphere. The bullet entered here, resulting in the darker hematoma you see. You can see the bone fissure, and the way the blood vessels of the pia mater have hemorrhaged. It's hard to say whether the bullet's path was altered by the skull, or if it was fired from the corresponding angle, but you can see that it traveled downward and lodged here, beside the foramen magnum—that's the opening in the skull where the spinal cord exits. It missed the veins of Galen, which lie in this large triangular fold in the pia mater known as the velum interpositum. It missed the major cranial nerves—the vagas, optic, trigeminal, etcetera. It missed the internal capsule of the brain itself, which controls motor function."

Dr. Stebbins frowned at the x ray. Then he looked at Merci and Zamorra. "Unfortunately, it did not miss the right amygdala. You can see the largest part of the bullet right here, about two inches in from the ear."

"What's it do?" asked Merci.

"In a male, the right amygdala processes the emotion of memory. Not the memory itself, but the feeling surrounding the memory. In women, it's the left."

"He has no emotions attached to his memories?"

"His recent memories. And to memories that he's now attempting to construct—every waking moment—with the fragment lodged in his amygdala. His long-term memories will begin to lose their emotional content, also. They're stored elsewhere in the brain, but when the links connecting present and past emotion are destroyed, recognition fails along with reproduction and retrieval."

"Meaning what?" asked Merci.

"His recent memories will be fragmented and incomplete, and he'll have little emotion attached. His long-term memory will weaken, in terms of clarity and emotional content."

Stebbins circled his red dot, then it vanished.

"So, if he can't form emotions as he experiences things, he'll be detached from what those things mean to him," said Zamorra.

"Yes."

"Like a zombie?" asked Merci.

Stebbins smiled.

Rayborn smiled back, lifting her eyebrows. "Look, I'm a cop, not a brain surgeon."

"No, your idea was workable. Just the language was amusing. But to answer your question, he's going to be detached from the emotional components of his recent past. Confused, too, because the emotional weight of memory is what we use to form our ideas of right and wrong, good and bad. Of what is threatening or loving. Dangerous or benign."

"He's got no emotional rudder," said Zamorra.

"No *recent* emotional rudder," said Stebbins, circling the x ray of Archie's amygdala once again. "He's only got his past to go on."

"But that's going away, too," said Rayborn. "Because there's nothing new for it to connect with, to keep it . . . living."

Stebbins nodded. "Of course, a certain amount of healing is possible. If the edema subsides and the pressure is lowered, we can expect some of his short-term memory to return. Whether or not the damaged amygdala will still be able to supply him with appropriate emotions again, I can't say."

"Will some parts of his brain be ruined forever?" asked Merci.

"Changed forever," said Stebbins. "He's lucky to be alive."

Merci wondered at the angle, the way the bullet went down through Wildcraft's brain, rather than across it. She wondered how tall Size Sixteen was, and thought about the light that Archie had remembered just that morning, and how he said it came from above him.

"That's just the amygdala," said Merci. "What other physical damage does he have?"

"Impossible to say without more tests and observation. Certainly the swelling here, near the optic nerve, might give him focus and depth-perception problems. Maybe his colors are dulled or transposed or exaggerated. Seizures are possible—mostly the smaller, focal seizures, but also some general convulsions. Seizures are caused by pressure and pressure is caused by swelling. The skull has very little give in it. There's also a chance that he won't feel crude pain or light touch as quickly and specifically as before, because of a small fragment against his thalamus."

"He seems to have forgotten a lot of what happened that night," said Zamorra. "Not just emotions, but whole . . . scenes, segments."

"That's traumatic amnesia and it's common. Even a mild concussion can leave someone with no memory of the injury. Full retrograde amnesia, where he loses large portions of older memory, is certainly possible here. It would take a great deal of observation to even diagnose him. Personally, I'd very much like to have that time to spend with him."

He looked at them with disappointment and an air of blame. "There's also the difficult area of psychogenic memory disorders."

"Psychogenic memory disorders," said Merci.

"Yes. That means disorders of the memory that are not tied to organic damage or disease."

"Psychological."

"Basically, yes. See, Mr. Wildcraft knows what happened. He remembers some of it. And the more time goes by, if the edema and bleeding subside, he will remember more. But the more he remembers, the better chance he has of developing various forms of hysterical amnesia. Hysterical amnesia is brought about by psychological stress and trauma, as opposed to strictly organic damage. Its range is wide and unpredictable."

Merci thought about this. "So, the part of his brain that forgot will start to remember. And the part that remembered will start to forget."

He smiled. "That's roughly true."

"Sounds tiring," she said.

"My patients undergoing that kind of retention-loss pattern tell me it's exhausting."

Stebbins sat back down and swiveled his chair around to face them. Merci watched the fan lift the paper corners, heard the quiet hiss of moving air, saw the collar of Dr. Stebbins's lab coat flutter briefly.

She tried to imagine what it would be like to be remembering and forgetting at the same time. Remembering and forgetting the *same event* at the same time. What, she wondered: you remembered the coat collar fluttering but you forgot there was a fan in the room? How did you explain things?

"Dr. Stebbins," she asked, "will he make things up?"

Stebbins started to answer, then caught himself. He looked at Merci, then Zamorra, then back to Merci again. "I'd hate to find myself on a witness stand against a patient. I'm not sure I would do that."

"You would if the court ordered you to."

"Is that how it works?"

"That's how it works. But we're not asking you to," she said. "We're trying to understand this man. We don't think he killed his wife, but some people do. What you tell me here might keep you off the stand, Doctor. And keep Archie out of jail."

Stebbins sighed quietly and shifted some papers. "We call it confabulation," he said. "Invention, exaggeration, chronological transposition. Some amnesic patients can invent perfectly logical and believable events that never took place. Some, when you ask them what they did the day before, will tell you in great detail—but it was what they did on a day twelve years ago. Some get fanciful and the inventions are very easy to identify as spurious."

"So which is Archie?"

"I didn't have time to find out," he said quietly. "And it may change—as the edema comes and goes, and as the psychological trauma runs its course. Confabulation is unpredictable. Generally, we see that patients with damage to the right temporal lobe are prone to feelings of déjà vu, which we consider a form of confabulation. Generally, we find that the more a patient is aware of his own amnesia, the less he will confabulate. Those who most strongly deny having amnesia are most likely to invent. But these are generalizations, so they won't turn out to be true in every case."

"Archie recognizes that he's lost memory," said Zamorra. "He admits it. He seems to remember things a little at a time, like he's retrieving the pieces of a puzzle."

"That's exactly what he's doing."

"Is it selective?"

"He's not consciously controlling the amount and quality of his recall, no. But Archie's memory is being filtered through, and certainly guided by, his general emotional state. Absolutely. He's gone through a profoundly traumatic experience. It's possible that he'll never fully recall some of what happened, that he'll remember in painful detail other aspects of that night. When all is said and done, we have difficulty differentiating organic from psychogenic amnesia. When you factor in the damage to the amygdala, it gets almost impossibly complex to make a sound prognosis."

"When will he be healed?" asked Merci. "I mean, physically? If nothing more goes wrong?"

Stebbins shook his head and exhaled. "Probably *never* if you don't get him proper medical care."

"And if we can do that?"

"It's impossible for me to say. I'm sorry."

"Two weeks? Two months? Two years?"

He looked at her. "If he develops no infection, and if the edema is controlled by the steroids, he'll likely have recovered what memory he's going to recover within a year. But you have to understand that he's had tissue damage. Some of his memory has been lost. It's not retrievable. It's gone. The same can be said of the psychogenic amnesia—if the psychological trauma was severe enough, he may never recover certain memories."

"But they're in there," said Zamorra. "Those memories are inside him."

"Yes."

"How do you get them out?"

"Hypnosis."

Merci thought of Dr. Joan Cash and the terrific results she'd gotten from a witness using hypnosis. She wrote *J. Cash?*

"Understand," said Dr. Stebbins, "that using hypnosis on a subject like Mr. Wildcraft could be damaging to him. You would be bringing forth memories that he is not presently able to process, emotionally. You'd be overriding his mechanisms of self-defense and self-preservation. It would be tantamount to trying to remove that bullet from his brain surgically. It would be ill-advised, destructive, possibly catastrophic."

In the quiet that followed, Merci listened to the fan-blown air tapping at the surfaces of the room, heard the footsteps and the echoes of footsteps in the hall outside. She wondered how many tough decisions had been made by people sitting right here where she was. How many people had looked down at the same floor, heard the same sounds, prayed to their gods for guidance.

"We couldn't use him in court if he'd been hypnotized," she said. "California law."

"Well," said Stebbins, "as I've said, that's getting ahead of what's really feasible now."

"Can you get us exact measurements on the bullet fragments?"

"I can get you measurements accurate to one millimeter, which would be acceptably accurate if the bullet was in one perfectly shaped piece. But there are three fragments visible on the spiral CT, and there are probably more that are too small for us to see. So there's no way to tell which dimension we're measuring—diameter, length? A combination of the two? I can't get an accurate caliber for the bullet—I assume that's what you're after. After talking to Sheriff Abelera I did some measurements. All I can say with reasonable certainty is that the caliber of the bullet is probably between a twenty-two and a thirty-eight."

"You're not even sure of that?"

"No. It's possible that the bullet fragmented on entry and part of it never penetrated. It's even possible that a fragment left his skull and came to rest somewhere else in his body. We only had time to take pictures of his head before he so foolishly checked himself out."

"If we got him back, could you try an MRI?"

"We can't do an MRI because of the metal in the bullet."

"What about positron emission tomography?" asked Zamorra.

"Wonderful for the biochemical activities in the brain, but not for space and volume measurements that precise. I'm sorry."

"I just exhausted my medical scan knowledge," said Rayborn.

"I did, too," said Zamorra.

"Believe me, I'd get you a caliber on the bullet if I could. An autopsy would be the only way. We'd literally have to put the pieces back together."

A moment of acknowledged possibility passed between them— three blinks and a small stretch of silence.

"Thanks for your help on everything else," said Merci. "And for your honesty."

"I don't know any other way to practice medicine."

Dr. Stebbins met her stare for a moment and neither looked away. Then he swiveled his chair and looked again at the x ray of Archie Wildcraft. "The human brain weighs about three pounds. It's small. You can hold one in your hands. But it's hugely complex. The harder you look the bigger it gets. It's like looking at the night sky through a telescope. The more you see the more there is to see. The more you learn the more there is to learn. It goes on forever, and there's so much we don't know."

He turned back to Merci. "But, Sergeant Rayborn and Sergeant Zamorra, I do know that Archie belongs under medical care. Too much can go wrong. I strongly advise you to get him back into this hospital."

NINETEEN

They walked across the Sheriff's Headquarters parking lot. Heat waves shimmered up from the cars into a humid brown sky. Merci looked up at the building—large, concrete and impersonal—of little more architectural flair than a home-improvement center. She'd always liked it because it was a no-nonsense building. It promised nothing except an attempt to enforce the law, and it sheltered people who were willing to die for this idea.

Sheriff Vincent Abelera's office was on the fourth floor. It was large and sunny and had two adjacent walls of windows. The carpet was light blue and the wood was all dark walnut, which Merci thought was a superb combination of texture and color. Especially the way the brass of the plaques and trophies and awards shined in the beams of the recessed lights. Abelera had a big desk in the far corner. A computer monitor sat where the former sheriff used to have a blotter and a marble two-pen holder. There was a sink and counter, bookshelves, two sitting areas with couches and coffee tables, and a big TV on a wheeled stand.

Walking into this office, Merci thought of the several agonizing meetings she'd had here late last year with Chuck Brighton, the previous sheriff. He had held the position for almost four decades. She had liked Brighton and she'd come to see how he bore the ills of his department as if he'd somehow caused them all himself. But she'd brought his career down by solving a homicide that had been unsolved for thirty years, a murder that Brighton and his inside circle had never wanted solved for reasons that became obvious. It was the same case that had disgraced her father and some other deputies, both retired and active. Walking across the pale blue carpet now sent a familiar ripple of nerves down her back and brought her senses to a keen and heightened edge. And it made her swallow hard as she was reminded of the terrible price of loyalty.

They were two minutes early, and the last ones to arrive. They sat on a sofa along one windowed wall, facing District Attorney Clayton Brenkus and Assistant DA Ryan Dawes. The lawyers had claimed a sofa of their own, as well as the view. Sheriff Abelera himself, as if to establish independence and superiority, sat in a leather armchair at the head of and exactly midway between the two couches.

Abelera was in uniform today. Brenkus wore dark trousers and a blue shirt. Dawes was his fashionable self, Merci noted: a soft olive-colored suit with a crisp abstract tie. He looked tanned from the weekend. She looked down at her black pants and white blouse and gray sport coat and figured they'd do.

Marilyn, the sheriff's secretary, offered coffee all around but no one accepted. She was an elegant, older woman with gray-black hair she only wore one way: in a bun. "Too hot for coffee today," she noted. She said they had juice and soft drinks but nobody wanted those, either.

"How about a beer after work?" asked Dawes.

Marilyn smiled and blushed a little, closing the door behind her.

Abelera, an arm on each rest, sat up straight and considered Brenkus. Then he looked at Merci.

"I've been working law enforcement for almost thirty years," he said. "And I've never seen the DA eager to file and the detectives not. It's *always* the other way around. So, here I am, not yet a year on the job, and you're making department history."

"It's our way of welcoming you," said Brenkus.

"I feel very welcomed, then," said Abelera. His face was sharp angles and his smile looked easy and genuine. "Merci, Paul, I want to start with the prosecutors because I know they're ready to file. After that, I'll hear from you, okay? Clay, Ryan—tell me why we should arrest and charge my deputy."

The district attorney looked at his assistant and nodded.

"Because he murdered his wife and tried to murder himself," said Dawes, looking at Abelera. "Why did he do that? Because he's a manipulator, and like most manipulators, when things didn't go his way he turned into a coward. A violent coward. First, the deputy and Gwen were under financial duress—they'd spent almost nine hundred grand in the last six months, and they were living on one income—a deputy's. Which is about fifty grand a year if he works overtime. And the deputy worked a lot of overtime in the last two years. He knew the whole financial burden was on him. New home, new cars, trips all over the place. This is easy enough to establish.

"Second, I'll prove that Archie Wildcraft was a jealous and manipulative husband. He had a temper. Gwen was beautiful and knew how to use it—her friends will attest to that part of her character. Archie was angry a lot. Gwen couldn't figure out why he was so angry all the time. It must have been kind of scary. But I can figure it. Any of us can. It's because he was going broke and he's losing his wife. *Losing his wife. His prize. His trophy.* They get in a fight and he throws a rock through a window. They yell at each other. The neighbors hear them. That night he's planned a big party for her, but she doesn't appreciate it. She flirts shamelessly. She drinks a little too much. At home he demands sex, she won't do it. He forces her. She gives in against her will because she can't fight him physically. He's six-three and weighs two hundred and five pounds. Besides, this has happened before. So she gives in to him, but that's not enough for this guy because nothing's ever been enough for this guy because he's a manipulator and a coward. He drinks, he broods, he wants sex again and she locks herself in the bathroom with a cell phone because she thinks he might be losing it and she's afraid. She's right but not right enough. The guy comes through the door with a lot more than sex in mind. He's got his nine, he pulls. She falls and he jams it against her head and pulls again. It's a mess in there. It smells like blood and gunpowder and his beautiful wife's dying on the floor. So he leaves her there, goes outside and kills himself too. That's what he wanted all along, was just to get out of this, end it, but he couldn't leave his wife alive for his friends to take care of, could he? Not when she's the cause of most of this. Trouble is, the bullet takes a lucky turn inside his head and he doesn't die. He wakes up and realizes, hey, I'm alive and I've got another chance at things. He figures out that he can say anything he wants about that night and there's nobody to contradict him. So he *remembers* certain things. But then again, he also *forgets* other things. Guess what—he can even *make things up*. This is what he's doing, ladies and gentlemen of the jury: he's manipulating you just like he manipulated his wife."

Dawes turned to Merci. "But guess what? None of that really matters too much because this case will be decided on physical evidence. Here are some things that the deputy cannot deny, because they are proven facts. We have no evidence that there was another person *on the property* that night, let alone inside the deputy's house. We know the deputy was home that night. We know that the deputy owned the gun that killed her. We know the gun was in his possession that night. We know it was in his *hand* that night. We know he *fired* it that night. We know his fingerprints are not only on the gun that killed her but *on the brass that contained the bullets that killed her*. That means he loaded it as well as fired it. And again, who owned that nine millimeter? Whose gun was it? The deputy's. That, ladies and gentlemen of the jury, is why you have to reach a verdict of guilty. That, Sheriff Abelera and District Attorney Brenkus, is why you need to file. *That*, Sergeants Rayborn and Zamorra, is why you have to *do your job* and arrest him."

"Good," said Abelera. "The defense?"

"He can't prove all that," said Merci, ignoring the assistant DA. "He can't prove they were going broke, because they weren't. They'd spent a lot of money in the last year because they'd made two million in a legitimate investment. It left the Wildcrafts about a million two after taxes. There are still almost two hundred grand in investments and accounts. Dawes can't prove that Archie was homicidally jealous— we're not getting that picture from friends and family at all. We're also not getting that she was an outrageous flirt, or that he was angry, or that he was losing her. It wasn't Archie and Gwen arguing that day at all, and neither one of them threw anything through a window. The whole rape scene is bullshit. There's not a shred of evidence that it wasn't consensual sex. Next thing he's coming through the bathroom door with a gun, ready to shoot her? Why? There's no motivation to do that, if you realize they weren't going broke and they were happy and in love with each other. We've got three separate witnesses to two men in a black Cadillac STS leaving the scene. We've got footprints—big, size sixteens—in *exactly the place a shooter would hide* if he was waiting to take out Archie. We've got Archie Wildcraft's prints on his own gun, but no proof that he was even conscious when his fingers touched that gun. Of course his prints are on the brass—he loaded his own gun, for cryin' out loud. We need more time, sir. We think we found the black Caddy. Huge footprints all around it, just like under the tree at the Wildcrafts'. We've got some indication that it could have been a contract hit by *La Eme*. Dr. Stebbins said the bullet in Wildcraft's head *could* be anything from a twenty-two to a thirty-eight, which means a second weapon is possible. Which, if true, would sink Dawes's theory all the way to the bottom of the ocean. And Archie is remembering more about that night and events that led up to it. We need to polygraph him—which he's agreed to—and we might want to consider hypnosis, when he's had a few more days to equalize emotionally. We need time to investigate further. We're not ready. It's a loser in court and I won't put my name on it. Pure and simple."

Dawes didn't wait before he commented, "Besides the potty mouth, you'd make a decent defense counsel."

"Decent enough to beat you."

"I can't wait."

"You'll have to wait," said Merci. "Because I'll make an arrest when I've got the facts. Not just to give an assistant DA a headline maker."

"Merci," said Abelera.

"Another headline maker," said Dawes.

"Cool it, Ryan," said Brenkus.

"Do you want the truth, Rayborn, or just hugs and kisses from your department?" asked Dawes.

"Shut up, Ryan," said Brenkus. "This won't take us anywhere we need to go. Vince—let me speak now. There's some truth in what Dawes said, some truth in what Rayborn said. But be aware that we're getting a lot of calls about this. I know you are, too. The public is angry about it and they want action. Fine, we can put them off until we're ready—a pissed-off public never made a case. But I'm getting pressure from the news media, too, and we don't want that. They're speculating already that your department is being slow to investigate because you're covering for the deputy. If that gets into the air—if people start to believe that—you set up an adversarial mood in this county, and I'm not convinced we're ready for that. Your predecessor brought some genuine distrust onto your department and it hasn't just vanished. That was bad cops covering for bad cops. People are eager to give you a chance, Vince, but they're going to be just as quick to hang you if they smell more secrecy and dishonesty coming from this office. Even if they just *think* they smell it."

"Well said. Paul?"

"Nothing I've learned about Wildcraft yet puts him in an at-risk category for suicide. He's not fitting the profile. But I'll tell you what I told Merci, I don't trust him. I think he's trying to run something on us. More reason to keep on him. Keep on him, sir. That's all we can do. Don't go off with a half-cooked case. We need to polygraph him and hypnotize him, like Merci said. We also need to surveil him. I think it's worth the time and money, sir."

"Consider it approved. Clay?"

Brenkus stood. "We'll stay busy. We'll keep Al Madden busy. We'd like swift communication between your people and ours. Gilliam's been slow. Don't leave us out of the loop, Vince."

"I wouldn't consider it. Would you, Merci?"

"No, sir. Absolutely not."

The sheriff stood and shook hands with Brenkus. "Clay, thank you. We're working hard on this one. Give us a few more days."

"Absolutely, Vince."

"Mr. Dawes?" asked Abelera.

Dawes stood straight and buttoned his suit coat. He looked at Merci. "We could grand jury it. Let them decide whether or not to indict. And if they want a longer investigation, then we're right back to where we are now."

"No," said Merci. "There's no way we're letting twenty-one people question a guy with a bullet in his head and no lawyer."

"Why not?" asked Dawes.

"Because his memory is coming back, that's why."

"Gwen Wildcraft was a human being," he said. "This isn't a game, Sergeant."

"Then don't turn it into—"

Merci was about to say "one" when the door flew open and Assistant Sheriff Dale Knox blasted in. "Boss, you better see CNB, right now. Unbelievable."

Abelera nodded, Knox slammed the door shut and hustled across the big room to the TV.

County News Bureau—the television wing of Gary Brice's Orange County *Journal*—came in loud and clear.

Wildcraft aimed the riot gun at the camera, said, *You're trespassing.*

Brice's off-camera voice: *I wanted you to tell me what happened.*

Merci couldn't believe Archie Wildcraft's face. His eyes were wide and shot with red. His stubble was black. A big vein rose under the skin of his forehead. His clothes were wrinkled and disheveled and there was a dirty pink-brown stain on the bandage wrapped around his head. He looked like a soldier at Antietam, or some malevolent genie just escaped from his bottle.

Get off my property, he said.

Brice backed away and the camera jiggled and Archie held the shotgun at an angle that threatened to blow away the CNB viewer.

"Where the hell are they?" asked Vince.

"His house," said Merci, putting together the pieces. "Brice found him. He's got snitches at the medical center."

The camera was in retreat now, jiggling and moving farther away.

Brice: *Did you see who killed your wife?*

Archie: *Get out.*

Brice: *What are you going to do?*

Archie: *I'll kill . . . myself.*

Halfway through that sentence the camera jerked wildly and Archie's face flew out of the frame. When the camera steadied, he offered a demented smile.

Brice: *Did you shoot her and yourself, sir?*

Archie: *Go to hell, you little BLEEP.*

Merci felt her heart fall and she got a quick, bitter taste of what it would feel like to be wrong about this man.

The last few seconds of footage showed Archie way up on his property, shotgun still in hand, staring down at the camera. He looked like a menace.

"Oh, man," said Merci, but what she was thinking was considerably worse.

"He certainly looks and acts innocent," said Dawes.

Merci heard Brice ask, *Maybe someone should explain why the police haven't formally questioned this man.*

"Pick him up right now," Abelera ordered Knox.

"Wait," said Merci. "Let us go get him. We've got rapport and he might be ready to talk. Please, sir—don't send in the uniforms. He's very . . . extremely messed up."

"Oh, really?" asked Dawes.

Rayborn saw the anger flash in Abelera's eyes. "Arrest him, Sergeant. Before he kills himself, or someone else."

"Yes, sir."

She swung around the couch and followed Zamorra out the door, her heart pounding out three beats of anger at herself for every one at Dawes and Gary Brice.

TWENTY

The two Sheriff's Department cruisers were still blocking the Wildcraft driveway. The four deputies stood beside them, beating the heat. They said that Archie had been inside the whole time, no one had tried to come or go except for his parents, who parked on the street at noon and left at ten after one.

No answer at the front door, so Merci knocked again. She tried the door and found it unlocked.

She pushed in, popping the thumb snap on her hip rig. With her left arm she reached behind her back and gathered a low handful of jacket material out of the way of the gun. She didn't think Wildcraft would come out shooting but she wasn't wearing armor and didn't want the ceiling to be the last thing she saw on Earth.

"Archie!" she called with kind authority, as if she was hupping a wayward pointer. "Archie—it's Rayborn and Paul Zamorra!"

Silence. She moved across the entryway, noting that Wildcraft's cut-down shotgun no longer rested in the corner. She leaned through the kitchen entry then angled quickly in. "Arch?"

She looked to the counter and saw that his prescription bottles were gone. Through the mullioned windows of the breakfast nook she looked out to the pool, where Archie had conducted his press conference with Gary Brice. Sky-blue water, the yellow hibiscus in bloom, no Wildcraft.

They quickly searched the house. Still no Wildcraft. There were two photographs missing from the music room wall, and three stones missing from the rock room. The master bedroom looked the same to Merci, except for a blank spot on one wall where a portrait of Gwen Wildcraft had hung.

In the master bath Merci found a loose wad of faintly bloodstained gauze lying on the counter.

"He took rocks, pictures, the riot gun and split," said Merci.

The garage still housed Archie's silver Boxster and Gwen's new white Durango. They checked the pool area and the grounds around the house.

They stood in the shade, not far from where Wildcraft had fallen. "What did he do, Paul, *walk* out of here?"

Zamorra looked at her.

They picked up a set of footprints leading down to the steps that wound through the wildflowers. The steps led to the gate. It was easy to see where the gate had been opened because it was out of plumb and had scraped a fresh gash in the earth.

"That's where Brice came in this morning," she said.

"And probably where Archie went out. There's a car rental franchise down on Moulton Drive," said Zamorra. "It's not far. Put the stuff in a duffel. Leave it by the gate, walk down, get a car and come back for it. The deputies wouldn't even know he'd left the house."

"Goddamnit, Paul. I should have seen this one coming."

"I didn't think he'd run. He had plenty of opportunity to do it earlier."

"It didn't cross my mind until Brice's stunt."

"It might not have crossed Archie's until then, either," said Zamorra. "That's why he didn't tell us Brice had been here. And Archie might have thought we didn't buy all his stories this morning. Which we didn't."

"It's too much to hope that he checked himself back into UCI Med Center, isn't it? Or went to his parents, or out to the Kuerners in Norco?"

"We'll see," he said, pulling the phone from his pocket.

"Dawes is going to love this."

"Everyone's going to—detectives let armed and dangerous murder suspect drive away." Zamorra mimicked the grave tone of a TV news intro: *"Or did the cops want him to get away?"*

"Dial Abelera, Paul. And don't forget the partner, Damon Reese. Archie saved his life."

She looked out to the pale blue sky and listened to a hawk crying and cursed herself again for letting this happen.

They walked back to the driveway so Merci could quiz the deputies again. While Merci learned nothing at all, Zamorra used his cell phone and found out that the Wildcrafts hadn't seen Archie since leaving here just after one.

William Jones, legs spindly but head purposefully angled, crossed the street toward them. Merci saw the huge purple plastic tumbler in his hand, heard the clink of the ice as he raised it in salute to the uniforms.

"Detective Rayborn," he said. "And of course, Detective Zamorra over there with the phone."

"Hello, Mr. Jones," she said.

"Archie was home last night, wasn't he?"

"Yes."

"The news said he checked himself out yesterday afternoon. Got a ride home from Gwen's sister."

"Can I help you, Mr. Jones?"

He sipped his drink and eyed her. "I just came over to tell you a couple of things. One, the gardener works Tuesdays. I know that because Tuesdays are trash days and I remember seeing him putting the empty trash cans back on the curb so he could park his truck. So, soon as he gets here tomorrow, I'll call you."

"I'd appreciate it."

Jones gave her his cagey, sideways look. "CNB made it sound like he killed her. You saw the show, didn't you?"

"Part of it."

"First they had that guy here with his camera, pestering Arch. Archie said he'd kill himself. Then afterwards they had him on—the reporter, I mean—saying how scary Archie was. How he thought Arch was going to blast him. Then the prick says what he thinks happened that night. He thinks Archie killed Gwen and tried to kill himself, and now he's trying to get out of it. And he says you guys don't want to arrest him because he's a cop. Because of the big scandal last year. But you'll get a chance to see the whole thing because they'll show it again. You know how they do at CNB."

Zamorra walked toward her, pressing down the antenna of the cell phone and shaking his head.

"Good evening, Detective Zamorra."

"Jones."

Jones smiled wickedly, turned away from Zamorra then looked at Merci. "I got a tip for you, young lady."

"Shoot."

"Two and a half hours ago, four o'clock this afternoon. I went down to get some smokes and vodka. I ride my bike because they took my license away. So I coast down and push the thing back up, right? Well, down the road about three hundred yards there's a little park with a table and some trees. Seen it?"

"I've noticed it," said Merci.

"Well, on my way down, there was nobody in the park. On my way back up the hill, pushing the bike, I saw a guy standing by the table, looking back through the trees. He had binoculars and he didn't hear me until I was almost across from him. When he heard me, he turned, gave me a drop-dead look and raised the binoculars the other way. This is what I'm saying: go down to that park and stand beside the table—the south end of it—and look through the trees. What you see is the back of Archie and Gwen's place."

"Describe him," said Merci.

"Second biggest guy I've ever seen in my life. I met Refrigerator Perry once. Anyway, he was dressed in a blue jogging suit, dark hair and beard, sunglasses. Not a big mountain-man beard, but a close-cropped one. Ugly and huge is how I'd describe him."

"What about his car?"

"White Lincoln Town Car. There was another guy in the driver's seat, blond hair, staring at me, face like a stone. I did not look at the plates."

"Why not?"

"I had this feeling they'd kill me if I did."

"Mr. Jones," said Merci, "if we had a couple thousand more citizens like you in this county, we'd be crime-free."

"Thank you. I was about to call you when Archie came on the TV. After that I figured it would take you about fifty minutes to get here. It took you thirty-four."

"You're something," she said.

"I'm a harmless drunk trying to help the cops catch the guy who shot my neighbors. Tell your partner I'm not a bad guy, no reason to look at me like I'm an unflushed toilet."

"I'll tell him."

Jones drank from his enormous purple tumbler and winked at her, then turned and headed back across the street toward his son's garage, his white legs faintly luminous in the early-evening light.

On their way down the hill Rayborn and Zamorra stopped at the little park. There was a concrete picnic table and benches, a green mesh trash can holder with a lidded steel can in it and a drinking fountain back by the trees. Merci stood to the south side of the concrete bench and looked through the sycamore trees. In the middle distance she could see the slope of wildflowers in Archie's backyard, the gate through which he had escaped, the roof of the house, some of the windows and the pool area surrounded by the big Canary Island palms.

Zamorra rang off his cell phone, then paced the grass with his head down and his hands behind his back. Merci walked into the little grove of sycamore and oak. She found a crumpled soft drink can that had been there for a lot more than three hours, a couple of old cigarette butts, a horse magazine with its pages dimpled and cracked by dew and sun. She lifted the trash can lid by its edges and set it on the grass. Inside she saw a bicycle inner tube, a fast-food sandwich box with the sauce stains gone almost to black, a white fast-food bag beside it, a black banana peel, a paper soft drink container with the lid still on and the straw stuck through it. The drink container was from a different fast-food chain than the box and bag.

Ike Sumich got there half an hour later. She explained what William Jones had told her.

"Size Sixteen again," said Ike.

"Maybe."

"These guys aren't birdwatchers."

"Dust the tabletop," she said. "Extra careful on the south end. Get the stainless push-button on the drinking fountain and the bottom *and* top side of the trash can lid handle. I hate to send you on a wild-goose chase, Ike, but there's a drink container with a straw in the can over there. There might be saliva or epithelial cells on that straw. If Size Sixteen used it, we can DNA print him, then check the markers against the shop rag we got at the STS on Sand Canyon. Shoot some stills of this place, will you, show the angle up to the Wildcraft house. Maybe stand by that smaller sycamore and shoot up at the pool area."

Ike nodded and grinned. "And I thought *I* was an anal-retentive control freak with grandiose delusions of power."

"We control freaks are still the best at what we do, Ike. No matter what they say."

"Where do you think Wildcraft got to?"

"I've got no idea. Do you?"

"I take it you tried partner, friends and family?"

"No luck, or one of them was lying."

Sumich shook his head. "When's her funeral?"

"Not until Wednesday. I think they wanted to wait until he was out of the hospital."

"I'll bet you a hundred bucks he'll show."

Rayborn tried to guess the chances of Wildcraft showing his face at the funeral now. Slim and none? "I want him before then."

"I can see why. Disaster on CNB today, and you know the networks will pick it up."

Rayborn hadn't thought it through quite that far until now. The idea of Archie all over the networks made her heart feel heavy. And who would they be coming after for statements, to answer why the cops hadn't arrested him—or at least brought him in for a formal interview—before he could vanish?

"I watched it with Abelera and Clay Brenkus," she said. "It was right up there with the stupidest I've felt in my life. Here I am, half defending this guy and he shows up on TV ready to blow away a reporter. I wondered, Ike. I wondered if I completely misread the man and what happened up there."

Sumich looked up toward the Wildcraft house, then shook his head. "Brice spooked him. Archie's not right. Not your fault, but it made him look bad. Us too. I hope to God he doesn't kill himself. Or someone else."

"He can't. I won't let him."

Ike turned his attention to the table, then up at the lowering sun. "Well, I need to get started while there's still some sunlight left. Any dog shit in that trash container you want me to process for possible latent fingerprints?"

"Actually, Ike, you're standing in it."

Sumich looked down and Merci clipped his forehead with her knuckle.

"Grandiose delusions of power my ass," she said.

Twenty minutes later, Todd at Economy confirmed that they had rented a vehicle to Archibald Franklin Wildcraft that afternoon at 3:05.

"That would have been a white Durango," he said, fingers flying over a keyboard. "One week at eighty-nine a day with the Auto Club discount. He didn't take the insurance."

TWENTY-ONE

Archie checked into a hotel off Interstate 5 in Irvine at four that afternoon. He wore an Angels cap to cover his shaved head and a big Band-Aid to hide the bullet hole, a stick-on mustache and dark sunglasses to change his face. The desk girl was polite and professional and gave not the slightest sign that she recognized him or found him odd.

He used the name Jim Green but otherwise filled out the application truthfully. He used the name Green because the girl's face was green. He paid cash for three nights plus a one-hundred-dollar deposit. She gave Archie a map to his room.

The hotel was a big barn-shaped concrete structure originally used as a granary and packinghouse. Archie remembered his father and mother staying here and liking it years ago when they visited over Christmas. He was upstairs on the end. The room was pentagonal in shape—once a silo, according to the illustrated history in the lobby. From the window he could see red railroad tracks and a blue field and foothills in the distance. The blue hills were beautiful. There was a burger joint across the parking lot and a gas station across the street.

He easily carried the two big suitcases upstairs, then unpacked them: three portraits of Gwen, the shotgun and a box of ammunition, a couple of handguns, his three favorite *suiseki*, a laptop computer, his clothes and uniform, the pills, his shave kit and some miscellaneous things he'd just thrown in. He was surprised that carrying so much weight upstairs

fatigued him so little. He'd come out of the hospital stronger, no doubt
about it. He felt like he could pick up a car and throw it if he wanted to.

He put one of Gwen's old demo tapes in a little cassette player
and turned the volume down low. Then tapped out his afternoon dose
of Decadron and washed them down with some orange juice from the
mini-bar, took an extra because of the colors getting mixed up.

But now my mind is playing tricks on me
I close my eyes and you're all I see

God, isn't that true, he thought. It seemed that every line she wrote
meant something more, or something different, now that she was dead.
He propped her portraits along the wall beside the air conditioner and
stared.

I won't let them take you away from me, he thought. I won't.

For every ounce of trouble
I gotta pound of cure

When the tape was over he got the phone book from the nightstand
and looked up medical supplies. He wrote down the two closest addresses, confirming by phone that both supply houses carried aluminum crutches for sale or rent. Specifically, he asked for the kind that
have braces for the upper arm to give more strength and stability. The
clerks referred to them as Canadian crutches and yes, they both carried
them.

He thanked them and hung up and thought for a moment, staring
out at the lapis blue hills. Red crows bickered in a yellow enamel
sky. Wow.

Then Archie thumbed forward in the phone book to limousine services and called the first number.

"Hello," he said. "My name is Jim Green. I found five hundred-
dollar bills in my limo last night on our way back from a party. I picked
up the roll and figured finders keepers, but I was drunk. I can't keep
them. I probably earn ten times what your drivers do, not that I deserve
to. Anyway, if it was your guy, I'd like to get them back to him."

"What was your driver's name?"

"I don't remember. One of my friends sent the car as a surprise, but I don't know which friend or which service he used. All I can tell you is the driver was a great big guy with dark hair and a beard. I mean very big. And he's five bills short."

"He wasn't ours."

"Thanks, I'll try the other services."

Half an hour later Archie hit pay dirt. The heavily accented front man for Air Glide Limousine in Newport Beach said, yes, they have one very large driver. This driver had in fact said something about ending the night short.

"What was his name again?" asked Archie.

"Al Apin."

He pronounced it *Ah-peen*.

Archie said he'd either drop by with the bills or mail them, thank you very much.

"I will be in the office until eight tonight. I will see that he gets these money."

I bet you will, thought Archie.

He sat at the table by the window, where he'd arranged his three *sui-seki*. He looked at them, trying to concentrate on their grace and beauty. He knew that looking at them had once been enjoyable to him. The same way that putting big cool boulders in his garden had been enjoyable, which was the same way that carrying around pocketfuls of rocks had been enjoyable when he was a kid. And just when he was ready to look away, the *suiseki* shaped like a water buffalo sparked something in his mind and for a few moments Archie understood everything about the an-imal—that he was a warrior, a leader, a patriarch.

Archie sat for a while, hardly moving, hardly blinking, lost in the leafy green world of the buffalo.

Doctors Medical Supply sold Archie one pair of adjustable aluminum Canadian crutches for ninety-eight dollars. In the still-hot shade of the parking lot, Archie grabbed the padded rubber handles in each of his hands, then worked his upper arms into the c-cup braces. He realized he'd have to widen the braces a little to accommodate his biceps and raise them about three inches.

He stood there for a moment beside what looked very much like Gwen's Durango. Feet together, legs straight. Then he raised his arms and the crutches. He turned his head to look down each aluminum length, to the pale green rubber knob at each end.

He raised and lowered his arms together. The crutches were surprisingly light. And they gave him well over three feet of extra reach on each side. Adjusted to their maximum length, he'd get even more.

From the nearby home-improvement store Archie bought three six-by-six waterproof tarps. The package said they were blue, but they looked rust colored. He also bought a six-foot-by-sixteen-foot piece of wool-poly blend Berber carpet that was advertised as "sand." Then, a good pair of shears, some lightweight nylon straps with quick release clips, two bottles of epoxy glue, forty feet of one-inch PVC irrigation pipe in eight-foot lengths, a cutter, an assortment of joints—angles, straight, caps, Ts, four-ways—and two pots of pipe cement.

He rolled his loaded barge into the parking lot and found the Durango. He unloaded his purchases, wiping the sweat and tears from his face after he finally slammed the liftgate shut.

He sat in the driver's seat and took off the cap and aimed the air conditioner at his face. It felt funny on his naked scalp, extra icy around the bullet hole.

Don't cry, Archie.

"Oh, damn, honey."

Come get me, Arch. I'm up here. I'm waiting.

"I'm coming, honey. I just have a few things to do."

I'm going to be here for you.

Then he headed for Air Glide Limousine Service in Newport Beach.

TWENTY-TWO

Cancun is a deputy hangout on Seventeenth Street in Santa Ana, not far from headquarters. The food is Yucatecan, good and cheap, the drinks are strong. At any hour there may be from one to twenty deputies there, and though they dress in plain clothes, there is still the bulge of weapons under jackets and trouser calves. Eyes are sharp, conversation is quiet, and hearty smiles issue from beneath mustaches. The restaurant is crime-free.

Merci walked in at six-fifty and found Brad Eccles waiting in a corner booth. Some of the deputies nodded or smiled to her as she went past the entrance to the cantina, some of them stared through her. The restaurant was a microcosm of the department itself, divided in its opinions. She hated the feeling of walking a gauntlet, but stubbornly patronized the place so as not to surrender. She would never forget the first time she'd gone in with Hess, and the smug looks she'd gotten from the men. That was before she'd come to love him, and it still irked her that people could assume things about her that proved to be true.

Eccles was Archie Wildcraft's best friend in the department, according to everyone Merci had talked to. He was thirty-two, just off patrol and assigned to Fraud Detail. He'd been the first to toast Gwen at the party at the Rex that night.

"So I raised my glass and said there was no way anyone as beautiful and smart as her deserved a guy like Wildcraft," he said. He took a drink off his beer and shook his head. "Just one of the ten million things I've said in my life that I wouldn't mind taking back."

"It was a joke," she said, writing in her blue notebook.

"Yeah."

"Have you seen him today?"

"No."

"Has he called?"

"No."

"Anyone called you about him?"

"Well, people wondering if I'd talked to him. Nobody knows where he is and they're worried. He didn't look too good on CNB this afternoon. He said he'd kill himself and it looked believable."

Eccles was balding and stocky, with dark hair combed straight back. Mustache, short-sleeved blue shirt with a paisley tie, corduroy coat. Thick fingers, wedding ring. He took another drink and wiped a beer bubble off his mustache with his palm.

Rayborn, who didn't drink unless she was at home, sipped a lemonade. "Was he a jealous husband?"

He looked at her with a gentle frown. "Some. He was extremely proud of her. He never said anything bad about her. Gwen wasn't . . . um . . . a topic of humor with Archie. He never said this, Sergeant Rayborn, but I knew that if anyone messed with Gwen, Archie would put an end to it real quick. You didn't monkey around with Gwen, is what I'm saying. But you know, I never saw him threaten anyone, or say anything to anyone about, you know, what he'd do to them. It just wasn't a topic. Archie wasn't the kind of guy you messed with that way. Not about his wife. Very intense about her. Very serious."

"So how did he take your toast?"

"No problem. Archie can take a ribbing about himself. He knows who he is."

"Was Gwen a flirt?"

"Well . . . happy, cheerful. She'd touch you while she talked to you. You know, a hand on your arm or something. Hug you hello and goodbye. But not a flirt. Not a woman who would tempt you on purpose."

"How about on accident?"

"She was really beautiful. A guy could maybe get the wrong idea."

"Which guy?"

"No, that's not what I'm saying. I never saw that."

"But you could imagine it."

Eccles nodded.

"What did your wife think of her?"

He looked at her, shook his head quickly. "They got along. No problem. My wife was a little envious of their house, all the money they made. That's all."

"What did the other wives think of her?"

"I really can't say. I don't know."

"How was Gwen that night?"

"Embarrassed at first. You know, twenty people for drinks and dinner. All these packages at her place at the table. Probably a three- or four-thousand-dollar evening. She grew up poor. Wasn't used to things like that."

"And after her embarrassment?"

"She was just . . . happy. Lit up. Very thankful that Archie would organize something like that. Thankful for their friends and all."

"Drink a lot?"

"A fair amount. We all did. Not Archie, though. He never overdoes it, that I've seen."

"What was he like that night?"

Eccles looked at her and drank again. He started to speak, then stopped. Another drink.

"A little on edge. Something was bothering him. I asked him and he said just some money shit."

"Those were his words?"

"Yes. Exactly. He didn't want to talk about it. But Archie worries a lot, so I figured it was just, well . . . another worry."

She wrote *money shit* and underlined it twice. Then she circled it twice, the pen carving deep into the paper. She felt a warm flood of anger come through her. It had been building for almost a week now, quietly multiplying while she was busy with other things.

Merci sat back and looked at the cane chairs and tables, the wait-resses in their short skirts, the palm trees and ceiling fans. She wanted to throw something at something.

"This is wrong," she said. "I talk to you, I talk to his partner, I talk to his parents, his in-laws and his neighbor, and you all tell me the same thing. You tell me how great Archie is. Archie saved my life. Archie adored his wife. Archie's not overly jealous. Archie struck it rich but it didn't go to his head. Archie pays his taxes. Archie never drinks too much. Archie always sticks up for women. According to all of you, Archie's perfect. I don't believe it. I don't believe that about anybody."

Eccles smirked, no teeth, just his mouth curving up and the mustache going with it. "Then there you have it," he said.

"Have *what*?"

He sighed and shook his head. He put his hands on the table and looked down at them.

"Archie is . . . different. He's got a wall around him ten feet high. And the outside of that wall is perfect. It's totally bizarre that everyone told you I'm his best friend, because I don't know him very well at all. I like him. I respect him. I even try to be a friend. Like when I asked him what was bothering him that night. But I felt like I was prying, really pushing it, asking him something that simple. I don't talk to Archie about real things. He doesn't talk to me about them. We talked baseball and work and cars, you know—guy stuff."

Eccles sat back and looked at her. She saw a hundred years of disappointment in his thirty-two-year-old eyes. "Maybe that's why I like him. Because I know there's so much more to him, things he won't tell me. Archie has weight, Sergeant Rayborn. He's got depth. Maybe he has secrets. Maybe some not-so-good secrets."

"What about his temper?"

"Oh yeah, short fuse. That's what gives him away. He's smiling and perfect, then look out. He usually controls it. He's got strong willpower. But sometimes not enough. You should have seen him take out Mark when they argued about you."

She waited and he said nothing. Instead, he sighed, watched a waitress go by. "Are you going to arrest him?"

"Yes."

"Did he kill her?" Eccles asked.

Merci sighed and watched two Burg-Theft Detail detectives head for the cantina. Burg-Theft was Clark's old detail. She leaned in close to Eccles.

"Shit, Brad," she said quietly, "he's your best friend and you're asking *me* that?"

As soon as she said this she realized that she'd made the same mistake before—sold her trust in a man too easily and too quickly.

Eccles leaned forward. "He's not my best friend, Sergeant. I'm *his* best friend. And when he was smiling at Mark one second and knocking him out the next, I wondered what else he might be capable of."

And when Mike McNally had confessed to falling in love with a nineteen-year-old prostitute who turned up dead after one of their secret little dinners at her place, Merci had wondered the same of him.

She nodded. Suspicion. Wonder. Surprise. Certainly, Eccles was entitled to them. "Okay. What do you think—Archie and Gwen, bottom line?"

Eccles tapped his beer glass on the table. He looked at her with a cold hurt in his eyes.

"I don't know, Detective—that's what I'm trying to say. Based on what I've heard of the evidence, and what I know of Archie, *I just goddamn don't know what to think.*"

His face colored and his gaze caromed off of hers.

"Well, if CNB and Gary Brice come snooping around, you don't need to say that to them," she said. "You can give him the benefit of the doubt."

"Don't worry. I'm just suspicious, Sergeant. I don't understand people who hold out. Especially on people who are trying to be their friends. But I'm not dumb enough to talk about it on TV. Listen— how do you think this sits with me? To say what I just said about him? My friend's got a bullet in his head. I feel like Judas. But I had to say it because it's what I've seen and it's what I believe. And because Gwen's dead. Maybe Fraud is getting to me. All you hear are lies and scams."

She considered this, laying some money on the table. "What you said was hard to admit. I respect it."

"I hope I'm wrong. Like you were."

She looked at him sharply but what was the point? "I do, too."

A long silence then, observed by the ghosts of Rayborn's memory. Eccles brought out his wallet. "By the way, McNally's a racquetball friend of mine. He talks about you. Not a lot, but more than a little."

"Don't."

It was Merci's turn to color now, and she felt it happen.

Eccles shrugged. "He admires you."

"That's not possible."

He looked at her with a level, open expression. "Maybe you know less than you think you do. I know you're a good detective. Everybody knows that. But you ought to open up a little and see what's around you. What's possible. What can happen. People are surprising. Give him a call sometime."

Merci looked at him, allowing some pleasantness into her face. "You don't sound like a Fraud guy now. Sure you're cut out for that detail?"

Eccles shrugged and smiled. "That was the old me talking. I was a Boy Scout—literally. That boy's not quite extinct, yet."

"Hang on to him."

"I'm trying."

She got home that night after eight. Clark and Tim were at the dinner table, facing each other, Tim in his booster seat and Clark leaning forward on his elbows.

Clark looked at her with concern. Tim didn't look her way at all. It was a typical Monday, Tim displeased by his mother's absence after two days of togetherness.

She hugged him and he ignored her, turning his head away when she went to kiss him.

"Thanks a lot, you ungrateful little monster," she said.

"He just missed you."

"Funny way to show it."

Tim turned to look at her now. "Hi, Mom!"

She attacked him with kisses and hugs and Tim endured it, giggling as she tickled him under his chin. Merci plopped into the chair at the head of the table, Tim to her left and Clark to her right.

"Whew," she said. "That was a day."

Clark stood and put his hand on her shoulder as he pivoted around her and into the kitchen. "Monkfish tonight," he said. "The poor man's lobster."

"We're poor," she said. "Perfect."

"I saw the CNB story this afternoon. Tim watched it, too."

"Great, Dad." She shot a glance at her father, but Clark dodged it by looking into his skillet. He let Tim see and do things that she would not, and that was simply the way it was. She'd spent a year scolding her father for his permissiveness, then given up. So far as the TV was concerned, anything went.

"Awchie is not okay?"

"No, Archie is not okay. He's missing."

"He is missing?"

"Yes. For now he's missing."

"Is not missing?"

"You're exhausting, Tim," said Merci. "Cute, but exhausting."

"Gary Brice called here twice," said Clark.

"That asshole." Too late.

"Not an asshole?"

"I quit."

After dinner she bathed her son. She put short pajamas on him for the heat but he insisted on wearing his cowboy boots. He sat on her lap in the bedroom rocker while she read to him. The first three stories kept him intensely focused, but then his boot heels started sliding down her leg and his body grew heavier as he tired.

The last story was *Da Grouchy Moocher Boogie Man*, which Merci found too dark and coincidental for her taste. But Tim liked it, studying the colorful illustrations as the old man dies and the young girl holds his craggy head.

Tim yawned and clumped across the floor to bed. Merci pulled off his boots and put them on the floor where he could see them. She pulled a sheet and one light blanket over him and turned off the light. She went back to the rocker then, for the last few words she'd have with Tim that day. This was a favorite time for her, talking to her son with the room darkened but the light from the hallway coming in. She wished it could last for hours.

"Grouchy Moocher Boogie Man is dead?"

"Yes, he dies in the story."

"He is all gone?"

"All gone. But he's just a character in a story."

"He is not real?"

"Exactly."

"Daddy is all gone?"

Her heart sank again because she'd heard this line of questioning before. There seemed to be no satisfying it for Tim, and she had come to realize that this is how the dead remain active on Earth.

"Yes, Daddy is all gone."

"Is dead also?"

"Yes."

"Is not a character in a story?"

"Correct. He was real. Your daddy was real."

"Name is Tim?"

Was Tim or is Tim? She sighed quietly and felt a warm wetness in her eyes.

"Yes. His name is Tim."

"And he is all gone?"

"Yes."

"Oh."

A few minutes later she said good night, I love you, and pulled the sheet up to his neck. Tim was silent but not asleep.

A few minutes after nine the phone rang. It was Captain Greg Matson of Willits PD, returning her call.

"Awfully sorry it's so late," he said. "It took me a while to get the file, then we had a shooting in a bar downtown. We get a shooting about every other year, but today was the day."

"Get the guy?"

"He was still in the bar when we got there. Jealous boyfriend. The woman's okay though, took a twenty-two slug through her arm."

It had always puzzled Rayborn that jealous boyfriends often shot their women first and their rivals second, or not at all. "Shooter have a record?"

"Couple of D and Ds. Decent guy, really. Wife died on Lake Mendocino a few years ago. Boating accident. He never got it together after that."

"Those are tough."

"Yeah, but Julia Santos was even tougher."

"Tell me."

Captain Matson said he'd been with the Willits PD Homicide Unit back then, which led him into missing persons when foul play was suspected. Foul play was definitely suspected in the disappearance of Julia Santos, age ten. She'd left for school one morning at seven-fifty and was never seen or heard from again. Neighbors had seen an unfamiliar pickup truck but nobody got plates or even agreed on make and model.

"The parents were clean," said Matson. "Single mom, Anna. Good lady. The father lived over in Fort Bragg but it wasn't him. He went to work that morning at seven-thirty, punched in, twenty people on the dock said he was there until ten o'clock, which was when I got there to question him.

"We interviewed every neighbor in Julia's apartment complex. We interviewed every property owner between that apartment and the school. We polygraphed a few. We got some bloodhounds out of Santa Rosa and they followed a scent trail from Julia's front door to a place on Highway 101, about where it goes over the river. I always figured he got her there on the bridge, where she had less room to run."

Merci thought for a moment. "What did you get with the polygraph? Anybody look good at all?"

"No. I figured him for an out-of-towner, probably took her far away. By the time two days went by and we didn't have a girl or a body, I had this damned awful feeling we'd never close it."

"What about Archie Wildcraft?"

"First of all, how is he?"

"Wounded in the head, presently missing, possibly suicidal."

"We got that video of him up here on ABC."

"Grim."

"I guess . . . well, I guess you would have arrested him before then if you had the goods."

Merci heard the kindly accusation, but she didn't let it rattle her. "That's exactly right. I don't think he did it. But when his folks told me about Julia, it seemed worth asking you about him."

Matson was quiet for a moment. Merci heard ice clinking in a glass. "He was eleven at the time. Big strong kid, quite an athlete. You know, it's funny. If that crime happened today I'd look at the boy real hard. I'd bring a lot of pressure. But back then, well, it was only eighteen, twenty years ago, but it was a different world. I never seriously suspected him, to be honest. I interviewed him and he struck me as a young boy who had a big crush on a cute girl. He was stunned. He was very, very serious about her and about what happened. And he never gave up hope, either. I kept in touch with George and Natalie for a few months after that, they told me about him going to the library to read news about her. He wrote her letters for half a year or so after she disappeared. Anna Santos let me read some of them—just break your heart. Like Julia had gone away on purpose and the kid was trying to talk her into coming home. But you know, the letters stopped and Archie got older and history became history."

"Did you ever tail him?"

Matson hesitated before he answered. "Actually, I did. He liked to take a shortcut to school through the woods, and I did follow him a couple of times."

"Was the shortcut before or after you get to the bridge on the highway?"

"Before."

"And?"

"Just a kid walking through the woods. That's all I saw. You know something—I never put that in my reports because I was ashamed I did it. But I was desperate."

"Like you said, though, Captain, it was a different world."

"I like the old one."

"Me too," she said. She thought for a moment, now understanding that she was feeling like Matson had felt eighteen years ago—about the same man. "What do I need to know about Wildcraft? Captain, can you tell me anything at all?"

Matson was quiet again. More ice. "I remember one thing very clearly about him. I'll never forget the look on his face after I'd finished talking to him the first time. He looked at me very calmly and told me if he couldn't be a professional baseball player when he grew up, he was going to be a detective. A missing-persons detective is how he put it. I believed him. That's how much conviction he had. My own son was thirteen at the time, and he didn't have that kind of conviction about anything. He still doesn't. I remember it was a little unsettling, the way that boy kept things inside. Meaning Archie. Very strong-willed boy. Intense. Sergeant, I'm sorry I can't help you more."

"I'm glad you can't."

"If Archie does something crazy like coming back here, I'll take good care of him and call you ASAP. Take care of George and Natalie. They're good folks. Tell them I'm keeping an eye on the house. Everything's fine. The dogs and everything."

"I will."

She was just about to go sit with Tim and watch him sleep when her phone rang again.

"This is Archie Wildcraft."

"Where are you?" She started down the hall for the living room.

"No, I'm not telling. I can't let you arrest me for Gwen. I'm positive I didn't kill her. And I've got some things to take care of, you know, things I can't do from jail or the hospital. I just wanted you to know I'm okay, taking my meds and all that."

"On TV you said you'd kill yourself, Archie."

"No, that was some kind of problem with the videotape. I said I'd kill *them* myself."

"Whoever shot Gwen."

"Yeah, Gwen."

"Is that what you're doing, Archie? Are you trying to track down the shooter yourself?"

There was a pause then and Merci listened to the traffic on Wild-craft's end of the line.

"Wouldn't you?" he asked.

"That's ridiculous."

"You didn't answer my question."

She thought about it but didn't take long. She knew what she would do.

"I might try."

"Especially if your own department was thinking you did it."

"I'm the lead investigator on Gwen's case, and I don't think you did it."

"Tell that to Al Madden. He called me at home. He questioned my mom and dad. It's him and Dawes. I may have a bullet in my head but I know when someone's out to cook me."

"Archie, we're not going to charge you. So meet me at UCI Medical. Or I'll drive you over. We'll get you checked in and let the doctors fix you up. You were bleeding on the CNB segment."

"It was minor."

"How do you know?"

"I'm actually kind of worried about it. I've been, well, when the pressure goes up I see colors that aren't logical. You know, like a red face or a blue hill. But I'm remembering things, and the feelings of things, so maybe the swelling's gone down. The doctor, Stebbins, he told me in the hospital that this could happen."

"Archie, goddamnit, will you tell me where you are and let me pick you up? Nobody's going to charge you with Gwen. Dawes just smells an easy winner because you can't remember that night. Madden's just doing his job. But I know you didn't do it and I know I can catch the people who did. You can trust me on that, Archie. I'm good at what I do. And listen to this, Archie—*there's a way to help you remember exactly what happened that night.*"

Silence, and she knew she had him.

"Hypnosis," she said.

"Who told you that?"

"Stebbins. It's risky, because it puts you through the trauma again. But it lets you remember everything, just how it went down."

"Really?"

"Really, Archie."

"I'd see her again. Gwen, in memory."

"Yeah."

"I think there's a chance I got a look at the shooter."

"Jesus, Arch—good of you to mention it."

"But I'm not sure. I'm starting to see this face behind the light. I wonder if it's something I saw or something I'm making up."

"That's what the hypnosis can sort out."

"And when I see that face I keep thinking the word *reversible*."

"Reversible what?" she asked him. Damage?

"Just reversible."

"That's not hugely evidentiary. Help me out, Arch. Help me help you get back to Gwen. Those doctors can make you better, get all those memories and feelings back for you."

Another silence, this one longer. "I'll think about it. But I still won't tell you where I am."

"Think, Archie—you want your job back when you're feeling better, how's it going to look if we had to bring you in like a creep?"

"Sergeant Rayborn, I loved my job, but I don't care if I ever get it back. I have to get the man, the shooter aiming that light down at me, the guy hiding in the trees. And I have to go get Gwen."

"Go get Gwen. What do you mean?"

"I told you I hear her voice. And I guarantee you it's not in my head. It's right here, in the room or wherever I am, and it comes from above me. Not high above me, not like high up in the air, but right there, like she's hovering, say . . . eight feet up. Eight to twelve feet above my head, and over my left shoulder. Every time she talks she's a little bit farther away. The first time she spoke I felt her breath on my neck. But the last time, which was about an hour ago, it sounded like she was, well, approximately twelve feet up, behind me and to my left."

"Archie, they shot you in the head. You need medical attention."

"I don't have time for it right now. When this is over, I'll let them poke and prod all they want. It doesn't hurt at all, you know. Just a lot of itching around the hole. That means it's healing."

"Come on, Arch. Tell me where you are. You're going to get your-self into worse trouble if you're not careful."

"I'm going to get my man, Sergeant. Deputy Two Wildcraft always gets his man."

Archie laughed quietly. She heard a Harley whapping past from Archie's end, then another. She thought of Cook's Corner, the biker hangout in the hills, but so many guys owned Harley-Davidson mo-torcycles now that Archie could just as well be calling from Irvine or Laguna Beach.

"You tried to be there for Julia, too, didn't you?"

"Julia? How do you know about Julia?"

"Your parents. Then Matson, from up in Willits."

"Oh, Julia," he whispered.

She heard the three light syllables of Julia's name, and the tonnage of loss behind it.

"Julia was what made me want to be a cop. That and my forkball going south."

"I had a nice talk with your mother and father. Lee and Earla Kuerner, too."

"They're all good people," he said quietly. "I'm lucky."

Rayborn heard exhaustion in his voice. "Did Julia ever talk to you, Archie, after she was gone? Like Gwen is?"

"No," Wildcraft said curtly.

"Why not?"

"Because they took her *away*, Sergeant. Gwen's different. They killed her, but she came right back to where she was. With me."

"The same guys, do you think, Arch? The same ones that took Julia also killed Gwen?"

"Fuck all of you."

He hung up. She tried the star-sixty-nine trick, but as usual it didn't work. She waited right there, in the warm living room of the orange grove house, for Wildcraft to call back. What a stupid thing to have said.

Three hours later she woke up. Her neck was sore from the couch and the police scanner was still turned to low.

She checked Tim then sat in the rocker, wondering how Wildcraft must feel with large pieces of his recent past blasted from his mind. Specifically, memories of what had happened on the night that left his wife dead and a bullet lodged too deep in his brain for the surgeons to take out.

Infuriated.

Frustrated.

Confused.

Helpless.

Alone.

Like he's in hell, she thought, whether or not he still remembers what hell is.

But he still hears her voice.

TWENTY-THREE

The next morning Merci had the coffee cup almost to her lips when she saw the lead story in the business section of the Orange County *Journal*:

SNAKES GO SOUTH AT SISTEL
Venom-based Cancer Treatment Slithers Away

Drug giant B. B. Sistel Laboratories yesterday announced an immediate end to the development of MiraVen, a snake-venom-based antitumor treatment.

Company vice president Carol Spenser said that all Sistel plans for manufacturing and marketing the treatment have been "suspended immediately," and that the OrganiVen Division of Sistel, which was responsible for bringing MiraVen to market, will be restructured.

Wall Street reacted to the announcement with a huge sell-off, bringing Sistel stock down to $45 per share, off from Friday's close of $55, a loss of almost twenty percent.

Of further concern within Sistel is the fate of the 100-plus OrganiVen Division employees, and the nearly $400 million paid for OrganiVen late last year.

Sistel Laboratories is based in Minneapolis and valued at close to $3 billion. Sistel holds patent, manufacturing and distribution rights to some of the world's most effective and profitable drugs.

"We'll try our best to absorb the OrganiVen Division into our work force," said Spenser. "We have a history of taking care of our own."

The much publicized cancer "cure" was based on the tissue-destroying effects of snake venom. The idea, decades old, yielded dramatic animal trial results for San Diego–based OrganiVen.

OrganiVen researchers used the tumor treatment in combination with an antivenom "immunity" program that allowed cancer patients to tolerate high levels of toxicity.

The tiny OrganiVen start-up company originally raised capital through a friends-and-family offering of shares sold for twenty-five cents each.

When OrganiVen—founded by UCSD-based doctors—showed dramatic results in animal testing with its cancer treatment MiraVen, venture capitalists such as CEIDNA, Trident Capital and Brown Brothers invested heavily.

PricewaterhouseCoopers, the accounting firm that released a recent survey on venture capital, put the combined venture investment in OrganiVen at $56 million.

Sistel purchased OrganiVen for $400 million in cash and stock in September of last year, planning to take MiraVen through the uncertain and costly human trials necessary to bring a new drug to market.

"There's some sense of disappointment over MiraVen," said Spenser. "But there's simply no way we could see an effective human cancer treatment within the timeline necessary to insure profitability. We have shareholders to consider, and we ran into some development glitches that just weren't solvable. It's too bad."

Of the total number of new human treatment drugs researched and developed each year by pharmaceutical companies, less than one percent ever find their way into production, industry sources say.

Merci read the article twice, her coffee untouched. "Archie and Gwen's company got canceled," she said.

Her father sat at the opposite end of the table, his gray hair in a storm and his eyes on the sports page. "I saw that."

"How can it be worth millions then nothing?"

"Those problems the lady talked about."

"What the hell is a four-hundred-million-dollar glitch?"

Clark looked over his glasses at her. "Ask her."

With little hope of getting through to industry captain Carol Spenser, Merci took the B. B. Sistel general number from the operator, then dialed. The receptionist put her through to Public Information. Carol Spenser's assistant answered the phone. Merci identified herself as an Orange County Sheriff's Homicide Detective and asked to speak to Ms. Spenser.

"Just a moment, Detective."

"This is Carol Spenser." She had a sweet, middle-aged voice with the distinct ring of intelligence in it.

Merci explained that one of her homicide cases involved OrganiVen investors, and she wanted to know just a little more about OrganiVen's restructuring.

"That just means we keep the people and the equipment but drop the division," said Spenser.

"But why? I saw the MiraVen video—it worked great."

"Those were animal trials, as you know, and human ones would have turned out to be much more complicated and expensive."

"What was the development glitch, Ms. Spenser?"

"Detective Rayborn, I can't tell you that. I am a vice president and the head of public information for a multinational company, and part of my job is to protect proprietary information about our company and its employees. We're under no legal obligation to reveal that kind of information unless we're under subpoena in a United States court. Some of that information we are not required to disclose under any circumstances. To do so would be like you giving out details of an investigation."

"I understand. But I've got a murder case to close."

"Well, certainly, our decision to restructure a division here at Sistel can't have had anything to do with a murder? I mean, we just made the announcement yesterday, and your case must have begun before then. Correct?"

"A week ago. The victim was an OrganiVen start-up investor named Gwen Wildcraft. She and her husband made two million dollars when you bought the company last September."

"And?"

And, Merci thought: her husband, shot in the attack and perhaps a suspect, now suffering brain damage, said that a huge man he *believed* to be connected somehow to that investment met with his wife in a bar and *may* have had something to do with the killing.

Think fast, she thought. She thought as fast as she could and came up with almost nothing.

"I thank you for your time," she said.

"Feel free to call again if there's anything I *can* help you with. I wish you success in solving your case."

Merci hung up, hit redial and asked for the B. B. Sistel security department. The receptionist put her through to Plant Security, which transferred her to Personnel Security, which transferred her to the Legal Department, Patents and Infringements.

"Ron Billingham," a smooth voice announced.

Merci identified herself and told Mr. Billingham that she was investigating a Southern California homicide, Gwen Wildcraft, a woman who had invested substantially in OrganiVen before it was bought by Sistel.

There was a pause, then Billingham put her on hold for nearly two full minutes. Merci listened to music and drank her coffee.

He came back with an apology, then, "Sergeant Rayborn, I'm going to give you a number for Ardith Day at the Federal Trade Commission in Washington, D.C. After you've talked to her, you can call me back if you need to."

Merci took down the number and called Ardith Day. Day took her call immediately and gave her the number of FBI Special Agent Nicholas Behrens in Washington. Behrens took her call immediately and gave her the number of Special Agent Carl Komer in the FBI Investigative Resident Agency in Orange County.

She left a message with the Santa Ana RA and Komer called back
in less than one minute.

"We should talk," he said. "How about my office, eleven-thirty?"

"Thank you. I'll be there."

Sheriff Vince Abelera looked at her unhappily as she walked across
the blue carpet of his office and sat in front of his desk. Marilyn shut
the door behind her and Merci felt the familiar hush of the office.

"Have you heard from Wildcraft?" the sheriff began.

"Last night, sir, at ten-fifteen. He called. He would not tell me
where he was. He would not let me come get him. He refused to
surrender himself or go to UCI Medical Center for treatment. His mental condition seemed . . . unstable. Physically, he claims to be feeling
fine."

"Why did he call you?"

"To tell us that he's okay, not to worry about him."

"Feeling okay, now that he's threatened a reporter with a shotgun
on television and said he'd kill himself?"

"Archie told me he didn't say that. He said he told Brice that he'd
'kill them myself,' but somehow the 'them' got lost on the tape. To
Archie's credit, sir, Brice was falling into the orange tree when Archie
was talking. I remember the noise that caused when I watched the
broadcast again."

Abelera's sharp dark eyes bored into hers. She broke the connection
and looked out the window to the hazy August morning.

"We've got an all-unit alert for him," said the sheriff. "All-agency,
all-unit. Nobody's seen him. Yet. We've got surveillance teams watching both sets of parents and the sister."

"He called from a pay phone, I believe. I heard road noise, two
Harley-Davidsons."

Abelera eyed her. "I've called a press conference for one o'clock
today. That's enough time to get it out onto the evening news. I've
got Public Information blowing up two department photographs of
Wildcraft, to be put on easels beside the podium. I've got stills from

the CNB video to show. I've got Dr. John Stebbins coming in to explain Wildcraft's precarious medical condition. And *you* will conduct the conference, telling our community that we need the deputy's whereabouts reported *immediately*. You have his trust."

"I think so, at least some of it."

"Then I want you to use it to get him in here."

"Yes, sir."

"You will indicate that we have no plans to charge Wildcraft with the murder of his wife. You may indicate that we do wish to question him in this matter. You will deny that the district attorney plans to charge him with threatening Mr. Brice but you will express deep concern about Mr. Wildcraft's apparently suicidal statement. You will be telling Mr. Wildcraft—because that's who this damned circus is really for—that we are concerned first and foremost for his well-being. You will order him to please report to the nearest law enforcement or medical facility as soon as possible. And when we get him, Sergeant Rayborn, I'll be turning this case over to Wheeler and Teague. Am I not clear on any of this?"

"I think you're making a mistake, sir."

"That's not what I asked you."

"No, sir, you're very clear on what you want."

"Sergeant, I don't care about your personal feelings regarding this deputy. He's a suspect, whether you choose to believe it or not. His prints are on his gun. His gun was used to kill his wife. He fired that gun. He left the hospital without our authorization and then he ran and hid. Those are *facts*."

"Yes, sir, they are. But, sir, please let me continue as lead investigator. I've made mistakes but I'll correct them. I'll close it. This isn't a matter of feelings. Forget my feelings. I don't like them any more than you do. But I have to be successful on this case. It's absolutely necessary. If you pull me, you may as well write me out of Homicide Detail. That would be two disasters in a row, sir. Don't do that to me."

In the silence that followed, Merci tried to think loud. Tried to make her thoughts clearly audible, because she would go to her grave never putting these thoughts into words, never saying the words to another living soul, true as they were. But Abelera needed to hear them, and she willed those thoughts into his ears while her dark brown eyes stared into his.

I put you here. My blood and shame opened this office for you. I almost died for you. I need your help now. Give me your help.

The sheriff broke off this time, looking out the same window Merci had looked out of, at the same damp, warming morning. He pushed back in the rolling chair and stood.

"All right, Rayborn. All right."

TWENTY-FOUR

The FBI Orange County Investigative Resident Agency is housed in a four-story building not far from Sheriff's Headquarters. The building has other tenants besides the FBI, one of which is the Government/Courts Bureau of the Orange County *Journal*. The building wraps around a ground-floor courtyard that is shaded by potted palms and is cool even on late-August mornings. Merci was early enough to try the ground-floor ladies' room, but it was secured with a brawny lock system and she didn't have the numbers.

Komer led Merci and Zamorra to his office on the second floor and closed the door. He poured three coffees from a pot on a stand and offered it black and without questions.

"Well, it's obvious by now that Sistel is having some problems with MiraVen," he said.

"I didn't know until this morning," said Merci.

"Almost nobody did. Sistel kept it quiet as long as they could—no reason to worry the shareholders until you have to."

"What happened?" asked Zamorra.

"I don't know yet. But Sistel is claiming that there's a major problem obtaining the snake poison. The short supply—they say—was conveniently omitted by OrganiVen during the purchase negotiations."

"Fraudulently omitted?" Zamorra asked.

"Sistel would like us to use that word. Then we can go after the OrganiVen people. That's my job, to determine if there's been fraud or not. And if so, take down the fraudsters. It takes time. Everybody's got a line. And the good fraudsters, they can steal a lot of money without leaving a trail."

Komer folded his hands and leaned on his elbows. He was younger than Merci had expected, forty, maybe, with short straight brown hair, brown shoes and brown leather on his hip with what looked like a Smith nine inside it.

"I've been looking at OrganiVen for almost a week now. I didn't connect Gwen and Archie Wildcraft with OrganiVen until yesterday."

"They made almost two million from it," said Merci.

Komer nodded. "And you'll be interested to know they were more involved than just as investors. Gwen was, anyway. She became an employee for almost six months. She helped raise capital. I'm not sure how much. I'm not sure what her arrangement was. But she spent a lot of time at the OrganiVen building."

"We wondered," said Zamorra. "With all the promotional material we found in their home office."

Komer sat back and looked at them. "OrganiVen received early money from a venture company called SunCo Capital. Heard of it?"

Merci shook her head and saw Zamorra doing the same.

"You're not alone," said Komer. "It existed for roughly two years, then evaporated. I ran across it when I got into the financial side of OrganiVen. I recognized the players immediately. SunCo is actually spelled ROC."

"Russian Organized Crime," said Zamorra.

Komer was already nodding. "Right here in the home of Disneyland and the master-planned community. SunCo was just two guys, as far as I can tell. Sonny Charles is an Anglicized alias for Sergei Cherbrenko. Nice guy. Came to the United States when he was twenty years old. A gay man. Did okay in insurance fraud up in L.A.—standard car accident stuff. But he really scored here in Orange County when he started up a company that bought out the life insurance policies of AIDS patients for fifty cents on the dollar. He called the company Rescue Financial. Heroic, isn't it? It was even legal. He was the scourge of Laguna Beach in the early eighties, made a lot of money watching his customers die. We got him on a boiler-room scam eight years ago—working senior citizens on a phony group medical insurance deal. He's been out for three years, so he obviously found gainful employment with SunCo Capital."

Komer handed Merci a file. Attached to the inside of the front cover were reasonably good booking shots—two profiles and a frontal. Sonny Charles was a sharp-faced blond who looked about as trustworthy as a scorpion.

"Of course Sonny didn't accomplish all this alone," said Komer. "He's got a helper—Zlatan Vorapin. Vorapin's got half a dozen aliases, one of which is Al Apin—which he used for his SunCo dealings. He's also got a Soviet jacket—robbery, extortion, debt collection, extortive moneylending. He came west in eighty-two. In eighty-eight we had a high-level ROC captain *cold* on an extortion case. But the victim was shot in the head before he could testify. We think Zlatan was the shooter but we couldn't prove it. LAPD got him on assault back in ninety—a nineteen-year-old girl. He was bringing poor young women in from the Balkans, making them work as prostitutes to pay off their transport. Nobody would talk to us, especially the women. Since then, nothing. We heard that he and Cherbrenko moved here to Orange County for a more affluent and trusting work environment. They're supposedly more into the white-collar things. Less violence, more profit. Vorapin's a hard guy to find, considering that he's six-ten, three-thirty."

Merci's heart was beating steady and true and she felt it in her temples. Vora*peen*, she thought: like a hammer. She looked over at Zamorra, who wore a cold smile.

"We got size sixteen shoe prints by the Wildcrafts' walkway," she said. "About eight feet from where Archie went down."

Komer looked at her and said nothing.

"And more prints by an abandoned Cadillac with plates similar to one seen leaving the Wildcraft crime scene. Two witnesses say huge, dark hair, short beard, thick glasses. The other blond and slender."

A smile crossed Komer's face as he handed Merci another file. She opened it and studied the enormous head, the unimpressed eyes and the wronged, infantile lips of Zlatan Vorapin. The top set of mugs showed him with his shaded rectangular eyeglasses, the bottom set without.

"Oh, man," she said quietly. *Vorapeen.*

Komer just shook his head.

"SunCo is long gone, Sergeant. Hit and run, these guys—they start a new company for every new scam. Our last contact with Cherbrenko was early nineteen ninety-nine. For Vorapin, two years before that. They're the most accomplished bureau-rats in the world. They just vanish into the system—multiple ID's, driver's licenses, credit cards. Burn companies within burn companies. The whole thing. We got four different sets of pretty good ID off of Vorapin. *Five* off of Cherbrenko. And that's just what we found."

"I don't imagine their fellow Russians are too helpful in finding them for you."

"Nobody knows anything. Let me tell you, the Russians are great at stock scams because they're educated to survive in a bureaucracy. So they can find a way to use the system. They love the taste of red tape. Seventy years of life under the KGB makes you resourceful. Life *as* KGB makes you ruthless. Put people like that together and you get very effective bad guys."

"But you don't know what the scam was?"

"I'm looking. I'm working it. Sistel's squawking about the supply of the venom, and that's all I should say right now."

"You'd think rattlesnakes are pretty easy to get," said Rayborn. "All those reptile farms in Florida with the big ugly things crawling over each other. Those roundups in Texas and Oklahoma. You know, belts and key chains and snake chili."

"Yeah. But according to Sistel, not true."

Merci tried to think this one out—can't they milk the damned things, put the stuff in the refrigerator with the butter and cheese?

"I know the scam was good," said Komer. "It had to be to fool B. B. Sistel. Whatever it was, it just started coming home to roost a couple of months ago. That's when Sistel launched their own investigation. A month later they contacted the FTC, which vetted the story,

then contacted us. Sistel tried to time the announcement of the restructure with an optimistic earnings forecast for the fourth quarter. Didn't
really work. I know for a fact that when Sistel cries foul and guys like
Charles and Apin are involved, it spells fraud. Capital letters. And
when a murder victim was working for these guys, well, I don't know
what to think. Nothing good, I can tell you that."

Komer shook his head and sat back.

Merci looked at the pictures again. "Can I get file copies?"

"You're looking at them. They're yours."

"Thank you."

"Sergeant, as far as I'm concerned, this is your murder and my
stock fraud. I'll help you all I can. And I'd sure appreciate your help
back."

"You'll have it."

"May I have a copy of your file, when it's convenient?"

"I'll have one on your desk by two this afternoon. Would it be
possible for you to clear Ron Billingham over at Sistel to talk with
me? He asked me to call back when I'd talked to Ardith Day."

He looked hard at her. "I'll clear it. Ron's a good guy. He was
with us for quite a few years."

"Can you connect Apin to a local limousine service?"

Komer thought for a moment, eyes roving the ceiling. "No. But
the ROC had their hands in some of the Los Angeles limo operations
back in the early nineties. Give me a couple of days, I'll see if there's
a local angle."

"Agent Komer, thanks again."

They stood. Komer regarded her with the casually optimistic look
that in law enforcement always means suspicion. "Is Deputy Wildcraft
still at large?"

She nodded.

"That video was damaging. I understand the evidence against him
is strong, and he talked suicide. But if the size sixteens were Vorapin's,
maybe he was there that night. Maybe these gentlemen framed Wildcraft for it."

"I think it's possible," she said. And she thought: nobody's framing a fellow deputy on me again, *ever*. She felt the skin on her face betray her but she didn't care.

Komer offered his hand and she shook it.

They walked down Flower toward the Sheriff's Headquarters. The noon heat was close and personal, and Rayborn was thinking about the Russians.

"I talked to Priscilla after work yesterday," said Zamorra. "I don't think she was after Archie. I think she had her hands full with her own husband."

"Does she seem like the type who'd yell about him to her brother-in-law?"

"The night before Gwen's birthday Brock told Priscilla that he was having an affair. She was furious about it. Still is. When she picked up Archie the next day, she snapped, blew off steam."

"You believe that?"

"Yeah. She had to do something, or go crazy."

"I'd have blown it off on Brock."

"She couldn't. He spent the night with the new girl."

The press conference was held in a first-floor courthouse conference room. Merci stopped in the doorway, unhappily baffled by the crowd.

George and Natalie Wildcraft were there, sitting with Gwen's parents, Lee and Earla Kuerner. Who told them?

Likewise, civil rights lawyer Connie Astrahan and a cadre of three women who sat at the end of the front row of fold-up chairs, murmuring like conspirators.

Likewise, the head of the Sheriff Deputy Association, an attorney named Dave Dunphy, who glanced at her dismissively then turned back to his group of deputies. She knew them—all sergeants or higher—loyal remnants of Chuck Brighton's old guard who thought that she had betrayed the department by telling the truth about it.

Likewise, at the other end of the chairs, a loose coalition of what

Merci privately referred to as "my people," mostly younger deputies who had stuck with her through those dark and agonizing days last winter.

Dr. John Stebbins sat at a table beside the podium, talking with Gary Brice.

CNB's pretty Michelle Howland was there, as were reporters from two of the networks. Merci recognized half a dozen print journalists who specialized in the crime beat, and attendant photogs. And two columnists who specialized in human interest, cheer-the-underdog stories. A magazine writer. And the publisher of Orange County's alternative newspaper, *County Weekly*. CBS and KFWB radio were there, even a reporter from the campus PBS station at UC Irvine.

The podium was already awash in light, the twin blow-ups of Wildcraft easeled on either side like candidate posters at a political rally. The one on the right was taken from Brice's video footage, and showed Archie by the pool in one of his less maniacal moments, cropped at the shoulders to omit the shotgun.

"I hate these things," she muttered to Zamorra.

"Never let 'em see you sweat."

"That's *all* they see me do."

Merci butted between Stebbins and Brice, nodding to the surgeon and turning to the reporter. "That stunk, what you did to Wildcraft."

"I didn't plan it that way."

"You made him look crazy for a story."

"I did? But not the shotgun or the threats or the somewhat destabilized glare in his eyes?"

"I wish you knew your place," she said. "But you don't, and it's too late for you to learn. Will you excuse me for a minute while I talk with the doctor? Beat it, Gary."

Brice tried to cover his humiliation with a smile but his face was a red giveaway. Merci looked at Stebbins and shrugged. She didn't have anything to say to him, her words to Brice were just a way of shoving him around a little.

"Sorry about this," she said.

"It's okay. Do I have to answer questions?"

"You can tell them about Archie's medical condition, then walk out of here if you want. The marshal will let you through the back door."

"I'm going to take you up on that."

She walked over to the Kuerners and the Wildcrafts and said hello to them. The men shook her hand, but Earla looked away and Natalie peered at her like a wolverine ready to jump. Merci felt the new chill, the clear message that *she* was out to get Archie, under the guise of wanting to protect him.

Rayborn reluctantly squared herself behind the podium and waited for everyone to take a seat.

She thanked them for coming.

She introduced Dr. John Stebbins, who nervously took Merci's place at the microphone and spoke of Deputy Wildcraft's medical condition: threat of infection, threat of edema, threat of seizure, threat of bleeding; loss of memory, possible hallucination, confabulation and erratic behavior.

"Is he suicidal?" asked Michelle Howland.

"That's not my area. I can't answer that."

"Is he dangerous?"

Stebbins cast a panicked glance at Rayborn, who shrugged encouragingly, trying to indicate the doctor could answer or not, up to him.

"I can't answer that, either. He's unpredictable," said Stebbins. "We just don't know. We've got to get him back under medical care. That is the only thing I can tell you for certain. I'm due in surgery in one hour. Thank you."

Stebbins banged his knee on the table leg on his way toward the back door, but the marshal had it open and waiting, and the doctor sidled out like a spy.

Rayborn went to the podium, looked up and focused on the CNB shooter because she'd never met him and he was a neutral being to her. She tried her best to sound like the cops she'd seen on TV, but she wasn't very good at talking that talk.

"We called this conference because we need Deputy Wildcraft to turn himself in to the nearest medical or law enforcement facility as

soon as possible. We ask that anyone who has information on Mr.
Wildcraft's whereabouts contact us immediately. It's for his own good.
Mr. Wildcraft has a bad head wound, and as you know, the bullet is
still lodged in him. He needs medical attention, as Dr. Stebbins said.
I want to stress that Deputy Wildcraft is not under warrant for arrest.
We want to talk to him about the murder of his wife, Gwen, because
he's a possible witness. No charges have been filed in regard to the
confrontation with Mr. Brice on Monday morning. We need to question Deputy Wildcraft. We understand that the deputy is despondent
over the death of his wife, is suffering a bad wound, and possibly feels
hounded by certain members of the media. We're with you, Archie,"
she said, mustering a small smile. "Come back and talk to us. Questions?"

Perfect, she thought: that came out just right.

CBS News Radio: "Has Deputy Wildcraft contacted you since dis-
appearing?"

Rayborn: "Yes. He appears to be feeling fine but is reluctant to
seek medical care."

"Why?"

"He is angered by a reporter trespassing on his property early on
Monday morning. He thinks he may be seen as a suspect in the death
of his wife."

*He thinks his wife is talking to him and he thinks he can track
down a three-hundred-pound killer named Vorapin but I'm not at liberty to tell you this. And if I were, I wouldn't anyway.*

"Is he a suspect in Gwen Wildcraft's murder?"

"I already told you he isn't."

"Sergeant Rayborn! Sergeant Rayborn—Michelle Howland, CNB.
Can you tell us why Deputy Wildcraft is *not* a suspect in the death of
his wife, if his gun was used to kill her, and his fingerprints were on
that weapon, and a paraffin test for gunshot residue came up *positive*?"

Rayborn could have killed her, would have if there weren't so
many witnesses around. She felt like blood was boiling out of her ears.
She imagined Howland being run over by a speeding armored car,
then by a steamroller, then by a . . .

"Sure," she said evenly. "Because there's a lot more to a homicide case than fingerprints and gunshot residue. Come on, even you know that."

A hush, then.

"That's all you're going to say?"

"What else is there to say?"

Merci had already traced the invisible path of disclosure from Jim Gilliam's crime lab to the rosy red lips of Michelle Howland: DA Clay Brenkus to ADA Ryan Dawes to news rat Gary Brice to Michelle the Belle. She imagined Dawes freefalling through a canyon again, his extreme-sports shorts tightly gripping his butt in the fatal descent.

But Michelle wasn't done: "I was wondering why you claimed recently that the weapon was stolen from Arizona, and that the fingerprinting was inconclusive. We have those statements on tape. Which of your stories is the true one, Detective?"

"Those were preliminary findings, later disproven," she said calmly. "I did say those things, but I shouldn't have. It was too early for a statement. One of these days I'll learn to keep my mouth shut around you people."

This, meant as a self-deprecating joke, drew a weak media chuckle.

Then, Natalie Wildcraft, her voice cutting through the tension like a rusty ax: "Archie didn't kill her, you stupid women."

Cameras swung toward her, shooters re-aiming at the far end of the seats, where the Wildcrafts and Kuerners sat in a sudden wash of bright light. A chair tipped over and landed with a metallic bang that was louder than it should have been.

"She's right," said Earla Kuerner. "You people ought to be ashamed. All of you."

The nonreporters—Merci's friends and enemies—stood simultaneously for a better look, which gave a sense of things unraveling.

Natalie shielded her face from the lights with her small, bony hand, her big engagement ring flashing. "Good gracious, turn those damned things off."

The shooters pressed in close and fast, not about to lose position to each other. The reporters fired questions at the same time, then fired them louder, then began shouting them as the marshal at the back door shook his head and hustled bulkily around the table to restore order.

Natalie Wildcraft rasped furiously through the din, *"Get away, you leeches, you gutless leeches!"*

Rayborn, thankful for something physical, rounded the podium to help the marshal.

"Be easy," said Zamorra, also stepping toward the little riot.

Merci restrained Michelle Howland by the arm but Howland wheeled and hissed, *"Take your hands off me or I'll sue you out of the department, bitch."*

"Cool it, Sergeant," snapped the marshal, moving toward her. Shocked and accelerating toward anger, Merci veered into Natalie Wildcraft, who had fought her way through the bristle of bodies and mikes to make for the door.

Natalie Wildcraft slapped her hard in the face, left side. Rayborn saw it coming but couldn't pull herself away from the focused fury of the mother's eyes.

"Stupid women," Natalie barked again. "She acts like a judge and you act like a *friend*."

She raised her hand again but Zamorra in one impossible motion caught the wrist and delivered it with something like grace into the beckoning paw of her husband. George Wildcraft eased out of the room, pulling her behind him.

Rayborn looked over at the video shooter who, alone in his group, had turned to watch her and catch the action.

She shook her head and looked down to avoid the glare of the video light.

The slap and the words and the exit of Natalie Wildcraft left a sudden silence in the room.

Earla and Lee Kuerner scuttled away like cold refugees.

Rayborn got behind the podium, threw back her thick dark hair and took a deep breath. She wondered if her cheek was as red as it felt.

"Any *more* questions? Good. We'll talk again in, oh, how about . . . never. Does never work for you?"

At that moment the door opened and a sunny, overweight woman in a blue dress smiled at Merci. A legion of girls, all dressed in identical brown uniforms, swarmed in ahead of her.

"Brownie Troop seven-eight-eight, Tustin," she said. "Courthouse tour?"

"Please retreat to the information desk," said Merci.

The Brownies had come to a communal stop when they saw Merci and the podium and the posters of Wildcraft and the video shooters and celebrity reporters.

"Girls! Girls—this way, please!"

Merci sat in the pen, waiting for Abelera to call or come over, fire her, take her badge and her gun, maybe whip her with his Sam Browne in the middle of the homicide pen.

She stared down at the recent arrivals on her desk: a department-wide notice of a birthday party for Assistant Sheriff Collins, suggested gift donation, twenty dollars; this month's newsletter from the Deputy Association; the "FBI Law Enforcement Bulletin"; blank timecards for the coming week.

She pushed them all aside for a look at Don Leitzel's neatly written note regarding the addresses in the navigational computer of the abandoned Cadillac STS.

Sgt. Rayborn—

Addresses contained in Sand Canyon car, in order of entry into the navigation system, are 83 Osler Lane, La Jolla (University of San Diego School of Medicine); 212 Saltair, Newport Beach; 4143 Agate, La Jolla.

I took the liberty of hitting the Orange and San Diego counties assessor's offices to see who the owners of these places are—hope you don't mind. These addresses belong to 1) the University of California, 2) Mr. Wyatt Wright, a single man, and 3) Dr. Sean Moss, a single man. The Wright and Moss home purchases were both within the last year, 6.8 and 4.5 million dollars, respectively.

Don L.

"I'll be damned," she said out loud. Inside her the embarrassment of the press conference was whirling up against the excitement of this new evidence, and Merci felt a giddiness that went straight to her head. "Cherbrenko and Vorapin used the Caddy."

"Huh?"

Sergeant Teague wheeled in his chair and looked at her.

"Those creeps that Crowder and Dobbs saw coming down the hill from Wildcraft's in a Cadillac at the crack of dawn—the same creeps were dialed in with home addresses for two of the OrganiVen founders, and the UCSD medical school, where another founder was working. The arrogant shitheads stole an STS for transportation and dumped it out on Sand Canyon."

"So?" Teague, large and only apparently sluggish, specialized in dumb skepticism and Rayborn generally loved him for it.

"Gwen *worked* for OrganiVen. It's a stock fraud," she said. She was thinking out loud now, and things were making sense. "Everybody got rich, but now something's going wrong. Archie didn't kill her. And he didn't shoot himself. I'm damned sure of it now."

"What are you going to do with all his fingerprints on the gun?"

"Wipe them off."

"Good. I knew Arch didn't do it. He's a good kid."

Teague wheeled back around and burped quietly. "But let me guess—they wiped the STS clean."

"They sure did. Ike and Leitzel couldn't get a single print."

"Pros."

"But still dumb enough to leave the addresses on the navigational system."

"Geniuses don't go into crime."

"A goddamned stock fraud," said Merci, still thinking out loud.

Teague spun around again. "So Archie's got the proof in the back of his mind, you might say. But nobody can get to it. Because to take out the bullet, it would probably kill him."

"The brain scans can't tell a thirty-eight from a thirty-two or twenty-two or a twenty-five or a nine. They're not quite precise enough to show an exact diameter, with the mushrooming and fragging and all. But yeah, if you could get it out, you'd see it didn't come from his nine. It came from something one of those two guys in the car was packing. I'd bet my house on it."

Teague shrugged. "So, when Archie dies of natural causes at the age of ninety-six, they can autopsy him, get the bullet and button down this case once and for all."

"Give me a break, Teague, I'm going to button this thing down by the time you quit burping."

"Feels like that could be a month."

"Give me a week."

"Get 'em, Rayborn."

"I'll get 'em cold."

But Leitzel the Thorough wasn't the only good fairy to have visited Merci's desk while she was being slapped and cussed and pushed around by a *marshal*.

A note from Ike Sumich lay just under Leitzel's:

Sergeant R—After many long-distance phone minutes I was able to determine that the shoe imprints were left by a size 16 Foot Rite "Comfort Strider." Two tread patterns were marketed in this country. What we found at Wildcraft's is the "Versa-Terra" by Markham. NOTE: FOOT RITE ONLY SOLD THE COMFORT STRIDER IN SIZE 16 THROUGH CATALOGUES. NOT EVEN SPECIALTY BIG AND TALL STORES CARRIED SUCH A LARGE SIZE IN STOCK. Here are the six most popular catalogues through which Foot Rite offered the shoe for sale in California.

Sumich listed the catalogue companies, their addresses, phone and fax numbers and Web site addresses.

"I love our crime lab guys," she said.

"They're all cuties." Teague turned back to his desk.

She got Sumich on the phone and thanked him for the good work. "This is what I need now," she said. "Get back to Foot Rite and find out if any of their catalogue retailers are specialty outfits."

"The ones I gave you are all specialty outfits—big and tall."

"Go a step further. Big and tall *executives*, because this guy might see himself as a businessman. Big and tall, ethnically targeted—look for European, Russian, Balkan, Slav. Try military surplus because a lot of them have been selling Soviet stuff since the breakup. Try big and tall outdoorsmen, too—hunters and fishermen."

"Got it. Why a European businessman who likes Soviet surplus catalogues and loves to hunt and fish?"

"He's a Russian, Ike. A gangster, a fraudster and probably a killer. The hunting and fishing idea is pure hunch. Nothing more."

"Do you have a weight on him, by any chance?"

"I heard three-thirty, but that was as of a few years ago."

"I estimated three-fifty from the soil and the print depth. I didn't want to say anything because it was so much. I figured my estimate was just flat-out wrong."

"Vorapin. Zlatan Vorapin. Also known as Al Apin."

"Al Apeman."

"He's going to be hard to find."

"Set a trap. Use bananas."

"I'll think about it."

TWENTY-FIVE

Merci opened the French doors of Gwen Wildcraft's music room to let out the afternoon heat. She smelled hay and horses as she stood on the patio and looked out at the houses and the hills. This is what two million dollars gets you, she thought, and then it gets you dead.

Zamorra booted up the computer and Merci went to one of the tall oak file cabinets.

Something, she thought: *Sistel says OrganiVen cheated them and its investors. SunCo was there. Gwen worked there. Gwen was murdered. . . .*

The files were clearly labeled and hung in alphabetical order. She found four thick red folders for OrganiVen—labeled I through IV in roman numerals. And one yellow folder for each of the four principal founders, Wyatt Wright, Cody Carlson, Sean Moss and Stephen Monford. There were separate blue folders for the venture capitalists who had come aboard, CEIDNA, Trident Capital, and Brown Brothers. No folder for SunCo. Too small? Or did she keep the toxic dirt somewhere safer?

Merci rolled the chair to put her back to the window and opened the red OrganiVen I folder. Taped to the inside of the folder was a three-by-five-inch sheet of notepaper, lined, the top edge raggedly torn from its binder, one corner left behind.

Quaint, thought Merci, to begin all this fancy stock stuff with a handwritten note:

232

OrganiVen
great potential
tip of decade
555-5839/Trent Gentry

The tip that changed their lives, she thought. Temptation. Serpent coming through, courtesy of Trent Gentry. The writing was probably Gentry's also, because Merci had seen samples of both Wildcrafts' and they looked nothing like this.

She recognized the name immediately—from one of Archie's arrest records. Drunken driving, wasn't it? Something uninteresting. The only reason she'd noted it in the first place was because Trent Gentry worked in the Newport Beach office of Ritter-Dunne-Davis Financial.

She looked at the simple sheet, wondering at the grand damage a few words can cause.

It was an outside shot, but she went to the car, unlocked the trunk and brought the Wildcraft case file back into the music room. She found Archie's inexpensive green notebook, the one where he'd looked for the plate numbers of the car driven by two Russian gangsters to a meeting with his beautiful, worried young wife.

She set the open OrganiVen folder on one of Gwen Wildcraft's keyboard instruments, a Yamaha. Looking down, she then flipped slowly through Archie's notebook, looking for the small missing right corner of the page in the folder. She found it between the fourth and fifth pages. Holding up the notebook to the inside of the folder cover, she eyeballed the pieces. They looked good, very good. Ike or Leitzel could nail it, but for now she'd call it a match.

So, what had happened?

Archie had pulled over a drunk stockbroker. Hoping for a break, the broker offered the arresting officer a hot stock pick, even wrote down the name and his own number on the officer's notebook. The officer arrested him anyway. The officer then did what? Checked out the tip with his brother-in-law? Asked his wife to check it out? At some point, the Wildcrafts must have liked what they heard because they kept going. Moving forward. Gentry to Archie to Gwen to Charlie to OrganiVen. . . .

Did it piss off Trent Gentry to give a two-million-dollar stock tip and still get a DUI? Served him right for trying to bribe a deputy.

She called Gentry's number and got a receptionist. The receptionist said that Mr. Gentry was on vacation now and would not be back until mid-September. Mr. Carnahan was handling Mr. Gentry's clients in his absence. Could Mr. Carnahan be of help?

"No, thanks," said Merci. "But where can I reach Trent?"

"I'm sorry, Mr. Gentry is not reachable until he returns."

Merci knew that he was reachable but the battle it would take her to get the number wasn't worth it. Yet. She ran one finger across the silent white keys of Gwen's synthesizer, thanked the lady and hung up.

She looked at Zamorra. "It looks like Archie did get the original stock tip from Trent Gentry. Gentry tried to grease his way out of a DUI with it. Archie told Gwen. Gwen took it to her brother-in-law, Charlie Brock."

"So Brock was telling us the truth."

"Must have killed him."

She knelt down and opened one of the black guitar cases, five spring-loaded latches snapping open at her touch. The case was lined in thick red velvet. The instrument inside was shiny wood and bright chrome. It smelled good to her. It had old-fashioned looking toggles and dials, and F-holes cut into the body. At the top it said "Guild."

"I like people who can make up something out of nothing," she said.

Zamorra looked at her, then at the instrument. "It's a gift."

"I don't have a gift," she said, "so I joined the system. I'm better off in a system. I need one. But people like Gwen, they don't need all that. She could make music."

"She should have paid closer attention to what was going on around her."

"It looks that way, doesn't it?"

She ran her fingernail over the strings. The sound was metallic but whole, and almost beautiful. The lid closed with a velvet harmonic whisper. Latches back in their plates with a heavy click.

Sitting down again with her back to the sunlight, she continued leafing through the OrganiVen I folder, then quickly through folders II, III and IV. She saw that Gwen had organized them in chronological order except for OrganiVen IV, which was dedicated to research.

In the beginning—nearly two years ago—the company was called VenFriendly. Two months later it was SeruCure. She dug further down to get her first look at the company as OrganiVen: January of last year, nearly twenty months ago. So, she thought, they kept changing their name.

She set down the folder and went to the Wyatt Wright file. Scanning through, she found what she was looking for, a later interview with biz-whiz Wyatt.

"It took us a while to come up with a name that seemed right. We kept trying to blend a biomedical flavor with something descriptive of our product. It's hard to put a positive spin on snake poison."

She agreed with Wyatt on that one. She heard Zamorra's lazy tapping on the keyboard and looked over.

"What do you know, Paul?"

"Gwen was representing OrganiVen. I don't know for how long, or how much, but she was selling start-up shares. And I've got two years of e-mail here, coming and going."

"Anything good?"

"Lots of correspondence with Sean Moss. He was one of the four founders. Their talks seem to relate to one or two topics, but their language is vague. Like they're worried about privacy."

"Read a couple."

" 'Hello Gwen: No problem at all on the *cerastes* rum. We've got some ideas on how to keep plenty around. Don't worry. Be happy. Later, Sean.'

" 'Hello Sean: I'm sure there's a way to get more. I'll leave it to you guys and do my job. Brought in another eight K today—some good friends from high school. Thanks for being cool. *You* be happy. Best, GW.' "

Merci asked Zamorra to spell *cerastes* and he did. She pictured the word, knew she'd never seen it, frowned. "What's *cerastes* rum?"

"No idea. I've got a friend who's a bartender at the Ritz-Carlton, though. He'd know. It comes up a lot in these e-mails. I think they liked each other, Gwen and Sean."

"Is he married?"

"The company bios said he was single. Here—Gwen refers to getting twenty dollars an hour to 'rep a treatment I've come to believe in.' Then Sean, he says she's worth fifty and he'll see about getting her a raise. Then she makes a joke about bringing in one hundred and eighty thousand dollars for OrganiVen 'so far.' "

Merci looked up at the four remaining photographic portraits of Gwen and Archie through the years. "She brought in eight thousand dollars for OrganiVen in one day, and didn't make that big a deal about it. I wonder how much she got for them, total. I wonder how much she got for herself."

"I'll let you know. But at twenty bucks an hour it wasn't a fortune."

"Unless she took the payment in stock."

Zamorra looked at her. "Then it's a different story."

Ten minutes later Merci's cell phone rang.

"Hello, Sergeant, this is Bill Jones. Archie's gardener just pulled up in front of his house. Is that your unmarked in his driveway?"

"Yes, Bill, it is."

"I haven't seen that big ugly guy or his ugly little partner since they were at the park."

"Meet me in the driveway in one minute."

"Consider it done."

Merci held back the file cover to show Jones the FBI photographs of Sonny Charles and Al Apin. Jones angled them to catch the sun better. He moved to one side, then the other. He never took his eyes off them.

"That's them. The ones I saw at the park."

"Any doubt?"

"None. They're older now."

"Thank you, Mr. Jones."

"I'm here to help. If I see them again, I think I know what to do. I've got your numbers in my wallet."

"Keep me posted."

"I will. I don't have anything better to do. By the way, when you ask the gardener about Archie and Gwen yelling at each other the day she died, remember that he wears ear protection when he's blowing leaves and a tape player when he's pulling weeds."

"Thank you, Mr. Jones."

"Bring you coffee, a soft drink, anything?"

"No again. But thanks."

"Doughnut? Heh, heh, just kidding. Ten-four."

The gardener was small and stout, tan jeans and a white T-shirt, not a size sixteen. He was looking around like he wasn't sure what to do. He's heard, she thought. He's heard what happened and doesn't know if he's still got a job.

"Over here," she called, waving.

He came her way, stopped six feet away. Black hair and eyes, a nice smile, two silver-capped teeth front and top.

Merci told him who she was. He nodded and said he was Jesus, and that he spoke English.

"Let me show you something."

She led him down the walk to the Chinese flame tree where Size Sixteen had stood. "Did you rake in here last Tuesday?"

"Yes."

"Did you stand under this tree—right here, like this—and face in this direction?"

She stooped under the foliage and arranged herself where the man had stood.

"Here, like this?"

"No."

"You're sure?"

"I don't stand. I rake."

Merci considered. "What shoes were you wearing?"

He looked down at his worn brown boots. "This boots."

"Did you wear some other boots over them? Mud boots, maybe, or boots to repel water?"

"No. I wear this boots. I don't stand there."

"Did you hear Archie and a woman arguing that day?"

"No. Did not hear argue."

"Did you see a woman here?"

"Gwen sister. I don't know her name."

Jesus said that he first saw the sister around three. He heard no argument, no conversation. He said he had a cassette player he listened to when he worked.

Merci led him around the walkway, past the pool and into the rear yard. She pointed to the hole in the window, now blocked by a piece of plywood held in place by duct tape.

"Was this glass broken when you were here last week?"

Jesus stared mournfully. "I don't see. I don't look at this."

"You don't know."

"I don't know. Mrs. Gwen is dead?"

"Yes."

"Oh. Bad. Mr. Archie get shot, too?"

"He's alive. That's about all I can tell you, Jesus."

"I like. Archie and Gwen is good family."

"Yeah. I know."

She asked him about people looking onto the property, very big men in specific, but Jesus had not noticed any. No unfamiliar vehicles, nothing out of the ordinary with Archie or Gwen. He had worked for Archie for six months, and for the previous owners for six years.

She got his full name, address and phone number, and thanked him.

Rayborn closed by saying *Vaya con Dios* because she thought the expression was elegant and meaningful, but Jesus himself looked at her as if the words were pointless.

Two hours later, midway through OrganiVen I, Merci picked up the trail she was looking for. In yellow highlighter, Gwen had begun to mark certain passages in the promotional literature, then keyed those passages to the research stats found in the research folder.

From the OrganiVen Company Overview brochure, dated March 2001: *OrganiVen researchers have found the extracted pure-form venoms of many vipers to be effective in the animal trials, especially those from animals indigenous to the deserts of the American southwest.*

Gwen's handwritten note referenced the SeruCure research data from October of the previous year: *The results of double-blind test series 12-C and 12-D strongly suggest that the serum obtained from C. cerastes is the only serum with toxicity levels necessary to destroy carcinoma cells at an acceptable rate with acceptable damage to surrounding tissue. Venom compounds using C. ruber, C. viridis and C. atrox resulted in significantly lower anaerobic reactions but higher healthy cell destruction. See charts for comparative venom strengths and collateral tissue damage.*

"Paul," she said. "*Cerastes* rum isn't liquor, it's a kind of venom. *Serum.*"

He looked at her. "Okay, that tracks with what I'm getting here through the e-mail. Gwen was worried there wasn't enough of it, or wasn't going to be enough of it. Lots of correspondence between her and Sean Moss. Something about a breeding program to make sure the supply would last."

Rayborn's heart jumped when she read one of the cross-referenced statements in an OrganiVen brochure. "She's marked up the promotional lit and cross-referenced statements to the research. All it talks about here is viper serum, nothing specific. So the research and the brochures are saying two different things. Let me see what I can find on a breeding program."

"Look for Dailey, or Dan, or Harvesters—all three seem to be in the game."

God rest Gwen Wildcraft's orderly soul, thought Merci, because she found a purple folder dedicated to Harvest Specialists. Inside was what looked like a hastily produced company brochure and a letter to Sean Moss from Harvest Specialists president Dan Dailey of Temecula, California.

In the letter, Mr. Dailey talked about his education as a biologist, his lifelong interest in herpetology, and his familiarity with the reptiles of the American Southwest.

Two months later, he wrote Sean Moss a short note saying that *of all the rattlesnakes we can supply you, only the sidewinder (Crotalus cerastes) is difficult to harvest in significant numbers. They're small, nocturnal, spend their days under the sand or in rock burrows, do not overwinter in "dens". Their venom glands are small. It figures they're the ones with the best juice. I'll see what I can do!*

Shortly thereafter, Dan Dailey began a breeding program for the sidewinders. His start-up costs totaled $5,345, billed to OrganiVen: lamps, tanks, "hot rocks and heating elements," water dishes, plastic-coated aquarium gravel, individual cage thermometers, reptile vitamins, breeding mice for food, etc. He promised results—twenty grams of pure fresh *cerastes* venom each week—beginning in six months. More after that, as the captive *cerastes* bred.

"How much does a gram weigh in English?" she asked.

"Three one-hundredths of an ounce. A little over."

"Wow. That's not much. I've got the breeding stuff here, Paul. Stand by."

A series of brief printed e-mails over the next five months chronicled the ups and downs of Dan Dailey's Harvest Specialists sidewinder breeding program. He had trouble harvesting the necessary specimens. He blew up the engine of a new pickup in the one-hundred-and-ten-degree Snow Creek heat. He had trouble telling the males from the females. He got bit by one and spent half a day in the hospital, billing OrganiVen for the expense. The specimens failed to eat in captivity and Dailey spent "significant hours" catching lizards for them because they wouldn't eat the mice, live or frozen. The sidewinders wouldn't eat the lizards, either. Only two mated females became gravid, and of the fourteen newborn rattlesnakes, only six were living at birth. Four of these died within one hour, the other two within twenty-four. The older snakes faced starvation and were released.

I'm totally frustrated by these fuckin' sidewinders, man, Dailey wrote to Sean Moss in March of the previous year. *If you had asked me for atrox or viridis venom I could have gotten you a gallon of it by now. I'll keep trying.*

"He struck out," said Merci. "Sidewinders are what OrganiVen needed, but Dailey couldn't catch enough of them and they wouldn't breed in captivity. He even got bit by one."

"That tracks," said Zamorra. "Listen to this:

Dear Sean, All I can tell you is the more control SunCo gets of your company and the less cerastes rum comes in from DD, I'm getting nervouser and nervouser about repping us. I've got a golden touch for you, but I can't sell what I don't believe in. Imagine if the Feds found out that you (and I) knew the rum bummer—they'd hang us. I strongly advise you to get the SunCo heavies to back off and put the rum problem back into the current prospectus and business plan, or find a solution fast. Charles and Apin are talking about redrafting all the research results to leave out the distinction in base serums. They think I'm nothing more than the typist, and they'll say anything around me. I just may set up a meeting and confront them. Don't redraft the research—that would be criminal. You should spend more time in the office and less in the lab if you really want to know what jerks these guys are. If it was my company I'd give SunCo their money back and tell them to get lost. Al Apin is not human, and I don't mean to insult dogs, pigs, dolphins, doves, millipedes or sidewinders.
Your Pal, Gwen.

"The date on that one is April of last year. Five months before the sale to Sistel."

Even though Merci's heart was beating fast with excitement, it sank at the end of Gwen's e-mail to Moss.

"If the Russians knew she knew this, Paul, if they even dreamed that Gwen might spill, that's motive to kill her."

"But why would they wait until last week to do it? The scam was over. The OrganiVen sale to Sistel went through back in September of last year. Everybody got rich, including Cherbrenko and Vorapin. They're long gone. Sistel's left holding the bag, they fold the loss into their annual billions, call it a restructure."

Merci thought it through. "Well, Sistel is just now starting to cry foul. Maybe she had just started singing. For a while, she played along, made her money."

Zamorra was nodding. "Which might be her inclination, after getting friends and family to invest."

"But she changed her mind. She did something they found out about. Or they *thought* she was going to do something, went proactive."

He looked at her. "With these guys, you don't change your mind. You don't get in the way of business."

"Then why did she, Paul? Why change her mind when everybody's paid, fat and sassy? Why would she do that?"

"A guilty conscience."

"It wasn't that guilty when she was making the money."

"Pressure," said Zamorra.

"From where?"

"Family?"

"She'd never tell them what she'd done. Especially if they'd invested, or loaned her and Archie money to invest."

"Friends?" he asked.

"The same."

"Maybe she didn't understand good old Sonny and Al. Didn't know how dangerous they were."

Merci knew that ignorance often supplies the opportunity for a murder. Not seeing the threat. *I didn't know.* "I'd give her more credit than that. And you know Archie would have understood it."

"But did Archie know? Did Archie know his wife was elbow deep in a stock fraud while she was making them rich?"

Rayborn, a believer in the right to keep and bear secrets, had to think about that one. What she came up with surprised her. "He was a cop. A straight arrow. She might have told him she was worried. She *did* tell him the SunCo guys were creeps—he told us that. But she wouldn't have told him details. Because he would never have let her do it. No. Archie never knew what these guys were up to. Because Gwen could never bring herself to tell him."

A moment of silence in Gwen Wildcraft's music room. Then an

understanding came to Merci as clearly as one of Gwen's melodies coming through the speaker.

"They weren't after Archie that night," she said, quietly. "They were after Gwen. They got him out of the house because they knew he was a cop and he was dangerous. Then they went in and took care of business. Because she changed her mind."

Why did she change her mind?

TWENTY-SIX

Dr. Sean Moss lived in a bashful mansion overlooking the Pacific at La Jolla. It was redwood and smoked glass, horizontal layers hugging the hillside, trying to look inconspicuous. The winding driveway was concrete, lined with Torrey pines and breeze-swayed grasses.

The voice from the gate speaker was youthful and high-pitched: "Yeah?"

"Detectives Rayborn and Zamorra, OCSD. We want to ask some questions about Gwen."

"You didn't make an appointment."

"You didn't answer your phone. Open the gate, Doctor, we don't have all day."

"This is not cool."

But the gate shuddered and began its slow roll across the concrete.

Beyond the gate the lot was level. Merci saw the tennis court, the helipad, the rock-climbing arena, the swimming pool with a ten-meter board, the sand volleyball court complete with a sunning beach with bright yellow umbrellas. These playing areas were connected to each other by lawns of thick green grass. Merci thought Ryan Dawes would probably wet his extreme shorts just seeing Sean Moss's setup. She wondered why men were slow to give up boyhood while girls raced to be women.

The house was bigger than it looked from down the drive, segmented into three stories that rose and dipped with the hill face. There were decks and more yellow umbrellas, clay pots of tropical plants on the rails. Merci parked near the volleyball court and they walked up a gravel trail bordered by the dense damp grass.

The front door was enormous and slotted with windows of tinted glass. One side of it opened and a skinny young man in shorts, a bright shirt and clunky sandals with ankle straps came to the front of the porch. He looked down at them. His hair was thick and straight, hanging down from the top of his head, then cut straight across his forehead and ears, as if the barber had used a mixing bowl as a template. His legs were dark and bony.

"I'm Sergeant Rayborn and this is Sergeant Zamorra. Are you Dr. Moss?"

"Yes. I only have like ten minutes."

"You young hotshots are always in a hurry," said Rayborn. "What are you a doctor of, anyway?"

"Organic chemistry." Moss smiled either boyishly or nervously and let them into his house.

The entryway was towering, three stories to the skylights, Rayborn guessed. Lacquered redwood floors, huge redwood stanchions rising to the distant ceiling. Moss lifted the lid of what looked like an old steamer trunk.

"Shoes, please."

They sat on a redwood bench along the entryway wall and took off their shoes. Moss kept his sandals on. Merci looked to the opposite wall, where shining, colorful surfboards rose in ranks of six across. She padded across to look closer at the writing on them: Wardy, Greg Noll, Hobie, Velzy, Dewey Weber.

"Surf up today?" she asked.

"It's a weak south. Trestles was okay."

Sean Moss, bowlegged as a bull rider, led them through to the kitchen that was done up in new stainless appliances and white everything else. Shiny blond wood floor. An island work table with a checkerboard hardwood top. He opened a wooden slider that led outside to a deck, offering them chairs at a long redwood table under a yellow umbrella.

Moss sat with his back to the sea, giving them the ocean view. He slipped on a pair of thin silver sunglasses that, with the bowl haircut, gave him a mushroom-from-outer-space look. He had a neat goatee.

"We think Gwen Wildcraft might have gotten herself into some hot water at OrganiVen," said Merci.

Moss looked at her and said nothing.

"Any thoughts on that?" Zamorra asked.

"Gwen and her husband bought some shares during our friends-and-family offering, then she became involved in the company. Really liked the idea of fighting cancer. She brought in over a quarter of a million in start-up money. We offered her hourly compensation, but she took her pay in stock. You don't think her work with OrganiVen had anything to do with her murder, do you?"

"It had everything to do with it," said Merci. "Who was the friend who got them in?"

"A stockbroker named Trent Gentry. I mean, the 'friends' definition was loose. I went to school with Trent, and he was vouching for the Wildcrafts."

Rayborn wrote. "Tell us about SunCo."

Moss had a tight mouth and a hard jaw. With the sunglasses he was hard to read. "Well," he said, "we graduated from friends and family to small venture capital companies, and SunCo was one of the first to come to us."

Moss sat back, crossed his arms over his bright yellow Hawaiian shirt.

"Did you deal with Sonny Charles and Al Apin?"

He nodded.

"How much did they come in for?"

"They put up roughly one million dollars."

"Friends-and-family rates?"

"Slightly higher. I think we were up to a dollar a share by then."

"What did you think when Sistel dumped the OrganiVen division yesterday?"

"It surprised me."

"They'd talked to you about the venom supply, though, the *cerastes* serum?"

Moss gulped. "Yeah."

"Dr. Moss," said Zamorra, "take off your glasses and talk to us. We're trying to find out who murdered your friend Gwen. We don't really care if you were short of sidewinders, except in how that relates to Mrs. Wildcraft."

He gave a small nod and took off the glasses. Glanced at Rayborn with truculent sun-bleached blue eyes. He looked about eighteen but Merci knew he was twenty-eight.

"Yeah. Okay. It's been almost a year since we said adios to SunCo," he said. "When Sistel bought us out, that was the end of those dudes. I mean, I didn't have to deal with them anymore."

"You may have parted ways with Sonny and Al, but you saw them last week, right? That's our information, anyway."

"Why would you think that?" he asked faintly.

"Look, Moss," said Zamorra, "we can go back to Santa Ana and sit you down in an interview room with a fake mirror, a videotape running and a cup of really bad coffee. You want to do it that way, fine. We're going back there anyway, so we'd be happy to give you a ride."

"No, no. Not really."

"Then cut the bullshit and talk."

Dr. Moss looked at them resentfully, then sighed and looked down at the table. "Yeah. I saw Sonny and Al on Monday. The day before Gwen was killed."

"Tell us about that."

"They just showed up here. Parked on the grass. They wanted to remind me that they had nothing to do with reorganizing our research statistics to . . . minimize the *cerastes* problem. That was *if* there was any reorganizing done at all. They wanted me to know that if Sistel or the FTC started asking questions about SunCo's part in the R and D of MiraVen, to leave them out of that discussion."

"Or what?" asked Merci.

"Or they'd cut out my tongue and replace it with my balls."

"Direct quote?"

"Word for word, minus the Russian accent."

"Who said that?"

"Al. That was pure Al, once you got to know him."

Rayborn made sure she had the words right in her blue notebook. She underlined them, but there was no reason to write *CK* next to a quote like that.

"Dr. Moss, describe the *cerastes* problem," she said.

"Fairly simple. Viper venom is mainly hemotoxic, it destroys blood and tissue. But it also has neurotoxic components, which means it also attacks the nervous system. The key to MiraVen wasn't so much the way it attacked cancerous cells, but the process that allowed us to use sufficient levels to destroy the cells almost instantly. That's important in surgery, for obvious reasons. The riddle was, how do you kill the malignancy quickly but spare the healthy cells? The solution was actually my idea. I'd read about the human antivenin process, where horses are injected with low doses—then increasingly higher doses—of venom. Then, when their immune systems had reached a certain strength, their blood was then taken and used to create antivenin for humans. When a human is envenomed by snakebite, then administered the horse blood serum, the venom is very quickly neutralized. Our key was developing a strong immunity in the test subjects *before* introducing the venom to the lesion. That way, the collateral damage was minimized, the side effects were small and the tumorous cells were destroyed, like, extremely quickly. But here's the deal—you don't want to immunize mammals with high levels of neurotoxic venom because it's too dangerous. And you don't want neuro levels too low, or the overall effect on the lesion—for reasons I still don't understand—isn't sufficient. So the right neuro-hemo mix, that was the goal. *Crotalus cerastes* had the right proportions. But it's hard to get. We tried to collect it, breed it, replicate it and synthesize it. I just couldn't get the results. I thought a cloning program might work. Millions of dollars, to do that. We left that to Sistel."

"Without really spelling out the problem ahead of time."

"Right."

"Sonny and Al made you rewrite the promotional literature and revamp the research to hide that problem."

"Well . . . no, not exactly. We just omitted the species *cerastes* from the genus *Crotalus*. Sistel never thought to get down to that level of taxonomy."

"Until a couple of months ago."

"I guess."

"Why did you do what SunCo asked? You knew it was at least misleading, possibly illegal."

"Exactly."

"Then why? The tongue thing again?"

"They were more subtle back then. They said it had to do with hundreds of millions of dollars."

"And they were right about that, weren't they?"

Moss nodded. "The thing is, I really believed that our harvesters would come through on a breeding program. We tried collecting enough sidewinders. We tried breeding them. We tried buying them. We tried every viper venom we could get our hands on to equal the *cerastes* reactions. We bought two hundred hand-collected eyelash vipers from Costa Rica to see how their serum would work. Too weak in terms of anaerobic capacity. We tried water moccasins from a snake farm in Florida. But the neurotoxins were high. I went out to the desert with our harvesters myself, to see if I'd have any luck finding the sidewinders. I stepped on a cholla cactus and had a minor heatstroke. What I'm saying is, the harder SunCo pushed us to adjust the test results the faster I tried to find a solution. I always thought I'd find that solution."

"But you agreed to keep quiet about the problem."

He sighed and nodded. "I can still make a legitimate case for the research, the way it was presented. I mean, it's kind of complicated, but you can organize trials to emphasize or minimize—even exclude— certain variables. It's like . . . if you change the angles a little, you get the same amount of square footage, but in a different *shape*. I also think I could make a case for SunCo coercion. They threatened to report *us* for defrauding *them* unless we downplayed the serum problem enough to bring in the big, big money. They made physical threats, too."

"Such as?"

"Al dropped a tooth in one of my beakers in the lab one day. Rolled it out of a handkerchief. A silver amalgam filling. Meat and blood on the root."

"What did he say?"

"Nothing."

Moss looked down at the backs of his hands.

"Then came CEIDNA, Trident, Brown Brothers," said Zamorra. "Around fifty-six million in venture capital."

"Yes."

"Bringing OrganiVen to the auction block at a cool four hundred million."

"Four ten, actually."

"What was your take?"

He looked at the table. "Twenty-eight."

"Twenty-eight at twenty-eight," said Zamorra. "Set for life."

"Exactly."

Zamorra, leaning forward: "Gwen didn't like the research redrafts, or the changes in the promo lit. She loved the idea of curing cancer. And she loved the idea of making some money at it. But she was wise to what Sonny and Al were doing."

"Yes," Moss said quietly.

"Dr. Moss," said Merci, "listen very carefully to this: we've got her e-mails to you. We've got your e-mails back to her. To us, she sounded ready to talk. She sounded capable of blowing the whistle on SunCo. To your knowledge, did she do that, or threaten to do that?"

Moss looked at her, then at Zamorra, then back at Rayborn. "I don't know."

"You must have seen that she was thinking about it."

"Yes. We became good friends."

"What did you tell her about SunCo? Did you encourage her, discourage her, what?"

"I told her that Charles and Apin were definitely not to be messed with. That we'd work out the problem. That she should be happy with the thousand percent return she made for herself and her husband and their friends and family. And pray the FTC doesn't open a probe. And if it did, to just say she didn't know there was any problem at all. Let them come to the founders. We were the ones who brought in SunCo. We were the ones who . . . fuckin' haired out when they got tough on us."

"I don't understand," said Rayborn. "Gwen knew early last year that there was a supply problem. She e-mailed you about it in April. She knew SunCo was pushing for the cover-up. But she didn't do anything. She played along, collected her money. Bought a nice new house. A couple of nice new cars. Then, months after the deal, Sistel finds the problem, Sonny and Al hit the campaign trail. They threaten you on Monday and kill Gwen on Tuesday. What did she do, Sean? *What did Gwen do?*"

"Sonny and Al were afraid of an investigation. I don't know what their information was, or how they got it. But what did Gwen *do*? I can't answer that. I don't know."

"When was the last time you talked to her?"

"Monday evening. I called to tell her about the visit."

"What did she say?"

"They'd talked to her that day, too. Told her to forget any irregularities she might have seen if anyone asked her about the *cerastes* problem. She laughed and badmouthed them."

"After they threatened you with a tongue-dick transplant, she laughed?"

"I didn't tell her they said that."

And Rayborn began to understand. It came over her just fleetingly at first, like a cool draft in an old room. Then she understood it all at once as the truth broke over her in a cold wave.

"You didn't tell her much of anything, did you?"

"She never took them seriously. Not seriously enough, anyway. Funny Sonny and Al the Apeman, she called them. I . . . the total worst thing I've done in my life is I didn't impress upon her how dangerous those men were. I . . . believed that if Gwen knew that OrganiVen was being eaten alive by Russian gangsters she'd head straight for the cops. She'd probably start with her own husband. So I . . . never came right out with what I thought of SunCo. I actually, maybe sort of covered for them a little. Told her they came from a different culture, had a different way of doing things."

"So you let her discover it just a little at a time, figuring she'd get in too deep financially to back out."

Moss was nodding again. "That's how they got me. It wasn't like they came in and announced they were animals. They were actually quite knowledgeable and occasionally funny and charming. They put up more money than we'd ever seen. And I knew Gwen was going to get rich. I wanted the best for her."

"And you wanted her to see you as an honorable research scientist on the verge of a cancer treatment."

Dr. Sean Moss looked at Merci. She saw a look of painful nostalgia in his eyes. "I actually was that, once. I can almost remember it. I was relatively poor and honest and proud of myself and what I was doing."

He reached an accommodation with himself. "Yeah," he said. "In the beginning, that's what I was. Proud to be me, and in the same room as Gwen. I loved her. I don't mind admitting it. Never told her. Never told anyone. Never did anything about it, that way. I just loved her."

"But not enough to tell her she was working with gangsters."

"I couldn't admit I'd become a greedy coward."

"Oh, man," said Rayborn.

"Exactly," said Sean Moss.

Zamorra tapped the tabletop with his fingers and sat back. Moss looked at him then away, shaking his head.

"I was trying to warn her when I called," said Moss. "Not trying to get her killed."

"She was *your* warning, Moss."

"Exactly."

"Have you talked to Wright, Carlson and Monford?"

"Well, two of them. Sonny and Al looked them up, too. Told them what they told me. Cody's surfing down in Fiji. Man, I wish I was, too."

Merci looked out at the glistening ocean, at Sean Moss's private playground, at the gnarled Torrey pines winding their way down his drive.

"Tough it out right here, Sean," she said. "Be ready to take a stand, tell what you know. Show everybody you're not the gutless little dweeb you seem to be."

TWENTY-SEVEN

Archie pushed Dr. Sondra Pearlman's "Harnessing Your Subconscious—Adventures in Auto-Hypnosis" into the tape player of the Durango. He liked that he was *in* an auto. He listened to the soft hiss, then to Dr. Pearlman's soothing voice.

"Welcome to the world of auto-hypnosis," said the doctor of psychology. "Welcome to yourself. In the next hour I'll be showing you how to put yourself into a deeply relaxed state so that you can gain access to the thoughts, memories and emotions that are with you all the time, but you never know about. This is your subconscious. Unlocking your subconscious can give you insight into who you really are, and who you can become. . . ."

The night was warm and humid and he could see the neon glow of the Air Glide Limousine sign in the parking lot across the street. The letters were hot aqua blue and the Air Glide logo—a long low car tilting upward, with contrails wisping off it to suggest flight—was red and pink. At least it looked that way to Archie.

He was parked in front of a surfboard shop down on Pacific Coast Highway, near the border of Newport and Huntington Beach. The surf shop was closed but Archie had found a spot beside a listing Volkswagen van that looked like it hadn't been moved in years. The traffic on PCH was steady and fast, but from the high interior of the SUV he could see perfectly the Air Glide lot and the front door of the business.

This was the same lot but not the same space where he'd parked the night before. He'd seen what he wanted to see then, a few minutes after midnight. Just terrifically good luck, he'd thought. He hadn't quite known what to do so he didn't do anything. Just went back to the hotel that used to be a packinghouse, stared at pictures of Gwen and thought about it.

The Air Glide window blinds were down but not closed and he could see a counter and a desk behind it and the same pudgy, dark-haired man sitting at the desk. A row of shining silver stretch cars waited out front, angled in unison like a school of barracuda, facing the highway. He wondered if he was seeing them wrong and they were actually black, or if Air Glide favored silver to fit in with the flight theme.

"This is what we'll need to get started," said Dr. Sondra Pearlman. "First, make yourself comfortable and get ready to relax. I'd suggest a reclining chair or a comfortable sofa in a darkened area. You can lie on a bed or on the floor with a pillow under your knees and head for support. The key is to be comfortable. If you're prone to falling asleep, don't try the bed or floor positions. Once you're comfortable, you can either choose a small, preferably bright object to concentrate upon, or you can simply close your eyes and imagine a candle flame, an orange-and-blue lilting candle flame."

Archie reclined the driver's seat. Not far, just enough to ease his head against the rest and give him a level sightline to the red neon car zooming through the sky. Without even moving his eyes he could see the front door of the business and the guy at his desk, now nodding, a phone to his ear.

One week ago tonight, he thought. We were here in Newport, at the Rex. Now he could remember how beautiful she was, how surprised and embarrassed, then grateful and happy. Only a few days ago, that memory—and its emotional echoes—would not have come to him. Thank God for modern medicine, thought Archie. Thank God for pills. He remembered the way her dress clung to her body, the great volume of her life pressing against thin fabric. He remembered being impatient and worried and nervous inside, and he was sorry to have spent her birthday that way. The truth was, he was like that a lot.

Sometimes she called him Worry King, as in welcome to *Worry King Live....*

He tasted Gwen's sweat and lotion in his mouth, though that had happened hours later.

"I'm still here," she said.

"I know," he said back. He looked at her and smiled. Gwen was wearing a short yellow dress and yellow sandals, dark hair pulled back on one side. She had her dark August tan. "I wish I could touch you."

"Soon, Arch. Don't worry."

Now Dr. Pearlman asked Archie to focus on his chosen object, or just close his eyes, and imagine his favorite place. It should be a place outdoors, a place of stillness and beauty. It should be a place of peace and understanding. She told Archie to include his chosen object into the landscape as a focal point. For instance, if he was staring at a candle, the candle could become the sun, or the reflection of light off a lake.

Archie stared at the neon sign and imagined it was a bank of night-lights at a big-league baseball park. He imagined the other light banks to the left and right, then moved his mind's eye downward to the empty grandstands, the dark green wall with the white numbers on it, the warning track and the outer edge of grass, the crosscut emerald expanse of the outfield, the orange gravel of the infield, the white bases in their holy shape and the perfectly chalked baselines and boxes. Then the flawless infield, crowned by the pitcher's mound with its neat white rubber and the concentric furrows of the groundskeeper's rake. Finally, the elegant pentagon of home plate.

"Now," said Dr. Pearlman. Her voice had become softer and slightly more commanding. "As you imagine your place of peace and understanding, breathe deeply and slowly. In and out. In and out. With every breath you take in, let go of all your thoughts. With every breath you let out, let go of all your thoughts once again. In and out. Thoughts going, thoughts vanishing. All you see is your place of peace. All you hear are the sounds of peace, if there are any sounds at all. Breathe in. Breathe out. Thoughts going, thoughts vanishing. Again. Again. And as you continue, imagine that you are not just visiting this place of peace and understanding, *you are becoming a part of it. You are joining it. You are becoming peace. You are becoming understanding.*"

"I apologize," he whispered. "For being so uptight on your birthday. I wanted everything to be just right."

"You can't apologize for anything that generous and wonderful, Arch. I won't allow it."

"That's a beautiful ballpark."

"It really is."

"I always loved the crunch of the gravel under my cleats. The first step I took onto the mound, if we were home. The mounds were perfect then."

"I liked the first time I saw you against Dominguez Hills. I couldn't believe you looked at me during a game. But you did."

Archie smiled. "Two-hit 'em that day."

"It was gorgeous. I was sixteen years old and in love with the most beautiful man God ever made."

"I'd have died for you then. And on any day since then."

"Oh, Arch. Don't get on a bummer. Not now, when we have so much to be thankful for."

Archie thought about that as a seagull flew through the outfield lights, white against the blue plastic seats of the grandstand.

"They want me to give up. Go back to the hospital. Probably arrest me."

"You have to do what you think is right."

"I want to be together."

"We'll be together soon. Then always together. Listen to this tape. It really sounds good. . . ."

". . . this state of total relaxation, you will allow your thoughts to speak to you. Try not to direct your thoughts. Try not to order them. Simply experience this peace that you have become. Simply feel the understanding that is you. Let your mind wander relaxed, like a deep wide river, and follow it to the places it is inviting you to go."

Archie looked at Gwen beside him, pretended for a moment that he didn't know her. He'd been doing that for ten years, since the first time she'd sat in his car beside him. Such a funny, subversive little thrill to see someone who moved your heart like Gwen moved his, and wonder what it would be like to touch someone like her. Well, not *like* her, but *her*. To touch her. To touch her every way you could dream of. Then again. Year after year after year. What a game, then, you suddenly unpretend and let the memories flood back. Let them carry you along your own past, rush away with you like a river, Dr. Sondra is right on about a river: *Gwen looking at me outside the theater that first time with eyes that took away some of what I was and gave back some of what she was, holding her hand in the living room of her parents' house in Norco, and that first time I brought my face to hers to see if she would let me kiss her and she dug her nails into the scalp above my ears and kissed me so hard and after that it was a storm that didn't happen all at once but still a storm like the laundry room of the Kuerners' place that first summer so damned hot and steamed up from the dryer and we locked the door and let the dryer pound away while we did the same with the washer groaning and thumping under my bare ass and Gwen deep in my lap and oh man that had to be one of the strongest I ever felt but there was also the tent in Yosemite and the sleeping bag in Sequoia and the beach at Thousand Steps and Crescent Bay and Diver's Cove and the bench seat of my pickup at the drive-in and the motels her senior year when we were engaged but didn't have a good place to go and we'd make love five or six times in four or five hours and still get to laugh and eat fast food and drink a little beer and tell each other every dumb little thing that had happened since the last time we'd seen each other and still be back in Norco by midnight and don't forget the Hotel Laguna and the Newport Marriott and the Hyatt Newporter on those special nights when we had enough bucks for a good room and room service breakfast at midnight and eight in the morning and definitely don't forget the first honeymoon night in the Disneyland Hotel the black lacy things and the great champagne, oh man, all you men out there who were not loved by Gwen Ellen Kuerner Wildcraft that night have never been loved at all and as long as I'm alive you never will be.*

"Remember the honeymoon suite?"

"You don't forget something like that."

"Let's get together right now."

"Okay!"

Archie put his hand on her leg, felt it warm through her dress. He was still looking out at the ballpark so he didn't turn to Gwen, but his hand felt the familiar shape of her thigh and he could smell the milk-and-orange-blossoms smell that Gwen had when he was close to her. He felt her hands on his service belt and the zipper going down, then the cool air below his belly.

". . . and in this deeply relaxed and receiving state your subconscious mind will fill with the thoughts that are most important to you. Let these thoughts come. Experience these emotions. Become truly and totally who you are."

"Wish we were home for this one," he said.

"We could use that old pickup now," said Gwen.

He relaxed a little, let her get comfortable, not easy with the center console in the way. His hand in her soft dark hair now, feeling the wonderful shape of her skull, then the physical sweetness, intensely specific but oddly general too, like his entire body was being swallowed.

Archie saw the giant and the blond man walking across the Air Glide parking lot at two minutes until midnight on the Durango clock. They were the men from the meeting with Gwen in the El Ranchito bar, absolutely no question about it. Something to do with OrganiVen. Marketing concerns, Gwen had said, right? The big one turned sideways to get in the front door, then, as he had done last night, pivoted his enormous head to scan the lot before yanking the door shut.

Archie closed his eyes for just a moment and tried to remember what it was he had seen behind the bright light that aimed down at him before the bullet smashed into his life: a man's face, possibly, but . . . this man? That face? He remembered the cartoon he and Kevin had drawn in third grade, a bearded man with rectangular glasses. The man's beard and hair were identical opposites, and his ears were rounded and sprung from the middle of his head, so that when you turned him upside down he looked almost exactly the same. They'd named him "Reversible Man."

And that was what this giant looked like. Archie had realized this over a year ago when he sat in his sunglasses and ball cap and baggy hula-girl shirt in the El Ranchito bar and watched with knots in his stomach and a forty-five automatic Colt pistol digging against his ribs as his young wife nervously sat down with two obvious monsters. Yes, she'd said *marketing concerns*, he could remember that clearly now. Reversible Man. Pretty Blond. But was it Reversible Man's head behind the glaring light that night? Archie opened his eyes. It was impossible to say.

He'd need to talk with them to determine that. With at least one of them. It wouldn't be easy and it wouldn't be pleasant, but it was easy to pick which one he'd interview.

At one-sixteen, what looked like a black Lincoln Town Car came into the parking lot from behind the building. It passed behind the silver stretch limousines and stopped at the entrance of Coast Highway. Archie saw Reversible Man deep in the darkened interior, and as if to confirm his ID, the driver's side of the car rode slightly lower than the other. No signal, but a break in the swift traffic and Reversible Man gunned the Town Car northbound on PCH. Just like the night before.

Pretty Blond came to the window and the blinds angled down to block Archie's vision. The lights stayed on for a few minutes—he could see the yellow outline between the blinds and the window frame. Then the lights went off and nothing that Archie could see stirred within the Air Glide office for twenty-four minutes. At which time the lights came back on.

A few minutes later another black Lincoln—this one a Mark VII—rounded into view from behind the office. Pretty Blond, alone, waited and signaled and turned south on Coast Highway.

Archie moved the gumball from the floor to the seat beside him, then followed. It was an easy tail, the traffic moving fast with plenty of cars to put between them. Pretty Blond was considerate, obeying the speed limit and signaling his lane changes. He turned east on Jamboree, headed past the big hotel where he and Gwen had played all those years ago, past Newport Center and Fashion Island toward Irvine.

Archie put the gumball on the Durango roof and pulled over Pretty Blond outside the Tuscany Apartments. There was a nice entry lane away from the traffic and he could see the man tilt to his left, probably to get a wallet or a gun.

Wildcraft filled his lungs as he approached the idling Mark VII, flashlight in his left hand.

The window of the Mark went down.

Archie stood beside it, but just slightly back of the driver's easy angle of vision, just like they taught you for patrol. Make them turn to you.

"Step out of the car, please."

Maybe it was Archie's summer-weight green cotton/poly-blend uniform. Or the name Wildcraft on the brass nameplate over his left chest pocket. Maybe it was the badge. Or the barrel of the forty-five ACP he touched to the lashes of Pretty Blond's left eye.

"Yes."

An hour later, Archie was standing just outside the master bathroom in his home. Sonny Charles leaned in the corner of the bathroom proper, in the same spot where Gwen had lain. She was with them, behind and slightly above Archie.

"She died right where you are," said Archie. "Isn't that right, honey?"

"Yes. Right there."

Charles looked at him without moving his head. He was sweating hard and his blond hair was shiny in the overhead track lighting of the bath. He had a narrow face and reminded Archie of the guy who painted the soup can. His eyes were blue and dry and extremely skeptical.

Archie unwound the duct tape from Charles's face and pulled the tennis ball from his mouth.

"Let this man tell us what happened."

"I was not here," he said. His voice was clear and brittle, like it could break. "I have never been in this house."

"Apin, the big guy," said Gwen. "He was the one who crashed in and shot me."

"Is that right, Mr. Charles? Was it Mr. Apin who did it?"

"Apin? I don't know any man named Apin."

"Oh." Archie sounded disappointed, even to himself. He slid his left hand into his pocket and slipped out the S&W S.W.A.T. knife, thumbing it open. It was a never-used First Millennium Run with a short black blade, incomprehensibly sharp. He put the point on Charles's forehead, mid-latitude, far left side.

"Mr. Charles, we have a situation. This is it: you will tell me what happened that night, or I'll cut your throat with this knife and let you bleed out in the bathroom here. Your blood on Gwen's."

"That's awful," she said.

"I know it's awful, and I don't want to do it," said Archie. "But if he tells me everything I want to know, I'll let him go."

The blue eyes looked uncertain, as if the man wasn't sure he was being spoken to.

"Now," said Archie, "look in the mirror."

He swept the knife lightly. Charles wrenched his head but couldn't move it far because he was contained, chin to tiptoes, by the carpet roll from the home-improvement center. The roll was snugged up to him with ten triple-wrapped belts of duct tape and five flat nylon straps with quick-release fasteners. Inside, his hands and ankles were secured by plastic department-issue restraints. He leaned upright in the bathroom corner, stiff as a mummy. Out in the bedroom was the mechanic's creeper on which Archie had wheeled him from the garage, along the side walkway, into the kitchen, down the hall and into the master bath. And the gag, freshly cut away to encourage free speech.

A line of blood jumped to Sonny's forehead, then washed down over and ran into his eyes.

"God," said Gwen.

"Be strong," said Archie. He reached over the carpet collar to touch the blade to Charles's carotid. A tight fit. Blood from the cut forehead eased over the knife blade and Archie's knuckles. "You've got five seconds to start talking. I don't really like this kind of thing, so I'm getting it over quick either way."

"I drove," said Pretty Blond. "Zlatan shot you and killed her. There, now you will let me go?"

"He put the gun in my hand?"

"Yes."

"And her blood on my robe."

"Yes."

Archie stared into the hard blue eyes, now blinking through the curtain of blood.

"What kind of bullet is in my head?"

"Twenty-two."

"A silenced automatic?"

Sonny nodded as the blood ran off his chin and onto the backing of the carpet.

"You'll need to tell me every detail of that night. Every small detail. And where I can find Mr. Apin when I need to. Then, if what you say turns out to be true, I'll let you go. But you'll never drive a getaway car for another murder, I can promise you that."

Archie watched the hope drain away from Sonny Charles's eyes. He turned on the small tape recorder that he'd set on the bathroom counter between the sinks.

"You've got my word, Mr. Charles. Here, let's get a bandage on that cut while you tell me what you did. Honey, do we have any rubbing alcohol?"

TWENTY-EIGHT

Rayborn and Zamorra sat in the blue department sedan outside Ascension Cemetery on the hope that Archie would cruise his wife's funeral. They got there half an hour early for the eleven o'clock service, rolled down the windows and waited.

A few minutes later the guests began arriving. Merci watched them park near the chapel for the memorial service, saw the black suits and dresses moving with slow respect through the inland heat.

The Kuerners and the Wildcrafts arrived separately but walked into the chapel together. George drove the Mercedes, a gift from his son, with an almost sacred caution. Rayborn saw Brad Eccles—Archie's alleged best friend—arrive with a big-hipped woman in a wide black hat. A moment later Damon Reese pulled up in a new black pickup truck with pipes that made it rumble and a vinyl bed cover that gave off heat waves. Merci watched him shut the door and make his way alone into the chapel. She felt his touch on her forehead again, wondered if he'd call like he said he would, wondered if she'd answer it.

"How's Kirsten?" Merci asked. She asked about Kirsten irregularly, but now seemed as good a time as ever.

"She's fine. She told me we should get married."

"What did you say back?"

"That I'm not ready."

"It's only been a year."

Zamorra was quiet for a long beat. Then, "Funny how the same amount of time can seem like a year or five minutes, depending on your mood. How about you and Frank?"

"I see him occasionally. Movies, dinner. He's real good with Tim."

"I'd like to meet him."

"One of these days we'll have you two over for dinner. Dad's a good cook. Tim would like to see you again."

"I'd like that."

"How about when we catch these Russian gangsters? That'll give all of us reason to celebrate."

"Perfect."

But she wouldn't invite Paul and Kirsten over, and she knew it, and that was fine with Rayborn. When she looked at Zamorra she felt interest and attraction, but less than before. She felt disappointment, but less of that, too. Merci did not believe that people came together "for a reason," or, certainly, that things always "happened for the best." She thought a lot of decent people got together for bad reasons, that much was obvious. But she also thought that she and Paul would be good, and it dented her pride to think that she somehow hadn't made the grade. But what *exactly* was missing? Ask him, she thought.

Priscilla Brock arrived with her husband. Merci watched them walk in, nominally together, Charles ahead by two steps, oblivious to her. Priscilla seemed not to care. Merci wondered if Gwen had had the same casual radiance.

A minute later a panel van with a wheelchair lift parked and an orderly helped a very old woman position her chair. The lift engine groaned and the woman descended to the asphalt. Merci watched her: white hair and white hands, head cocked sideways, brand-new black shoes that had never been and never would be walked in. The orderly slammed the van door shut and pushed the woman toward the chapel.

Then a group of young deputies who looked about Archie's age, fashionable guys, not meat-and-potatoes cops like Damon Reese. The kind of men who liked a little style and could pull it off. Archie's friends, she thought, and Gwen's admirers. She gave them credit for coming.

"I've heard lots of talk about this funeral the last couple of days," said Zamorra. "Half the deputies have Archie good for the murder. The other half thinks he got himself mixed up in something he shouldn't have."

Merci watched as one of the cool young cops conferred with the woman in the wheelchair, then took over for the nodding orderly.

"That's what I got, too," said Merci.

Left unspoken was the fact that half the department wouldn't talk to Rayborn in the first place. Those who did tended to be the younger men and women who had advanced and profited from Rayborn's testimony about a corrupt phalanx in Chuck Brighton's old guard. The most awful side effect of that testimony, in Rayborn's opinion, was that some good old deputies had gone down with Brighton while some undeserving younger ones had risen to replace them. By the end of her grand jury appearance Merci had been ready to disclaim everybody, cash out her meager savings and take Tim down to Mexico in search of the pink house on the white beach that she had often thought about but never seen. Zamorra had not allowed her to throw away her badge.

"These deputies who've come," she said, "I respect them for showing."

Merci had never seen admin so quiet on such a hot department issue as the Wildcraft case. There had been no official guidance, no meetings or memos, none of the unofficial "policy" that often leaked from behind the closed doors of the sheriff's office. Those who thought Archie was innocent were staying low, and the ones who thought he was guilty were staying even lower. Lots of I-told-you-sos waiting to be spoken, Merci thought. Lots of bets covered.

She watched a couple of young deputies and their wives or girlfriends stepping out of a van. The driver waited until they were out then locked the vehicle with a chirp. He looked at one of the dark windows and ran his fingertips along the hair behind his ear.

Maybe it was Wildcraft's own fault, she thought: he had built the wall around himself, he had brandished his weapon at Brice, he had the temper and the pretty wife and had stubbed his toe on more money than the guys he worked with would ever see. Maybe if Archie had been a little more open, a little more forthcoming, then people could rally behind him now, take up his cause. She had long suspected that being open and forthcoming were often methods for self-advancement rather than signs of good character, but what did this matter?

More opinions, she thought. More loud, useless opinions.

Rayborn, too young for wisdom but old enough to become tired of herself, sighed and shook her head slowly and stared out through the heat as the door of the chapel swung closed.

"So you get a deputy shot in the head," she said. "And his wife takes two in her own bathroom. He can't go to his wife's funeral because he thinks we'll put him in the hospital or under arrest or both. He's out trying to catch the creeps himself because he doesn't think we are. That isn't right."

After the memorial service the mourners drove to the grave site. The cortege moved slowly through the cemetery and Merci stayed far behind so as not to annoy the Wildcraft and Kuerner families any more than she had to. She wanted to march over there to the hole in the ground and tell them she was sorry about Gwen, that she was really pulling for Archie every way she could, really wanted to button down this case and get a little justice done for their girl. But instead she parked by the rounded curb and endured a long hostile stare from Natalie Wildcraft as she walked from her Mercedes to the grave.

From the car Merci could see the dark mourners and the green hillock and a pile of red earth covered by a blue tarp. There were two big black boxes that looked like loudspeakers—far too much power, she thought, for the meager audience. The casket was gunmetal gray with gold accents. She flashed on Gwen in her bathroom—the robe and her blood and the cell phone in the sink, and thought: what a way to go to the satin. Twenty-six years old.

She was too far away to hear what the preacher was saying. Merci caught the earnest baritone coming across the grass and asphalt to her and it seemed like that sound must always be here, part of nature, like the breeze. Why not use the speakers?

At eleven fifty-seven Merci saw the helicopter waver into view and she wondered if Archie had friends with the air patrol. Her second thought was network news. The bird squatted in the blue sky and lowered upon the graveyard, tail swinging around like a cat's as it came closer to the ground.

By then she saw it wasn't a Sheriff's Department or a news chopper, at least it wasn't marked that way. She wrote down the numbers on the tail.

It leveled off a couple of hundred feet above the grave and she could see hair and black clothes rippling and jumping in the rotor wind, and hear the bone-tickling *whump whump whump* of the blades. Down it came, another fifty feet. The dirt swirled up from the edges of the tarp and the tarp jittered against the mound.

Then the oddest thing: Natalie Wildcraft beside the preacher, holding him by the arm with one hand and raising her other one high, waving it back and forth as she tried to shout above the roar to the mourners.

Merci could see the guy in the chopper, not the pilot but the man behind him in a baseball cap, bracing himself behind the open door of the passenger bay. He threw something from what looked like a bucket. A faint pink burst spotted the air, then exploded in the turbulent wind from the rotors.

Two of the deputies drew down on one knee, aiming up with their sidearms.

Some of the mourners covered their heads and ran in one direction, others running the opposite way.

Rayborn scrambled out of the car, popped the thumb brake and started to draw her H&K, but it didn't make sense so she left her hand on the grip and watched. Another burst from above, and another. It looked like the man was airing out a bedsheet next, and the air filled again with a pale storm of color that blew apart like a pastel firework when it hit the chopper's wind.

Natalie Wildcraft stood with both hands raised to the machine.

Merci understood. The mourners who hadn't run were waving and cheering and the helicopter dipped a little lower. More buckets of color dumped into the sky then, as the first bits settled down over the grave site and the mourners, and the deputies stood with their sidearms now literally at their sides.

Rayborn was trotting toward the chopper, looking up as Wildcraft threw another bucket into the air. She watched the confetti wobble down, and when she was close enough to catch some she got flower blossoms and rose petals and bits of curled gold ribbon. Daisies and marigolds and periwinkles and zinnias and gazanias and geraniums and a lot she couldn't ID.

Natalie went over to the speakers, bent for a moment, then music burst forth. Merci recognized Gwen Wildcraft's soft clear voice through the mechanical percussion of the blades. Archie threw out another bucket of blossoms, then another, then what looked like another bedsheet full. Where had he gotten them all?

I've got to get through to you
I've got to get next to you

Zamorra stood beside her, a red rose petal stuck in his black hair and a look of disapproving awe on his face.

"Sonofabitch," he said quietly.

"Son of a something," said Rayborn.

She watched the sky rain flowers, jumped forward to catch a few more, but it was harder than it looked, the way the petals zigzagged in the wind and the blossoms bobbed like parachutes.

Tiny Natalie Wildcraft faced her from the grave site, her fists clenched and raised over her head like a new flyweight champion, her mouth open in exultation or challenge—no way to tell over the hugely amplified post-mortem voice of Gwen Wildcraft or the thump of the helo—but what Merci got out of it was that Natalie was offering Archie's attendance as the latest proof of his love and devotion and innocence.

A white-and-orange CNB van leaned around a curve behind them and skidded to a stop. Out spilled a shooter and Michelle Howland.

"We're in the air for this," said Zamorra. "Abelera wanted a helo on call in case the news people used choppers."

"Call them."

But she made no move to call them herself. The chopper was already banking away and lifting fast. In a windblown flourish the last of the flowers showered down on the mourners while Archie shot toward the straight-up noonday sun.

TWENTY-NINE

They stood on the porch of Sonny Charles's last known address, a neat town house in Costa Mesa, over by the fairgrounds.

"I've never heard of Sonny Charles," said Ruth Greider. She was red-haired, mid-fifties, stocky. "I bought this home from a very nice couple."

Merci explained in humorless terms how important it was to find a man who had once lived here. She implied that lives might be at stake. "Were the couple eastern Europeans?" she asked.

"Russian. The Selatsins—Jerry and Mary."

One hour later they sat in the cool living room of the Huntington Beach home of Mr. and Mrs. Vsevolod "Jerry" Selatsin, who admitted to buying the Costa Mesa town house from Sonny Charles in March of 1999 and selling it to Ruth Greider eight months ago.

"It's in good condition when we buy," said Jerry. "And good condition when we sell." He was thick-boned and white-haired, with a strong neck and jolly blue eyes that looked like they could change weather in a heartbeat. Sixty. His wife, whom he introduced as Marina, was slender and svelte, with a pale face and dark eyes. Half of Jerry's age. Her smile was sad.

"We need to talk to Mr. Charles," said Merci. "Do you know where we can find him?"

"We don't know Mr. Charles. We just buy his house," said Jerry.

Marina's already dark features darkened more as she sank back into a leather chair. She moved loosely, like a cat or a weasel, Merci thought.

"You had never met him before you bought his home?"

"No."

"Ever hear *about* him, Mr. Selatsin?"

Jerry Selatsin rolled his strong shoulders and then his pale blue eyes. "You know, everyone knew about Mr. Charles. He made the big money with the homosexuals in Laguna. All legal."

"How did you hear about Mr. Charles's town house being for sale?"

Jerry nodded and Marina sank still further into her chair. "Friends of mine, they know Sonny. They put us together for the sale."

"Who? I need their names. I need to see them, quickly."

Marina Selatsin rattled off a sentence that Merci assumed was Russian. It sounded spiteful and confessional at the same time. She thought she recognized something in it.

"Zlatan Vorapin?" Merci asked. "Al Apin?"

Jerry iced his wife with a stare, then tried to soften it as he turned to Merci.

"Mr. Al Apin was the one. He was always coming to my office. I do American taxes and IRS for recent immigrants, they don't understand the complexity of the system. He have work for me. He works in immigration, helps people come to U.S. We talk about Moscow. I need a house."

"He set you up with Sonny."

Marina shifted in the seat and lit a cigarette. She coughed quietly. Merci felt the waves of anger coming off her, tried to figure the rough outline of why.

Because Apin set Marina up in the States, too, Merci thought. And she worked off the debt like the other young women did. Until she found her husband, questionably a move up.

Jerry's hearty eyes had gone downward now and Merci saw the tension lines cross his forehead.

"And you bought the Costa Mesa town house for a very, very low price, because Sonny had taken it from a dying man for about half what it was worth."

"This is true. And legal."

"Where's Apin?"

"I don't know. I never know. He is here. He is gone."

Marina curled up into the chair like a cat, bringing her legs under her.

"He is a fucking criminal, like Sonny Charles," she said, not much more than a whisper. "Criminals in Vladivostok and criminals here, the same. Tell him about the Bar Czar, Vsevolod. Or I will."

Big Jerry Selatsin shrugged and looked from his seething wife to Merci, to Zamorra. "Bar Czar, a joke on America that has czar for this and czar for that. On a Lincoln Street up in Anaheim. Little place. Russians, Russians and Russians."

"Al?"

"Maybe, maybe not. You don't tell him I say hello. You don't tell him Marina talk about him. She would like to forget about him. I want to remain alive. Correct?"

Vic Elbe, who owned and managed the Bar Czar, was a short, slight man with a bald tanned head and green eyes. He wore jeans and a broadly striped shirt like a country singer, a tremendous belt buckle in the shape of a bear.

He said he had not seen Al Apin or Sonny Charles in years, though Merci suspected he had. He said he'd call her immediately if he saw them, though Merci knew he wouldn't. He suggested they try the Hot Zone strip club in Santa Ana because everyone knows Al likes the girls.

The Hot Zone was in a nondescript industrial park near the 55 Freeway. It was owned by Johnny Reno, a dapper young man with a scar that ran from the side of his forehead to the bottom of his ear. Reno—no relation to Janet, he said—told them that he hadn't seen Al Apin since the last time he threw him out of the Hot Zone for trying to muscle in with his own talent. Real funny of Vic, he said, to send them over here.

Apin had told Reno that he had European girls who could dance, beautiful girls, blondes, not the dark ethnic stuff you usually found in Southern California. Reno had told Apin that he and his customers *liked* the dark ethnic women usually found in Southern California and threw Apin out. That was the last he'd heard of him. They kept a list by the door, said Reno, of guys the bouncers won't let in. Apin was number one.

"How do you throw out a guy who's six-ten, three-fifty?" Merci asked him.

"He put three of my bouncers in the hospital. After that, we just called you guys. He didn't want to talk to the cops."

"Where can we find him? And don't say talk to Vic Elbe."

Reno smiled, the big scar shifting back a little on his head. "Sergeant, if I knew where to find Al Apin I'd tent the place and fumigate it."

"That's exactly what we'd like to do."

Smiling still, shaking his head: "I heard he's got four girls and a lock on the Camino Newport Hotel. The girls are getting five hundred for a quick half and half, three or four times each on a good night. Figure *that* math. I wouldn't look for him in the lounge, but you might draw a girl. Sergeant Zamorra might, I mean. I'm not sure—that's only what I heard. I don't keep up with that stuff. I run a clean place and you can ask any of my dancers."

"Yeah," said Merci. "If it gets any cleaner they'll want to do Brownie tours."

She could tell by his perplexed smile that he had no idea what she was talking about.

They were on the way to the Camino Newport when Merci's phone rang. It was Grant Nolan, owner of Pace Charters and the helicopter that had flown Wildcraft over the cemetery, returning Rayborn's call.

When she explained what had happened and what she needed, Grant Nolan went silent, then asked her to hold for just a moment.

He was back a minute later. He sighed. "Yes, we chartered that flight to Larry Gray of Laguna Hills. One hour at five hundred and sixty dollars for a birthday party surprise. He paid in cash and we took him up. The pilot wasn't that happy about buzzing a funeral."

He gave her the information that Wildcraft had used to charter the helo—his own address and number.

"What kind of car was he driving?"

"A late-model Durango."

"Thank you. If he contacts you again, I want you to call me immediately."

She gave him her numbers and punched off.

Zamorra was approached by a young woman exactly fourteen minutes after he sat down in the Camino Newport Hotel bar. The Camino was up at Fashion Island and catered to wealthy tourists. The parking attendants wore tan safari suits with red piping and the concierge could cheerfully exchange into dollars the currencies of twelve prosperous nations at rates only slightly higher than the banks offered.

Merci, who had come in before her partner, loitered at a window table for two. Her cell phone lay on the table in front of her, turned off. She looked out the window and checked her watch often, trying to look like someone losing a tremendously valuable boyfriend.

The woman got out of a black Porsche. She looked mid-twenties and carried a Neiman-Marcus shopping bag. Her figure was excellent in a calf-length black dress. Heels with straps and a handbag that glittered and her honey-blonde hair restrained in a strict French braid. Heavy mouth. Her dark blue earrings caught the light when she looked at Merci, vaporizing her with a glance. She sat one stool apart from the sleek, black-suited Zamorra. A few minutes later she laughed. Merci could hear their voices but not their words. Zamorra smiled and motioned over the barkeep. The woman moved next to him and got what looked like a martini, something clear in a stemmed triangular glass. When the woman's drink was gone she took Zamorra's arm and the handsome couple walked out of the lounge and into the lobby. Merci could see them heading for the elevator, heads tilted toward each other like lovers taking their time on their way to ecstasy. She thought of Mike and the call girl he'd fallen in love with, wondered if they'd ever tilted their heads toward each other like that, then men-tally kicked her own ass for wondering it.

Ten minutes later they stepped back out of the elevator. The woman touched Zamorra's cheek, then kissed it lightly, then strode across the lobby. She palmed something to the doorman, who whistled for the valet. Through her window Merci saw the valet pull a set of keys from the box behind his stand, then hustle around a big potted juniper and disappear.

Zamorra sat down.

"How was it?" she asked.

"Perfect in every way. Vorapin runs two women here and two more at the Castaway. They pay him once at one o'clock, then again at nine in the morning. The good news is the payout is at the same place every time—the Bar Czar. The bad news is Vorapin only shows once a week, maybe less. The rest of the time they pay whoever he sends to collect. Various associates. Sometimes Sonny, sometimes not. She's never sure who."

Rayborn groaned quietly. The black Porsche rounded the juniper with a dry growl and the valet sprung out.

"We could spend a lot of nights waiting at the Czar," she said.

"That was the best she could do. It cost the department a hundred."

"No wonder she pecked your cheek. Want a baby wipe?"

"Nice woman, actually."

"No phone for her boss? No address, nothing?"

"Vorapin just comes and goes. You weigh three-fifty you get good at hiding."

"Paul, Vorapin's a pro. Selatsin probably tipped him. Elbe defi-nitely did. Reno might have. That girl will. We're not going to surprise these guys. We're getting farther away, not closer."

"We need to light their cuffs on fire."

"You present it to Abelera. I'm not high on his list right now."

As soon as they stepped outside the hotel and Merci turned her phone back on, Ike Sumich called. He'd found a Russian-language catalogue, published in New York and nationally distributed, that fea-tured a big-and-tall section and offered Foot Rite products for sale. He'd found two big-and-tall catalogues that specialized in upper-end business attire, also distributed in California, also selling Foot Rite. He'd found a military surplus catalogue specializing in Soviet products and memorabilia that *occasionally* offered discontinued or closed-out goods from mainstream manufacturers. This catalogue—Dinky Durkee's Surplus—had offered the Foot Rite Comfort Strider in "extra, extra-extra and extra-extra-extra large sizes" in their January, February and March issues of this year.

Rayborn knew she couldn't subpoena the catalogue retailers without a search warrant on Vorapin. She knew the catalogue retailers would be extremely reluctant to part with any subscriber or sales information. Occasionally, they would confirm a name. Very occasionally, a shipping address.

"Call them all back," she said. "Ask them for a customer list for Orange County if they have it. For the whole state of California, if they don't have it broken down to county."

"They'll say no."

"I know. You're just softening them up for me."

"Ike, the *picador*."

"Right. Then I sweep down upon them with my incredible charm and they cave."

"Hmm."

She thanked Sumich and punched off.

An hour later they were making their case to Abelera and Brenkus. It was five o'clock and the shifts were changing downstairs. Merci looked down from the sheriff's fourth-floor office at the county streets, thick with traffic. There were so many people in the county now it could take you hours to commute from one end of it to the other. She remembered Clark telling her that in the early part of his career he made the drive from south Orange County to *Los Angeles* in forty-five minutes.

Zamorra outlined the evidence for suspicion and Merci could see Abelera nudge the bait, but not take it. Brenkus was a tougher read.

"Bring them in here and talk to them," said Abelera. "That can't hurt."

"We'd like to," said Zamorra. "But it might take weeks to find them. They're way underground. That's where they live. By now they know we're asking questions. What we need to do is splash their faces everywhere, get the public helping. Smoke them out."

The sheriff stared at Zamorra, still uncertain.

"The timing is good," said Zamorra. "The public cares about Gwen Wildcraft. People are talking about Archie after the shotgun thing and the press conference yesterday. Tonight's news is going to have the funeral stunt with the flowers. What people are going to be thinking is, this crazy deputy *couldn't* have shot his own wife. He loves her too much. So now's the time, drop the bomb that we need to question two possible witnesses to the Gwen Wildcraft murder. Use the FBI file photos. Go big with it. Conduct the press conference yourself, sir. Really let people know we need the Russians. The citizens out there will help us. They're worked up about this. That, or we stake out the Bar Czar for the next month and wait. Maybe longer."

Merci said nothing, but she watched Abelera consider. She could see relief stirring behind his face, as the idea of an innocent deputy sank in.

"And there may be another benefit," said Zamorra. "If Archie thinks the temperature's down, maybe he'll come to us. We can get him to the hospital, we can question him again about that night. If he's strong enough, and willing, we can hypnotize him and find out everything he saw and heard. To hear Stebbins tell it, it's that easy to unlock his traumatic amnesia. It's done all the time."

Brenkus sat back, laced his fingers over his neat gut. "Paul, Merci, do you honestly think these guys framed Archie?"

"I do," said Merci.

"I think there's a damned good chance they did," said Zamorra.

"Why frame a guy and then kill him, or try to kill him?"

"To cover their own butts," said Rayborn. "But I don't think they planned it. The opportunity just presented itself and they took it. When Archie went down, Vorapin saw the chance to make the thing look like a murder-suicide. He grabbed Archie's gun and went to work. When they were done with Gwen they wiped their goddamned gloves off on Archie's robe, put his hand on the gun while he bled on the walkway, pulled the trigger using his finger. Messy, but simple."

Brenkus raised his eyebrows, a man skeptical but optimistic. "I'd love prosecuting two Russian gangsters rather than one Orange County deputy. Talk to the Russians. I don't have a problem with that, especially if it gets Wildcraft back to us." Brenkus looked over at Abelera. "And I'll make a cameo at your press conference if you want, Vince."

"Maybe Ryan would like to do it," said Merci.

She sat at her desk and looked through Ike Sumich's handwritten notes on the catalogue companies. All had refused his request for Orange County addresses of their subscribers. Two had asked to speak to his superior, indicating they might cooperate with someone more important than CSI Ike Sumich.

She called them back and made her case—not for an entire county's worth of subscribers, but for the confirmation of just one name: Al Apin.

One of the executive big-and-tall catalogues refused again, referring Merci to a lawyer.

The other agreed to look up this one name, but no Al Apin appeared on their customer lists for the last two years.

The offices for the Russian-language catalogue out of New York were closed.

Gail Durkee, the sales manager for Dinky Durkee's Surplus out of Portland, Oregon, pleasantly refused to search her database for the name.

"It would be a huge help to me if you would, Ms. Durkee."

"I'm so sorry, Detective. But I can't do it. It's against our policy. Dinky—I mean Ernie—would kill me."

"I understand, Ms. Durkee, but, please, let me tell you just a little something about this case."

Rayborn hated to play the gender card, but she played it anyway. She explained that a young wife had been murdered in very cold blood, a girl who'd married her high school sweetheart—a law enforcement officer in good standing with her department—and together they'd

struggled to make a good life. Merci even explained that it looked like
this young woman had gotten involved with organized gangsters who
took over a company she was working for. When this woman resisted
their corruption, she was murdered in her own home, and her loving
husband was shot and left for dead.

Zamorra offered Merci a small smile.

"Oh, the lady with the funny last name?" Durkee asked. "Wildman
or Wildflower or something like that?"

"In strictest confidence, Gail—yes. Gwen Wildcraft."

"We've had the story up here. I thought the husband was the *suspect*."

"Not anymore. The name we need is Apin. Al Apin."

She spelled it. A silence then, and Merci heard the tapping of a
keyboard.

"Sergeant, can I call you back in exactly five minutes?"

"Please don't disappoint me, Ms. Durkee. I need your help."

"Five minutes."

Rayborn hung up, predisappointed because she knew Gail Durkee
was not going to call. She sat back and thought about Archie Wildcraft
dumping pounds of flowers over his wife's grave site while friends
scattered and flummoxed deputies drew their weapons on him. She
wondered what it would look like on CNB.

Pounds of flowers.

She thought of something then, and went over to Teague's desk to
use his phone. From her blue notebook she got the number of Archie's
gardener, Jesus, who had looked at her so forlornly when she asked
him to go with God.

When he answered she identified herself, then told Jesus that it was
his duty to tell her what number Archie had given him to call regarding
the flowers.

"Flowers?"

"The flowers he wanted you to collect. You know the ones I mean,
Jesus—he asked you to get a whole bunch of flowers. Just the blossoms and blooms, not the whole stem."

"He no want me to say nothing."

"You can say something to me, Jesus. It's important. Where was he? How were you supposed to contact him when you had the flowers?"

The phone on Rayborn's desk started ringing. Zamorra moved to answer it but she waved him off. "Jesus? I'm going to tell you what you're going to do. You're going to go get that address and phone number, and you're going to hold that telephone to your ear until I come back. Is this clear?"

"Yes, is clear."

"Can you do it?"

"Yes, okay."

She punched the hold button and got to her own desk on the fourth ring.

"Sergeant, this is Gail at Dinky's? We sold a pair of Foot Rite Comfort Striders to an Al Apin of Fullerton last March. I've got the shipping address and a phone."

"Shoot."

She was half astonished to find Jesus still waiting. Jesus gave her an address in Irvine and a phone number.

"He is in a room two . . . seventeen."

"Thank you, Jesus, *vaya con Dios*."

"*Vaya con Dios*, police woman."

She pulled her blazer off the back of her chair and slung it over her shoulder. "I just got addresses for Archie and Vorapin."

Archie's address was for La Quinta Inn, right off the interstate. It looked to Merci like an old agricultural or industrial building of some kind, or maybe just made up to look like one. She drove around and tried to spot room 217 from the parking lot but the doors were all inside. No Durango.

She parked in a corner of the lot and followed Zamorra inside. She glanced at the display of some old piece of canning or packing machinery, scanned the sign that told about it, watched the family that burst suddenly from the elevator. There was a bawling boy with tears jetting from his eyes, a woman loaded with baggage scolding a man loaded with luggage, who also pushed a stroller containing a shrieking baby. Zamorra leaned in, holding open the door for them.

When the elevator was finally empty he picked something off the floor and gave it to Merci: a small white flower with a yellow center. She looked at him and said nothing.

The maid's cart was parked outside the open front door. A short stocky woman ran a loud vacuum cleaner and Merci looked in at the made bed, the paper-wrapped water glasses on the counter, the drawn drapes. She opened the trash can on the cart and saw the most recent load: wads of tissues, some faintly pinked by blood, and a collection of now-wilting flowers. No stems or stalks, just flowers and loose petals. She reached in and pulled out a long scrap of blue tarp. It was almost a yard long and roughly a foot wide. One side was cut straight, the other curved. One end was squared, the other rounded gracefully like the tip of a sword. She had no idea what it was for so she dropped it back in the trash can, then unhinged the liner bag, knotted it and slung it over her shoulder.

She nodded at the maid as if she was obeying orders from the woman. She cursed Jesus for tipping off his boss that she had called. On her way to the lobby her temper ebbed as she realized that Jesus might just be innocent and that Archie might just be luckier—or more clever—than she had thought.

At the desk Zamorra badged the manager and found out that Jim Green had paid cash for room 217 for three nights, but only stayed two. He had checked out at four, just a few hours ago. The manager said that Mr. Green wore a baseball cap and sunglasses and did not make conversation. Mr. Green loaded several large framed pictures of beautiful women into his Durango. Not provocative pictures, nothing obscene, more like portraits. They may even have been of the same woman. He had also loaded some fairly long, flat objects that were covered with what looked like old bedsheets. Roughly, he said, the objects were the shape and size of surfboards, but appeared to be very lightweight. He had loaded several rocks that sat on stands. Earlier today—in the morning, around ten—Mr. Green had talked with a Mexican-looking man who drove a small pickup truck with gunnysacks full of something in the back. It was a gardener's truck, with rakes and hoes upright in holders on the side of the bed. They had loaded the gunnysacks into Mr. Green's Durango and he had driven off, wearing his baseball cap and sunglasses.

Merci read the registration card. Wildcraft had used his real address and phone number, changing only his name. She pocketed the card then grabbed the knotted trash bag and headed for her Impala, leaving her partner to thank the manager.

They called for backup on Vorapin. The four uniforms met them on Imperial Highway behind a convenience store, where Zamorra briefed them. One of the deputies would carry the twelve-gauge riot gun from his cruiser, one other a Taser, and the remaining two were instructed to have their pepper spray in hand and ready. The youngest deputy told Sergeant Rayborn that the newly issued spray was "incredibly effective."

On the drive through the Fullerton hills Merci unsnapped the thumb brake on her Bianchi. She thought of a man she'd killed and the bullet hole he'd put in her. She felt the taut pull of the scar on her side as she leaned forward to make sure her little .40-caliber ankle cannon was snug against her left leg. She sat back and banished these memories. She refused to be haunted by what she had done. Killing another human alters the soul, though, and Rayborn knew this.

It was a little after seven. She looked out at the big houses, the circular driveways filled with shiny new cars, the old palms that towered and drooped like they'd seen it all before. They passed a Florentine palazzo, a small Norman castle and a Greek temple.

"Left side," said Zamorra. "The ranch house under the big pine."

They passed it. It was large and rambling, with dark windows recessed under the deep overhang of roof. The shingles were warped and lifting. In front was an enormous Norfolk Island pine going dry in the August heat. The driveway was cracked and littered with browned needles and led to a garage almost invisible from the road. The place had an air of neglected nobility that made Rayborn uneasy. The bullet scar on her side was still tight and throbbing, like a patch put on too tight. Why now?

Zamorra made a left on the next side street, then a U-turn, then a right, heading back the way they'd come. He parked along the curb, two doors short of Vorapin's address. As arranged, the two patrol cars came by a few minutes later and took their time ambling into position, one unit in front of the unmarked, and one across the street facing the other direction.

Rayborn sent one deputy around the left side of the house, another around the right. Then she walked up the drive, with Zamorra two steps behind and to her left, and Taser and Twelve Gauge behind him. She stepped up to the porch, and as her hand went to the grip of the nine she registered: cobwebs in the eaves and dust on the side windows and cracks in the plaster and most of the shrubs dying.

She rang the doorbell, heard the muted chime from inside. A long wait, then she rang again. And again.

Merci was about to turn away when the door opened and a woman in a tight green dress looked at her. Thirty-something, auburn hair pinned up, eyes the shineless green of cash.

"No," the woman said.

"No what?" asked Merci.

"To whatever you want."

The woman moved to close the door and Merci straight-armed the wood. "I'm Sergeant Rayborn, County Sheriff's. We're looking for Zlatan Vorapin, also known as Al Apin."

Rayborn got her duty boot between the door and the floorboard, swung back her coat to show the badge and the nine. Money-eyes looked impressed. There was a hallway behind her.

"Open this door and invite us in, lady," she said. "Get Vorapin. This is about a murder and you do *not* want to make me angry right now."

Rayborn looked past the woman's shoulders, ready for movement. The hallway opened to a living room.

"He is not here." Her voice was strong and thick with accent, but of which language Rayborn had no way of knowing.

"Then you don't mind if we look around, is that what you're saying? That's okay, sure, we'll come in if you say we can, just swing that door open for me. . . ."

"He is only here not very often."

"My name's Merci. What's yours?"

"Irene."

"Irene, just let me in, will you, dear?"

"I am leaving."

"I won't make you late. Just give us a few minutes."

Irene turned away and Merci wasted not one second, pressing in ahead of Zamorra, then turning to wave in Taser and Twelve Gauge. She kept her palm on the Pachmayr grip of the H&K as she followed Irene into the living room.

A lamp turned low, weak light, gray leather sofa and love seat, a glass coffee table. Zamorra moved into the kitchen. Irene watched the big-armed deputies jangle down a long hallway toward the bedrooms.

"You work for him?" asked Merci.

Irene shook her head quickly. "Yes and no."

"You help out."

"I help out."

"Are you his girlfriend?"

"This is not a word I use."

"Where is he?"

"Zlatan never tells. He comes when he comes. This house is one he bought for me. There are others. I don't know them and I don't want to know them."

"Do you make his pickups at the Bar Czar at one and nine?"

"Only sometimes."

"Tonight?"

"I am not told until."

Merci flipped on a wall switch and the overhead track lighting came on. She could see that Irene was probably late thirties. Her makeup was half finished, her eyes tired. One pearl earring. Irene looked at her, then away.

"Where can we find him?"

"Always moving."

"Where does he sleep?"

"I don't know. This is the truth. Sometimes here but not often. One time each week, perhaps."

"And you don't know one single other place he might lay down for the night?"

"I do not."

"Or one single other place he does business, collects money, hangs out and drinks with his friends?"

"Bar Czar."

"When?"

"Impossible. I am not often there."

"What about Cherbrenko?"

"I have met him and seen him with Zlatan. Partners in business."

"Show me his room."

Without a word Irene led her down the hallway to the end, then opened a door and flicked on a light. Merci followed down two steps that led to a big bedroom. There was a gaudy brass bed with black sheets and covers, a gold ice bucket on a stand by one side, a huge television rising from beyond the foot of the bedstand. The room smelled of cologne and BO and cigarette smoke.

"Does he have an office here in the house?"

"Yes. This way."

She led Merci through the bedroom, past a huge master bath with a red-tile shower and whirlpool, toilet and bidet, all with gold fixtures.

"He's got horrible taste," said Merci.

Irene shrugged.

"Why don't you quit?"

"He knows where to find my daughter."

"Maybe I'll arrest him for murder, get him out of your hair."

Irene looked at her, the planes of her face weighted by fear. "He's everywhere. You must arrest them all."

"I'd like to."

They went through French doors and into a faintly lit back room paneled in dark wood, with a cluttered desk along one wall, a black leather sofa pushed against another. A big TV dominated a corner, viewable from sofa or desk. Irene turned on the lights and a ceiling fan began to turn. More smoke and cologne.

"What's he watch on all these big screens?"

"Shopping channels and pornography."

"Does he make his own movies?"

Irene actually colored. "No. They show amputated people and violence."

"Irene, are you going to tell me where to find this guy?"

"I can not."

"You can call me as soon as you know where he'll be."

"I should risk my child for you?"

"He'd never know."

"He will know, Sergeant. I am not a foolish girl anymore. Please do not behave that way to me."

Merci walked around the desk and stood by the chair. The seat was adjusted so high it came almost to her hips. The desk legs rested on cinder blocks, apparently spray-painted gold. On the desktop was a clean blotter, a small Russian flag upright in a holder, a notepad, an ashtray filled with butts, a calendar with August's model reclining invitingly in the back of a black stretch limousine. The promotional header above the photograph was of a neon car swooping through the sky. The name of the company was in hot blue text: Air Glide Limousines.

"Air Glide," said Merci.

"Friends of his," said Irene.

"No wonder they told me they didn't have any giants for drivers."

"No one talks about Zlatan. You must understand."

"Understand what?"

Irene stared at her and Merci stared back. "How he is without restraint."

"I'm beginning to."

"Then get out, please."

Serve and protect, thought Rayborn.

She pulled at the center desk drawer but it caught against its lock. The side drawers were locked also.

"Give me the key," she said.

Irene sighed, then moved to the door and reached above the frame. She brought it to Rayborn, dropped it onto the blotter.

Top drawer: pencils, pens, a notepad promoting a company called NexLess. Merci held the pad to the light, saw no imprints on the top sheet but stripped it off and put it in her pocket anyway. There was a magnifying glass with a nice wooden handle. Matches, rubber bands, paper clips. A key chain with a clear acrylic disk that said *OrganiVen*.

"What did he say about Gwen Wildcraft?"

"Nothing."

"Archie Wildcraft."

"Nothing. I read the papers about them."

"Don't tell me he never said anything about OrganiVen."

"He did not. Why would he talk business with me?"

"Except the girls."

Merci looked at her, tried to figure the bend of Irene's psyche that accommodated Zlatan Vorapin in whatever way she did. Came up with nothing but fear. Confirmed by the flatness of Irene's green eyes as she stared through her.

"He was here. The man with the bullet in his head."

Rayborn felt her pulse jump, then the cool fingers of adrenaline moving through her. "When?"

"Afternoon today. He waited across the street in a sports utility car. I watched from a window. When he took off his hat and looked at his head in the mirror, I knew it was him. From television."

Irene shook her head, looked at her watch and brought her hand to the ear without the pearl. "I must finish and go."

"Thank you. Just so you know, Vorapin put that bullet in the man's head. Murdered his wife in her own bathroom, shot her once in the heart and once in the brain."

She offered Irene a card and the woman backed away.

"That would be foolish."

"Yes, it would. You'll remember my name. The operator will give you the department number."

"I've done too much for you. You can do nothing good for me. Go and never say to Zlatan that we talked."

Rayborn pocketed her card and turned to find Zamorra and the two uniforms examining the shower in Vorapin's bathroom. Twelve Gauge pointed at the gold nozzle, situated a full foot higher than the standard. Merci joined them, disturbed by the height of the thing.

"He's got some newspapers in his laundry room," said Zamorra. "Just certain sections, not the whole paper. They go back a week, and every one of them has something about Archie or Gwen in it."

"OrganiVen stuff in his desk," said Merci. She looked at Irene, who stared through a window like she wanted to fly out of it.

On the way down the hall Merci stopped and glanced into one of the bedrooms. There was a makeup table set up along one wall, with a lighted mirror and a chair in front of it. The chair was pushed back. A cigarette had burned down in the ashtray and the dead ash snaked from the filter down into the glass. A pearl earring sat next to a large tumbler of something clear over ice.

By the time they got back to headquarters, Zamorra had called Sheriff Abelera at home and talked him into authorizing twelve-hour after-dark undercover surveillance on the Bar Czar, Air Glide Limousine, Vorapin's home in the Fullerton hills and Archie Wildcraft's million-five spread in Hunter Ranch.

"I know, sir. I understand. Thank you."

When Zamorra punched off Merci asked him what the sheriff had said.

"He said he was holding a press conference tomorrow at noon. He's going to do the talking himself. We'll have a dedicated line for information and people to answer it twenty-four/seven. I can tell he's not convinced on the Russians, but he wants to be. The last thing he wants is Archie guilty. But he's got to *act* like he wants Archie guilty so he doesn't look like he's covering his own. Like Brighton did. He's got the Deputy Association pulling him one way, that prick Dawes leaking our evidence to the media, guys like Gary Brice making entertainment out of it."

Merci said nothing, just looked out the window at the darkened county, the taillights, the signs flipping past overhead.

"I wouldn't want his job," said Zamorra.

"Neither would I."

A lie, but she'd never told him of her plan. It wasn't something you could tell someone without sounding crudely ambitious. But that was the old plan anyhow. It went exactly like this: head of Homicide Detail by age forty; head of the Crimes Against Persons Section by age fifty; elected sheriff by fifty-eight. There had been a time when she believed it was possible. It was the plan of her life.

"You'd make a good sheriff," said Zamorra. "But you'd have to polish your press conference performances."

"Man, would I."

"You've thought about that, haven't you—the job?"

"I used to."

"Don't stop. Things change. Then they change again. That's what you told me when Janine died, and you were right."

She looked out at the county buildings along Flower Street, solid in the fading light. Funny, she thought, how she used to believe that her ninety-two percent conviction rate on homicide cases would pave her way to the office of the sheriff. Simple cause and effect. Girlhood dreams. She felt so much older now. But more real, more keenly attuned to the signals of all that can go wrong.

THIRTY

Tim had dressed himself for his mother's return home: plaid shorts, rubber rain boots, a suede cowboy vest with fringe and a red cowboy hat with his name embroidered on the crown. Stringless bow in one hand, rubber-tipped arrow in the other.

He met her at the screen door as she came across the porch in the lingering heat.

"Awchie threw flowers from the heckilopter."

"Yes, he sure did."

Good to know that her father and son had been monitoring the Wildcraft case. She could see Clark in the depths of the kitchen, looking out at her, keeping an eye on his grandson, too.

Tim banged the door open and clomped across the porch. She swept him up—it took real leg strength to lift him now—and he hugged her as much as the bow and arrow would allow. She tilted back the cowboy hat to reveal a face stained by something orange.

"Awchie is gone in the heckilopter?"

"Gone for now."

"Can you find him?"

"I hope so, Tim. He needs a doctor."

Merci elbowed her way past the screen door, reached up and locked the little deadbolt when they got inside. She set him down and he dropped his bow.

"Can I have your gun?"

"No. Never touch the gun. You know the rule."

"I never touch the gun?"

"Never touch the gun."

"I *can* touch the gun?"

"What do you guys do all day, Dad," she said over Tim. "Just stay home and figure out ways to defy me?"

"Pretty much," he said. "They've been showing Archie and the helicopter over and over on CNB."

"Slow news day."

"You ought to see it. You can't tell at first what's coming out of the chopper, then they zoom in and you see it's flowers. Then they show petals on the coffin. It really gets you. After that they interview the families."

In his rubber boots Tim waded to the TV and turned it on, but it was a commercial for a local car dealership.

"New car?" he asked.

"No, thanks, Tim. The Impala's running fine."

It was too hot and humid to be inside, so they sat on the backyard patio. Merci shooed one of the cats off an Adirondack chair and huffed down into it, wondering why an allegedly classic design was so uncomfortable. Clark had made lemonade but Merci asked for a "hearty" scotch and water over ice. In the near dark, Tim played with a hose on the grass, watering down his hat, vest, shorts, everything. He chased one of the cats but it outran him and his spray. He found a gopher hole, put the hose down it and squatted down to watch the bubbles and mud froth out. She loved the way he squatted.

Merci looked out at Tim and the deep green Valencia orange trees beyond. She wasn't much of an orange eater, but she loved the smell of the trees, and not just the orange blossoms that narcotized you in late winter and early spring, but the astringent summertime smell of leaves and fruit. She was content for a moment, then the feeling was gone.

"Gary Brice left two messages. And Mike called a few minutes ago."

"Mike? What about?"

"Well, not to talk to me."

"Pretty obvious, Dad."

"I really don't know. I'm just telling you he called."

Merci heard a vehicle out on the dirt road that led to their driveway. Probably the grove manager, she thought. Odd that Mike would call, but one of them was bound to break the silence. You don't love someone then arrest that person for a murder he didn't commit, then just ignore each other for the next fifty years.

Clark checked his watch, popped up and headed back toward the house. "I'm going to go get the evening paper," he said. "See if they got pictures of Wildcraft in the chopper."

The screen slider slapped shut and Merci saw Mike McNally's pickup truck bump onto the driveway concrete. She quickly connected the phone call, the watch check, the need for a newspaper and Mike's arrival into a loose conspiracy theory.

She watched the truck come up the drive and park under the floodlights she'd had installed. Mike got out and waved at her, same as he used to. His blond hair was shiny in the light. She saw from the way his hands went suddenly to his hips and the chesty posture that he was nervous.

Danny came around from the passenger's side carrying a small clear box by a handle. Danny was eight now, an intense and humorless boy who had gone far out of his way to ignore Merci when she and his father were together. She'd admired Danny's loyalty to his mother, a woman who treated Mike pretty much like shit so far as Merci saw. Tim spoke often of Mike and Danny, having easily attached himself to a friendly man and a big brother. Merci had explained their departure in vague terms that had never satisfied him. Tim was precise, forgot little, and it angered him to get soft answers to hard questions. She despised herself for taking them out of his life and told herself that someday he would understand. Mike had taken up with CSI Lynda Coiner after the arrest and she'd wondered what Mike told Danny.

Tim bolted for the backyard gate.

Here goes, she thought, taking a large gulp of her drink and pouring the rest into a potted rose tree, leaving the glass upended against the trunk and the ice cubes in the soil.

Merci slid the bolt and Tim pushed open the gate. Danny gave Tim the clear box: a small terrarium containing an alligator lizard he'd caught. Danny didn't look at Merci. Mike extended his hand like a salesman and she shook it, increasingly flummoxed and wishing she'd had some warning on this, then feeling her anger brew because Mike and good old Dad had not extended that common courtesy.

"Thanks for the warning," she said.

"We can't stay, Merci. I told Clark we were just going to drop the lizard off for Tim."

"Well, okay, there's no harm done, Mike. It's great to see you. You too, Danny."

He glanced at her.

"Play with the hose?" Tim asked, pulling Danny by the shirtsleeve. The boy looked to his father for an answer, and Mike looked at Merci.

"Okay," she said. Tim pretty much threw the lizard box at her and the boys bolted.

"We can't stay," Mike said again. "We were just, look, Merci, I know I should have said something to you before we bombed in. I didn't. But I need to talk to you and I thought . . . I figured you'd say no and I didn't want to hear that."

"Okay, okay. Come on in. Let's sit."

Mike lowered himself into one of the torturous Adirondack chairs and Merci offered lemonade.

"No, thanks, really," he said. "I won't be here long."

She sat in the chair next to his and for just a flash felt like a real couple, watching their children play in the yard. Tim had turned the hose on Danny, who dodged in and out of range. She could smell the dogs on Mike because Mike was the department bloodhound handler and three of the hulking monsters—Dolly, Molly and Polly—lived with him.

"It seems like a thousand years since I sat here," he said.

"It does. How are you, Mike?"

"Just fine, really. I'm glad to be out of Vice. Burg-Theft is hopping. You?"

"Hands full with Wildcraft." She had the lizard box on her lap and she saw the creature peeking out at her from under a piece of bark.

"The press conference was bad. Sorry."

"Yup."

"But that's one of the reasons I'm here. I mean, not directly, but related."

"What's up?"

"It's time for the Deputy Association to elect its reps for next year. Pretty much whoever gets nominated gets elected. I'm on the nominating committee and I want to nominate you."

A wrinkle of joy wobbled through her, followed by a hot flatiron of suspicion. She set the terrarium beside her chair.

"Why me, Mike? Half the department hates me."

"It's kind of hard to explain. I'll try, though."

She watched Mike's forehead knit, saw in his clear blue eyes his enduring struggle with words. He'd told her once that he liked being around dogs more than people and meant it.

"Merci, some of it's about you and me. See, what happened wasn't all your fault. And not all Evan O'Brien's fault, either. Some of it was *mine*. So, skip forward until now, and a lot of the deputies, they blame you. And a lot of them took my side, like you just said. But not many of them knew that I fell in love with that girl, and that I deserved to get my ass kicked for it. Not that I deserved exactly how it went down, but . . . well, they just don't know. Am I making sense?"

"Some."

"So I hate it like this, half the guys pulling for me when they don't know what happened, and half of them hating you for no good reason. It's all . . . simplified and stupidified. Like a bunch of children. It's like we're symbols for something. But what you did with Brighton and my dad and yours, God, it must have been hard for you. And it had to be done, Merci. I know it did. I'm glad you did it, even though my dad suffered. He deserved to suffer. Clark deserved to. Brighton deserved to. So what I'm saying is, I was behind you then, even though everybody pulled us apart. And I was too wrapped up in you and the girl and getting arrested to see clear, you know? I just let the crowd carry me along like some kind of wounded hero. It was easy. But I'm sick of it now. It's degrading. I don't want the department torn like this. I want us all at least halfway together. What you did, it cleaned us out, but now nobody gets along. I can't write a memo about all this because it's hard to explain all the emotions I was going through back then. Too personal. I'm sick of my emotions, I really am. But I want you on the board of deputy reps. And if I'm the one to make the nomination, then that just sets all this stuff straight. It says two people who disagreed now agree. I don't mean to sound like I'm important or anything, but it sends a message. I can send a message to this department—forget, forgive, move on. Actually, I can send half that message to the department. And you can send the other half by accepting the nomination and letting it go to a vote. I'll be explaining to the other deputies what happened, as much as I can. I'll be pulling for you. For us. You know, I mean, for the whole department."

He was a little breathless by then, blinking fast like he did when his mind was working hard.

"I haven't said that much at one time in my whole life," he said, smiling. His forehead was relaxed now, but covered in a shine of sweat. "Except maybe to one of my dogs."

A large and basic movement took place inside Rayborn then, and she could feel it, plates of hope and history in realignment. It was like breathing a new way, or having your nerves cleaned and straightened and freshly laid into place.

"I accept."

"You've got a couple of weeks to think about it."

"I accept."

Mike stood but said nothing.

She opened her mouth to say she was sorry, that she was so sorry for everything that had happened, but this was not quite true and she knew it; and she was also about to say she thought he was a good man, really a very good man, but there were a million wrong ways to take that; and she wanted to hold him like you'd hold a brother or an old dear friend or an aging mother or father, but again there was so much that could go wrong. She wiped away a small tear and called upon all her will to keep more from coming.

"Goddamned *hot* today, wasn't it?"

He turned and looked at her. "Ninety-two at Civic Center, about

average for this time of year. Good seeing you, Merci. You look terrific."

"Thanks. How's Lynda?"

"She said she'd break it off if I came over here and asked you to
run. I told her it was off already, then. It shouldn't have gotten to that
point. Even I'm smart enough to know that."

She let Tim stay up an extra hour to watch the late CNB report. Clark
settled in early for it, like it was a playoff game. Merci sat on the
couch beside Tim and stroked his soft hair while Michelle Howland
blabbed her intro over a montage of the annual portraits that the Wildcrafts commissioned of themselves:

*"Was it love or hate? Did the deputy kill his wife? Or did he try
to save her—and get the bullet that is still lodged in his brain? This
is Michelle Howland and tonight we'll have a special look inside the
life of county Sheriff Deputy Archibald Wildcraft—a man many believe was responsible for shooting to death his beautiful young wife,
Gwen. But whom many others believe is a man misunderstood, a
man too deeply in love with his wife to ever do her harm. In the next
hour we'll talk to Archie's and Gwen's parents and friends, to the
people they worked with. You'll hear from doctors and lawyers.
We'll show you how Deputy Wildcraft attended Gwen's funeral today without touching the ground, and we'll show you exclusive CNB
footage of Wildcraft himself, taken just hours after his dramatic funeral appearance. Stay tuned for 'Hero or Killer—the Mystery of
Archie Wildcraft.' "*

That *shithead* Brice, Merci thought, even as she was dialing the
reporter's home number. Brice had located Wildcraft but not bothered
to call her, not even *after* he'd gotten his interview. She got the machine and tried his *Journal*, cell and CNB numbers but got machines
for those also.

"Maybe he was calling here to tell you," said Clark.

"Unbelievable."

Tim looked at her hopefully. "Awchie throws the flowers?"

"Yeah. Right."

She stood abruptly and walked into the kitchen, her bare heels heavy on the hardwood floor. Tim thumped in behind her, still in his rubber mud boots. His brow was furrowed, his eyes wide with alarm.

"You are mad?" .

"I'm not mad at you."

He looked away from her and his bottom lip swelled, then trembled. She picked him up but it was too late. The tears jumped from his eyes like living diamonds. Plenty of volume to his wail. She hugged him and told him over and over that she was mad at *Gary* not at *Timmy* and after a while this worked. She silently cursed her temper and her selfishness. She felt her heart beating against his little pot belly. He stopped crying as quickly as he'd begun, pushed away and looked at her very seriously.

"Why did Awchie throw flowers?"

"Because he loved Gwen."

"Loved Gwen?"

"Yes."

"I down, please."

She set him on the floor and watched him pad purposefully along the hallway toward his room. Another mission. When she got back to the sofa Michelle was interviewing the Kuerners and the Wildcrafts.

"Tell me how Archie and Gwen first met. Mrs. Kuerner, was it love at first sight?"

God, thought Merci. She tried the CNB after-hours number but the receptionist wouldn't say whether Brice was in the studio or not. She tried his cell and *Journal* numbers again but there was still no answer. Zamorra answered and she gave the news to him.

She tossed the phone into the sofa cushion and paced while she watched, too rattled to sit. Earla Kuerner had tears in her eyes. Natalie sat still and sharp-eyed as a kestrel. Lee talked about his daughter falling in love with a college ballplayer, smiling at the memory while his hands wrung themselves in a dissenting agony. George Wildcraft stared at the floor.

"Watch," said Clark. "Here comes the grave."

Merci saw the cars filing into the memorial park, then longshots of the mourners disembarking for the chapel. She had not been aware of the CNB van coming up behind them and it angered her now that she hadn't thought to look for them. But what would she have done? It wasn't Michelle Howland's or Gary Brice's fault that Wildcraft had put on a show. Maybe Archie enjoyed the attention, she thought, maybe he was courting public opinion like everyone else on Earth.

Take a deep breath, she told herself. She took two. Didn't help, never did.

She heard Tim pulling his wheeled suitcase down the hallway. It was one of his favorite things, easily transporting small toys, snails, fallen oranges. Or the heavy newspaper, which he would roll right up to the kitchen table and deliver to Merci on Sunday mornings. Then the kitchen slider rasped open and slammed shut. Merci saw that the patio lights were on, noting that she'd need to look out on Tim in a minute, two at the outside.

On-screen the helicopter lowered and sent some of the mourners running. The deputies drew down and hats flew and the orange dirt dusted up around the blue tarp. Then the first faint bomb of color burst in the air and Archie Wildcraft waved down at the crowd. Merci hadn't seen him do that. Gwen's music kicked in and the flowers fell and Archie was back at the open cargo door of the chopper disgorging an entire bedsheet full of blossoms.

"Incredible," said Clark. "Look at that."

Thanks to the beauties of zoom and stop-action the incident was more detailed on video than it had been live.

"Natalie Wildcraft, what did you think when you saw that?"

"I thought, get 'em, Arch. Show 'em what you're made of!"

"What is he made of, Mrs. Wildcraft?"

"Guts and flowers, lady."

Clark turned and smiled back at her. Merci caught the pride of fandom in it and she realized that Clark was pulling for Archie the way he'd pull for the Angels or the Dodgers or the Lakers.

The TV picture changed to the back view of the Wildcraft property.

Merci went to the window and saw Tim out on the edge of the patio, trying to catch the moths that rose up from the margarita daisies whenever the back lights were on. The suitcase lay behind him, zipped open and waiting for the treasures he might find.

"But is Archie Wildcraft truly the wounded hero he appears to be?"

Then came the video footage of Archie and his twelve-gauge and Gary Brice. Merci watched again as Wildcraft, unshaven and bandaged, the head wrap dirty and bleeding, his clothes wrinkled and his eyes furious, leveled the big barrel at the reporter's chest and hissed out something about killing himself or killing *them* himself or whatever it was. Try as she could, Merci couldn't make out his words because of Brice's near fall and the air crackling around the mike.

Then the press conference in which Michelle Howland tried to pin Merci on the specifics of the physical evidence:

"Can you tell us why Deputy Wildcraft is not *a suspect in the death of his wife if his gun was used to kill her, and his fingerprints were on that weapon, and a test for gunshot residue came up* positive?"

Merci listened to her reasoned, slightly condescending answer:

"Because there's more to a homicide case than fingerprints and gunshot residue."

A shot then of a dapper, gray-haired man sitting in a law library, with Michelle Howland's voice-over.

"But is there? Attorney Giles Newman has prosecuted scores of murder cases, and defended hundreds more. As a private attorney now working in Denver, Colorado, Newman is immersed in the details of homicide virtually every working day of his life."

Dapper gray: *"Fingerprints and residue tests positive? Suspect apprehended at the scene with the weapon in his hand? That's powerful evidence in a courtroom. I'm not going to comment on this case or any other, but generally, when a prosecutor gets his hands on that kind of evidence, you're looking at a conviction."*

Merci shook her head and looked back through the window. Tim was over by the roses now, suitcase still open. It looked like he was brushing ladybugs off into his luggage.

Then a forensic expert from Washington, D.C.; a psychiatrist from Los Angeles; a neurosurgeon from Baltimore. Michelle explained that neither Assistant DA Ryan Dawes, Sheriff Vince Abelera nor Dr. John Stebbins were able to go on record for this CNB report.

"And what does Archie Wildcraft have to say? He requested an interview with CNB just a few hours after showering his wife's grave with flowers. . . ."

Merci took a deep breath as Archie appeared on the screen. Free of the gauze turban, his head was close-shaven and somehow vulnerable rather than menacing. His eyes were pale and he looked exhausted. He wore a shortsleeved white shirt buttoned all the way up, like a youngster. There was a big beige bandage over his wound, the kind you can get at a drug store. Merci tried to make out the background but all she could identify with certainty was a brick wall. They were outside.

"I want to tell Mom and Dad and Lee and Earla that I'm fine. I'll have this case wrapped up pretty quick now. Just don't worry, guys."

He smiled a smile such as Merci had never seen: innocence, cunning, danger and serenity all in one brief flash.

"And everybody? Gwen says hello. She's just fine. I promise you that."

"Deputy Wildcraft, did you murder your wife?"

The same perfectly contradictory smile.

"After reviewing all the evidence, I'm now certain, beyond a shadow of a doubt, that I did not. Turn off the camera now. That was the agreement. Now."

"Oh wow," said Clark.

Back to Michelle in the studio, sitting with, of course, Gary Brice.

"Gary, what do you make of Deputy Wildcraft's strangely unemotional and less-than-positive defense?"

Merci shook her head and looked back outside. Tim had zipped up the little suitcase and extended the handle, which he now used to pull it across the patio toward the slider.

"I think he's delusional. And he's probably an extremely unreliable witness to the events of that night. I don't mean to condemn him, but the man has a bullet lodged in his brain."

"Why isn't he in custody?"

"I think what's really interesting here is the way the Sheriff's De-

partment moved so slowly to question and arrest him. Now he's out
there, maybe a danger to others, certainly a danger to himself. . . ."

"It's a heartbreaking story."

"Yes, it is, Michelle. And it's far from over."

"What were you thinking when he had that shotgun aimed at you?"

"To be honest? I thought I'd be meeting my maker in about two
seconds."

"We're glad you're still with us, Gary."

"I am, too."

"I'm not," said Merci.

She called Zamorra.

She read Tim *Cars and Trucks and Things that Go* and let him find
the Goldbug character hidden in the vehicles. He knew exactly where
Goldbug was on every page, but pretended to be uncertain. She put
him in bed. He was quiet, perhaps still mistaking her anger at Brice
for anger at him. She sat down in the darkened room and watched the
light from the hallway softly illuminate her son's face.

"Lay down here," he said.

Sometimes she lay beside his little bed and talked to him through
the mesh of the safety rail. She understood that he wanted her to be
closer tonight, so she lay down on her back and looked up at him.

"Stay," he said.

He climbed out of bed. She heard him extend the handle of his suitcase and roll it over beside her. She heard him zip it open. By the time
she'd turned her head to see what he was plotting he was standing beside
her, dropping little handfuls of damp cool flowers onto her body. She
caught a few in her hand and tilted them toward the hall light: rose petals, margarita daisies, dandelions from the lawn, geranium.

"I love you," he said.

She couldn't speak.

Late that night she poured another scotch, got a flashlight and went
out to see Frank.

She walked across the back patio, then the lawn, then through the gate to the far side of the garage. The orange trees made shadows in the moonlight. She stood before the pile of cinder blocks and tumbleweeds then set the light and her tumbler on the ground. Squatting, she pulled away the cinder blocks. She tilted up the plywood planks one at a time, dragged them over to the garage wall and propped them against the stucco. The tumbleweeds, tethered to the plywood with dental floss, remained fixed to the wood. She brushed off her hands and went back to the trench. She pulled away the bubble wrap then sat down cross-legged on the ground and shined the light in.

There was Francisco. Ancient and still, a startlingly small human skeleton with a conquistador's helmet over the skull. The front of the helmet swept up like the prow of a tiny ship. From deep within its recess Francisco's bottomless eye sockets looked back at her. His teeth were enormous. His hands were monkeylike but his sword was huge. Beneath the chest plate and the Spanish armor his bones were brown and helpless.

"Hello, Frank," she said. She'd named him Francisco out of general probability. She'd discovered him here one day while trying to locate a leach line, and had no idea what to do with him. She felt possessive and protective. She'd fashioned the cinder-block-plywood-tumbleweed-bubble-wrap security system to protect him from dogs, kids, coyotes. She had only shown him to one other person—Hess, of course—who had pronounced him "alone."

She sipped her drink, then ran the flashlight beam over Frank's skeleton. It bothered her that she couldn't determine his eye or hair color, what kind of mustache he might have worn, the shade of his living skin. She harbored a baseless hope that Frank had been in law enforcement of some kind. The badge would have rusted away by now, right? Even the big sword was half eaten by decay.

Every time she decided to call the university and rat him out, she'd think of them dismantling and cataloguing him, taking their instruments to him, touching him.

So he remained here, where he had been buried some five centuries ago.

She never actually said much to him. What could you? But she found something inspiring in him, in his literal embodiment of the idea of a life of action. She loved it that even after death, Francisco remained suited up, armed and ready. Talk about eternal vigilance. She had read about the ferocity of the Spanish conquerors and admired him for it. And she understood something of what Francisco's sword had cost his soul.

She thought about Mike and Hess and Evan O'Brien, but mostly about Hess.

She sipped, checked the moon, turned to see the dark treeline against the sky and the orange fruit surprisingly clear in the darkness. Then back to Frank. She wondered if, after Francisco's death, someone had willed him back to life the way Archie had willed Gwen. The way she tried to imagine Hess back but never could, except that one time in the dream when he came into her bedroom while she was sleeping to tell her everything was okay.

She looked down again at the conqueror and felt comforted by his patience.

"You know Archie didn't do it. Don't you?"

Just before midnight Merci dumped the contents of the La Quinta Inn trash bag onto the floor of her garage and rummaged through it in the bright fluorescent light: wadded tissue, some of it stained with bloody discharge; used bandages, folded into quarters; two days' worth of newspapers; fast-food bags and cups; a plastic bag from a pharmacy and one from a market; balls of lined yellow paper; three of the little waxy sacks used to cover hotel water glasses.

In addition to the long, sword-shaped swatch of blue tarp that she had noted earlier she found several smaller scraps of the same material. There were also six short lengths of one-inch PVC pipe—four of them jointed together with dark blue pipe cement—and dozens of wilted blossoms and flower petals.

She separated the pipe and the tarp fragments and considered them. Something to do with the flower drop? Maybe. But what? Archie hadn't used anything but what had looked like a bedsheet. It certainly wasn't a blue plastic tarp. Something to do with transporting the flowers? Something to do with Gwen? With his wound? With snaring Vorapin and Cherbrenko? With . . . *what?*

It was the same material used to hold down the earth from Gwen's grave, she thought. She pictured the burial scene, the orange dirt and the unnaturally blue tarp covering it, and the black mourners against the green grass.

She picked up one of the tarp scraps and saw the darker blue of PVC cement stuck to one of the straight sides. One of the pipe pieces had glue along its length also, and the telltale blue plastic debris where the tarp had been affixed, then torn off.

She tried to arrange the PVC into a meaningful shape but could not. Ditto the scraps of material. She thought they looked like the remnants of some sixth-grader's science project, but what was he trying to make? Had he completed or abandoned it?

The balled-up legal sheets were all pencil drawings, apparently made by Archie. Most were childishly inept renderings of Gwen. One sketch showed a latticework of some kind—a long rectangle cross-hatched with short support beams. For all Merci could tell it might have been anything from a retaining wall to a new board game.

She spiked the sketches to a nail in the drywall and turned her attention to the largest piece of tarp. Shaped roughly like a sword. Or a wing. Or a surfboard skeg. Or a jib. The long rectangle again, but with one end sharpened.

She pulled out a dusty old folding chair, whacked it open and sat. She stared at the potential evidence. A few minutes later she moved the chair, and a few minutes after that she moved it again.

But it didn't work. No matter what angle she looked from, nothing about the pipe and the glue and the tarp suggested anything she could use to figure what Archie Wildcraft was up to.

Half an hour later she put everything back in the bag, tied it shut and leaned it in the corner before turning off the lights.

She called Brice on his cell phone and he answered, slurry with drink.

"Where was Wildcraft when you saw him?" she demanded.

"Up against the wall, Sergeant."

"What wall and where, Gary? I can't believe you wouldn't tell me where he was."

"I called you four times, Merci. I *tried* to tell you where he was."

"You could have tried Zamorra. Or the watch captain. You could have called Vince, for that matter."

"I wanted you to get the exclusive."

Merci heard a female voice in the background, teasing and chipper. "Where was he?"

"He sent me to a pay phone in Santa Ana, then to another one. Then to a closed-up body shop down on First Street. When he saw I hadn't brought along any company—such as *you*, Sergeant—he led me around to the back and let me shoot him. He said if I told anybody where he'd been, he'd never call me again with an interview. He took off real fast when it was over."

Giggling in the background, the sound of a slap.

Rayborn felt her anger abating, replaced by curiosity over the condition of Archie Wildcraft.

"He looked a little . . . unbalanced on the TV," she said.

"*Unbalanced?* Merci, that guy's crazier than a shithouse rat. Tell me about the Russians."

"What did he say?"

"Said he'd be taking care of them real soon. What gives? Do you have some suspects I should know about?"

"Abelera's on at noon. Pictures, everything."

"Shit, no kidding? Fucking ROC in OC? That's a story I'd like to run with."

"Too late for the morning final," she said. "You'll have to break it along with everybody else."

"You could really help me out here."

"I was saying that to you two minutes ago."

"Forgive me. Forgive me, and when we meet again, punish me severely. In any way you want. *Whip me. Beat me.* But until then give

me the names of the suspects and some of the evidence you've got
against them. E-mail me the pictures and I'll get them into the Art
Department ASAP. Give me just a two-line statement I can use.
Please, please, *please* help me get this story out before the *Times* and
Register do."

She hung up on him and didn't answer when he called back.

THIRTY-ONE

While Merci puzzled over tarp and PVC, Archie Wildcraft pulled the Durango into a parking space outside the Fifteenth Street Surf Shop in Newport Beach. He sat for a moment, looking at the lavender light cast by the streetlamp, the red moths arcing against the bulb. He couldn't get the smell of burned flesh and phosphorous out of his head. He'd blown his nose three times and wiped his nostrils with a wet napkin from a foil pouch but nothing helped. He tried to feel bad for Sonny Charles but didn't.

He took a deep breath and got out. A blue fog hung over the sand and he could hear the waves roaring up the shore. A bright green kid on a skateboard thunked down the sidewalk.

Archie went to the rear liftgate and opened it. He pulled out the Canadian crutches one at a time and propped them against the vehicle. Then the wings. Slipped a screwdriver into his shirt pocket. Swung the door shut and locked up with the key pad.

He carried his things down the sidewalk, past the restrooms and onto the sand. He was pleased at how light the wings were, yet so eager to perform: even the faint breeze off the ocean caught the skin of tarp, wrapped tightly and glued to the bones of the PVC. Ingenious.

"They'll work," he said.

"I hope so," said Gwen, hovering in the fog behind and above him.

"Sorry you had to hear Sonny scream like that."

"The gag helped," she said. "But he won't drive another getaway car."

"No."

"Won't he tip Vorapin?"

"That's okay. Let the big man be afraid. He *should* be afraid."

He walked across the sand until he saw the orange, luminescent waterline. There, he knelt in the cool sand and laid out the wings, upside down. He fitted the right crutch against the underside of the right wing and screwed it tight with the hose-clamps he'd built into the crossbeams of PVC. Then the left.

"That's a good fit," said Gwen.

Archie reached a hand back to touch her. She took it and held it against her warm cheek.

"I can't wait to try them," he said.

"Go for it."

He slid his right hand down along the crutch leg, worked his upper arm into the big C-clip, closed his fist around the padded handle.

"It really feels good."

"It really looks good, Arch."

Archie lifted his right wing and felt for the first time its slight weight and powerful lift. Then he felt a gentle upward nudge from a breeze so light it never registered on his skin. What power!

"Oh," he muttered.

"Oh, my," echoed Gwen.

Carefully as a newborn creature, he folded the great yellow wing to his side.

"It's indescribable, Gwen."

"I'm proud of you. You're beautiful. And so were the flowers at the funeral. And the ones you put by my pictures in the hotel."

He was too excited to answer. He leaned over to get his left arm into place. It was a little precarious but he felt Gwen holding him and he got his hand onto the soft grip and his arm into the C-clip. He righted himself and stood.

Archie looked out at the bright golden water. Slowly he lifted his wings. The spread was sixteen feet—seven for each wing and twenty-four inches across his back, just below the shoulders. First he felt the emancipation of weight from his feet. Then the diminished load on his legs. Next, the lightening of his bony middle, then the joyful buoyancy of his back, the tickling freedom of his chest and neck. He felt like a big helium balloon held down by a weight only slightly heavier than himself. Like he could glide along for miles between effortless steps. Like he could fly.

He walked down to the waterline and turned south. Felt the lift. Broke into a trot. Felt the uneven pull of the wings, like a marionette. Heard the *slap-slap-slap* of his shoes in the water.

"How's it feel, Arch?"

"They want to fly. I just need more speed and more air under me."

He kicked the trot into a gallop then to a sprint. The *slap-slap-slap* came fast and his horizon line jiggled and he felt the great long muscles of his ballplayer's legs rejoicing in the effort. He veered up onto the embankment of the beach, then turned back downhill. He was running on his toes, then on nothing at all. The *slap-slap-slap* had suddenly stopped and Archie felt as if someone was trying to hook him into the sky. An enjoyable confusion broke over him as he suddenly realized the dimensionality of flight: the heartstopping ups and downs, the quease of pitch and yaw, the wild potentials of attitude and azimuth of a body in space.

"God, Gwen!"

"Arch, it's working!"

"I'll be coming soon, girl!"

"Oh, Archie, I can't wait!"

Then he plunked down to heavy Earth again and came to a panting stop ankle-deep in the Pacific.

"Totally cool, man," said a young male voice. Archie hadn't noticed anyone. The boy came out of the ocean with his surfboard, then turned north and ran through the whitewater.

"Thanks!"

Archie got his breath back quickly, then turned around and walked back to the lifeguard tower at Fifteenth Street. He wanted to get up onto the platform from which the lifeguards observed, but they took

the ladder with them at night. Archie had to remove his wings and
reach them one at a time onto the platform before climbing one of the
legs and chinning himself up and over.

He worked his arms back into the wings and stood at the edge of
the platform facing the ocean. The sand looked to be about eight feet
down from his feet. He spread his arms, then started pumping. He felt
lighter with each big downthrust. He jumped. Out and up. Timed it
with the downstroke and saw the ocean move a small notch away and
felt the air-starved tarp lifting him upward.

Then the sudden exhilaration of ascendance.

Moving not on Earth but above it, wings stiff and alive with air.

Gwen out there somewhere, close and touchable.

And this great new strength that gave him all the lightness and
endurance of a bird.

The next thing he knew the ocean was rushing up at him. *Cold!*
He got his feet under him and stood waist-deep in the bright gold
water.

"Whoa," he said quietly. "*Whoa.* Hon?"

Gwen didn't answer. She had a way of coming and going, which
was the reason for this whole project to begin with.

"Gwen?"

Just the ocean rustling on the sand.

More speed, he thought.

More air.

Catch her.

Take care of the giant first.

The brine stung the bullet hole in his head but it wasn't an alto-
gether unpleasant sting. He pushed through the icy ocean toward shore,
dragging his yellow wingtips through the golden sea.

THIRTY-TWO

Hours later, just after sunrise, a stumbling, disoriented man was picked up by two sheriff's deputies cruising the Ortega Highway outside of San Juan Capistrano. Both deputies dropped from the unit and drew down on him in the uncertain light. When they saw that he was completely blind and in tremendous agony they holstered their weapons with a sense of relief and awe.

"At first I thought he was drunk," Deputy Maxwell told Rayborn and Zamorra. He was waiting for them at the entrance of Western Medical Center in Anaheim. "Then I saw his face."

The detectives hustled up the steps and Maxwell stayed abreast of them, his belt jangling with gadgetry. "All he's got left of his eyes are black pits."

"And his CDL said what?"

"Steve Charles. But the burns and his accent made me think, so we ran the name through the Feds and came up with Sergei Cherbrenko. He's a gangster. Dobbs heard it at the morning roll and called you guys."

Yes, Dobbs again. Marching through the automatic doors of the hospital entrance Merci wondered: how could one formerly hostile Deputy 1 get so lucky? He'd spotted Cherbrenko and Vorapin coming down the hill from the Wildcraft home. He'd found the abandoned STS Cadillac they'd used. Now, he'd smelled the connection between a freshly blinded man wandering the Ortega and the murder of Gwen Wildcraft.

She was suspicious of fortune this good. She wondered if Dobbs might be connected up with the Russians, might be running interference for them. How? By ID'ing them in the car, and sealing off the STS crime scene like a pro? Idiotic. Maybe he was fingering them for a rival. Maybe the sun would rise blue next Tuesday. Was she still pissed about him not protecting the Wildcraft driveway?

God, woman, she thought: you'd shoot an angel out of the sky to make sure she was real.

And the problem here wasn't that Deputy Dobbs had made a nice leap from Cherbrenko to Gwen. The problem was that Deputy Wildcraft had probably tortured him.

"Road flares?" she asked.

"I've never seen anything like it," said Maxwell. "Well, actually, I have, in college. The end of one of those old tragedies, where they put the guy's eyes out."

"But he wouldn't tell you who did it?" asked Zamorra.

"No. He just blubbered and cried. Does this have to do with Archie?"

"We're about to find out."

Cherbrenko lay in the burn unit with his head and face wrapped in white gauze and his hands in wrist restraints. His fingers were cupped and still. His pale hair was bunched behind the bandage, loose as a pile of straw.

"He's on a strong painkiller and sedative," said the doctor. He referred to Cherbrenko as if he was absent but would be back soon. "He can answer your questions if he wishes. Do not be surprised if he falls asleep."

Rayborn stood and looked down at the gauze mask. There were no eyeholes. She thought she should be quiet, but the doctor hadn't been. She wondered what it would be like to have roaring road flares be the last thing you ever saw in your life.

She told him who she was. The mask moved slightly to the right, toward her. A sigh elongated from the nose opening but that was all.

"You're Sergei Cherbrenko and you worked for OrganiVen," she said. "Gwen Wildcraft worked there with you."

No movement, no sound. The head moved again, but away from her this time.

Then a sigh and a soft whisper. *"Wildcraft."*

"Did he do this to you?"

"Yes."

"What did he want?"

"Facts."

"Of?"

"Murder."

"Of Gwen, his wife."

"Yes."

Rayborn thought she knew why Archie had done this, but she wanted to hear it from Cherbrenko. "He said he'd let you go if you told him who did it and how it happened."

A nod.

"You told him."

Another.

"And the truth is, you didn't do it."

"No, I did not."

Merci tried to square her knowledge of Archie Wildcraft against the hideous thing he had done to the man below her. She understood murder but not mutilation. It took her a moment to find the logic. "Deputy Wildcraft didn't kill you. You told him you didn't shoot her, and he believed you, didn't he?"

"Yes."

"Because it was Vorapin who shot her. And Archie."

No reply. Her mind raced ahead through the possibilities, tasting and rejecting, moving on.

"You told him it was Vorapin."

"No. We did nothing."

"But Archie did this to you anyway?"

Just a whisper: *"He told me I would never drive a car again."*

He was right about that, Merci thought. And she realized why

Wildcraft had done what he had done. There was only one more thing he could have wanted. "He let you live because he wanted something from you. And you gave it to him."

A nod.

"And you understand, don't you, Mr. Cherbrenko, that if you tell me what you told him, there's a good chance we can get to Zlatan before Wildcraft does."

"Yes."

"Where is he? Where's Vorapin?"

It was a long time before Cherbrenko answered. The fingers on both his hands slowly opened and closed, then clenched into fists.

"His private house."

"The Fullerton house, with Irene?"

"No. His other."

"What's the address, Mr. Cherbrenko? Help me save your friend something worse than what happened to you."

Another pause. Cherbrenko lay still as a dead man, his fingers again open and relaxed on his tethered hands.

"We did nothing."

"I believe you. Now give me the address."

"Two-two-seven Palacio. Newport Beach."

Zamorra broke for the door but Merci waited. Another light went on: friends don't let friends die. "The nurse dialed his number for you."

Another nod.

"Was he home?"

"No."

"You left him a message."

"Yes. I told him to call the police and let them handle this mistake."

"I'll bet you did."

"This is true."

"And what else?"

"To pull out his eyes and step on them."

"You're a sweetheart, Sonny. You two killed her because you thought she was going to blow the whistle on you about the MiraVen."

"We did nothing."

Rayborn and Zamorra made the Newport Beach address in half an hour. Palacio was up in the hills off of Coast Highway, servicing Bella Villagio, one of the new Italianate developments. The homes were built in clusters of three, which allowed them to face away from each other and into the tan canyons.

Vorapin's address had a courtyard and garage behind a gate. The gate was closed but the garage was open. She could see the back end of a clean black car and that was it.

They walked to the gate and looked through the wrought-iron rail. Merci noted the chrome-heavy back end of the Lincoln Town Car and the livery plates, the Air Glide plate frame.

"He's home," she said.

"You want to camp or knock?"

"I'll knock."

She popped the snap on her hip leather and drew the Heckler & Koch, holding it down against her leg as she walked around the court-yard wall and into the narrow cones of shade cast by three Italian cypresses. The front door was recessed and rounded at the top, with iron bands bolted to the timbers top and bottom. The knocker was black iron, heavy and warm against her fingers.

One rap, two, nothing.

Three, four, nothing.

She tried the doorbell next but it chimed back with distance and emptiness.

Then again.

Then back to Zamorra, shaking her head, her nerves buzzing, the nine tapping against her thigh.

Zamorra jumped the gate with the bored grace of a cat and hit the manual opener. It slid open and Rayborn angled in, taking the left side of the walkway while her partner took the right.

Into the dappled shade of the courtyard and the spicy aroma of the cypresses. The walkway made an elegant curve toward the house and that was where they found Vorapin, facedown and motionless in a lake of blood, holes gaping from the back of his head, the upper middle of his suit coat and the center of his buttocks.

Merci stared at him, figuring the high hump of his back would come about to her knees. Why would God make a man that big?

Vorapin groaned and Merci felt her heart leap into the sky. He coughed a mouthful of black blood onto the pavers.

"Oh, Christ," she said, staring down the sights of the automatic, which had reflexively jumped into her sightline.

Vorapin's fingers tightened and slid. His cratered, misshapen head rose and wobbled, like he was a baby trying to crawl. He turned a little, just enough to curse Rayborn with one magnificent, furious eye.

Then he blew another storm of blood, gave an enormous animal shudder and his head landed with a heavy wet crunch.

For just a moment Merci couldn't hold thoughts. They swam at her dreamily, only to vanish like spooked tarpon in a bright silver sea. Then her attention refocused with blazing clarity on the soles of Zlatan Vorapin's gigantic shoes.

"I'll call paramedics," said Zamorra.

"Versa-Terra."

"What?"

"Used by Foot Rite."

She lowered her gun and looked at Zamorra blankly.

"Take five, Merci. He isn't going anywhere."

"In their popular Comfort Strider."

She half listened as Zamorra made the call. She couldn't take her eyes off of Vorapin. His bulk was obscene, absolutely. But he was majestic, too, like Ahab's whale or a Tsavo man-eater.

Her own phone rang three times before she flipped open the mouthpiece and spoke from her heart: *"Who are you and what do you want?"*

"Hi. It's Archie."

A sudden reentry for Merci, swift and complete, all of her attention now focused on the voice in her ear. "Where are you?"

"I'll be at the top of Santiago Peak in about ten minutes. I'm going to get Gwen. Meet me and we can clear some things up."

"You blinded Sonny and murdered Vorapin."

"Hurry up, Sergeant. I'm kind of eager to get going."

THIRTY-THREE

He got the wings out of the back of the Durango and carried them to the edge. There was a natural platform of sandstone to step out on, warning signs all over the place, and above him a fenced-off area bristling with radio and communications antennae and more signs. It was windy and hot, and when he looked out he could see Orange County spread out in front of him, the blue houses creeping up the purple hillside below like soldiers storming a fort. According to his map the peak was 5,687 feet above sea level, the highest point in the county.

"It's beautiful," he said.

"It really is."

At the sound of her voice he swung around, but she wasn't there.

"Sweetie, I'm sorry you had to see all that. But they made me do it. They started all of this."

"I know," she said quietly. "They deserved it."

"I didn't feel anything while I was doing it."

"It's the bullet."

"What a thing to happen."

He sat at the edge of the sandstone, legs dangling in air. He watched the wind work the manzanita, shifting the branches in terse unison. He looked down at the beautiful yellow tarp of his wings, checked the fittings and the fasteners into which the Canadian crutches were locked.

"What I'm going to do is head off toward the ocean then turn south. The wind coming up the peak is strong, and I'll ride it up and back toward you. Then, well, it's just us. Hold on to my shoulders. It'll be nothing but blue skies."

"I'm ready, Arch. I'll be here. You look terrific."

Archie had used the hotel iron and board to press his uniform, getting the seams crisp and the difficult pleats of his shirt pockets flat before reattaching his badge and nameplate. Concerned about weight, he stripped his duty belt down to the essentials: holster, handgun and plastic wrist restraints; no extra clips of ammunition, no flashlight or radio, no spray and no stick. He'd polished his boots with a miniature shoeshine kit from a drugstore. Shaved his face, of course, and affixed a fresh bandage over his wound, which, in the stress of Sonny and the giant, began emitting a steady flow of pink fluid. Since the giant, it had been getting worse.

"I called Rayborn, Gwen."

She didn't answer right away. "Why?"

"I want to see something."

"Her?"

"Not her, Gwen. Me. I want to see something about me."

"Be careful."

"I think I got into a fight because of her. I can't quite remember."

He felt the warm trickle down his neck and knew the bandage pad was full again. He fished a fresh square out of his shirt pocket and peeled away the old one, which he flicked sideways off the cliff. It spun out and caught the updraft, then downward out of sight.

"Better," he said.

He gathered up the wings and lay them across his lap. He could feel the sun on the back of his uniform and the sharp breeze drying his sweat. Below him, the colors of the county had changed: now the foliage was red and the houses were a pale turquoise that reminded him of a Baja village he'd visited with Gwen once, years ago, driving the old pickup truck slowly over the pitted asphalt and looking for a lobster restaurant to eat in.

Archie sighed and looked out at the sky in which he would soon be reconnected to his wife.

In the awful confusion after his shooting he had clung to two hopes: that he would see Gwen soon, and that he would kill the men who had brutalized her. To him these seemed to be reasonable and just desires. True, he'd spared Sonny, because it had been the right thing to do. Sonny had driven, not shot. Sonny would never drive again. Strange, though, how unsatisfying it all had been. Archie remembered saying to the giant *this is for Gwen*, though it caused none of the exhilaration he was expecting. All he really felt as he did these things was that he'd done his job fairly well, taking a rational satisfaction in details: apprehending Mr. Charles without struggle; jumping the giant's gate in the early-morning darkness and landing without a sound; the performance of the noise suppression device. This crude silencer, which he had painstakingly created from two PVC pipes of differing diameters, steel wool and duct tape—all fixed to the barrel of his Smith forty-five with a powerful epoxy cement billed as Squeeze-a-Bolt— had turned out almost comically large. But it had worked well. After five shots, only a small part of the end had melted. So that was that. Sonny and the Giant were accounted for. But his liberation from numbness had failed.

And now, with half of his desires fulfilled, Archie felt pinioned and exhausted and alone and he missed his wife even more terribly than before. He thought about his faraway life because he could still feel the moments, though just barely: walking Julia to school with that big sweet lump in his heart, and the Little League years when he first understood that he had a gift for the game, and high school ball when he set all the county records; then Gwen and college ball and later the months when she put him through the academy and the skinny first years when he worked the jail at odd hours and she built her schedule around his and they lived only to love each other; then later the friends on the department and the regular shifts and the feeling that he was getting good at his job; even the dizzying spiral into wealth, all the worry and scrounging of money to invest, not knowing if it was going to pay off or not; then the house and the new cars and he and Gwen still in love and it seemed like life couldn't get better. These were true memories, not the neutered snapshots that the Russians had left him with. But the emotions accompanying even these were harder and harder to recall. He remembered now, slowly and with a grim resolve, how it felt the first time he saw Gwen Kuerner in the multiplex out in Riverside.

Suddenly the tears were rushing out of him as a great spasm of loss cracked through him like a whip. It felt like his soul was caving in upon itself. He could hear his scream, feeble in the wind, but inside him it was deafening as the roar he'd heard standing by the tracks near Willits, when he was a boy with Kevin and they'd seen how close they could get to the train as it howled clattering past, inhaling their thin boys' bodies toward the fatal rails.

"We shouldn't have messed with the snake stuff," he sobbed.

"It was a terrible mistake, Arch. But I was trying to make things go our way. Really go our way."

The tears kept pouring down his face and he stared through them at the sky and wondered why his life had come down to empty air.

"It's okay, Archie," she whispered. "Come on, now. Come get me."

He turned and saw Rayborn climbing up the crest of the peak toward him. Zamorra was behind her ten yards, carrying a shotgun.

Merci slipped on the loose rocks, steadied herself by grabbing the branch of a low manzanita. She was breathing hard with the elevation and the heat and the uncertainty of what Deputy Wildcraft was doing up here.

She could see him out at the edge, looking back at her. Two large blue curves dangled where his arms should have been, like wings. She recognized the shape instantly: the swordlike piece of tarp from the hotel trash can was a model version of what Archie now wore at his sides. The cemented joints she had found were prototypes of what must be holding those things together.

And she thought: *Oh shit, he thinks they're wings.*

Experience failed her but she knew it was important to get him talking.

"Archie! Arch! Thanks for calling."

She stumbled again, grabbed another branch, then pulled herself to a stop on a small level spot fifty feet away. She heard Zamorra twenty steps behind her and she calculated that he was within effective shotgun range. That she would take the time to figure this irked her but she couldn't help herself: it was in her training and in her spirit.

He looked down at her, wings tucked, wobbling in the capricious mountain breeze.

"Thanks for coming," he said.

"What exactly are you up to?"

"Going to get Gwen."

"She's up here?"

"Yes."

"You make those yourself?"

"I got the idea in the hospital."

She glanced back at Zamorra, who stood spread-legged, one foot uphill and the other braced down, holding the shotgun across his chest like a bird hunter. He'd moved to her left to get a clean line at Wildcraft.

She turned back to the deputy. "Hey, Arch, we know the Russians did it. You did what you had to do. You put out Sonny's eyes and shot up Vorapin, didn't you?"

"Yes. Sonny told me everything. It's on a tape recorder in my bathroom. But I'd remembered the giant's face by then—the face that was behind the light that night. When I saw him, I knew he was the one."

"Archie, there's a whole department waiting for you to get healed up and back on duty."

"I can't. You know that."

"Then take the disability. You can get yourself a little airplane, get rid of those funky wings."

"I like them."

"They won't take you far."

Wildcraft looked out over the cliff then, and Merci saw the breeze sway his body.

"I don't have that far to go," he said.

"I'll tell you one thing—if Gwen was alive she'd kick your butt for even thinking about this."

"Not true. We've talked it over."

"And what does she say you'll get out of it?"

"Just that she's up there."

"Up *where*?"

He looked out again. "There."

"What about your mom and dad, Arch? And the Kuerners. And Priscilla. And Damon Reese and Brad Eccles. Those people love you. You can't just jump off the end of the world when they're counting on you."

Wildcraft seemed to consider this. He looked into the abyss, then back at her. "I love them and they're going to have to understand."

"Understand what?"

"That I can't just let them fade away. Gwen. Everybody."

"Of course you can't. But it's going to take time. You're going to heal, Archie. You're going to feel like you used to, someday. Gwen would want that. You say you talk to her? Then ask her if she wants you to jump, or not. Ask her what you should do."

Merci had the horrible inkling that she'd just said the absolute wrong thing, that Wildcraft would ask Gwen what to do and his imagination, or his memory of her, or the bullet inside him or whatever it was that was guiding him would say, yes, Arch, jump.

Her heart sank when Archie looked up over his shoulder, away from her, and said something to the air. He nodded. He nodded again.

"Archie! Goddamnit, you've got a bullet in your brain and you're not thinking straight. Gwen's dead, Arch. She isn't coming back and she isn't in the sky and she doesn't want you to jump off and die. Trust me on this, Archie. I'm telling you the truth."

"I'm coming," he said, but Merci couldn't tell if he was talking to her or not. He was still turned, looking up and behind him. "But I need to do one thing first."

"What?" Merci asked.

Archie answered, but the wind snapped the words from the air before they could get to her. It looked like he was having a conversation with himself.

"I'm coming," he said to Gwen. "But I need to do one thing first."

"What?"

"Just to see. Just to see what happens if I do it."

Gwen didn't answer.

He turned, spread his blue wings and glided down to Merci. She couldn't believe the damn things actually worked. He landed softly, duty boots sliding to a stop on the sandstone gravel. The wings folded down and back. She saw that his bandage was soaked in pink and his pupils were grossly dilated. His head and neck were shiny with sweat, but his uniform was pressed.

He came toward her. She glanced back at Zamorra, who had the gun raised in the relaxed manner of a man who doesn't miss.

Archie stepped up close, then spread the wings around her. The breeze hissed against the polypropylene and she could smell fear and aftershave. She brought the nine up and out of the leather.

He held her close now, moving her—she was sure of this—into Zamorra's sightline. Though with Wildcraft so close to her, there was no way that Zamorra could fire. She held the barrel of her automatic against one of his ribs. She heard Zamorra crashing through the brush behind her. Slowly, she raised her left hand above the outstretched wing and turned the palm back toward her partner.

Archie gulped hard and kissed her lightly on the right cheek. Then the left. Then he brushed his lips against hers, drew a long, deep breath and pulled away.

"Nothing," he said.

Her heart was thrumming fast and light as a bird's and she felt an awful heaviness in her legs.

She lowered her hand and put the tip of her forefinger into the pit of one dimple, set her thumb under the good hard line of his chin, and pulled his mouth against hers. His body went rigid and his weight began to shift away so she wrapped the gun hand around his back, held on tight and kissed him like she'd once kissed Hess, without thought or method or even a nod to consequence. She ended it when her breath was gone.

"No," he whispered. "I don't feel anything."

"I feel everything, Archie."

"Thank you."

She dropped the gun, tried to get one hand on the shoulder of his uniform and one around his belt but he was too fast and much too strong for a takedown.

Wildcraft wrenched himself away and scrambled back up to his perch on the cliff. He looked down at her. Then he turned and spread his wings and hopped into the abyss. He rose in the draft. Hovering, he looked at her again, then gained elevation with two strokes of his powerful arms. He floated out and away and she saw the hopeful concentration on his face as he lifted gracefully in the breeze and drifted out over the great space. Then he fell. By the time she made it to the edge and looked over he was beating hard but falling fast. He hit a rock outcropping a couple of hundred feet down, bounced off it with a terrible sound then careened wing-over-boot another hundred feet, colliding with a huge boulder that spun him the other way into the deep black canyon and out of sight.

THIRTY-FOUR

Merci carried a heavy, overfilled silence through the rest of her shift. It felt like her blood had turned to lead, her bones to iron.

She volunteered to call on George and Natalie Wildcraft and the Kuerners. It was her first line-of-duty death notification and her training had instructed her to be informative, helpful and soft-spoken.

She told them unflinchingly what had happened, enduring first their questions then their silences. She omitted the part when Archie felt nothing and she felt everything. When they were finished she and Zamorra left without lingering. As a messenger she was killed twice; as a detective formerly suspicious of the deputy's actions she was killed twice again.

Sheriff Abelera asked her to make "the Wildcraft statement." This, in lieu of the noon press conference originally meant to deal with the Russians and the probable innocence of Archie.

She stood there in the courthouse conference room, feeling heavy and thick as an Easter Island statue, telling the lights and the restless reporters that the best efforts of her partner and herself were not enough to bring Deputy Wildcraft down from the precipice of Santiago Peak. She told them that rescuers had recovered his body about halfway down the mountain. She said nothing of wings, only that the deputy had been shattered by the death of his wife. At the word "shattered" she saw in her mind's eye the pinwheeling descent, then Archie's broken body careening into the maw of shadow and stone.

"How did you find him?" asked Gary Brice. "I mean, before he jumped."

"He informed us of his whereabouts."

"Why wasn't a negotiator brought in, or a rescue team assembled?" asked Michelle Howland.

"We had no indication of his purpose. There was no time."

"How long did you talk to him?" asked KTLA.

"Less than a minute."

"What, exactly, were his last words?" asked Brice.

"Thank you."

"For what? What had you done?"

"Nothing. I think that, by then, he was . . . completely disoriented."

"Were you close enough to physically restrain him?"

"My attempt failed."

"There was contact, then, a scuffle?"

"Yes."

"How would you describe his expression when he jumped?"

"It can't be described."

"How was he dressed?"

"In his summer-weight uniform."

"Was he armed?"

"His sidearm was holstered."

Abelera had instructed her to leave the Russians out of all this for now while the lab corroborated Wildcraft's confession with evidence.

"This press conference is over," she said. "But you can stay and ask all the questions you want."

She turned off the mike and walked out the back door with Zamorra.

For a long while she sat in her office cubicle, staring at the phone, her picture of Tim, the calendar. She had a small stack of mail but no heart to open it or even look through it. Zamorra left the homicide pen without a good-bye.

Around three, a couple of uniformed deputies stopped by to tell her they were sorry about Wildcraft, but wanted to thank her for taking Archie's side. They knew all along he hadn't killed Gwen, but it was good of her to believe in him even when the evidence was against him. She asked them to sit a minute, but they excused themselves with a nervy curtness that she respected.

By four o'clock she'd received two calls—both from deputies she knew were hostile to her—telling her they were pleasantly surprised/ proud to see the way she stuck by her department as far as Wildcraft was concerned, and pleased/honored that she'd accepted the nomination for the Deputy Association. She would have their votes. Merci felt Mike's unsubtle hand in this but the calls helped slow the thick ice she felt closing in around her heart.

Dobbs came by to ask if there was anything he could do. "You half cracked this case, Deputy," Merci said. "Thank you."

"Last time I'll turn a crime scene into a parking lot."

"Dobbs, you're going to be just fine."

"Thank you, Sergeant. I'm headed here, you know. Homicide. That's my goal. That's what I want."

"Careful what you wish for."

"I will be."

Gilliam called.

Her father called.

Ryan Dawes called to tell her she had good instincts about this case and had been right to follow them. He sounded like a movie critic praising a trashy blockbuster, so she hung up on him.

Al Madden called and said he was sorry about Archie, but gratified that the deputy had been innocent all along. He wondered if his investigation had helped drive Wildcraft to suicide and she said she didn't think so. Madden apologized for having to get involved and remarked that her fieldwork was, in his opinion, flawless.

Neighbor William Jones called to find out if the press conference account of Archie's suicide was accurate, if there was anything else she could tell him. She told him that Archie believed he was going to join Gwen. Jones said if he was Archie he'd go and join her, too. Merci excused herself and rang off.

George Wildcraft called to ask about his son. He wanted to know how he'd looked, what his state of mind had been before he did it.

She told him what she'd told Jones. She told him she tried her best to take him down, get him off that mountain alive. Her throat went hard and her eyes hurt and she could barely get the words out.

He thanked her and said he was impressed by her and always believed she had had justice and his son's best interest at heart. He apologized for Natalie "throwing herself around." His voice was soft and Merci figured he was sneaking the call on her.

"He was a good man, Detective. Such a good man."

"Yes, I know he was."

Abelera stopped by and told her to take a few days off. She agreed.

Zamorra appeared at five-thirty. "I went to the market. I'd like to make dinner for you and Tim and Clark."

She looked at him, a little surprised. "Great. Tell Kirsten to come."

"Okay. Let Frank know, too."

She wondered why her old affection for Zamorra hadn't drawn him closer but her recent affection for Wildcraft apparently had. Or was it simple sympathy? Either way, it wasn't the kind of question that really riveted you after watching a fellow deputy fall five thousand feet because he had a bullet in his brain and missed his wife. Or talked to a guy just blinded by road flares.

Mike came quietly into the homicide pen, like a man unwelcome. He shook Zamorra's hand and then offered it to Merci. She shook it while she looked into Mike's clear blue eyes and saw the gears of his heart grinding away behind them.

"I was hoping to drop by this evening with Danny," he said. "Bring some meal worms for the alligator lizard."

"Okay," she said.

"We've got plenty of food," said Zamorra. "Bring some wine if you'd like, stay for dinner."

Mike released her hand and nodded at Zamorra like the boy he was, competent in the male world but largely ignorant of the female. He looked at her with an inquisitive expression.

"Fine with me," she said. "Lynda's welcome, if you want."

"No."

When they had gone, Merci picked up her mail, crammed it into her purse and walked out.

———

Home at six-ten on a warm August evening, Merci slinging her purse onto the little breakfast table while Tim clunked across the floor to meet her: red shorts, black cowboy boots, skinned knees showing between them, a plastic gladiator's vest and an Angels baseball cap.

Her heart lightened when she saw him. Purity. Innocence. The Man. No amount of violence could smother the love; it was always there, like a sweet bolt of lightning crackling through the dark.

Clark hugged her, regarding Zamorra and his groceries for an extra second before nodding. "The Weber's on the patio."

Tim stared frankly at dark Zamorra.

"Good to see you again, Tim. Nice vest."

The boy nodded. Paul gravely shook his hand then headed for the barbecue.

Merci swung her son up onto her shoulder and mouthed the word *Wildcraft* to her father, a big silent question mark at the end.

"No, I figured that was for you." He turned to watch Mike's pickup come up the drive. "Oh, I see you invited Mike too."

"More or less."

"You okay, honey?"

"I'm okay, Dad."

"I'll run these guys off if you just want to be with us tonight."

"I'm okay."

He looked at her with his bottomless calm. His glasses caught the light and magnified his eyes into faux astonishment. She leaned into her father and hugged him with her available arm. He smiled, then ambled to the front door.

"And how about you, little man?" she asked. "How are you today?"

"Good," said Tim. "I'm fine. Is Awchie in the heckilopter?"

"He's done with the helicopter."

"And the flowers?"

"And the flowers."

"Because he loves his wife."

"Yes, he . . . does."

"Danny's here!"

He struggled off her shoulder and she set him to the floor with a thud of boot heels. He ran to Danny and Mike as they came through the door. Danny dropped the tub of meal worms and the top popped off, leaving a pile of meal and worms on the floor.

"I'll get that," said Mike. "Here."

The boys bolted off for the backyard, Clark behind them. Mike set down a heavy plastic grocery bag and knelt, using the lid to sweep the worms back into the container. "Thanks for the invite," he said.

"You're welcome."

"Three or four of these a day," he said.

She hesitated, uncertain.

"For the lizard," he said.

"Ah. Got it."

"Keep the container in the freezer but warm the worms in your hand before feeding. If the worms are too cold, the lizard could get indigestion."

"Okay."

"And fresh water at least once a week."

"We can do that, sure."

Mike stood and held up the plastic bag. "I brought a box of wine so there'd be plenty for all of us."

"I'll get that, Mike," said Zamorra, coming through, coat gone, tie loosened. "Cocktails?"

"Definitely," said Merci.

"Make mine light," said Mike.

All three of them turned when Damon Reese, a big bouquet of flowers in his hand, stepped onto the porch and up to the screen door. He wore a Hawaiian shirt brighter than the sun.

"Damn, I'm sorry to interrupt, Merci," he said. "I just wanted to drop these off."

Mike looked somewhat confusedly at her.

Zamorra opened the screen door and handed Reese the boxed Chablis. "Put this in the kitchen sink and shoot a hole in it with your service weapon."

"And I'll take those," said Mike, ears reddening, reaching for the flowers.

He looked at Merci as his attempt at competitive gallantry backfired and he was left standing with a bouquet of flowers in one hand and the container of meal worms in the other.

Reese clapped him on the shoulder on his way by.

Merci smiled. A sit-com. But what a feeling. She felt like she hadn't been amused in a couple of centuries.

She sat in the shade of the backyard patio, increasingly plastered to the Adirondack chair by Zamorra's martini. It made her usual scotch and water seem feeble, and the lemon gave it a bright flavor. She'd changed her slacks and boots for shorts, an ancient blue dress shirt stolen from her father and a pair of clogs that a salesman said flattered her legs. She divided her attention three ways: part to Tim and Danny and Mike playing in the grove beyond the fence; part to Zamorra and Reese differing on the best placement of coals for indirect cooking in the Weber; part to the awful memory of Archie Wildcraft and his hapless blue wings.

Clark creaked into the chair beside her. "These drinks are strong."

"Very."

"I heard he'd built some wings or something."

She looked at him. Her father's pipeline for department information never failed to surprise her. She imagined geezers cawing into their telephones all day.

"Not or something, Dad. They were *wings*."

"Wow. Did they work?"

"At first, then it seemed like he fell through them. By the time I got to the edge where I could see, he was really going fast, straight down. He hit so hard."

Clark frowned and shook his head. He sipped his drink and looked out to the boys.

"Did he really think he could fly? Or was it a straight suicide?"

"He thought he could fly up and find her, I guess. He actually called me on the cell, said he was on his way to get her."

"I thought that for a while with your mother. Not the flying part, but you know, going to the other side to see them."

"Human optimism," she said.

"Who knows? Maybe it works. None of us will ever know until it's too late to report back."

"Maybe that's good."

"Mysteries are good. So is this drink." He took another sip and chuckled. "It's kind of funny that three guys showed up here all at once, hoping for your attention."

"They think they're taking care of me."

"Let 'em."

Merci thought again about Wildcraft spreading his wings around her. She thought about Hess and his cancer. She saw Archie's body falling through the sky and Hess's hair falling through her fingers and she realized she'd loved them out of some blurry notion that love could heal.

"Arrogant," she said.

"What is?"

"Just thinking out loud."

She watched Tim trudging through the orange grove and knew that there was something else in what she'd felt, though, something more than cures and miracles. It was big and straightforward and simple. But what—desire? Passion? What was the word? What was it that your heart yearned to take big bites of, ingest and surround and own? What was the word for that powerful hunger?

Archie knew, she thought. Whether he had the word for it or not. Because if you think you can fly to it then you know. If it takes you that far then you know. If you act then you know. If you feel it then you know, and for a second there on that mountain, I felt it.

For a crazy lilting moment she felt light and blessed, and understood that Archie had worked a miracle on her and not the other way around.

"Get you another drink, Dad?"

"How about a plain soda with some lemon? One of these things is enough for me."

In the kitchen she leaned against the cool counter and poured the soda over ice. She remembered how the tip of her finger fit in Wildcraft's dimple. The words *loss* and *waste* came to her again as her lightness fell.

I felt everything.

"Hey. I'm sorry I didn't call."

She turned to find Damon Reese behind her, grinning with a touch of wickedness. He came right up to her and brushed the hair from her forehead again, just like he'd done that day in his front yard. She smelled cologne instead of fish and gasoline.

"You okay, Merci?"

"I'm okay."

"Rough, what you went through."

"Yeah."

"I've thought about you a lot," he said. "Every day."

"That's nice," she said. She thumbed the opening of the soda bottle, gave it a quick two shakes and shot Reese in the face with it.

"Yeah, no kidding," he said. "I deserved that. Okay."

"You had me for a second."

"Things are complicated."

"No, they're simple, Damon. Do me a favor. Take this drink out to Dad."

Reese took the drink, glancing down at his soda-blasted Aloha shirt. "Let's start over."

"Let's drop it and go outside."

"I absolutely want to see you again. Bring the soda bottle if you want."

He smiled and took a step toward her.

"Damon, you're a real punk."

Something in Reese took this as a compliment. He gave her a conspiratorial grin and walked away with the drink.

It was then that she noticed that Mike had put Reese's bouquet in a vase on the breakfast table by her purse. The flowers were arranged upside down, blossoms drowning at the bottom, and the stiff green stems with their white supermarket tie jutting from the top.

Boys, she thought: my favorite ages are two to forty.

She sat down and looked through the window at Zamorra while he pondered the coals. She had not yet seen him place a call to Kirsten. Reese sat in the shade, examining his soaked shirt. Clark was where she had left him, fresh drink in hand. Mike and the boys were coming through the gate, back into the yard. A pink house on a white beach in Mexico, she thought: Tim and Hess and me.

She picked the office mail out of her purse and fanned through it quickly until her eye caught an interesting return name and address: Sean Moss, La Jolla.

Dr. Sean, she thought: surf dude, biochemical researcher, entrepreneur, friend and smitten admirer of Gwen Wildcraft, coward. She noted the post date—the same day they'd seen him at his mansion overlooking the ocean.

She opened it and read the handwritten note.

Sergeant Rayborn—I should have handed you this when you were here. It doesn't really contain anything I didn't tell you, but it's personal and physical and I felt at the time that it shouldn't go into a murder file. In fact I should have handed it to someone back when it might have done some good. I had no idea that all of our hard work could lead to this. I'm leaving for a surf camp on Tavarua tomorrow, and won't be gettable for three months. The BD present she refers to was a disc she'd made of her songs—SM

The attached letter was postmarked on August 20, Gwen Wildcraft's birthday:

Dear Sean,

I'm truly happy to know you've found someone to love, and earned the fifty million it will take to keep her happy. Just kidding. All's fine here. Archie's working hard, ready to move off patrol this year sometime, we hope. The home is just beautiful, many improvements since you saw it. Sick, and I love it. I was completely horrified to find Al and Sonny waiting by my car yesterday in the grocery store parking lot when I came out. Told me to keep my mouth shut about serum

problems I might have known about. Those random weirdos
actually threatened to report ME to the FTC for not divulging
the sidewinder problem unless . . . get this . . . unless I came
back to work for their latest company, some silicon molecule
engineering start-up in Irvine. Apeman said they needed a
"money-maker cover girl." Made it sound like he was
recruiting a whore, sure looked at me that way. They said
they'd pay me twelve an hour to do what I did for you. I told
them to quit leaning on my new Dodge and get out of my life
immediately or I'd report THEM to the FTC, the FBI, the INS,
and the Centers for Disease Control. They didn't laugh at that.
They never took one word I said at OrganiVen seriously. Hey,
I'm 26 today! Here's my BD present to you. It's my day, so I
can do what I feel like, right?
Talk soon,
Gwen

Rayborn sighed and read it again. There it was, a bluff called with
three bullets. A threat that cost three lives, two eyes and countless
sorrows. Gwen had fallen once, but she wouldn't fall twice. Her mistake was not going to the Bureau or the Sheriff's. Would that have
mattered? Maybe not. It had taken Al and Sonny less than twenty-four
hours to execute her.

All for the good life, Merci thought. All for the extra stuff when
you already have enough. She pictured the Wildcraft home—beautiful
and empty.

She put the letter back and looked through the window again at
her own life—somewhat chaotic at the moment, but very full. Her
heart was beating hard and strong, a beat of sadness for Archie and
Gwen, then a beat of promise for everyone left standing.

After dinner Mike had a third martini and passed out on the couch.
An hour later Merci woke him up, told him that Clark would give him
and Danny a lift home. Mike looked at her blearily, then at Zamorra,
finishing up the dishes. She thanked him for coming—the wine, the

worms, just fantastic. She hugged him and told him his flower arrangement was right on, too. He smiled and stumbled just a little on his
way out the door.

A few minutes later she carried Tim to his room, read to him and
felt him melt into sleep in her arms.

She came back out to find that Reese had put on some music and
poured more wine for himself. He offered Merci a series of winning
smiles.

When her father got back, he said he was beat and went to his
room. Damon asked Merci to dance but she just wasn't up for it. Then
Damon got loud and Zamorra told him to leave. There was a moment
of fight or flight but Reese put up his hands in mock surrender and
headed out.

Zamorra thanked her for the evening and put on his coat.

"Wait," she said. "Let's take a walk."

"I'd like to."

She got a flashlight and led Zamorra across the cool grass, through
the gate, and down the path along the grove. Her thoughts were a little
unusual from the gin and the good wine at dinner. The moon was
nearly full, dropping a faint silver light to the leaftops. Merci raised
her nose just a little to let in the stinging fresh smell of the citrus.

"I've got someone I'd like you to meet," she said. She hadn't fully
decided that she could go through with this but now the sentence hung
in the air, blatant and tactile, like a spider at the end of a strand.

"I could have put my tie back on," said Zamorra.

"It's casual, Paul."

"I made Mike's extra strong. Sorry."

"It's okay. He ODs kind of easy."

She led him across the weeds of the back lot, to the cinder blocks
and the floss-tethered tumbleweeds. When she lifted the plywood she
caught Zamorra's mute surprise that the weeds were attached. He
pitched in and helped her set the sheets against the garage.

"Bubble wrap?"

"You'll see."

She knelt and set the wrap aside, dirt digging into her bare knees.
Then she shined the light in.

"This is Frank."

"I'll be damned."

"I found him here. He's from Spain. He's real."

"He looks real."

"I make him for law enforcement. The sword, mainly. Maybe a *trabuco*, which was an early gun, but his department kept his weapon after Francisco bought the farm. I really don't know. It's speculative."

"Seems possible."

"What do you think of him?"

"He's well grounded."

She laughed quietly. "Hess said alone."

"That comes to mind too."

Zamorra continued to look down. He was squatting with his elbows on his knees and his chin on his fists, the way Tim did.

"Kirsten is a lot like him."

Merci was about to make a crack about both having tiny skulls when she felt the sweet awakening of becoming unfooled. "No."

"Yeah."

"You're really kidding."

"I made her up."

"Why?"

"To keep myself away from you."

She almost said something like *this changes things*, but for once she calculated her words against the situation and kept her mouth closed.

"I wanted to be more than just a furious widower," he said. "There were too many dangling nerves."

"Man, I know that feeling."

"I know you do. I admired the way you bulled right through the bad things that happened to you. I loitered around mine. When I saw you and Wildcraft today I understood how strong you are. And how tired I was of self-pity. Thank you."

She wanted to do something meaningful, but what, hold his hand?

Then her words jumped out and it was too late. "Let's go to Mexico and find a place on the beach for a couple of days. Pink walls, blue water, bougainvillea in clay pots. A good beach and a maid to clean up."

He looked at her. She saw the moonlight on his black hair, the glint in his eyes. Too soon, she thought. I just scared him off. *You're a stupid, selfish, greedy, idiotic . . .*

"Pack your things," he said. "I'll pick you up in one hour. Tim can sleep on the way down."

"Wait for me. I'll be ready in half of that."

"Even better. Would you make a pot of coffee? I'll sit here with Frank a minute. Tuck him in."

She got up and brushed the dirt off her knees, left the flashlight on the ground. She came around the grave and ran a hand through Zamorra's hair on her way past. An unexpected thrill, that. Always loved a man's hair.

Walking by the fragrant trees her thoughts split into familiar couples of hope and worry: Zamorra and stingrays, Tim and mosquitoes, love and the *Federales*.

She came through the gate onto the grass. Turned and looked back at Zamorra still squatting behind the streak of the flashlight beam, contemplating Frank. Smelled her fingers. Moving toward the house she felt full. Lucky. She felt like dozing with her head against the cool window glass of a car while the radio played low and a capable man drove her someplace she'd always wanted to go.

Felt a little bit of everything.